Praise for John Brady's MATT MINOGUE series:

A Stone of the Heart

"Towers above the mystery category as AN ELOQUENT, COMPELLING NOVEL . . . a tragic drama involving many characters, each so skillfully realized that one virtually sees and hears them in this extraordinary novel . . ." – PUBLISHERS WEEKLY

"A MASTERFULLY CRAFTED WORK of plot, atmosphere and especially characterization . . . Minogue, thoughtful, clear-eyed and perhaps too sensitive . . . is a full-blooded character built for the long haul of a series . . ." – MACLEAN'S

Unholy Ground

"RIVETING . . . The suspense builds to barely bearable intensity . . . crackles with pungent Irish idiom and its vignettes of the country's everyday life." – TORONTO STAR

"Excellent Sergeant Matt Minogue . . . MARVELLOUS DIALOGUE, as nearly surreal as a Magritte postcard the sergeant likes, and a twisting treacherous tale." – SUNDAY TIMES

Kaddish in Dublin

"MATT MINOGUE, THE MAGNETIC CENTRE OF THIS SUPERB SERIES . . . and Brady's tone of battered lyricism are the music which keep drawing us back to this haunting series." – NEW YORK TIMES

"Culchie Colombo with a liberal and urbane heart . . . like all the best detective stories it casts its net widely over its setting . . . [Minogue is] a character who should run and run." – IRISH TIMES

All Souls

"As lyrical and elegantly styled as the last three . . . A FIRST-RATE STORY WITH MARVELLOUS CHARACTERS . . . Another masterful tale from a superior author." – GLOBE AND MAIL

"Nothing gets in the way of pace, narrative thrust or intricate story-telling." – IRISH TIMES

"A KNOCKOUT." – KIRKUS REVIEWS

A Carra King   GLOBE AND MAIL TOP 100

"DENSE AND MULTILAYERED . . . a treasure of a crime novel."
– TORONTO STAR

"Brady has a great eye for the telling detail . . . and a lovely slow pace of storytelling. There's much talk and thought events and you can't read this book at warp speed. Instead, save it to savour"
– GLOBE AND MAIL

Wonderland   GLOBE AND MAIL TOP 100

"IF THERE ARE AUTHORS BETTER THAN JOHN BRADY at chronicling the events of modern Ireland, I HAVEN'T YET READ THEM . . . Brady's best so far." – GLOBE AND MAIL

"ANOTHER SUPERB NOVEL BY A WRITER OF INTERNATIONAL STATURE." – TORONTO STAR

"BRADY'S BEST: informed, subtle and intelligent, with Minogue revealing a hitherto unseen depth of soul, humour and emotion."
– THE TIMES UK

Islandbridge

A MATT MINOGUE MYSTERY

JOHN BRADY

Islandbridge

A MATT MINOGUE MYSTERY

McArthur & Company
Toronto

Published in Canada in 2005 by
McArthur & Company
322 King Street West, Suite 402
Toronto, ON M5V 1J2

Library and Archives Canada Cataloguing in Publication

Brady, John, 1955-
Islandbridge : a Matt Minogue mystery / John Brady.

ISBN 1-55278-520-3

I. Title.

PS8553.R245I84 2005   C813'.54   C2005-903711-3

Cover, Image & Composition by *Mad Dog Design*
Printed in Canada by *Webcom*

The publisher would like to acknowledge the financial support of
the Government of Canada through the Book Publishing Industry
Development Program (BPIDP) and the Canada Council for our publishing
activities. The publisher further wishes to acknowledge the financial
support of the Ontario Arts Council for our publishing program.

10 9 8 7 6 5 4 3 2 1

For Hanna, with love

What thou lovest well remains
The rest is dross
What thou lovest well shall not be reft from thee
What thou lovest best is thy true heritage.
— Ezra Pound, *Canto 81*

A Legend About Islandbridge

Islandbridge is an area in inner-city Dublin with a long past, perhaps even being where the Vikings first settled in the 800s.

WHEN THE VIKINGS SETTLED DUBLIN, they were being continually harried by chieftains from the nearby hills, and even from north of the settlement in the rich lands of Meath. The native Irish regarded them as barbarians. A Viking who wanted to settle in Dublin decided that marriage would be the solution. He set about finding himself an Irish wife from amongst the families and chieftains that were hostile to the Viking's growing presence. When he found one, he spoke with her father, a man who was reputed to be both wise and unrelenting in battle.

"I will build her the finest home on the whole island of Ireland," he told the chieftain. "It will be safe from raiders and brigands, because it will be an island itself, in the River Liffey."

"My daughter is not an island woman," the chieftain said. "She will find it confining more than reassuring."

The wooer had foreseen this objection.

"But it will have a bridge to the shore," said

"Well, if there is a bridge," the chieftain said, "it can hardly be an island, can it?"

"She can go forth and come back and go as she pleases, amongst her own. It is not my intention that she should be separated from her family and people."

"You are granting her a freedom that she has by birthright," said the chieftain. "Who are you to say whether she may come and go?"

At this, the Viking knew he was in a tight spot. Although he had learned many of the customs of the native Irish, he had not reckoned on how the Irish chieftains did not distinguish between the worth of a son and a daughter in their rights.

"She will have the riches of trade," he said. "Jewels and stones from the East. She will be the envy of all."

"She, like I, cares nothing for wealth," said the chieftain. "That is only for display amongst the vulgar classes who would wish to conceal their low character with their baubles."

The Viking was now in dire straits.

"I know your faith in God," he said to the chieftain. "I have given you my oath that I will become a Christian like your people."

"That goes without saying. She will not marry a pagan, or a barbarian."

Almost at the end of his rope, and seeing the chieftain's brow descending, the Viking came upon an idea. He had heard that, while Christians, the native Irish retained many of the old ways.

"The island I speak of is more than merely a place to live," he said. "I have been told the secret of the place and how to use it, by a holy man."

"And what is that?"

"That on the island, time is yours to do as you please. You can go back in time to youth, and the past, or forward in time to foretell what will happen. Of course those who do not live on the island, and who do not know the secret, will never know this and will live their lives as others, and the days and years will tax them with age and death."

"Are you saying that this island in the river is *Tír na nÓg?*"

"The holy man told me that it is an entry to that land of the young that your poets speak of, but it has never been known outside a few who guard its secret."

The chieftain thought for a long time before he looked to the wooer of his daughter again.

"Well," he said at last. "If what you say is true, then she could cross that bridge one day, and return to the past to undo a mistake, could she not?"

"She could."

"Such as her marriage vows?"

The Viking realized that he was caught, but he remembered that the Irish valued those who never stinted in their efforts, be it in horsemanship, battle, or argument.

"It is true," he said, looking boldly into the chieftain's eyes. "But she will never regret those vows for one moment of her life, I promise you."

The chieftain stared at him for several minutes.

"I think you have made your case," he said finally. "Whether this island can hold time as you say it can, we shall see. But one thing is certain: she will not be bored for lack of storytelling."

He leaned in over the table that divided the two men. The Viking did not know if a knife would suddenly spring into the chieftain's hand and he would be dispatched for his impertinence and casuistry.

"In telling the story itself, you yourself have held back time," said the chieftain.

"Your wisdom is beyond me, sir," said the Viking.

"What I am telling you is this," said the chieftain, standing up as a signal that his visitor should depart. "In your desire, you have already made this island with its bridge, an island that is not an island at all – Islandbridge we shall call it – true."

The Viking left, not knowing what the chieftain thought, or would decide.

Prologue

July 9, 1983

IT WAS COMING UP to midnight and the club was going strong. There was an hour to go yet on Declan Kelly's shift, but the tiredness had left him. That no longer surprised him. It usually did toward the end of the night. He figured it happened like this because there was less of a serious performance needed from him now. But it wasn't good to get too relaxed. He still had to be wide awake and to look deadly serious when they'd be emptying the club at closing time.

Kelly had plenty of ways to while the time away until the end of his shift, and tonight for some reason, making up names of books and films had come to him. *The Life of a Bouncer* by Declan Kelly. The Famous Garda Declan Kelly, that would be, Off-duty Garda Declan Kelly. Saving Up For The Big Day Declan Kelly. How about: Never Going To Do A Crappy Job As A Bouncer In This Dump Again, Declan Kelly? "You've read the book, now see the film." Who would he get to star in it, though? Clint Eastwood, with an Irish accent. That'd be something all right.

He watched a taxi approach in the dazzle of lights that flooded up from the oily, patched surface of Capel Street. It passed, and the street was empty again. There was the Liffey stink hanging in the air around here. It crept like poison gas all over the centre of Dublin, when the tide was out. There was always the smell of the Markets too, day and night. Somehow, the stray fragments and squashed pads of vegetables that lined the laneways here brought a quiet dismay to Garda Kelly. A farmer's son, they reminded him of the sure and certain fate of nature and its bounty, here in this city where he had once wished to be posted, but now was beginning to hate.

The thumping from the new speakers they'd put into the club last month gave way to tinnier noise and voices. He looked over and returned a wave from Mick, the inside man. Mick held the door open with his foot and raised his arm. He tapped on his watch face and gave Kelly the thumbs-up. He thought he saw Mick roll his eyes. The door closed slowly, swallowing back some of the noise.

Kelly had no idea how many were still in the club. It had been slow enough all evening and, after all, Wednesdays were not much better than Mondays here. He stared at the heavy galvanized plates that covered the door, and stifled a yawn. The doors were actually vibrating with the music: he was sure of it.

Mid-stretch, he thought about his fiancée. Eimear would be sound asleep in her flat over on South Circular Road. It was two weekends since her flatmate Breda had gone home to her folks in Longford, and left them to themselves. He wondered if one or the other of them had planned it like this. It seemed the most natural thing in the world when Eimear came out from her bath naked and then eased into bed beside him. Just like that, he'd said to himself over and over again for days afterwards. She had told him she'd heard his heart beating halfway across the room.

Breda had to have been in on it, he decided again. The same Breda was arranging most of the reception. "No backing out now, Declan," she had said before she'd headed down for the train, "The hotel is booked."

Well ha ha ha, Breda. Actually Breda was all right, most of the time. Lately he wondered if maybe, just maybe, she was a bit jealous.

The door to the club swung open again. Mick held it open for two girls to step out. They stumbled out arm in arm, and even above the music Kelly heard the clickety click of their heels. A cigarette from the one nearest the door caught in something and cascaded glowing pieces at their feet. These were right Dublin scrubbers, the pair of them. In his time in Dublin Declan Kelly had come to the conclusion early enough that there was and always would be an endless supply of these sneering, brassy, foul-mouthed young ones.

One stopped just outside the door. She yanked her friend back, and said something to Mick. Kelly wondered why the doors had stayed open. Then he saw that Mick was still there holding the door for a fella – wait, two fellas – to leave. The second one was wavering a lot. When he made for the footpath outside with sideways, lurching steps and abrupt halts, Kelly eyed him trying to flick back his long hair from time to time, almost falling back in the effort. He began to sway now too as he headed down the footpath, something that reminded Declan Kelly of a sailor on board ship in a storm. The glimpse of face Kelly saw said nineteen maybe twenty, but with that stunned, slack expression of some-one well into a stupor.

They hadn't noticed him, and that was just fine by him. One of the girls yanked the other around as she turned to shout some-thing, but Mick had the door pulled closed already. The first man was trying to light a cigarette now. Kelly couldn't help but smile at the effort. Even standing with his legs braced against his rolling world, every match the fella lit was going out, or dropping, or breaking. Then he turned his head, but it fell back, and he took several sudden, tottering steps to regain some footing. No sooner had he done that than the swaying started again. Then he seemed to get suddenly very interested in the night sky. God knows what he saw up there above these wet Dublin streets of this July night – morning – year of Our Lord 1983. This thick was more than just drunk, Kelly decided, more than stoned, even.

The girls seemed to be arguing with one another now. One of them laughed, with a cackle that ended in a smoker's cough. They lurched on, half pushing and half tugging at one another. One of the girls' heels clipped something on the footpath, and she skittered a few steps with a yelp and fell then against a car. The fella with the unlit cigarette called out to her, while the other girl buckled with laughter. The girl against the car started to laugh herself. She stayed leaning against the back door and looked up and down the street. She had seen him now, Kelly believed. She took out a cigarette, trying to watch him all the while. The flare of her lighter jolted her. She batted at her hair a few times. The other girl, beside her now, erupted into laughter again.

Kelly looked away from them now. As Clune used to tell him when they started foot patrol first, you don't have to stare to notice things. The trick was to look away down the road, while at the same time you keep an eye on people. It was a bit like a dog you couldn't trust, according to Clune. If you make eye contact, it sends a signal.

The two men had caught up to the girls now. The wobbly stargazer with the long hair was like a hospital patient taking his first steps after an operation.

"Sure who'd ever want to be in that dump?"

It was the girl on the car who had made the half-hearted yell. Her accent was that lazy, mocking whine Kelly had come to despise.

She seemed happy enough against the car now, settling onto it, wet or not from the showers earlier.

He kept his gaze on the lights by Capel Street Bridge. She drew on the cigarette again, coughed, and pushed her hair back. Then she looked at her friend rummaging in her handbag.

Kelly thought of the money he was making tonight, mentally rearranging it into pound notes and fivers. Then he did division on how many pints of stout that'd buy, or how many gallons of petrol for his new Toyota Starlet. Mostly, he fought off the urge to look over.

There was no sign of them pushing off yet. Jesus, he muttered under his breath. He felt a twinge of remorse at taking the Holy Name. There was something about people who were drunk, he'd come to believe, something that gave them some weird power of knowing what you were thinking, or what you wanted. He turned his mind to mental calculations again. There were three more of these jobs before the end of the month. That was three hundred quid. Furniture for the new house, or extra for the honeymoon?

He caught the movement out of the corner of his eye. He had been right: drunk people were mind readers. She was headed his way. The bitch, he murmured.

Her sugary breath preceded her and wafted across to Kelly. It was soon joined by a stink of stale smoke and worn-out perfume that had baked into her clothes in the club.

"You like being a bouncer, do you?" she said. "Isn't it fierce boring, like?"

"Go on," he said. "Your fellas are going on without you."

She had to steady herself when she turned to look back. The two men were staggering in some kind of unison now. The other girl was wavering a bit herself while she searched in a small handbag.

"Don't mind them," she said. "They're only gobshites. We can get other fellas."

Her sudden yell startled him then.

"Yvonne!!"

"What?"

"We can get any fella we want, can't we Yvonne?"

Now the other woman began to make her way back. Kelly almost groaned aloud.

"Give us a fag," the other girl called out. The first girl ignored her.

"You should put your uniform on," she said to Kelly instead. "Why don't you?"

He looked down the street.

"Shouldn't he, Yvonne?"

He stole a quick glance at Yvonne's face. Her mascara had gone astray and her pale face and empty eyes told Kelly she could puke any moment, without warning. He took a step back and turned to look down the street in the wake of another taxi.

"Shouldn't he put on his uniform, Yvonne, this copper?"

Yvonne shivered and nodded.

"That's where the money is, I'm telling you," said the first one.

"Where are the fags?" Yvonne asked through a shiver.

"Will you wait? Jesus, where are yours . . . !"

"You should buy some," the girl said. "You iijit."

"They'll be gone if you don't hurry up," Kelly said.

The Yvonne one lurched as she reached for the packet. Kelly turned at the sound of her sole scraping the pavement.

"Do the routine, you know?" the first one said. "Peel it off. They throw their knickers up at them in the one in Finglas. They throw money too."

Kelly returned to studying the far end of the street. The more sober, or less drunken, man had stopped now. He rested his mate against a car and drew on the cigarette he managed to light.

"Come on, will yous?" he shouted. Kelly didn't hear the rest of what he said, as the man reached over to right his tottering mate.

"You'll miss your lift home be late," he said to the girls.

"Home? Ha ha. Home . . .?! We're only starting! Isn't that right, Yvonne?"

The Yvonne one drew long on her cigarette. She couldn't focus on him, he saw. Puke could go six feet, easy. She began to move off in the direction of the two men.

"Where are you going," said the first one. She turned back to Kelly.

"Come here, I'll show you."

He brushed her hand away.

"Enough."

"What do you mean enough, here–"

"Bugger off home, you dirty scrubber."

Her face gave way to a sneer.

"Want me to run you in?" he said, and glared at her. "You and your pals?"

He enjoyed knowing she couldn't find the words to snap back at him. Slowly he headed back to the doorway.

"Did you hear that?" she managed at last, and her voice gave out at the end. It turned into a ragged shout.

"Yvonne! Yvonne!"

Kelly spotted a car coasting slowly down the street toward the club, the reflected lights from the shops and the street lights sliding over the windscreen every few moments.

"Kev!" the girl was shrieking while she walked away. "Come here, will you?"

The car slowed even more, and Kelly saw an arm resting in the open window. There were two men in the front seats, and another sitting behind. The front passenger pointed at something.

The club door opened and that same, stupid tune they always played this time of night poured out, louder than ever. That was another thing driving him bonkers here, how they played the same thing over and over again. The Police, "I'll Be Watching You." Ha, ha bloody ha. Not funny, never was.

The car accelerated and then suddenly braked, with a loud, hissing skid. The two women had noticed it. The driver leaned over to look out the passenger window. The women said something back, and they began scurrying awkwardly down the footpath.

"A spot of bother?"

"Almost," said Kelly.

Kelly heard the skittering heels as they tried to hurry, and tracked the red, arcing glows of their cigarettes. The car kept pace. There was shouting.

He stepped into the street and looked down at the taillights. The girls were trying to run now. Then they just disappeared. The taillights bounced once as the driver took it up the curb, and headlights swept over a wall before the car itself vanished into the laneway. He waited to hear shouts but none came to him over the steady hum and thumping from the club behind him.

"It was their own lookout," he muttered.

Slowly he walked back to the footpath himself. A motorbike passed, hissing over the tarmacadam, its springs squeaking as it took the bumps. Now he thought about the swimming pool in the picture of the hotel where he and Eimear had booked their honeymoon. They'd stick near that pool all day, for sure. You could swim in the sea, of course.

He cupped his ear. It might have been another shout.

The door of the club opened, and he watched a couple coming out. Sleazy wasn't enough of a word for it. The man looked old enough to be her da, for God's sake.

He looked back toward the laneway again. It was one of several, he knew, but of how many he wasn't sure. All he knew of this part of the inner city was that there were more than enough laneways that wormed their narrow winding ways through the Markets and on into Smithfield, places where everyone stopped to pee and anything else they felt like.

How did he ever wind up here, he wondered, with the clammy night air full of the stench of Dublin city seeping into his skin. And why did Guards have to take nixers like this, to moonlight, anyway? Half the force was at it, and everyone knew about it. It was almost expected, as if to say: "Here, welcome to the Guards. You'll get lousy pay, and have to do nixers like this for ages until you get sick of it. Or you can emigrate, like everyone else your age is doing." It would be ten years before they'd even look at you for Sergeant. The word was that you had to be in the know to get plainclothes too.

One of the women was back now.

It was the other one, the one who had been the drunkest. She was in a hurry now, and he saw that she had one shoe missing. Away she went, half hopping and half scurrying down toward the Liffey. She kept close to the shop windows, brushing against some of them, looking back every now and then. Then she stopped and she took off her remaining shoe.

He waited for the others to show up. A taxi passed. The woman had covered a lot of ground, and had broken into a clumsy run every now and then, with her hand out often to fend off parked cars along her way. Then she was out of sight.

Declan Kelly was surprised to find himself heading down the footpath. The frustration swirled in his thoughts and he muttered and swore. He passed dribbly streaks that reached out from the walls where the boozers had stopped for a leak. There were plenty of gaps between the parked cars here now. The music faded behind him, but he heard no voices coming from the mouth of the laneway ahead.

He stopped at the end of the footpath and looked up the laneway. There were cobblestones glistening, and little sprays of light from broken glass. A car had blocked the lane further up.

One of the doors was hanging open, and the headlights were on.

He rested his hand on a parking meter, and listened. Still he heard nothing. He yanked at the meter, and cursed, and looked at the drops of rain that fell from the meter when he shook it again. Then he saw someone, a man, holding the other girl by the arm. He yanked her around the open door and shoved her into the car. She wasn't putting up much of a fight. He heard her say things, loud, but couldn't hear the words. The man slammed the door and stood by it.

Kelly crossed and stood by the corner. Now he saw movement in a small gap that opened to his view beyond the car. Another fella was standing up there, and pointing at something. Someone called out, a name. Johnny? Tony?

The man who had stood by the car reached in and switched off the lights.

Kelly's neck began to itch. There was a phone in the club, he knew.

There was no sign of the woman in the car. She seemed to have keeled over in the back. Still he saw a figure detach itself from the darkness, still pointing. Now some small movement – a hand – from by the wall. Someone sitting down up there, waving?

Kelly's feet took him down the narrow footpath. The stale stink of the market rose up around him, its overripe and discarded fruits squashed into the gutters, along with the malty tang of urine. He heard voices, not words.

There was a door, or a gate, recessed in from the laneway, and there sat two men, their knees up. Over them stood another man, and behind him another, whose hand clutched the driver's side mirror as though to keep the car from running away.

Kelly heard the voices going up now, an argument. It was effin' this and effin' that, from the man standing. He was beginning to pace up and down a few steps now.

A few words came back from the two in the doorway, in that tone of crude, sing-song earnestness that Kelly had heard too often here in this city. Those words were cut short by more from the one standing. Told you, didn't I, Kelly heard. Effin' messers, he heard, and then something about always . . ., and never – never listen. He heard clearly when the man shouted then: keep you effin' mouth shut when I'm effin' talking to you . . .

This was no place to be. He began to turn away, but stopped as the man standing made a sudden move.

The flashes made the man's arm jump. He kept them coming as though to quell the shouts that erupted. Cracks echoed down the lane and spread between the buildings, and Kelly heard the sounds of something metal falling and rolling. It could only be a dream, he believed, when you are so tired to doze off a few moments even standing up. His legs wouldn't move.

Someone called out, Jesus, Jesus, Tony. The car shook a little as a head came up to the window. It was the woman, with her hair astray. There was a dull shout from inside the car, and a scream. The light went on as she opened the door, and he saw the hair twisted across her face. The other man pushed the door back at her. He reached around and shoved her head and she fell back. He stood by the door looking in.

A man was talking again now, but in a low voice. The dim light from the car showed legs at the foot of the wall. The feet were pointing at odd angles. The man with the gun stepped in, leaned, and shot again, once, twice. The one by the car jumped a little with each sound as he skipped to the driver's side and got in behind the wheel.

The man with the gun walked slowly to the car side and got into the back. The girl screamed and he yelled. It looked like she was hammering at him.

Kelly pushed himself harder into the wall. The car shot off and he stepped away. Then the brake lights came on. The tires sizzled to a stop. Kelly saw the door opening, and then his running legs were taking him back down toward the street.

There was no immediate pain, only surprise, when he found his cheek on the wet cobblestone next to the curb. He knew he had hit his head, and his knee. The pain tore up his leg and exploded in his head when he got up, but he pushed on, the slimy wetness from the stones all over his palms. The leg gave way when he put his weight on it, and he pitched sideways.

Kelly heard himself groan when he hit again, felt his palms

punch the stones as he tried to break the fall. Still he tried, the dread on him like a dead weight. He fought off believing that he couldn't run, and he begged that the clattering feet of the man running his way would lose their grip on this greasy laneway too.

His fingers brought him up, and he elbowed over and got his hands under him. He tried to get up, thinking in an instant of the three-legged races he'd run as a child. Even after falling, he and his best friend Donie had still carried on crablike, seized with shame and hilarity, but trying their best to scuttle to the finish line.

It was himself wheezing and talking, he knew, but he kept it up so he wouldn't hear the slowing footfalls or the sound of a gun that'd reach him, he understood, long after a bullet would.

He spun with his good leg to face him. He couldn't see a face but it was the same punk-rock hair in silhouette. Back up the lane, the driver was standing in the open door of the car.

The air seemed to quiver all about. He watched the man's arm.

"Look," he said, and had to pause. "Wait! I'm a Guard, a Garda officer."

The man's shoulders were heaving, and Kelly heard him trying not to pant. He smelled the car's exhaust settling over him. He looked down at the cobblestones. If he didn't look up, then he wouldn't see the gun, and that meant the man wouldn't shoot. Kelly wanted the other man to get out from behind the wheel of the car, and come over. It meant this one standing over him would stop, or think, or leave, or at least break this spell.

Kelly heard everything, saw everything, knew everything. The man's breath whistling through his nose. The perspiration and stale cigarette smoke off his clothes. The filth of Dublin here, the greasy stones that made up the lane. He even saw the labourers setting them in centuries ago. He saw Eimear sleeping, he saw the kids they were going to have. There were his mother's hands whitened with flour and him bursting into the kitchen from school. Now it was the passing out parade in Templemore, the rub of the new uniform cuffs above his thumb. He saw his father's moist eye when he was working alongside him in the fields. Now came his patrol partner O'Keefe's buck teeth, the car's tire treads shining down the lane, a smell of something he never smelled before, scuffed toes of the shoes that had stopped three feet from his.

The driver had kept the engine running. Kelly heard some wheezing or a muffled shout from the car, saw it move a bit on its shocks.

He was surprised that he could speak, that his voice was strong, even.

"I am," he said. "I'm a Guard."

The laboured breathing stop-started, and he heard breath sucked in between teeth.

"Jimmy," came the voice from beside the car. "Come on."

The feet turned, the man yelled.

"Will you shut up?"

Kelly's heart sank. The name he'd heard made everything worse. He kept his eyes on the shoes.

"I just wanted to see the girls were okay."

"What? What are you saying?"

"The girls—"

The man shouted again from the car.

"Are they all right?" Kelly asked.

"Is who all right?"

"I saw them leave, I wondered if they were okay, I'm a door-man."

"A doorman?"

Kelly watched the man's arm come around from behind and then fall back. When he tried to speak, nothing came. It was as if all his words had fallen away, and now even feeling was leaving too. Nothing mattered now, not the protesting the colossal unfairness of this, the bad luck, or even his own stupidity.

The man's breathing slowed. Kelly heard a crunch of gears and tires hissing. He looked over and saw lights turn into the lane.

The driver yelled again. Kelly watched the car skid to a stop and buck, as the driver let go the clutch early.

"Jesus, Jimmy. It's your old lad . . ."

A heavy-set man had launched himself out of the car and was half skipping, half rolling toward them now.

"What are you doing?" Kelly heard him say. "Who's that?"

"Go back, Da," the man answered, his voice rising. "I'm taking care of something."

"Jesus, put that away. That's not necessary. Put it away. Where'd you get that?"

"Leave it, Da!"

"Who's that?"

"I'm a Guard."

The man kicked him in the leg and then raised his arm.

"Stop it!" the father shouted. "Are you mad? Jesus! Put it down!"

"Shut up, Da. I have to do this."

"I swear," said Kelly, but his voice gave out. He cleared his throat. "I swear to God, I was just walking by."

"Jimmy put that away. In the name of God–"

"Da, you don't know anything! Just leave us."

"It was the girls," Kelly said. "I was worried–"

This time he kicked Kelly under the arm.

"I told you to shut up, I did."

"Who's in the car there?"

"Da, just get back in your car and go off home. I'll explain it all later okay?"

"Is that who I think it is . . . ?"

Kelly's panic surged when he saw the older man walk quickly toward the car.

"I was only trying to help!"

The arm went out again, pointing at him, Kelly rolled on his side and put his hands over his ear. He registered the kicks in his spine and back, wondered for an instant why they weren't hurting.

The kicks stopped. He heard raised voices, a car door being slammed. Then a girl's scream burst from the car, followed by the older man's muffled shouts.

♣ ♣ ♣

There were sports pages from a newspaper on the floor of the car, bits of potato crisps, empty cigarette packs, a plastic bag, half-crushed cans of Fanta. The hand was still on his neck, holding his head down behind the seat.

"I can't breathe," he said as the car leaned into a bend. "I can't."

The gun pushed harder into his neck.

"What did he say? What?"

"Nothing."

"He said something."

"He's complaining about something."

"I can't breathe here," Kelly said.

The barrel was shoved into his neck again.

"Shut up," the son said.

The car passed over broken roadway, and stopped. The red from the traffic light came to Kelly from its dull glow on the wrappers beside his face. He listened for other traffic.

The father didn't talk. He was driving cautiously, and stopping at all the traffic lights. His whistling breath and cigarette smoke filled the car. Kelly hoped it was a sign, that he was buying time to think. A man of the father's age wouldn't be a savage, he couldn't be. Any delay was good, moments even, to give this maniac son of his time to cool off. Jimmy. Jimmy who? Maybe the father knew the son was on drugs, and he was trying to calm him down by cruising around. But maybe he's afraid of his own kid, Kelly thought then. Maybe he's not in control of this at all.

Kelly's face felt like it was ready to burst with the heat. His ankle was warm and numb now. He was almost sure he'd blacked out for a while after the son kicked him getting him into the back of the car.

There was smooth pavement now. The father put it into top gear and the car seemed to be just cruising indefinitely now. Kelly felt the panic rise again: they were taking him out of the city. He tried to plot where they were and quickly settled on the Phoenix Park. They had gone down the Liffey quays, and now had miles and miles of clear road ahead, roadway that had hundreds of acres of woods and broad fields to both sides. The park was a place for

couples in cars, and carry-on at night, Kelly knew soon after starting here in Dublin. He remembered being amazed that there
could be such a huge, wild-looking place so close to the centre of
the city.

For several moments he imagined himself looking down on
this car, with the night sky overhead and the car's headlights
carving through the darkness. How easy to just keep driving, he
thought, just to keep going no matter what speed, until dawn and
into the morning, just to see light. Then they'd see his face,
they'd see how ordinary he was, how hurt he was. How could
they not see then in the daylight how big a mistake this was, how
they had to let him go?

"Are you a detective or what then?" from the father.

"No, I'm not, no."

"Liar," said the son. "You tailed the girls. Waiting for them,
you bastard."

"No, I swear."

"You wanted to get her, to get them. So's you could use it
on us."

"Jimmy," the father said, before a phlegmy cough scattered
his voice.

"You knew you could use her," the son went on. "You knew
you could get that dirty little scut with her."

"Jimmy, give over a minute."

"For Jesus' sake Da, will you just stop the car and get this
done? What are we doing driving around like this?"

"We wouldn't be driving around like iijits in this situation
– not if you'd of stopped for one bloody moment and consulted
me–"

"Consult? What the hell are you saying, 'consult'?"

"Don't you dare talk to me like that, you pup, you."

"You knew all about Breen, for ages, nosing around her. And
you did nothing!"

"Listen to you making a show of us in front of a Guard.
Making a show of your family! You haven't paid attention to a
damned thing I've tried to tell you!"

"I swear to God Da, you know nothing. Nothing! And you

don't *want* to know, do you? Yvonne would have been doing the business there on the canal if I'd let this go on any further, if you'd kept turning a blind eye! Something had to be done, don't you see?"

The voices turned to hoarse shouts, and Kelly's mind flooded with fear again.

The shouting stopped when the father had another fit of coughing. When he spoke again it was in a reedy voice.

"You and I need to talk," he said.

"Talk to Kevin Breen, why don't you."

"I can't believe what I'm hearing. Do you think we're going to just walk away and go home and go back to bed, get up in the morning, and everything's back to normal?"

"If you let me finish this, your worries are over."

"My worries? Mine . . . ? You've said every name this fella can remember now. And here we are, driving around in the middle of the night on some kind of mad I-don't-know-what, a crazy tour or something, and here you are, Mr. Genius, spilling out names and everything to a Guard. What do you think is going to come out of that?"

"At least I know what I'm doing."

"What about your pal driving the car, with Yvonne in it. Have you thought of that?"

"Yvonne would never rat on her own family, as mad as she does be."

"Wait a minute, what's this family thing? Do you think this is *The Godfather* or something here? Is that what's going on in that head of yours?"

"Yvonne would be shooting up if I hadn't woken you up with this."

"Don't! Don't say another word about my daughter! Just don't. Your own sister. You'll never know, never. Not until you're a parent. And actually, I wouldn't wish it on anyone. Your mother . . . ahh, what's the use of talking."

He slapped the wheel.

Kelly closed his eyes tight and held them for several seconds. He had to try, he told himself. Whatever happened, he had to try. The father knew it, that this son of his had painted them into a corner. Now he wanted to cry, but he held back.

He felt the car speed up, then turn as though it had found a purpose, that a decision had been made.

Kelly lost track of time. Several times he had tried to get his head up even a little. It had been the butt of the gun that had hit him on the spine the last time, he was sure of it. There had been stops, and more rough roadway, and quick turns. The car slowed, and then stopped, and the ignition was switched off.

There were stars in front of his eyes when they let him lift his head. Kelly saw that he had parked the car in the shadow of a tallish building. It looked like a warehouse. He felt pukey now, but breathed in deeply. His ankle was going from numb to a feeling that someone had fastened a clamp on it, with hot points that bit in tighter each minute.

He pretended he was stuck when Junior began to pull at his lapel, and he let himself fall over on his elbow across the back seat.

"It's my ankle," he said, "it's gone numb, it's broken."

Jimmy pulled harder, but lost his grip and had to step to steady himself. Then he began to shout, and raised the gun.

Kelly watched the father come around the back of the car, his shoes sliding on gravel.

"Wait, Jimmy," he called out. "Easy, now."

"They put him there," said the son. "The Drug Squad, somebody, whoever."

The father looked down at Kelly while he cupped his hands around a fresh cigarette and lit it.

"Well, you get him out, then. We have to do this, I'm telling you. He'll take us all down, you, me, Yvonne, me, everyone. Take him out or I'll do him right there in the car."

"We'll do what we have to do, don't worry. Just *listen*."

"Get him out of there. Or get out of the way and I'll do it, I'm not afraid to do it."

"I know you're not, I know. But I want to hear what he has to say first. Okay?"

Kelly felt a tiny glow of hope as he watched the smoke issue slowly from the man's mouth and nose. This man must know his son is wired. It can't have been the first time he'd seen something like this.

"Come out of the car there," said the father. "Out."

"I can't."

"Jimmy will take you out so. Do you want that? No. So get out."

Kelly looked at him, but he didn't move. He waited for the man to finish drawing on his cigarette to look over.

"Only if you–" Kelly started.

"No deals. This is serious. There's only so much we can do. Get out."

The weary tone that had come into the voice paralyzed Kelly. It was telling him that he'd been wrong about the father, that the time had run out.

Numbly he watched the father lift his cigarette to his mouth again and turn away.

"I'm trying here," he said, and he began to ease himself over the seat.

His palm dug into the top of the door as he grasped for balance. He hopped once, but kept his eye on Jimmy. He couldn't stray from the car, he was sure, or it was over. He held the door from swaying, and spread out his other hand on the coolness of the door panel. He needed the father to turn around, to protect him just by looking at him.

"I can't get anywhere with this ankle," he said, and the son rushed at him almost immediately. He flinched and braced himself.

The blow down on his arm didn't work the first time. He clung on to the door, but his foot had come down and he was blinded by the bolt of pain that ran up. He felt a glancing fist on his ear over his own cry and he fell, still hopping but trying to turn, he hoped, to fall on his good side.

"Look," he heard above him. He recognized the father's voice.

"You've got to listen to me here."

The grit under his forearms and biting into his elbow was sharp.

"What am I going to do with you?" the father went on. "You're Guard. You've got ears. You heard things. You saw things, whatever you saw earlier on. Didn't you?"

"I didn't see what happened."

It was his own voice, back again, speaking calmly from a place somewhere near him.

"What happened, then?" from the son.

"I don't know. I was just concerned, I was worried about the girls."

The mocking groan came from the son.

"I'm getting married," he blurted out.

"What?"

"I'm getting married; I was only working there to save up for the house."

Nobody said anything. Kelly heard the phlegmy rasp of the father's breath.

"It's the last time I'll go there to that club," he added. "I hated it, in actual fact."

"If you'd a knew this was going to happen you'd have stayed home. Is that what you're going to tell me next?"

It was the father's voice. Kelly didn't know if he should say anything.

"Turn over this way," went the father now. "Yeah, so's you can see me. Is that glass under you? It's car glass, don't worry. Yeah, here. Can you see me? Good. Now listen."

Kelly tried to see eyes in the silhouette of the man with the gun.

"Do you know who I am?"

"I do, I think."

"There's an honest answer for now. For a Guard."

"He's a plant," said the son. "They keep tags on Yvonne. It's to get at you, Da. Don't you see that yet?"

"Are you Drug Squad, any of them?"

"No. I'm not, I'm just uniform."

"Well, where are you? Your station, like."

"Ballymun. All I've ever done is patrol, since I started."

"Okay. Who am I then? Who's he?"

"Well he's your son, I think."

"'I think.' Is he or isn't he?"

"He must be."

"Oh right," said the father. "He's cursing at me and annoying the heart and soul out of me, so he must be my son. Right?"

"Da, will you shut up and let's get this fixed? What are we doing here, only walking into more trouble."

"You hear that," said the father, and flicked his cigarette again. He took a long drag on it and then threw it away. He watched it arc into the shadows and spark where it fell, and then it disappeared in the darkness.

"He's a good lad, you know. Behind it all. When he doesn't get his rag out over something and go mad entirely. Aren't you, Jimmy?"

"I'm giving this one more minute," said the son. "One. I swear. And then I'm doing what I should of done ten minutes ago. This is out of hand."

The father's head snapped around.

"You wait over there. You and your 'out of hand.' I can't even think with you jabbering on there."

"There's nothing to think about! It's time for doing something. Action."

In the quiet after the shout Kelly heard dull metal thumps from far off. Trains, he wondered, shunting.

"Well, we seen you in action tonight, didn't we," said the father slowly.

"It was time someone stepped in."

The father said nothing. He seemed to be searching the darkness where he had thrown the cigarette.

"It's him or it's us," said the son, his voice rising again. "He walks from here and he takes everything. I'd be getting life, and so would you."

"Wait in the car."

The voice had been low. The son didn't move.

"Please?"

Kelly heard a whispered curse, a mutter, but the son stayed. The father had a packet of cigarettes out again.

"You love this," he said to Kelly, behind the flare of a match. He drew hard on the new cigarette.

"Don't you? To hear us falling out."

"No," said Kelly.

"You know who I am?"

"Da! Are you a broken record or something?"

"Will you give over Da-ing me? Jesus, he knows who you are by now, if he has ears on him."

Kelly nodded. "Mr. Rynn."

"Come on now, you can do better. What do your crowd call me?"

"Jumbo Rynn, I think."

"You think. Come on. What is it, Guards don't use curse words anymore?"

"Well," was all Kelly could think to say.

"Where do you think it got started?" Rynn went on. "Except from one of yours. That sergeant giving the interview to that newspaper there years ago. Here, tell me, did he get a dressing down for that?"

"I don't know."

"Bet you he got a bonus, so he did. Anyway: what's the name, the full, official Garda name? Come on now. It's important. Didn't your ma tell you to tell the truth?"

"Jimmy . . . I don't want to say it."

"Say it."

"Jimmy . . . Bloody . . . Rynn"

"Right. Top of the class. Okay: to finish the test here. Ready? Who's going to win?"

"Jimmy Bloody Rynn."

"Yes! I'm famous. Sour grapes by the ton. The State, with all their wigs and gowns lined up. You know how much I paid barristers to walk from that one, with their European Court of Human Rights and all that due process stuff, and your search and seizure that?"

"Da, this is useless," the son called out.

Rynn spoke without taking his eyes off Kelly's. "You wait over there," he said. "And don't interrupt me again."

When the son didn't move this time, Rynn stood.

"Whatever I do, I do," he said to him. "Now go to the car."

Kelly did not try to turn to watch as the footfalls went away.

"How do you know me anyway?"

"It's just talk. Like, members talk."

"'Members'– oh, Guards, you mean. Only talk is it?"

"There's pictures. In the station."

"Junior too?"

The son, he meant, Kelly realized, Jimmy Junior.

"I never saw his there, no."

Rynn looked back into the deeper shadows that lay beyond the reach of the street lights.

"You keep tabs as to who goes in and out of that club, don't you?"

"Look," said Kelly. "It was my last shift, I was sick of it–"

"Answer the question."

"Only if I think there's something to it. If they look like they'd be trouble later."

"Who do you give that info to?"

"I don't. It's just a mental note, for myself. Nothing else, honestly."

"Why did you let those headers in, the ones with my daughter?"

Kelly let a few seconds go by trying to think what Rynn was getting at.

"Come on now. You're well able to talk."

"I thought the fella inside could handle that. On a weekday night, I mean."

"Who? His name."

"Mick. Weekends there's two on the door, there has to be."

Rynn let out a long, smoky breath from his nose. Then he turned aside and rubbed slowly at his face.

"Look," he said. "Don't try to cod me. You know what happened back there."

At these words, and the quiet, almost regretful way that Rynn had said them Kelly's mind rebelled. This was all an act. They had decided.

He felt that he weighed nothing now, that he could almost rise, and drift up into the night sky. He wondered if he was here at all, if maybe his mind hadn't caught up to what had happened to the rest of him, and had escaped on its own, after refusing to let this go on.

For a moment he saw himself floating over the city, seeing everything and everyone in it. He kept his eye on the dark form he took to be the son, just beyond the car. If the son was to sneak around behind to use the gun, he wanted to hear him, to be able to yell, at least.

"Right?"

Kelly felt his jaw beginning to go, his throat close with the urge to cry.

"You did your hero bit worrying about the two women. Brilliant move."

"Look, I can," and Kelly's voice broke. The sobs wrenched his chest. The father waited. Kelly almost heard the seconds tick.

"You can . . . ? You can what? Are you making me an offer? What have you got?"

Kelly could stare back through the tears into the Dubliner's face now. He wiped his nose with his sleeve, and tried again to stop the shivers running through his body.

"I'll tell you something new, mister," said Rynn. "If you live to see tomorrow's newspaper, you'd read this: two low-life drug pushers, dealers, whatever they call themselves, I don't know. Two low-lifes found de– what's the word? Deceased, yes, suddenly deceased. Can you hear it on the news? 'Deceased.' So maybe your mates will hear it, you know, in the cop shop. Do they do a roll-call thing like on *Hill Street Blues*?"

Kelly nodded.

"Good. Well maybe there'll be a little cheer will go up, do you think? Maybe your pals won't hear it though, because they'll be complaining about pay or Dublin or something. They're worse than the bloody farmers, or the teachers."

Kelly heard distant, slow thumps again, those same metallic clanks as before. There had to be a train station, or yards, near.

"They'll cheer because their job was done for them. I mean

27

to say, would you want your kid to be a heroin addict? Would you?"

The startled, sneering expression on that girl's face flashed through Kelly's mind.

"So don't you be thinking you're the family men, and we're the bad guys on this."

Kelly saw the dark form that was the son begin to move. Without taking his eyes from Kelly the father called out.

"Bring it over, Jimmy. It's time."

Kelly had already begun to move without even knowing it, but the kick caught him just under the ribs. It shocked him because it had come from the father. He tried again and this time it caught him in the shoulder. Still he heard no metallic click.

"Don't," he called out. "Don't! I never did anything, I couldn't!"

"Give it to me, Jimmy."

"I'll do it, Da. Get out of me way."

"No: you started, but I'm going to finish. I'll show you how things is done. Remember we're all in it now, up to our eyes. So give it to me."

Kelly didn't know if he was actually shouting or if it was all his thoughts.

The son said something he didn't hear.

"Wedding bells you're supposed to be hearing, isn't it?"

Kelly's eyes opened. Surprise, he felt, near a shock, that the dread had lifted, that everything was clear now. He wouldn't be crying, he wouldn't be pleading. He stared up beyond the end of the pistol to the shadowed face of Jimmy Rynn. Was it drops of rain he felt? He wondered why those kicks hadn't hurt. How the mind works, he thought, how little we know, how everything had led to this moment, one minute a kid by the tractor at home, another in school playing hurling, and then the time he'd met Eimear first.

Kelly caught the movement of the finger before everything went away in the flash and noise. He fell back, his thoughts still running, but calm too, wondering and surprised that that's how it was.

There was light against his eyelids, and still the grit and

pieces of rubble and broken granulated windscreen from where he had lain. He heard talk, a low grunting cry. Angels, he decided, and like humans too probably, so it was true all along what he had hoped, that you got to continue on your odd life now in the new place.

A voice came through the ringing still going through his head.

"That's called reality."

Kelly opened his eyes. Rynn let out the cigarette smoke in a thin plume.

"But it's postponed, for now," he added.

The son seemed to be kicking something.

"Do you hear me?"

The red glow of the cigarette glimmered and glowed bright, and Rynn's face appeared again in the red gloom behind.

"Did you hear me, Kelly? Mister Garda Declan Kelly. Did you?"

Kelly nodded.

"In an hour I'll know where your parents live. Where your fiancée lives. I'll know what time she leaves for work every day. I'll know if your ma has varicose veins. How much money you have in the bank."

Rynn went down on one knee. The pistol wavered in his hand. A sharp, smoky smell different from Rynn's cigarette stung Kelly's nose now.

"Yes, I'm taking a chance. A big chance. That's because two percent of me believes what you said about my daughter. Two percent is all I need to go on for now. Are you hearing me?"

Kelly's nod this time was more of a shudder.

"Okay, you're not in a position to call me a liar. That's fair enough. But just so's you know we're serious. That was a real bullet that did your hair for you. Remember that. And remember those two scumbags back at that place were the bane of many a family. They took the lives of people. They've ruined families. I don't do that. Whatever else I do, I don't do that."

He stood up slowly.

"Think about that," he said. "Think about that, when your

young one, let's say when you and your missus-to-be do the business in a few weeks – you know the next steps, right? So let's say you're scoring goals and not just dribbling, let's say you'll have a young one same age as my young one. What, in 2000? Isn't that seventeen years? Okay. See, I was thinking about things like that and us driving around here. Numbers. Sums. I was always good at them. So I see the year 2000, the start of the next I don't know what you call it, centuries or something. But it's important, for some reason. Maybe I'm gone mental, but I don't think so. Let's just say it'll be a fresh start. A turning point."

He nodded and grimaced as he drew hard on the cigarette.

"Just don't get me wrong, Garda Kelly. I've done stuff, whatever needed to be done. I'm afraid of no-one. No-one."

Kelly heard paper rustling. Rynn was rummaging in his pocket again. Rynn's arm shot out and Kelly flinched. Something landed softly near him.

"For your hardships tonight," said Rynn and he waved the pistol once. "You get the good with the bad."

"It'll pay for a taxi. It's better money than being a bouncer, I'm telling you."

Rynn turned and he looked around the small mounds of rubble, into the dark empty places high up on the walls where the windows had been.

"Leg or no leg, you'll manage," he said. "You're built to take a bit of a hiding."

Kelly saw the glow of a cigarette near the car. The son seemed to have gone quiet now.

"One last thing. The most important thing. Are you listening to me?"

Kelly nodded.

"I'm going to be phoning your place in the morning. No – not your cop shop. I'm not checking up on you. I don't need to do that. I mean your house or your flat or whatever you have. Be there when I phone. You know? I want to hear you say you understand."

"I do. I understand."

"And that you understand it's not just me, or him. If you get any more hero notions or run to your boss, even if I'm out of the picture, you're gone. You know that? Gone. No matter where you are. You, your missus, your parents. You hearing me?"

"Yes."

"I do, say. Pretend you're doing the business. Pretend I'm the priest."

"I do. Yes."

Rynn nodded. He seemed to concentrate on where he had thrown the money. Then he turned and walked away.

Kelly watched him become a darker shadow, and then fade into the gloom by the wall. He listened for the footfalls on the rough ground. He began to elbow his way toward what looked like a bigger mound of clay and bricks. His rib hurt with each flexing of his arm. He didn't care if his hands were over glass. He heard the son's voice now, a single shout, and then something from Rynn. A car door opened. Rynn shouted something and he pulled it shut. Kelly got to one knee, listening for the second door.

He tried to stretch out his toes but the pain flared. The engine started, and screeched as the ignition was turned again. Kelly got up on one foot. There was nothing here to balance against. He drew in deep breaths as quietly as he could, and held his bad leg to hang in the air.

The tires bit into loose gravel and then found something more solid. Soon it crossed the sharp box of yellow cast by the lights on the street side the building. Kelly watched the car wallow and saw the jig of dull reflections dance over the car's roof. Then it was gone.

He began to hop. His head was suddenly full of the smell of his own body, and the rank smell of the rubbish from somewhere about him. He couldn't stop in time when some rubble by his shoe caught his foot. The other foot came down, and he gasped and cried out, and let himself fall to the side. Back on the ground again, he felt vulnerable, everything rushing back at him from the yellow haze of Dublin's lights over him. He reached down to feel the swelling, that warmth and numbness that would give way anytime to pain. He rubbed at the ankle, watched where the car had disappeared, listened. He couldn't take the chance of staying to rest, even a minute.

He realized that he had been talking out loud. Now it was his own hurried breaths he was hearing in the air around him. He got up again, and a new pain sliced into his side.

He found a half-mashed piece of PVC piping to his right, half-buried under clay and sharply broken cement. He pulled one loose, and it held as he tested his weight with it jammed into the ground beside him.

He stopped every few steps and used it to test the ground ahead of him. He worked around the mounds and away from the torn track the Rynns had driven out. In one of his stops, he heard a distant squeak and the dull thumps again. Trains for sure. This was somewhere in the centre of Dublin then. There had to be people, traffic, taxis.

He found a gap in the chain-link long ago widened and trampled down. The pipe caught in it but he held onto the lip of the fence and then a concrete pillar that was hanging by its rebar core. There were weeds growing by the fence, burst bags of rubbish and the leftovers of someone's old bathroom tiles.

Here was a street he didn't know, with just a high wall opposite, made of stone and topped by barbed wire. For a moment he thought he was near Kingsbridge, or beside that army barracks, what was the name of it.

Lights swept along the roadway then, from his right. He crouched and turned his face away. The car passed. He took down his arm, and looked down at the sleeve of this jacket he'd never wear again. He felt his mind began to slide, to capsize, the way it had when he'd fainted years ago with that flu. It felt he was fading into the street. He had to sit down, no matter how much it'd hurt him on the way down or back up again. Time passed, he didn't know how much. The sound of a car, and its lights, had him getting up again. He squinted into the headlights and tried to see a taxi sign on the roof.

The car swept by, leaving a fine spray from the road in its wake. He stared at the wet roadway but didn't see it for several moments. He hadn't said a prayer, not even when it looked like

Rynn was going to kill him. But how could that be?

A sob escaped him. He felt numb now, and he wondered if he were about to pass out. A paralysis had come over him, one he couldn't break, and with it a terror that felt like it would only grow until it crushed him into the roadway here for ever. Maybe it had been too sudden, and he couldn't think? It was ridiculous to be thinking about this now, he knew, but still it pierced him. He understood that he was alone now.

The pain roaring up from his ankle brought him back. He realized he had sat back against the fence, his leg straight out ahead of him. He got up and used the broken pipe to get over the last of the chain-link. There was a doorway, a wide one, opposite, three-quarters of it in the gloom. A piece of the sign on the pad-locked door met the light from the street lamp farther on. Eblana Electro something, he made out. Electroplating. Islandbridge.

♣ ♣ ♣

July 10, 1983

Kelly's eyes burned. All across his chest lay a weight, like a tightening belt. He had lain on the bed where he got in, in his clothes, and he remembered the huge jolt that had shaken him as he went into sleep. It was seven, now. That meant he'd gotten three hours of sleep, or less. The traffic had started already, its muted hush rubbing across the window.

He managed to get through a small bit of breakfast, but he was bewildered by the terrible taste of everything. Now that he was home, he couldn't decide if it was a lousy coincidence that he was starting his two days off, or a bit of luck. He remembered staring at the phone when he'd gotten home, and the awful, numb indecision.

The taxi driver had taken him right up to the door of Casualty. He had spun him a story of being roughed up. When he got to the Casualty he changed it to falling. The doctor bandaging him had had a strong Indian accent. Kelly didn't mind the open skepticism on his face. A twisted ankle was manageable.

He took the leg down from the chair and reached down with

his hand to the ankle. It wasn't swollen at all. He sat up again, and looked around the flat. Everything here was the same but it wasn't. Now he eyed the cardboard boxes he'd begun to stack near the door. They held the books and tapes he hardly listened to, as well as the trophies from the country championships, and the medals from Cluain Caomhin, his school, when they'd made it to the Munster Finals. Maybe that's what had saved him then, the sports.

He forced himself to think of Eimear. Mostly it worked, but she faded as did everything else, and without warning too, and for a moment he was back on the road with the slick, gritty cobblestones under his palms and the voice over him. But his mind was working, that he was certain. If that's what the brain did, this shutting things out for a while, that's what he would go with. He was fairly sure that it was shock, or plain and simple fear, but he needed time to figure this thing out.

The main thing was that he was able to see things a bit clearer now. He knew that every minute he delayed telling what had happened last night made it worse. Several times already he had reached for the phone. In the end he had done nothing. He'd thought about an anonymous call, or telling someone who'd then tell for him – but no: he'd been through all the ways he could think of. Still he couldn't make the move. He had to do something. Something ran cold in him at the thought, and then there was a kind of fury. No matter what he did, it'd turn out bad.

He reached for a mug, and he had several moments to watch it wobble and hit the linoleum floor. He smacked the tabletop with his palms and he closed his eyes tight. He counted to five and opened them again. Everything was so strange in the room yet: the rings on the cooker, the angle of the taps over the sink; the half-empty wine bottle left from Sunday. He stared at the milk container near where his cup had been. Not phoning someone about this, not deciding even, they were decisions too. Time was running on: running out, really.

He swiped the milk container hard enough for it to clear the floor before it crashed against the door. He felt some drops on his nose, one near his eye. He watched as the remains of it drained slower onto the floor. The quiet of the room after the whack got to him. He sensed a wave of panic closing on him and he got up. He wouldn't be able to fight this off for much longer. Something had to be done: he had to talk to someone. He leaned against the cabinet and tried stretching out his toes. The splinter of pain shot up, seemed to hit him behind his eyes.

Through the wall he heard a door being shoved closed and then a radio. There were squeaks as a drawer was pulled open. He listened for the water and sure enough it was turned on hard in the kitchen. Maybe it was early lectures for the three students, the slobs that he'd come to half like in the two years since they'd moved in. They could just get up and go to their lectures and do a bit of this and a bit of that and come home.

There it was, that same goddamned tune they played toward the end at the club. "Every Breath You Take."

He pivoted to the sink and turned on the cold tap full. Drops reached his neck, and out over the lip of the sink onto his feet. He rested his hands flat on the bottom of the stainless steel sink and let his forehead rest on the cupboard door above. His eyes were sore even behind the closed lids. The tightness all over his body grabbed at his shoulders and his knees most.

The water rose in the sink and tickled his wrist and fore-arms. There was four hundred and fifty-odd quid four inches from his forehead, in the souvenir mug from Crete. He'd never go back to that club on Capel Street again, never go down these streets and lanes around the Markets. He'd never stay in Dublin to get a Sergeant's.

The stream from the tap shot into the rising water, making a deeper sound. It was like a drill, he thought, or like a bullet. They must have been found by now, the two men. Maybe Rynn had taken them away, or sent someone to take them away some-where. He saw himself then an hour from now hobbling into the station, soaking up some jibes about the leg and learning to dance and how was Eimear after it.

It was to O'Keefe, his patrol partner, he should be talking to first. He would lay out what had happened last night, right from the word go. O'Keefe would know what to do. The law ran the place, not people like the Rynns, and the full powers of the Gardai would have each and every one of Rynn's crowd swept off the streets. Then he remembered the father's face, standing behind the pistol barrel. That drunken bitch of a daughter of his was behind all this, and then another kid of his, this lunatic of a son, was going nuts shooting people. And all Rynn's remarks about family, and why it was okay to gun down two dealers, only made everything even worse.

He imagined watching the judge pronouncing sentences on the Rynns. It'd be life for sure, and none other that Declan Kelly would be staring at them when it happened: right in the eye. Who would be the boss then?

And then what?

He'd be looking over his shoulder every day, is what. Moving, uprooting. What would Eimear do? Rynn could work from jail, put a number on him and Eimear. He'd be after revenge in the worst way, after letting Declan Kelly walk from this. There'd be his parents, Eimear's family, anybody Rynn wanted.

He left the tap running full. After a few moments he reached down and pulled out the stopper, and he watched the swirl begin. He shouldn't have waited. He didn't really have a choice now. He'd tell them it had been shock, or that he'd been paralyzed with fear, that he couldn't think. It was true. First thing was make sure Eimear was safe, and he'd get them to let him go to somewhere. The States would be his first choice, or Canada maybe.

The doorbell startled him. He turned the tap off and waited. The bell went again, the last note off, as it always had been, and probably always would be, in this flat. Hardly anyone used the doorbell.

He headed for the hallway, using the chairs and then the wall to take the weight off the ankle. It was the postman's bike against the railing outside.

"Howiya boss?"

Kelly took the chain off and opened the door. This cheerful, skinny Dub had been doing the road for twenty years.

"I was asked to tell you something here, about your phone."

"What?"

"Well, a fella says you're related, or you will be. You're tying the knot soon?"

Kelly looked through the railings at the traffic.

"Who told you that?"

"A fella over there, sitting in a car. No, he's around the corner there."

"Who is he? Is he there now?"

A glaze came over the postman's eyes.

"You haven't a clue, have you?" he asked.

"No."

"He's your brother-in-law."

"My brother-in-law?"

"To be, in anyways," the postman replied. Then he cocked an eye at Kelly.

"Tell us now," he said. "Is there maybe a bit of a practical joke type of a thing going on here?"

Kelly realized that he'd been staring at the man's ruddy face.

"He's gone off to find a phone box anyway."

"A phone box. What phone box?"

The postman waited a moment.

"'I don't want to scare him banging on the door,' says he. 'A bit delicate this morning.' He says for you to put your phone back on the hook, or plug it back into the wall."

Kelly squeezed the door handle tighter. The postman was still eyeing him.

"Well maybe you better go back and sleep it off then," said the postman. "Celebrations and all the rest of it? . . . Declan, is it?"

"Yes."

The postman's smile crept back, but it was cautious now.

"You look like shite, if you don't mind me saying so, Declan. But she'll sort you out, I'm thinking."

"I don't get this."

"Ah come on now – you're joining the fold. Your brother-in-law gave it away. The accent? Marrying a Dublin girl is a great move, that's all I'm saying."

He winked.

"Eimear," he said. "Eimear Walsh? Did I get her name right?"

He shrugged and he grinned, and he walked away whistling.

Kelly closed the door, and made his way down the hall. The radio from the next-door flat seemed to have gotten louder. He couldn't think. Eimear, they knew her name. Or had he said her name sometime before? No, and not her second name, ever.

The coldness seemed to rain down inside, falling from his chest, and it left him weak and empty. He stared at the transistor radio by the fridge. Now he thought about Australia, what he'd been reading in that *National Geographic* at the dentist. They'd never find you in Australia. Wasn't it Australia where Kevin Heaney had gone to work in a bank?

His eyes drifted back to the phone. He had wrapped the cord around it and put it under the hall table. He hobbled over and eased himself down onto the lino there, his leg pointed back to the kitchen. He plugged in the connector.

He could not remember later what he had done, or thought, in the time he sat there. It might even have been hours. Later he saw that it had only been minutes until the phone rang. He let it ring twice.

"You know who this is. You don't need to say anything."

Kelly concentrated on the brown nick in the lino where someone had dropped a cigarette. The voice was quiet, and the Dublin accent almost friendly.

"I said I'd be in touch. I keep me promises. So here we are."

He wondered where Rynn was. Maybe he had stayed up all night.

"None of us wants to go through something like that again. Right?"

Kelly listened to the faint rasp in Rynn's breathing. He said nothing.

"Look," said Rynn finally. "I'm sure you've been thinking the same thing as me in that line. Nobody would wish that on anyone. No sane person."

He heard the inhalation of breath again, the soft pop of a cigarette being pulled from between Rynn's lips.

"You're on your own there now," Rynn went on. "I'm not in a phone box, so don't go looking. I had someone pass on a message, that's all. Look. I hope you haven't done anything stupid now. Have you?"

Kelly kept up his scrutiny of the dings on the hall door, the black marks where he and others had closed it a hundred times with their foot. He wondered if Rynn had someone outside here all night, watching.

"I know you're listening. Have you told anyone, I asked you?"

He could put down the phone. He saw himself walking out to the car, the door open in his wake, getting in, driving to the bank to pick up Eimear, going out the Naas Road, away, away to the far end of Kerry or Cork or somewhere nobody went. Just to think, to know what was best to do.

"You're tying the knot soon enough. A grand girl, I'm sure. A lady."

Kelly felt the weariness as a new kind of gravity pressing him flatter against the wall and into the floor.

"Now of course every little bit helps when you're starting out, we all know that. And I was thinking about you a long time last night. Does that sound peculiar to you?"

He should have gotten a tape recorder.

"I don't know," he managed to say.

"Or you don't want to know . . .? Well I'll tell you anyway. You're a decent fella. That's what I decided. I can tell, you know. Actually even before I decided – it's funny – that's what I was telling you-know-who last night. You know who I'm talking about, don't you? Remember what he wanted to do?"

Kelly counted to five.

"Yes. I do, yes."

"Are you wondering why I keep on yapping here? Why I'm not worrying about who else is listening in? I'll tell you why. It's like I said: you're not stupid. And your heart's in the right place. You don't want anyone getting hurt. Right? After all, no-one told you to go down there after them, did they? To see if they were all right? No. It was your instinct. You were well reared, I mean. Did anyone ever tell you that?"

He wondered if Rynn was sitting in the hall in his own home too.

"Look, I want to know if you can hear me. That you're not asleep there. Okay?"

"I hear you."

"Well Christ! You got your voice back . . . ! Is that all you're going to say?"

He began to imagine Guards bashing down the door behind Rynn, letting him have it with batons.

"I'm not asking you for anything," said Rynn. "Not a thing. That's always been my philosophy: if you're not involved, you're not involved. Circumstances, is all. Are you with me on this?"

Kelly remained silent.

"I'm a bit concerned here now that maybe you're not picking up on this. I'm telling you that so far as I'm concerned the matter is settled. You hear me? Do you?"

"I do."

Kelly stared at the skin on his instep where it met with the braid edging on his slipper. There were two big veins. He wondered how long a twisted ankle took to mend.

"I'm not saying what happened was right," said Rynn. "No. But I'm telling you that I'm taking a chance here, like I did yesterday. This is a big risk for me, you understand? I need you to hear that, and tell me you got it."

Kelly listened to the breathing as Rynn waited.

"I've made arrangements, see? For whatever happens. Do you know what that means? Yes, or no?"

"I do."

"Well good. I'm a family man. And I'm not half as thick as I look. So when I say I've covered both sides, you can take that as gospel. You think about that. Think long and hard, before you get ideas."

Kelly heard a lighter being thumbed a few times.

"Okay then," said Rynn. "It's like a train, see – you think 'Oh it's nice and calm in here, like we're hardly moving, I can just go and step off.' Right? But you can't just walk out, 'cause everything else is going fast – you mightn't be, but everything else is?

Do you get it?"

Kelly said he did.

"I'm glad," said Rynn. "Now you don't know this 'cause you're new, or newish, maybe. I can do lots of things. If there are times when you want something done, well then you just tell me. Or tell someone, and they'll tell me. I don't owe you anything, mind. But what's done is done. There's no going back. That's lesson number one in life. You see?"

♣ ♣ ♣

October 24, 1983

The week before Hallowe'en, Kelly started his longed-for month of day shifts. They kept him with O'Keefe. O'Keefe was a terror for the snacks still. You could depend on him going into a shop twice or more just to get a bag of crisps, or a bar of chocolate or something. There was never an apple, or milk even.

Kelly kept the engine running outside the newsagent. He adjusted the volume on the radio and surveyed the leaves scudding in under the parked cars. The pearly light that strained through the low clouds over Dublin would hardly give them bright spells today, any more than it had let even a few minutes of sunshine down in the past few days.

The days had gone short all right. It had been dark when he'd gotten out of bed this morning, and it surprised him that he had not noticed until now. A red-headed man with a flushed face eyed him from outside a bookie's. The radio chatter between patrol cars and Dispatch about the big traffic accident near South Circular Road went on still.

O'Keefe was out quick enough, with his fags and his KitKat and his Coke. He also had a newspaper under his arm. He sat in and opened the newspaper. Kelly glanced down at the headline as he turned to begin reversing out. Another factory closing?

"Well, there's my brother heading for the boat," said O'Keefe. "Or the plane, or whatever it is."

"How do you mean?"

"That factory was where he worked."

"Was he long in it?"

"Eleven years. He thought he was safe. But what can you do?"

They half-listened then to an assistance call to a printing shop. The staff had just come in and the place had been burglarized. A Finglas car took the call. Kelly sped up again and was soon turning into the industrial estate and beginning to coast down by the warehouses.

O'Keefe finished his KitKat. He sighed, and started up a cigarette. He rolled down the window a little after the first pull.

"He might try the States," he said. "The brother. But it won't be on a visa, I can tell you."

"There's work if you're willing, I hear," was all Kelly could muster.

O'Keefe took a long, meditative drag on the cigarette and he opened the paper again.

"Well, well, well," he said. "Some you win – or we do, I should say."

"The hurling, is it?"

"No, no. A different sport entirely. Things take care of themselves sometimes, is what I'm saying. But we shouldn't be clapping in public now, should we."

Kelly looked over.

"What are you talking about?"

"There are scumbags getting what was coming to them. A rare enough event in this kip."

"Something in the paper?"

O'Keefe folded the newspaper again and flattened it more on his knee.

"You're a muck savage," he said. "Don't you read the papers at all? Look, I'll read it out to you. But before I do, maybe I should tell you a bit about this fella, or his family. You probably heard of them, but a fella in the know in CDU was telling us some of their shenanigans."

"Who, or what are you on about?"

"Ah you know them, come on. Everyone does, every Guard – the Rynns."

Kelly felt surges moving up and down his arms, and his back locking up.

"I heard it on the radio this morning. What's the name of the crowd in *The Godfather* there, that film? Car– Corleones, that's it. The son was a maniac, I heard. Jimmy Rynn. Junior they call him. Surely to God you've heard of him, or his oul fella?"

Kelly nodded.

"The son was off the wall," he said. "Breaking legs, kneecapping, God knows what else. So he must have done it once too often. Here is it, listen: 'Garda sources have confirmed that the body found in a field near Blessington was that of James Rynn Junior. Preliminary reports suggest that Mr. Rynn died of gunshot wounds. He was on bail awaiting an appeal of a conviction for theft and several related charges. And blah-dee-blah more, suspects sought dah dee dah . . .'"

O'Keefe reached down for his Coke and pulled off the tab.

"I'll drink to that," he said. "God forgive me."

Kelly had the feeling that the patrol car was driving itself, and that the hands on the steering wheel worked independently of their owner.

O'Keefe stifled a soft belch.

"Plenty more where he came from," he said "But we shouldn't look a gift horse in the mouth, I suppose."

Kelly smelled O'Keefe's sugary breath wafting across to him. The flashes from the laneway that night, and the shouts ran through his mind again. He took his foot off the accelerator and stared at a van parked up on the curb.

"What's wrong? What do you see?"

Kelly shook his head. Everything had a strange light to it now, even a glare off the lorry coming his way. He saw then that a shaft of sunlight had somehow broken through the cloud.

"So, you heard of them," said O'Keefe. "The Rynns?"

"Who hasn't?"

"Tit-for-tat, I'll bet you. Maybe the father'll be next. Hope springs infernal?"

O'Keefe looked over for a reply, but Kelly said nothing.

"The father's not a thick by any manner or means though,"

O'Keefe went on. "No sir. He's a 'businessman.' You've seen *The Godfather*, haven't you?"

Kelly sped up. He swerved just in time to avoid a deep fissure that connected several potholes spanning the width of the road.

"Jesus, Dec, relax! You nearly spilled me thing! What's around here to rob?"

Kelly concentrated on Eimear now, and what had happened last night after they got home. He'd heard that tone in her voice earlier on in the pub, and she had that sort of lingering look when their eyes met. They had barely closed the door when she came at him. He was still not over the surprise that she could ask for it – just like that – or that she could come at him with her hands.

"Did you know that?"

It was O'Keefe.

"Did I know what?"

"Did you know that you're on the planet?"

"Sorry, I was thinking."

O'Keefe shifted in his seat.

"True as God," he muttered. "You're a candidate for NASA there, sure you're halfway to the moon already these days."

"What were you saying?"

"Well, what I was saying was it was Rynn or one of his crowd did insurance fires here. Did you know that?"

"No, I didn't."

"Serious? You should keep your ear working, there, Dec. You'd pick up a lot. The Rynns, they have a go at anything. Rob the crown of thorns off the head of Our Saviour. Ever hear that one before?"

"I think I did."

O'Keefe tilted the can up to drain it.

"Christ, what a system we have here," he said then. "It's a joke. They get hired to burn down a factory. Insurance pays up – and I swear some of them must be in on it too – and guess who pays in the end?"

"Okay," said Kelly. "I get it."

O'Keefe was looking at him.

"Are you all right, Dec?"

"I'm grand."

"Have you got a cold or something? The flu?"

"No, I don't."

"You don't look so hot, I'm telling you."

"Better than you though."

"You'd better not puke on me."

"Don't be worrying."

"Get more sleep. If you know what I mean."

"Ha ha. You're funny."

They went by the picket at the gates of the cardboard factory, and got a slow, half-derisory wave from two of the picketers.

"Yobs," said O'Keefe. "No wonder there's, what is it, twenty percent unemployed. Or is it more now? I swear to God. Ah, what's the use."

O'Keefe took up a Dispatch request to go to a disturbance near a betting office on Glenore Road.

Kelly turned the car around.

"A bit of a barney," O'Keefe said. "Is there anything else they do around here these days?"

Dispatch came back with an Immediate on it. O'Keefe gave him a rueful look before he reached for the siren.

Kelly was glad of the excuse to drive like hell. He and O'Keefe had a routine down pat for these kinds of things. O'Keefe used his size to do the opening act and put the hard look on them, but the trick was that he delivered it all in a friendly way. He had one of those faces that made you laugh, or expect to hear something funny.

Declan Kelly's job was to watch the reaction, to eye who tried to leave or, rarely enough, have a go at them. O'Keefe still laughed at a bang from August. They attended on a closing-time row that soon went wild, with squad cars piling in and batons flying. One of the less drunk ones had made a run at O'Keefe almost right away. Kelly had put his foot out and watched as the man took a nosedive into a parking meter. Broken teeth and a concussion were the least of it.

O'Keefe was humming now. It was his worst, most annoying habit. It also meant he was content and even looking forward to the call. Kelly replayed in his head again the advice that Clune, the duty sergeant, liked to repeat: Don't talk too long, just give 'em the state of play, and a warning to disperse. Kelly's father's counsel repeated often too on the visits home was darker, for all its resemblance to a coach advising tactics for a hurling match: Stay a step back so you can see their hands – all those Dublin gutties carry knives, every man jack of them.

Kelly drove even faster. He didn't ignore the glow of satisfaction that was beginning to spread through him. There was no way in the world he should feel guilty either. He hoped that it had been a long and painful death for Junior Rynn. For several moments he imagined Rynn pleading for his life, on his knees, after a good hiding too. So be it, if he had been slaughtered like a pig.

"Jesus, Dec," O'Keefe said. "Slow down, man. Starsky and Hutch we ain't."

He braked for a delivery van that didn't move aside. The van reminded him of a big biscuit tin on wheels, and his mind went to the tin where he had put the money, and the patch of grass that covered it next to the end of the clothesline in the back garden. The envelope with the thousand quid had been delivered to the house, and left right on the kitchen table. There had been no signs of a forced entry. The doors had been locked all the time, and so had the windows.

Whoever had done it also knew that he'd be home before Eimear. Kelly had searched over and over again for a note or some sign from Rynn, but there had been none. He had wrapped the money inside two plastic bags, and then slipped it into a tin that he buried at the end of the garden. It was the day they'd officially moved in.

More days passed now when he didn't think about that buried tin, but many he did still. Often before sleep he had imagined, or felt, that some part of him was on a slow, meandering escalator that led somewhere he wasn't sure, like a path into the woods in some children's storybook. He had dreams that he held the tin under his arm, and someone was waiting for him to answer a question, but one he hadn't heard and couldn't know. It was a month ago when he had woken up crying. He had managed to let Eimear sleep, however.

Kelly had written down the telephone number for the Garda member's assistance line and had even phoned once. It was after a night shift and he remembered sitting in the driveway outside the house, with the rare sunny morning flooding through the car. He persuaded himself that what his ma had always said would come to be true, and that he wouldn't have to sit there ever again looking at his own house and hold back his panic. Time, she'd say, it just takes time. Or maybe it was like O'Keefe had said: sometimes things just take care of themselves.

♣ ♣ ♣

October 28, 1983

They buried Junior Rynn out of Raheny Church on a Friday morning. It was one day after Eimear's birthday. Kelly parked out of the way, on a road behind the shops there. He had no umbrella, but the hood of his anorak soaked up enough of the steady drizzle. He bought the *Racing Post* and found a spot to stand in the bookie's office across from the church where he could see out of the fogged and barred window onto the road.

It struck him again that now he felt nothing, absolutely nothing. A thousand times in the past few days he had Junior Rynn being knifed, and shot, and slashed, and begging to be killed just to end his agony. In this endlessly revived play, Kelly poured acid on Junior Rynn's face, burned him bit by bit, put him on broken glass and walked on him. Then he shot him again and again, starting methodically from the toes up, and waiting a minute while between each shot, aiming six inches higher than the last shot. His shin, his knee, his groin: all the while alive and conscious, and roaring.

He had tried to find out more about what had happened to Rynn, but even O'Keefe had heard nothing more than the same rumour that Junior Rynn had tried to put one over on some people with connections to the IRA in the North. It was only speculation.

The church car park filled steadily. The group of men near the door grew larger, and the cigarette smoke gathered above them more. A heavy-set man in a leather jacket turned his fat, bright-red face every now and then to spit. In the door of a church, Kelly thought, if that didn't tell you something about this crew. He didn't doubt there'd be some Guards around the funeral somewhere, and not just the traffic men on point duty. He looked for vans where there'd be cameras, but he couldn't tell.

Two older men came into the bookies and began watching the screen.

"A big turnout," said one to the other, and coughed.

Kelly went out onto the footpath now. He stood by the hairdressers' and lit a cigarette. Eimear had told him again last night that she hoped that'd be his last package, what with the baby on the way. He didn't smoke in the house. It was temporary, he didn't know why, he told her. It had been nine years since he'd smoked. He'd be off them soon, no bother.

There was a light brown tinge to the cloud cover, and no sign of any change from the drizzle. It seemed to get in everywhere, no matter what you wore. Then, from the direction of the city centre, came the headlights of the funeral cortege. The hearse, an old American car, seemed to float in a watery gleam over the roadway in. The door to the hairdressers opened beside him, and a woman with a towel wrapped around her shoulders came out. He glanced at the wet curly hair, smelled burned hair from the dryers.

"Is it starting," she said. "God – there's tons of flowers, look."

The hearse drew up close, and driver and the sidekick stared ahead under their brims. Behind came four other funeral cars, one completely loaded with flowers.

Kelly thought of Junior Rynn lying in the coffin moving by a hundred feet from where he stood. If it was to be an open coffin at all, Rynn's face would be plastered with makeup, or whatever they did in the funeral director's. He'd be all dolled up in a suit too no doubt, and holding rosary beads, like was done for everyone nearly. These were the same hands that had held the pistol, flashing and bucking, blasting the life from those two men in the laneway.

There were three Garda motorbikes. One of them was dismounted already and holding up the city-bound traffic. Kelly saw him wipe the beads of drizzle off his visor; and his white gloves raised and lowered sharply against the greys, chopping the air as he signalled. So a gangster gets the Guards to help with a funeral – no: but they did it for any funeral, any big funeral.

Kelly watched the way the people outside the church turned to the arrival of the cars. Most blessed themselves. These people were blessing themselves for a killer, he thought, and they were passing condolences, some of them genuine. People who should and did know better were now sympathizing with the parents who'd raised a mad dog of a son, a man who'd only have gone on to worse if he'd lived.

O'Keefe had heard from a detective that Junior Rynn had been taken out of a car as he was parking at a pub down the Naas Road. Rynn's girlfriend told the police there had been three men dressed in balaclavas, and according to her, one of them spoke with a definite Northern accent. Kelly remembered O'Keefe raising an eyebrow and repeating the "definite." He told him that his friend-of-a-friend detective said that the Northern bit was only a screen. The Guards were quietly working on an assumption it was a turf war in Dublin.

The door of the bookies opened and the two men came out. As though it were a design laid on people everywhere, Kelly thought, they had to sidle over his way, to stand together in a group.

"There they are," said one.

"God rest him," said the woman of the interrupted hairdo. "The only son."

"Isn't there another one?"

"It's a girl. There – she's there. That's her in the car, I think."

"She's dug out of him, isn't she?" said the woman. One of the men coughed several times.

Kelly dropped his cigarette into a puddle. He watched the gaberdined men from Fanagan's open umbrellas over the doors to the cars.

"God forgive me." He heard one of the men, the cougher, say. "But it'd put you in mind of that film."

"Look at all the stuff in the car. Flowers, wreaths, what have you. Jaysus, there's hundreds of quid in it. Thousands, maybe!"

"No wonder they call him the Godfather," said the other. "But not to his face, bejases!"

Kelly knew the cougher was angling his comments to draw him in.

"The biggest one I ever seen, I'll tell you that – no, wait. No that was only on the telly, the Bobby Sands one. Was that last year?"

"It was two years back," said the other. "Eighty-one."

"Well, you remember Dev's funeral, don't you?"

"No. Why would I remember Devalera's funeral?"

"I'm only saying."

"I know. I'm only saying too, amn't I."

They fell into a touchy silence then. Kelly watched the umbrellas seem to carry the emerging legs and trousers and black coats across the pavement to the church door. It was quite unbelievable, he decided, and most of all it was because it looked so normal. Here were the lugs and thugs and low-lifes, every variety of the scuts that Dublin produced so effortlessly, all pretending reverence here at a church they'd gladly rob or set fire to, if the humour took them.

The cougher cleared his throat

"Oh, I'd say you'd have to be counted today," he said. "Put in an appearance, as they say. There'd be notes kept by some people, if you know what I mean. Both sides."

"You're dead on there. There's Rolo Murphy. He must be sixty now. Weren't the Rynns and Rolo on the outs for years?"

"I heard. But like you said. That's all by-the-by now – look, that's Yo-Yo Keogh, isn't it . . .? It is. Look there he is, Jumbo Rynn. The father. God, but he looks shook."

Kelly watched Rynn shrug off the offer of an umbrella and glance at an outstretched hand before he turned to wait for the coffin. He pulled the drawstrings on his hood tighter under his chin.

With the traffic stopped now, he heard the gurgle of rainwater from a drain, the grumbling transmission of the bus waiting for the Guard's white glove. The only movement by the church now was the slow, silent work of one of Fanagan's men to draw the coffin out to the waiting men.

Kelly watched them take the weight, saw the sways and bobs before they had their balance, the arms go out to the shoulder opposite.

"By God, that crowd must have practised," said one of the men. "They have the drill down pat."

Kelly's stomach felt like it was welling up under his ribs. He smelled the cigarette off his own breath still. Soon the praying and the holy water and the incense would get going in the packed church. There'd be people Rynn paid to do all his dirty work, who bided their time in jail over the years knowing he kept a place for them, people who thought nothing of taking a drill to your knees or selling heroin to your daughter. But there'd hardly be one member of a family who had suffered because of the bastard, no one to stand up and tell the truth: The man in that coffin deserves to be there on account of what the bastard has done to people.

"Ah well, we all get our turn, don't we?"

It was one of the men, Kelly realized. It was him they were talking to.

"You're right," he said.

"We'll hardly be shuffling off with this kind of a classy effort though, hah?"

Classy, Kelly thought. His arms tingled when he imagined grabbing this Dublin gouger beside him, and shoving him along with his mate into the window behind.

He nodded, and watched the church door. The long strands of hair that Rynn had tried to keep over his baldy head were now sliding down with the drizzle. Mrs. Rynn, to judge by the cut of her, had appeared now, and she was in a bad way, hanging off other women. Kelly was pretty sure that one of them was the daughter. With her dark, bruised-looking eyes and the ruination all over her face, the mother looked so doped up that she wouldn't see much beyond the tip of her nose.

Then Kelly sneezed. He hadn't felt it coming, and it wasn't going to be the only one. He turned away and pulled down on the strings of his hood just as the second sneeze came. He searched around his pockets for hankies and found some, fairly mashed, but unused. The one he tried to separate and spread out on his hand escaped his fingers and fell to the wet cement. He took another, and wiped his nose, and then balled up the hankie and put it back in his pocket.

When he let his eyes find the front of the church again, he froze. His blood began pounding in his ears. Slowly he let his eyes move to the trees and their sparse leaves to the side of the church car park. He did not want to make any sudden moves. He could see that Rynn had still not moved. He didn't want to look at him to check he had stopped staring. Had it been the sudden movement when he sneezed, he wondered, or the clumsiness with the hanky that had drawn Rynn's eye over here.

The two men beside him were blathering again, something about the 2:30 race at Cheltenham. For a moment he let his gaze go back toward Rynn's figure in the church door. Strangely, it was no surprise really, none at all, when he saw that Rynn was staring his way still.

♣ ♣ ♣

November 8, 1983

He was a half an hour from the end of the shift, with more than half of the statement typed when the phone call came. Cullen, the new Guard, held up the receiver.

"Something to do with a motorbike stolen?"

Kelly looked at the night pressing in on the window and then made a face.

"I don't know now," said Cullen. "But he sounds like he's had a few."

Kelly Tippexed the misspelling in "altercation" and blew on it, before he reached for the extension. Again he tried to remember: there had been the crash over near that pub, what was it, Healey's, but it was a van and a car.

He checked the clock again and jabbed at the glowing button.

"Garda Kelly?" he said.

"Yes, Garda Kelly."

The voice was a man's, a smoker's wheeze layered on a weary, Dublin drawl.

"Who is this?"

"You don't know me?"

Kelly felt himself go still, balancing at the front of the chair. He dug his elbows into the desk.

"Well? Open your mouth and say something."

"Yes."

He had almost made it, Kelly thought. In fifteen more minutes, he'd have been on his way home. A cup of tea, a bite of a sandwich, Eimear still awake maybe, after her twentieth trip to the toilet.

He stared at his incident book splayed out on the desk in front of him: Rynn knew his shift tonight. He had probably picked this time, exactly. He looked around the station. Cullen was scribbling something in a notepad and then turning back to the typewriter. Being new, he took pains to get everything perfect in his reports, and even had a dictionary in his locker. Fahy, the duty sergeant, was on his phone extension, smiling lazily about something and murmuring every now and then.

"Hey!"

Rynn's sudden growl startled Kelly.

"Are you awake there?" Rynn growled. "I'm expecting more than a 'yeah.' Okay?"

Kelly brought the phone to the near edge of his desk, and he turned aside.

"What?"

"What do you mean 'what'?"

"Well, I didn't expect–"

"–No, you didn't expect. Of course you didn't *expect*."

The words that cut off his were cut off in turn by a cough.

"You think I'm blind, is it?" Rynn went on, hoarsely. "Is that what you think?"

"Look," Kelly began, but he lost track as the panic took hold. Rynn said nothing. Kelly's nails dug harder into his palm.

"I'm at work," he said.

"Well aren't you great."

"I can– you can . . ."

"Go on. What can you do? Or are you going to tell me what I can do?"

"No. I meant now's not a good time."

It might have been humour more than mockery that he heard in Rynn's snort now.

"It never is, is it? What do you want?"

"I don't know what you mean. I don't want anything."

"I said: what do you want. What do you want from me? Or are you going to give me something, is that it? Jesus, wouldn't that be something now."

"Nothing," said Kelly. "I don't want anything from you. I don't."

"'Sell' then. What do you want to sell?"

"No. That was never, I mean, that'd never happen."

"Listen to me, Kelly. Whatever you could offer me I wouldn't want. Do you get that?"

He wondered how well Rynn could hold his drink. Maybe it was some drug, some sedative, they'd put him on.

"Yes."

"But that's wrong. No, no it's wrong. I'll tell you what I want, yeah, I will. Are you listening?"

He thought of Rynn's grey face from the church door that morning last week. It was like a dead man's really, the solid, squat bulk of him in a coat that could never suit him, and his whole body slack and sagging.

"Tell me why you were there. That's what I want. Tell me that."

Kelly's hand reached for the button to drop the call.

"Revenge, was it? To make sure, maybe?"

"No."

"Did you want to see him? To put a curse on him, was it, you Garda bastard? Was it?"

"No. I wouldn't."

"You would," said Rynn in a strangely calm voice. "You would if you could. Don't you think you have me codded, not one bit. Did you go there just to laugh at me, because if you did, you have to answer for that. Yes, you do."

"That's not it," Kelly said. "No."

"I lose my own son? And the other one, you, got to walk away? Because I took a chance on you?"

"No," Kelly said. Rynn did not seem to have heard him.

"So you can finish your little cop thing there, and go home and do the garden or something, or wash the bleeding car– Is that the way it is?"

"I have a baby coming."

Immediately he heard his own words, Kelly recoiled.

"What did you just say?"

"No, nothing, I was thinking of something else."

"A baby, I heard you say baby."

"No. I meant something else. No."

In the quiet at Rynn's end, Kelly imagined him pouring more whiskey.

"He's gone," said Rynn. "But you're not. You wanted to rub it in on me."

"No, I wouldn't."

"You wanted your revenge. You wanted to get back at him, at me."

"I would never do that. I'm not that kind of person. I'm not."

Rynn didn't speak for several moments.

"You're scared," he murmured. "Aren't you?"

Kelly leaned further over the desk pressing his elbows down harder.

"You are," Rynn said. "And so you should be. I'll tell you why. Are you listening to me?"

"Yes."

"You better be. 'Cause I do want something now. Oh yes I do. I never expected one thing out of you, not a thing. And I never said nothing to you after that. You got an envelope – and don't say you didn't – and your wedding, and your little house and what have you. But that wasn't good enough for you, was it?"

"I only went to– I was just curious," Kelly said.

"You were curious? Jesus."

"I don't know why I went, I don't. I really don't. Look, I've been having problems ever since then. I mean, it's been hard."

"Don't you start telling me about hard times. My son's dead."

"There's things going on, stress, that sort of thing. I've been learning a bit. It's the subconscious, I think."

"What in the name of Jesus are you on about? Are you mad, or something?"

Kelly's neck ached from the tension. He watched Cullen stretch again.

"I'm not sleeping right," he said. "So my thinking is off. That's all it was. But I'll be getting better. It was a mistake going, look, I don't know why I went. It wasn't what you think, what you said, I mean."

"You want me to feel sorry for you or something? Is that your game here?"

"No, no. I'm just saying, I'm in no position to, you know."

"To . . . ? To do something for me? For the man who saved your neck? How do I know you didn't rat on me for what happened back then, what is it now, only four months . . . it's like a million years ago. Anyway, how do I know you didn't?"

"I didn't," said Kelly. "I wouldn't, I swear."

"You swear, do you? What about your priest in confession, whatever your crowd do. What about that?"

"No. I mean I wouldn't. And now, well, it's gone by."

"What are you saying 'gone by'? It's too late to rat on me just because my son isn't here?"

"I mean there's no point. That's all I mean."

Rynn seemed to consider this.

"Well, you're starting to make sense a bit," said Rynn. "Just a tiny bit, mind you."

Kelly lowered his voice again.

"I didn't mean any harm there at the church," he said.

"So you say," said Rynn. "So you say. But those are only words."

"It's true."

"Now look. You have to realize something here. You have to see my position here. Jesus Christ, I can't believe I'm talking to a Guard like this, explaining things. This is madness. But I have a bad feeling that somebody's trying to rub my face in it here."

"I wouldn't–"

"–You keep on saying the same thing: 'I wouldn't, I didn't, I couldn't.' Let me tell you something, copper: you would if you could get away with it. All of you cops would. You hate me, us, all my people. You're jealous of us. You'd love to see us go down. Don't lie to me, I'm not an iijit?"

But staring now at the marks on the desk, the bottle of Tippex, his incident book, Kelly realized then that he had decided something. It had happened in an instant. He understood that he had made this decision long before tonight. It was just that he hadn't even admitted it to himself. It wasn't relief that flooded into him, no, but some feeling of clarity.

Yes, he'd work at anything. Toronto was nice he'd heard, but only go to a big city. Somewhere near the mountains and the sea, Vancouver? So much space – and the North, where hardly anyone lived?

"You get what I'm saying to you?"

"I do."

"Good. I want an address. Can you do that for me?"

"I don't know."

"Well try. And try hard. I'm trying to get in touch with someone but I've lost his address. So his sister would have it but she moved a few weeks ago herself. They're half-knackers, to be honest. Him, he's like a fart in a bottle, always running around, but I know he gets in touch with her. So I don't have time or energy to be running around. Write down her name."

Kelly wanted to say something. He watched his own hand scribble the name. Lorraine Smith.

"I know, I know," he heard Rynn say. The voice seemed to come from a great distance to him now. He loosened his grip on the telephone and took a deep breath, and then another. "There's tons of Smiths, I know. That's why I'm asking you, see. She had some connection with people in Arklow or some place. Knackers, the half of them, I think. I used to know her oul lad but he's otherwise occupied this past while."

"I don't think I can do this," he said.

"That's a load of bollocks. Just go to that new computer thing you have there somewhere and do it."

"There's a log of who uses it. There's requisitions and everything. I can't."

"Did I ask you the ins-and-outs of the thing? No I didn't. And let me tell you something else now. I want you to think long and hard about this. I'm not asking you to do impossible things. That's not my way. That'd be stupid to do that. You said stress, didn't you, pressure and all of that? Well, I'm not thick. I know all about that. People do mad things under stress. I'm going to tell you something now and you're hardly going to believe it, so you're not."

Rynn seemed to gather himself before going on. Kelly kept his eyes on the desktop but his mind was trying to piece together images from maps and travel brochures, and from the pictures he had formed from listening to people's descriptions.

The Rockies were so high they had snow all year long. They were different from Americans too, the people there, not loud or full of themselves, or that. There had been a bunch of them years ago, hitchhikers, in that pub there in Clifden.

"I'm going to consider what you done at the church as a good thing. Do you hear that?"

"Yes."

"I don't think you know what a big step that is. Do you have a clue, even?"

"I do."

"I'm going to think of it as a show of respect. Not as some kind of savage thing, a revenge thing."

Rynn paused then and waited. Kelly thought he heard some liquid swishing around.

"I bet you think I'm losing it," Rynn said then. "Don't you?"

"No, I don't."

"You wouldn't tell me anyway, would you? But just think

back for a minute how this conversation started, and then tell me it's not some kind of a miracle. I mean, I don't believe in that shite, don't get me wrong, okay? But it started out me wanting to nail you for that, for showing up. But I always had that doubt, wondering if maybe you didn't mean any harm. D'you get that, did you?"

These were the first slurred words, Kelly realized.

"Yes," he replied. "I think I do."

"Nobody asked for any of this to happen, okay? But there's something between us, yes there is. I don't know what it is. I don't believe in this fortune-telling crap, no way. But there we are. So there. Did you ever think you'd hear someone on my side of the fence talk to a Guard like that, did you?"

"No. I suppose not."

"Well, I'm telling you. I know myself. I don't have much schooling, but I know stuff. So I'm saying this: you save me time finding Lorraine Smith, and I'll push things your way. No, no, no – I can hear you thinking I'm trying to buy you off – it's not that. It's not. Not at all. I'm saying that I'll look after you, yes I will. In some shape or form. Okay? I'm going to just leave it with you for now. I don't want to hear from you saying you can't, and it's impossible, or whatever. Lorraine Smith, used to be in Walkinstown. Lorraine Smith."

Kelly's thoughts swarmed, and words skittered into nowhere. He definitely heard a glass, or ice at Rynn's end now. He listened harder and heard a sigh.

"Look," he said, but stopped. Rynn had hung up.

Kelly put down the receiver. Things went on around him, as though nothing had happened or changed. He heard the stutter of the typewriter still, and saw the piece of tongue Cullen held between his teeth in his efforts to concentrate.

Everything looked faded and tinted a pale grey by the fluorescent lights. Fahjy was off the phone himself, and he groaned and swore as he stood. After a stretch that lifted one shirt tail right up from his belt, he began that tuneless whistling he did with his tongue at the roof of his mouth. The happy man finishing his shift, just as he Declan Kelly should be.

JOHN BRADY

He heard his breath and felt a band around his forehead, tightening, pushing.

Fahy turned up the radio traffic to hear something about a motorbike accident. He turned away, heard a Guard talk a little breathlessly about some pub called Tracy's, a falling-down fight they'd need a wagon for three of them.

"What's with the long face there, Dec?"

He studied Fahy's tired smile. Fahy at least had the where-withal to stop the digs about women after the wedding.

"Not long now," said Fahy, and tilted his head and winked.

Kelly knew it was well meant, maybe even a joke, but he didn't know what it meant. Nor did he care, right now. Fahy was still eyeing him.

"Come on," he said. "Go home. Are you nodding off there?"

Kelly got up. Everything was suddenly heavy on him now, his limbs even.

"Are you all right there, Dec? Going to make it, are you?"

"If we were all right we wouldn't be here, would we."

Fahy smiled but it became a yawn. Then his face turned softer.

"Don't be overdoing it," he said. "Believe you me, there'll be plenty of time for that painting and decorating thing now. Conserve your energy, as they say. You'll be busy enough in no time, let me tell you. Mark my words, oh yes."

Kelly tried to hide his irritation. It was well meant. Fahy had three kids already, himself. Maybe he should have kept back the news about Eimear expecting until later. It was inexperience really, and there had been a little bit of embarrassment about how quickly she had gotten pregnant. Ahead of the rest of the field already, Fahy had said when he'd heard the news first, and hardly out of the starting gate.

"Thanks for telling me," he said to Fahy.

"I meant to ask you, Dec. How's the leg with you?"

Kelly didn't get it for several moments.

"The ankle?" Fahy went on. "You're back to the hurling, aren't you?"

Kelly was almost certain that Fahy'e eyes had done a quick

search of the desk for an ashtray.

"Oh, I nearly forgot."

"Well, that's a good sign then," said Fahy.

But Kelly knew that Fahy was still watching him as he put away his folders.

"Ever consider trying again, you know?" he asked.

"Twisting my ankle?"

"No, you thick– I meant looking for those fellas who did it."

"I haven't, to be honest. I suppose I should."

"It might be worth it, Dec. They might have come up since, for a similar."

His fury with Fahy's meandering talk that'd never stop was only growing. "Maybe," he said. He realized that he had been holding his breath.

"Dublin, huh," said Fahy then, with an air of finality, and began another long, slow stretch. His last words came out as a groan.

"Lucky it wasn't worse, I suppose."

Kelly finished the incident report but left the misspellings. Then he got up. His mouth felt acid, and the room seemed to have changed. He couldn't bear to look over at Fahy, but seeing Cullen's earnest, frowning attentions to what his typewriter was doing repelled him now.

"You look shagged," he heard Fahy say behind him. "Go on home."

Cullen looked up from his typing, and Kelly had to look away.

Fahy shoved the drawer closed as he always did when he had his shift done.

"You might be coming down with something," he said. "There's something going around, I hear."

♣ ♣ ♣

November 18, 1983

For the fourth night in a row, Declan Kelly kept waking up. It was almost always the same time. Eimear was beginning to sleep lighter too. Tonight, for some reason, she had woken up before him. He could tell by her breathing. He tried not to move.

There wasn't a hint of dawn on the curtains. The nights were so damned long now, and there was still a month yet to go before it turned again. Solstice, was that the word?

He listened, hoping for her breathing to lapse back into the steady, nasal pattern that had come on in the past few weeks. She didn't mind the odd kick during the day but at night it wasn't much fun.

Her voice was clear when she spoke, clear enough to startle him.

"You're awake."

"I am."

"Why are you waking up?"

"I don't know," he said.

She shifted a little, and drew up her leg. He had stopped wondering how much the skin on her belly, on any woman's belly, could stretch so much already.

A minute passed. He stared at the darker line where the curtains met, willing it to be brighter so he wouldn't have to look at his watch and see how early it was.

"What time is it?"

"I don't know," he replied. "I don't look."

She moved around and got her elbows under her. The bed warmth came up at him. Wait till the water breaks bejases, O'Keefe had told him: it's always at night!

"I might as well now as later," she said.

"Do you want a hand?"

"To pee? I'm not ready for that yet, love."

Kelly followed her form in the near dark, heard her labouring breath. The yellow landing light glowed at the bottom of the bedroom door, and he heard the door to the bathroom close.

He turned on his back and stared at the ceiling. The tots of whiskey hadn't helped a bit these last two nights. Eimear hadn't noticed, or if she had, she hadn't let on. He'd been careful, brushing and gargling. There was the soft clank of the lever pushed and the rush of water. He waited to hear her footsteps, and the click of the light switch.

"Don't be worrying," she said, and nestled against him.

"I'm not," he said. He took her arm under his and let it rest on his chest.

"Come on now, Dec," she murmured. "I'm not blind, you know. Or stupid."

He didn't know what to say.

"Go back to sleep, can't you," he managed. "Talk in the morning."

"Give us an oul squeeze first, but," she said.

He guided her leg up and felt the taut press of her belly against his side.

"Don't be getting excited now," she whispered.

From her voice he knew she was smiling. He stroked her back with his fingertips, felt her head shift a little in the crook of his arm. He had admitted to himself that part of him was annoyed at how fast things had happened. The thing was, it was nobody's fault. Even thinking that way about "fault" was stupid: a baby was good news, for God's sake. And when you think about it, it was way better to get started now and not to be waiting. The fact was, Eimear must have been pregnant at the altar. People would figure that out soon enough, no doubt.

He lay there for what seemed like a long time, until he thought her slack weight meant sleep. Then he began to work at freeing her arm.

"I can tell, you know, Dec."

"Aren't you asleep?"

"How can I sleep?"

"I'm sorry. Here, lie over."

"I can read your mind," she said. "Well, a bit anyways."

"Jesus, now I'll never sleep again."

"I'm only joking. But it's okay to be nervous, for men. You know that."

The flutter of resentment stirred, and stayed. How women were so all knowing, he thought, or so they thought. He rubbed at his eyes and for no reason he saw the flashes in that laneway and Junior Rynn's lit up with each shot.

"What," said Eimear. "What's that? Did I hit you?"

He felt his heart thumping. He tried harder to keep his breathing normal.

"No, no. I'm grand."

He could tell by the quiet then that it wasn't over, that she didn't believe him. His mind ran from place to place, through the years, in his search to banish the dim half-born images circling in his mind. He must never panic: never.

He forced himself to remember the beach where they had lain and had it off that night in Portugal. There had been that low wall with the nice places to sunbathe, he could remember. Then there were the umbrellas, the wooden walkway thing. A German couple, with the girl going topless, no big deal. His mind raced to the hurling that he had enjoyed all the way though secondary school, even the falls onto the grassy, soft surface of the pitch so often moist from rain. It had been an icy blue sky the day of the passing out parade in the Garda Depot in Templemore, though–

"What is it, Dec? No secrets, remember?"

He mustn't get angry, not even annoyed.

"Ah, it's just a situation at work. It'll work out. It will."

"It'll be different soon," she said after a while. "They'll know you have responsibilities, you know."

He stared harder at where the curtains met. If it was dawn here, then it was dusk on the far side of the planet. He had never quite figured that out: if the Earth was spinning so fast, well how come . . . ?

The question faded as a great longing came over him, a confused cascade of sky, and snow-capped mountains, and the wide highways – interstates, they were called – and skyscrapers and California beaches. He opened his eyes again.

It wouldn't even have to be more than five years away: that's how he'd sell it to Eimear. They could save pretty well everything they earned over there too, because stuff was cheap. He could try his hand at something there that'd look good when he came back – a course in computers would be good, the coming thing. Then, when they'd come back, this would be all out of their system, and they would build a house, their own house, down near Cahir. He'd never have to travel the stinking streets of Dublin again.

"When is your cousin visiting again?"

"What cousin?" she asked.

"Paddy Keane, him"

"From the States?"

She jerked upright, far faster than he imagined she could. Her voice had changed.

"Listen, Declan. Don't start that again. Don't. This is not the time, okay?"

"What am I starting?"

"You know my feelings on that score. It's a lot different now; with the way we'll be, God willing. There'll be three of us. Not two, three. Are you listening to me?"

He was annoyed enough now not to pretend otherwise.

"Declan, look. A woman doesn't think like a man, okay? She can't. I have all mine here. Ma, all my sisters. Everybody."

"Okay," he managed. "Okay."

She knew enough not to push it, he realized. Slowly she let herself down again.

"Of course we'll go," she said. "For a visit. I know you want to go. New York, Los Angeles wherever. Australia, wasn't that another one? Canada. I listen. I do."

He heard the little intake of breath. His mind rocked with guilt and love. He reached for her.

"I'm sorry," she said, and a sob broke. "I'm sorry."

"It's okay," he said. "It's me that's sorry. I shouldn't be talking."

The strange and frightening peace that took over in him then could have carried him off into sleep as it did Eimear. He didn't want to sleep now. He waited, watching the morning leak gradually into the room. The birds were so many fewer, or quieter now, than in the summer here.

Things detached themselves slowly from the gloom and took shape in the pale light. For a while he imagined their bedroom was its own world, and that when he'd open the door later, there'd be nothing out there. Or maybe it was an island that he could look down on, right through the roof and the clouds, and even from frozen space full of blinking stars. Was this what drugs were like, he wondered, the good bits that people don't like to admit?

He might have slept. He hit the alarm, felt her stir, and heard her swallow dryly. Things moved on, he understood as he swivelled his legs over the edge of the bed. He knew that whatever he'd been carrying since that night had grown, and that there'd be more spells of that panic, that kind of paralyzing helplessness. He welcomed the cold of the carpet underfoot. He looked back at Eimear, and at the squashed pillow and the turned back eiderdown where he had been. For a moment he imagined himself lying there still, as though part of him could stay there and the other just carry on, heading out to work, and coming home, and going to the shops, and thinking about their first Christmas together. . . . Had he become two people somehow, and was only noticing it now?

♣ ♣ ♣

December 14, 1983

It wasn't remorse Kelly felt, looking down into the remains of the Bushmills on the counter in front of him. He was used to pints after a game, and he could go fairly steady at them all night if there was company. He was still surprised that he had blurted out the order to the barman without even thinking about it beforehand. He had never just walked into a pub and ordered whiskey before. Now, like his father, he wouldn't adulterate it with water. Funny the things you do automatically, he thought, however you learn them. The Bushmills went fast. He ordered a pint, and then another Bushmills.

It had worked, he had to admit. He felt calm, and almost friendly. It certainly wasn't the anemic-looking Christmas decorations pinned on the edges of the shelves, or the "Welcome to 1984" card that only looked ridiculous and even almost pathetic here. He remembered that *1984* was a famous book, but not if he had read it back in school.

His stomach had been in rag order all week. A wormy, gaping ache working its way around his guts had kept him away from proper meals. The quick bang from the whiskey had taken the edge off things, and soon banished the aches entirely. The beer he now drank felt like it was falling from a tap straight into a stomach that wanted something to eat. It could wait. He'd stick with the package of peanuts.

He could have hit O'Keefe earlier on today. The same O'Keefe had been niggling away as they patrolled, thinking he was funny. Of course, you work with a fella, he's going to notice you're off your fodder. "A bit peaky today, Dec?" from O Keefe, and the sly look to him. "Finally sinking in is it, Dec?" Sure didn't he have the same thing himself, O'Keefe, the proud father of three, all the way to labour pains, bejases, can you believe that? And O'Keefe laughing in that rolling chuckle he had.

Eimear had noticed he wasn't up to par a few days ago. She was sort of charmed about it. She had said she'd heard that some husbands went through this, these sympathy symptoms, they were called. But he should talk it out, she'd said. Declan Kelly wasn't inclined to do that. Too often he imagined himself bursting out, shouting about the mess he was in, they were in, how he had to keep it to himself, how he couldn't sleep, how he nearly fell asleep at the wheel on patrol. How he was ready to give O'Keefe a clout if he started up again tomorrow.

He fished in the corner of the bag for any fragment of peanut, or for salt even, and licked his fingers. Then he took a small sip of the whiskey, and let it lie in a pool under his tongue. After a few moments he let it trickle and scorch its way down his throat. He felt his shoulders loosen even more now, their weight draw him down. He could almost sleep right here.

The barman continued to fill shelves and half-whistle a tune he was making up as he went along. He looked up to the mirror behind the counter when the door opened. Kelly didn't know the man entering. Still, he had the look about him, Kelly decided, that aggressive wariness and deliberately loose-limbed way of walking. But didn't every second man he saw in Dublin have that?

The man shook change in his pocket and took his time

heading to the bar. Kelly took in the scuffed elbows on the leather bomber jacket, the forehead that seemed to end in a line over small eyes, the wispy red-blond hair, the neck settled tight into the collar.

Kelly saw the door move again and Rynn's face appear. The man in the leather jacket was standing in the middle of the floor now, and he was staring at Kelly.

"Gentlemen?" from the barman.

"Remy Martin for me," said Rynn. "And another whatever for this man."

"I'm okay," said Kelly, his voice catching. He cleared his throat. The blood now pounding in his head seemed to deafen him. Rynn's minder had perched on a stool now, and he was watching him in the mirror.

"What's that," said Rynn. "A small one? Give him a small one."

"No."

"No nothing. Give him a small one."

Rynn leaned one elbow on the bar and turned to face Kelly. "You look like you need it, believe me."

Kelly had rehearsed this so many times so often in the past few days: the tone, the way he had to be sure to look Rynn right in the eye, the expression he'd put on his face.

"Ever see anything like it," Rynn said to the barman. "Poxiest week of rain I ever seen."

"You're right there. Absolutely right about that, Mr. Rynn."

The name was like a blow to Kelly. Barmen knew every-body. This one would be able to say he'd seen Garda Kelly and Rynn having a little chat.

Rynn skated his glass around in a slow arc, over and back on the counter, and then lifted it.

"Well now," he said.

Kelly shook his head. Rynn nodded back his first gulp of whiskey.

"What," he said then. "What are you shaking your head at me for?"

"Can't do it. I just can't."

Kelly looked away from the mirror.

"I can't," he said. He was surprised at how easily it came out.

"You can't," said Rynn. "One name? One address? What, you can't find it?"

"I can't do it."

"You can," said Rynn. "And you will, because you're not stupid."

Rynn's minder was no longer pretending not to listen. Kelly glanced his way and locked eyes for a moment.

"I'm a Guard," Kelly said. "That's why I can't do it."

Rynn looked into his glass, and then flicked it slowly from side to side.

"You're serious, I think," he said.

Kelly wondered if it was the whiskey had held the panic back, had given him his voice, the quiet exhilaration rising up in him. Again he saw himself phoning Eimear before the morning was out, telling her that he'd decided, and that they'd have to change everything. When she'd hear what he'd been going through, all her dismissals and her warnings would fall away. It'd be Canada he'd ask for, if they gave him a choice.

Rynn stopped rolling the brandy and stared at it.

"Have you gone and done something very stupid?" he murmured.

Kelly didn't answer.

"Who've you told?" Rynn asked, his voice even lower.

Kelly shook his head.

"How do I know that?"

Kelly glanced at him.

"You know," he said. "You know."

"Do I? How do you figure that?"

"If I didn't tell people that same night, then every day after that, every hour that I didn't make that call, looks bad. And you know that too."

There was a hint of thoughtful amusement in Rynn's gaze now.

"You don't hear me arguing, do you? But who knows you're here now, is what I'd like to know. I mean, you're a married man now."

"No-one. I would never involve my wife."

"Are you certain? 'Cause you better remember what I told you. This is bigger than you or me. It doesn't matter where you go, or even where I go. Things will be taken care of. Are you hearing me?"

Kelly studied the cigarette burns at the side of the counter.

"What's with this change of attitude then? Are you hinting at something?"

"It'll never let up," Kelly said. "If I do this. It'll just go on and on."

"Nobody's telling," said Rynn. "So what's the big problem? I get what I want, you get what you want. So?"

Kelly felt Rynn's eyes on him now.

"Oh, I get it," said Rynn then, and sat back. "You want something better, is it? How much?"

"No, it's not that."

"What do you want, then?"

"I want to, I want out."

"You want out? What does that mean, 'out'?"

"Just out. It's too much, the pressure. I can't function. It just gets worse and worse."

"You can't function, is it? Well, well."

"You could easily get it yourself," Kelly said. "You don't need me."

Rynn did not react.

"It'd be something else the next day. And the next. There'd be no end to it. So, I decided I can't start that."

"Have you been drinking all day?" Rynn said. "You look like it. And now you sound like it. That's the only explanation."

Then he sighed and stared into the mirror.

"Frankie," he said. "Meet you out in the car."

The red-haired man got up and threw a last glance at Kelly. Kelly looked to see if he was carrying anything, but his jacket stayed zipped.

"You put me in a spot," said Rynn. "I don't think you realize that."

Ree – ah – luy – is, Kelly heard, that guttural accent that was as bad as raking your nails down glass. His words were coming easy; this was going to work.

"I didn't ask for this," he said to Rynn. "I don't want any more of it."

"What, you don't want an envelope full of twenties, for a lousy address? You want to go back to your night-job at that dump where all this trouble started?"

Kelly shook his head.

Rynn waited while the barman fixed something under the counter nearby and then moved off.

"This isn't a bus," said Rynn. "You can't just ring the bell and get off, bye bye. You know?"

When Kelly said nothing, Rynn looked over sideways.

"You're a stubborn, stupid, thick bogman, Kelly. The Guards don't give a damn about you. I know what you get paid. I know that's the way it's going to be for years. Sergeants'? Hah, that's ten years."

"I didn't want that money."

"Yeah, but you kept it, didn't you?"

"It's yours, I'll give it back."

"What, you think money's dirty? Or you're too good for it? Or Eimear's too good for it?"

"Don't bring her into it."

"Oh now. I haven't seen this side of you. Are you going to rear up on me now, are you? Tell me something; does wearing a wire make you itchy? They use Elastoplast to hold it on, don't they?"

"I don't have any wire."

"You mean you haven't tried to rat me yet?"

Kelly stared back at him. Rynn's frown dissolved.

"You know what's weird?" he said. "I actually believe you. Don't ask me why or how, don't. But it's weird. All the things I learned, the hard way too, a lot of them, all the things that keep me on top of things, they should be telling me to take care of this . . . problem . . . a different way."

Kelly felt a quiet and slow sag start in his stomach. He grabbed the glass and sipped a mouthful of the whiskey.

"So now you get it," Rynn whispered. Kelly placed the glass carefully on the mat.

"Now let me see if I got this right," Rynn went on. "You are turning Turk on me. You turn up at my son's funeral. Now why is that. To rub my face in it? Because you feel sorry for something or somebody. I can't decide. So I give you the benefit of the doubt. That's twice. Right? That's twice I says to myself 'I must be around the twist. What in the name of Jaysus am I doing? Have I lost it, or what?'"

Kelly had felt the last belt of the whiskey. Maybe he had been just on the brink and that was enough to push him over. He felt for change in his pocket to phone Eimear, to tell her to get out of the house and meet him at the corner, inside that shop.

Rynn was talking again.

"You don't seem to see your situation here, copper. You better wake up here."

Something had changed around Rynn's face, Kelly saw. His voice had grown quieter.

"I think you're missing the boat here," said Rynn. "So let me tell you something. Right now, right here, I can give you two names and two addresses, and the days of the week you'll be able to nail these two people. What people, you say. Two middling big fences, is who. Two fellas who organize break-ins, move the stuff. They even rent out guns and boots for any jobs in the Dublin area. Red-handed, you get it? So, you pass that on, and you get to look good. People start thinking, that Kelly fella is not half as stupid as he looks. That's called promotion. That's called upholding the law. You know?"

Kelly studied Rynn's ear, the little hairs that stood out.

"There's your career. I give you that, and all I want is one lousy address. No dirty money. No comeback. Case closed. Okay? Are you taking this in at all?"

"I know why you want it," Kelly said. "The address. You think I'm stupid, and that I'm going to listen to all this and believe every word you say. Well, I know."

"What do you know?"

"I know."

"You're talking fierce tough for a fella who's in a jam here."

"It's her brother you want."

Rynn's eyes widened.

"And I know what you want to do to him."

"What's that?"

"You want to do for him."

"What does 'do for him' mean?"

Kelly met Rynn's eyes.

"You want to kill him."

"Really. I didn't realize how drunk you were."

"You do."

"Why would I want something like that?"

"'Cause he's one of them who– "

Rynn's hand shot out and his fingers pressed on Kelly's chest. It had been fast, a lot faster than Kelly had imagined he could move. He looked down the arm, back up into Rynn's face.

"You shut your hole now, pal," Rynn said. "You're getting to me. So just shut it. You're way worse than drunk, with your, I don't know what kind of rubbish."

Kelly found himself almost smiling.

"This is how you repay me?" Rynn whispered. "This is what you do, for me saving your skin?"

The barman's whistle had slowed. He seemed to become very intent on wiping something at the farthest end of the counter.

The tip of Rynn's tongue went along his lower lip once and back, and withdrew as he let his arm down. Then the arm was back up, a finger wavering in front of Kelly's face. But Kelly felt tall, expansive, strong now.

"You just screwed yourself," Rynn whispered. "And you don't even know it."

The finger began to wag.

"But by Jesus you'll find out. Oh yes you will."

Kelly turned back toward the bar, and watched in the mirror as Rynn yanked open the door and strode out. He stared at the door for a few moments. Rynn had looked shorter than he remembered him. And for being a Dublin gangster boss, chief, or whatever he called himself, there was a worn look to him.

He finished the whiskey, felt it flood into his chest.

"Where's your phone?" he said to the barman.

"There's a phone box halfway down to Lenehan's."

"Your phone, not Lenehan's."

The barman gave him a blank look, but said nothing.

"I'm a Guard," said Kelly. He finished the sentence in his mind while he stared at the barman: and I don't care who knows it. "I have to use it."

It felt strange to be behind the counter of a pub with the phone pushed hard to his ear, waiting. Everything looked different from here. A watery-eyed oul lad scuttled into the pub, with his cap pulled down over his eye and his collar up to his bristles. The barman served him a pint without a word exchanged. The man worked his lips around and Kelly saw that he was juggling his dentures with his tongue. He eyed Kelly; Kelly winked at him.

Eimear sounded sleepy. He didn't want to alarm her. Still, he knew by her voice that she had picked up on something right away. The strange flow and gathering of everything all around him now had him doing a hundred miles an hour in his head. Everything met and ran coursing through his mind as he spoke to her: how it took a week to just drive across Canada, the snow, the North he'd seen in the *National Geographic*, the fields of waving wheat on the Prairies. But also with them came the darkness and the flashes from Junior Rynn's arm that night, the thumping music that bounced around the street from the club as though to shake the whole filthy city loose, the wet grit ground into his palms in the laneway.

Eimear gave a little shriek, the start of her protest or shock or disbelief, but he interrupted it. He knew he was speaking louder, and that he was speaking forcefully and even angrily. He also knew that he was close to smiling, and that the man at the bar had not touched his pint because he couldn't stop staring at him.

It's a tin, a biscuit tin, he told her again. He'd written a letter and put it with the money, to prove he'd never used it. He told her again to go down to the shops, to the hairdressers that stayed open late, to just sit there. He heard the panic in her voice and told her again that he was on his way. She had known, she cried, that something had gone wrong, and why hadn't he told her, and now this was happening. Then she said that it couldn't be happening and that she never heard of these Rynns. She asked if he was drunk. He told her he'd packed their passports and papers in the car last night. Again he heard that sharp intake of breath that could only be her ready to burst into tears.

But how calm he felt, with this flow engulfing him. He'd never be back here, ever, and maybe never in Dublin itself. He thought of his parents. His first duty was to Eimear; the rest would be taken care of. It'd be bad, he knew, but that was okay. They'd get him out and they'd nail Rynn.

Eimear wanted to know what she was supposed to do about Breda who was supposed to drop in soon, and where were they going to go tonight if they couldn't be at home, and what about the arrangements and the baby. He told her there was no going back, that he'd burned his bridges now, that she needed to believe in him.

He didn't feel cruel telling her to stop her crying. He'd had no choice, he told her; things had come to a head. It could only get worse and worse until – well, that was his only mistake, saying that. Now she was almost hysterical. He told her to go now, not to wait. He told her he loved her. She was still talking when he hung up.

There was a glowing luminance from everything around him. Little sparkles and glints came to him from the glasses and the bottles. The barman was watching him, his towel still moving slowly and unnecessarily around a glass. The old man had settled his dentures, and his hand rested on the counter near the pint he hadn't yet touched. Kelly felt blood coursing through every part of his body stronger and stronger. He waited by the phone awhile, staring at it and the rubber bands and the pencil and the scraps of paper and the ashtray. He wanted to roar at the two men here, to frighten them, to laugh.

Okay, he heard himself say, and then a second time, actually shouting it enough for the barman to wince. Yes he'd had four glasses of whiskey and he was fairly flying on them now, but he was finally surfacing too, and bursting with strength and resolve.

He crossed the floor, almost gliding toward the door, ready to kick anything and anyone out of his path, to take the doors off their hinges too.

The rush hour was in full swing when he stepped out of the pub. He looked over the roofs of the cars coming from the lights at KCR. There was no end to it, but fifteen minutes would do it. A feeble mustard-coloured dusk was settling in behind the bare twigs and branches by the walls. Across the road his Escort had been joined by other parked cars. He put one foot out on the road and looked back to the Terenure end of the road to be sure he'd have a gap that side too. A cyclist went by eighteen inches from him as he turned back, with a curse. He stepped back on the foot-path, and took in a deep breath of the smoky diesel air all around him.

He waited, fighting back the impatience. Then he saw his chance far down the line of cars, with a lorry labouring under a small cloud of exhaust.

You're always a Guard, he remembered his da saying. Where would they put him up first, him and Eimear? He had done what he could. The money and the letter were waiting in the tin for when Rynn would pull that one. He imagined himself looking the Commissioner in the eye – or whoever this would lead to – and presenting the tin with the thousand quid in its three rubber bands, untouched. Never used, sir. I knew this day would come, I knew it. And the Commissioner would give one of those little smiles, and a nod.

But another thought came to Kelly then as his second foot found its way onto the roadway. What if they sent him back to Rynn to get more with a wiretap or something?

Rynn would know what was going on if they tried that: he'd have to persuade them that Rynn would know.

Where the hell did all this traffic come from? Wasn't there twenty percent unemployment or something like that? He remembered how fast Rynn's hand had shot out to poke him in the chest. He fought off thinking about Eimear, someone coming to the door.

"Ah come on, will you," he called out to the cars.

He let a car go by and he skipped out. He crossed the middle of the road, and looked to see what room the bastard who'd parked the van behind his Escort had left him. Enough, but barely. The shrieks that could only be tires made him turn his head. Declan Kelly had a moment for his mind to protest that there should be lights on the dark mass rushing up at him.

Chapter 1

Summer 2005

T HE DAY OF THE MIRACLE, the African Miracle, started late enough for the man who was to soon be driven mad by telephone calls from all over the world. Mr. Joseph McCann, accountant, of Malahide, County Dublin, noted the nine o'clock mark of the fourth day of his holidays with a study of the light scum of soap on the back of his hands. It had been left by the draining water of the hand basin. He had installed said basin all by himself the day before.

The track changed on the stereo downstairs: "Angel of Harlem," with the saxophones massed to lay it on heavy for the chorus. Brilliant, he thought: things only got better and better. He lifted his hands from the basin, spread out his fingers, and studied the cut he'd given himself yesterday. This was the first real holiday he enjoyed in a decade. He remembered his wife Anne's words, and he smiled before he murmured them.

"A man of simple pleasures, our Joey."

"Easily pleased" was another expression. It too had sting to it, at first, but it passed.

He hadn't known how to take these at first. Though he took them as a slight, they were always hard to answer, and harder still to bite back about. Face it, he decided yet again, on this morning when the world was finally going right, and the prospect of a free day and all its promise lay before him: he had no real complaints. No whinging. They had a great marriage. So what were a few "Try something different" or "Change is good" or "Live a little"? You had to have a bit of static in life.

He studied a corner of the garden reflected from the mirror that faced the open bathroom window. The garden had finally come into its own this year, and it presented itself to him today as a blooming, sun-drenched work of art. It was as nice as the South of France, so it was. Some credit was due to Anne. It was she who had persuaded him to let it run a bit astray, and not to be trimming and mowing so much. That went with her interest in wildflowers and naturopathic stuff, he believed, and maybe even the yoga she liked so much now.

Such is life; yes indeed.

He bared his teeth and leaned in toward the mirror. The caps on his teeth had definitely been worth it. He wiped his hands and forearms and set the towel folded again on the railing. He had a real holiday facing him, time to himself. Why pay to rent some-place, or to stagger around Prague looking into shop windows, when you could be here in your own place, with all the toys?

A little shadow drifted over his cheer when he remembered how Anne had said she couldn't take the week off like she'd hoped. It was because they were so busy. Yet McCann couldn't help wondering if she preferred to go to work now while he was at home. Was it because he'd put his foot down – nicely, mind you – and said they should just stay home a week and enjoy the weather?

He had time to himself at last, and that's what the "real" in real holiday meant. Orla was at the kayaking camp until Sunday, loving it, and Kevin – not little Kev anymore but a grouchy six-teen-year-old slug – was off with his mates at the Gaeltacht in Connemara. It was less to learn Irish from the native speakers than it was to go to dances and do a bit of courting – if that's what they called it these days. Everyone knew that. But there was no Grand Theft Auto in the house where Kev was lodged. What's more, he had to be out of bed by eight. And there was somebody else making him do it!

Joey McCann looked at his profile in the mirror. He drew in his belly, and pulled the T-shirt tighter to his waist. The

Gaeltacht, he reflected again, wasn't it hilarious that these days the kids actually wanted to go. He didn't think too hard about what Kev might be up to there. It'd be different if it were Orla, of course. God, the changes in Ireland in the past–

–Christ: there it was. He'd been right all along. He kept his eye on the mirror and he moved closer. It was right there on the top of his nose: that rogue hair again.

The hairs had started to sprout in odder places over the years. It wasn't much use asking why in the name of God, or evolution, or genes, why a man of forty-three would have a wiry red beard-hair growing from the tip of his nose.

He took out the shaver and started it. He drew the trimmer bit over his nose, and then he canted his head and squinted into the light to spot any more hairs on his ears. With the light behind them they showed up as glowing white wires. Ah – he might as well do a run over the sideburns while he was at it. There had to be grey hairs at this age, no big deal there.

Whether it was the shaver's buzzing resonance pushing into his cheekbone, or the noise of it trimming, it brought him back years, to the barbers where his father took him the first Wednesday of every month. His first memories were watching his da in the mirror down at the barber's. They didn't call them hairdressers then. Da always went in the chair after him, and young Joey would watch the proceedings, and listen to the banter. It was strange and almost mysterious, he recalled, almost like Mass in Lent. That was because he'd see in the chair before him a strange and yet-so-familiar man with a bristly neck, a man with Da's voice and words. Of course it was his da, but in that chair . . .? And it was always: "The usual Mickey: short back and sides. And don't draw any blood!"

McCann finished the left side and turned his head. He always had lists going on in his head. According to Anne, all accountants were born with lists and columns and rows imprinted into their brain. Ha ha. He bent down his ear, and eased the trimmer in over the sideburns and let his list unroll itself.

Price the blocks and preserved wood over at Woody's; Tesco for three bottles of Chilean red, meat for the kebabs, olives – who said men can't evolve, Anne, ha ha on you now. See about a tennis racquet for Orla and rent that DVD version of *Amelie* – either that or *LA Confidential* again – nearly forgot: check if that lawn furniture set is really on sale in Savanna, like Crowley said it was.

He looked down into the basin again. No, there was nothing more than the expected trimmings and flecks. But it wasn't his imagination: there had been something. He switched off the razor, and he focused on the mirror and looked around the garden again.

Whatever had flickered at the corner of his vision a few seconds ago had been followed by an odd noise. It was more of a vibration, actually. He wondered if a bird had flown into the window. It had happened often enough in the old house, flying smack dab into the upstairs one. Didn't some birds get drunk on berries, something on the Discovery Channel last month?

But the sound had stirred something more than curiosity in him. He turned and walked toward the open window where he stopped and listened. There was a drone of a plane coming in, or circling Dublin Airport a few miles to the west.

His list rolled again in his mind again: the Xbox magazine for Kev to put him in a biddable humour when he got back from Connemara. Wax for a proper job on the car: it really was time. Maybe go to the library, get books on making a patio.

His thoughts suddenly cleared. It had been something big. There had been a cracking sound too. Had it been a branch giving way, or swishing leaves? Maybe someone was working on the roof.

He looked hard at the tops of the trees by the lawn. The sound of the plane faded a little. The birds seemed to be chirping and chortling more. He pushed at the window and he saw the undersides of the shrubs, the exposed white sap where they had broken. There were gouges at the border by the one bit of lawn he'd kept.

Now McCann heard someone, an old person, a woman, talking louder. It must be Bridie Jennings, two houses down. Crazy Bridie, he murmured. Maybe something had happened to her husband, the diabetic. Someone was calling his name. It was Bridie for sure.

He took his time going downstairs. He thought about slipping out the front door and hopping into the car, with the radio up loud so he had cover, or an excuse if she got to him before his getaway. Lately he had less time for Bridie and the husband, a stooped, quiet man who rarely made it outdoors. It was uncharitable, to be sure, but still. Did they have no family or relations to come in and, say, clean the place up, or bring them out shopping? And, God, the house had been left run to crap, with the grass and the peeling paint on the garage. Worst of all, if she thought you were home, she'd be over, like the other day. Couldn't a person take holidays in their own home, for the love of God?

McCann went through the kitchen and toward the door to the side passage that led to the iron gate beside the garage. He picked up his keys and mobile from the counter and took a glance at the window.

Whatever had happened, it had come though the garden. McCann felt his heart start to race. Burglars, was his first thought, and they'd been interrupted,. They had just ploughed through here as part of their getaway. The sea-grass had been really badly done in. Talk about brazen. Well, where were the Guards then? McCann stared at the still foliage, listening harder for any sirens. But Bridie Jennings was caterwauling again.

Instead of heading for the front of the house, he went to the television room and lifted the poker from its stand. He considered how stupid this might be, but soon continued heading for the back door that opened out onto the cement path. He paused there and unlocked the keypad on his mobile, and keyed in 911. Then he poised his thumb over the Send button and pulled open the door. He stepped down onto the cement and listened again. Still the plane. He flourished the poker a little, and tightened his grip.

Accountant or not, he was no pushover. His father had been a civil service clerk all his life, his grandfather a deliveryman. There was no way in the wide world that anyone was going to take one bit of that back. Joey McCann was not one bit ashamed of that anymore than he was embarrassed to be doing well, or that he still had enough of a Dublin accent for people to comment on it.

He looked from the patch of grass with the small hollows between three torn-up pieces, over to the remains of the sea-grass. Then he saw the hand, and with it the arm, and a white, worn shirt-cuff halfway up to the elbow. There was a blue tinge to dark skin.

This is ridiculous, he heard himself say loudly. *Candid Camera*? He looked around the garden and back to the house. His eyes slipped out of focus for a moment. He wondered if he'd just had a heart attack. And there was Bridie Jennings' voice again, straining and breaking with her effort to yell. The smell of soap came to him stronger now.

He refocused his eyes, and looked back at the body splayed in the sea-grass. The limbs were bent at impossible angles. An Adidas jacket had pulled away from the man's trousers, to reveal the dark skin on his back. One foot was barefoot and the sole was bright like it had been scoured or scraped.

She was shouting again, but he could only make out the last words: fell out of a plane?

McCann lifted his mobile and looked at the screen for a moment. What was he going to say? There's a black man in my garden, and I think he fell out of a plane? A man with one shoe? He stepped back, taking deep breaths.

"I know, Bridie," he yelled then. "I know, now will you whisht a minute?"

Then he saw the shoe over by the wall. He tried not to think what the impact of this man's body must have been.

"Jesus, Jesus, Jesus," he said and turned away when the revulsion hit him, and he pushed Send.

It took forever for the network to connect. McCann squeezed the poker tighter and kept his eyes on the teak slats that made up the chairs by the wall. He had to fight not to think about this person who had mangled a corner of the garden, and the ways his body had been broken.

Was this an emergency call? the man's voice asked.

"It is," said McCann, suddenly aware of a sour, metallic taste in his mouth and his heaving chest.

"There's a dead man in my garden, he fell off a plane – out of a plane, I mean, I think. A black man it looks like, in my garden, it just happened. Just now."

Could he repeat that?

Chapter 2

"MOVE THAT BIG FAT HEAD of yours, will you?" Minogue was sure that the sardonic Dublin tone could only be the voice of Detective Garda Tommy Malone.

"Thanks very much," said Malone. "Boss."

Minogue gave his colleague – his former colleague – the eye before turning back toward the speaker. Light from the projector caught motes of dust circling above, and turned them to filaments of silver.

Minogue watched the presenter, *Inspektor* Peter Moser of the Austrian state police, aim a laser pointer at the map of Europe. Yes, he thought again, Moser might well be the type of policeman that Basically Lally, Superintendent Cormac Lally, host and convenor of the meeting, wanted to be.

Moser was yet another visiting Euro-cop from Vienna, and he was good. The man's English was simply brilliant, better than many native speakers on Minogue's own island of preening yappers. Here was a man who finished his sentences, and ambitious sentences they were too, grand long ones with clauses that never strayed far or long, but were instead reeled back to one powerful statement.

Moser had snappy clothes, and could tell jokes to beat the band too. It wasn't fair that Arnold Schwarzenegger kept popping up in Minogue's mind when Moser was speaking. But whose fault was that? It had been Moser who'd said it almost first thing, as an ice-breaker: *I sound like Ah-nold up there, don't I?* Were Austrians supposed to be this funny?

But had he been asked directly, Inspector Minogue would have readily admitted to his own misuse of this interdepartmental meeting for the purposes of daydreaming. It wasn't his first time so engaged, but his guilt quotient for this lapse was negligible. Minogue had learned that these monthly meetings he attended, representing his International Liaison Section, were not as useful as Lally, their convener, seemed to still believe. Anyway, there were always good notes available afterwards.

Try as he might, Lally could not seem to help saying "basically." Minogue liked to believe that Lally's recourse to this term was a sign of his desire to be candid and economical with words. It was not so for begrudgers and slaggers in the ranks, however, such as Minogue's old friend and tormentor, and former boss on the Murder Squad, James Kilmartin. It was from the same Kilmartin that he had heard Lally called The Powerpoint Prince of Darkness. Minogue still did not believe this was quite fair.

The same Lally was bound for big things, to be sure. And why not? Lally definitely had the lingo: relationships, interdiction, proactive. There was much reaching out, plenty of building bridges, a fair bit of empowering. The phrase "comfortable with" had showed up too often in the TV and radio interviews where Lally seemed to pop up quite often this past year. Minogue had even heard him say "win-win" twice, when he had introduced Moser earlier on.

Lally's law degree, his year at Europol, the live Internet feeds and video conferencing up on the big screen at his meetings – none of this had impressed Kilmartin much. He had confided to Minogue that he believed that Lally had set up these meetings as fodder for his own promotion. A trick bicyclist, was Kilmartin's irrevocable verdict on Lally: basically a media man, an operator, not a real copper anymore.

Well, little would impress Superintendent James Kilmartin these days, Minogue was beginning to believe. Indeed, he often wondered if Kilmartin was chafing even more than he was himself to get back to what he knew and liked. That consisted of chasing murderers and catching them, and dressing in his best suits to attend court, where he liked to stare at the defendant as he gave testimony, and particularly as a verdict was announced.

But Kilmartin's bluntness, and his ferocity, made up for his temperamental deficiencies. He was beyond ardent, a zealot in fact, and had often been brutal in tracking and seizing a killer. Shrewd enough to call on the right people, Kilmartin had not minded taking troublemakers on the Squad staff. It helped morale immeasurably that he wasn't shy about buying a round of drinks either. Even Tommy Malone, the first Dublin-born Guard that Kilmartin had inducted into the Murder Squad, had allowed that Kilmartin was bearable, some of the time.

This did not cause James Kilmartin to let up in his slagging of Dubliners and their accent, as personified in his final "hire" before the Squad was disbanded – Garda Thomas Malone. But Malone had proven as dogged and as smart and as capable as any who had ever come though the Squad. This was no small feat. Kilmartin in his cups was willing to quietly concede that fact also, to concede that Malone had been up with the likes of former Squad members Plateglass Fergal Sheehy, Jesus Tony Farrell, and Head-The-Ball John Murtagh.

Kilmartin didn't restrict himself to Dubliners, however. It was pretty much anyone not graced by fortune to have been born in his native County Mayo. Accordingly, Minogue routinely fell under the rubric of "a Clare savage," or perhaps a "buff," or "mucker." Kilmartin seemed oblivious to the fact these almost archaic terms of lethal understatement had resonance only for himself really. Minogue didn't mind one bit. Hiding within them remained a refuge, a strength, even a weapon.

Solely for the sake of a staged row, Minogue would occasionally affect to seek redress in the matter of Kilmartin's slurs. The scene for this mischief was usually licensed premises. The raillery itself was the point. It built thirst, and sooner or later it would end in a bit of play-acting, and elaborately fake umbrage to go with an extravagant show of bad language.

Minogue felt obliged to do some *pro forma* jabbing back at Kilmartin, and his reminders that County Mayo was no

Parnassus, and that Mayo men no standard bearers of civilization, only kept things simmering nicely. After all, Minogue liked to remind his friend, the same Jim Kilmartin's fellow Mayo men couldn't all be as thick as they were reputed to be. Hadn't they had the good sense to kick Kilmartin out of the county years ago, and up to annoy Dublin . . . ?

Moser had a remote in his other hand, and it acted like a mouse. Minogue squinted at the names that had appeared on the map. The walls on the squadroom had always been plastered with maps, even after a case had been cleared. Ambiance, was Kilmartin's explanation, and he even directed Eilís, the Squad secretary, to rearrange them rather than remove them.

Minogue shifted a little in his slouch in an effort to dislodge himself from this slide into reminiscence. A total waste of time, to be sure, and in all fairness, it had to be said that the closing of the Squad had been engineered with a grand, soft landing for them all in the land of Cushy Numbers, or Grand Strokes, as Kilmartin called their new posts.

Since the disbanding of the Garda Murder Squad, Kilmartin spent plenty of time in the monthly get-togethers down in Willie Ryan's Pub near the old Technical Bureau offices by Islandbridge, boasting about the perqs of gadgetry trials, and the budgeting and faraway conferences that were part of his new nine-to-five in Procurement. It was as cushy as Minogue's posting to Liaison, and his twice-a-week Alliance Française lessons to get him to become one of the Garda point men in for European police initiatives that were rolling into Ireland now. The Big Time, as Kilmartin called it: no more economy-class policing, no sir.

Maybe it was time to give the regular meetings of the old Squad members at the Willie Ryan's Pub a miss for a while then, Minogue reflected now. "Club Mad," John Murtagh's name for the get-togethers – it had come from his harrowing tale of food poisoning after a tryst with a Danish gymnast at his first, and only, Club Med holiday – had served its purpose. It had run its course, and everyone should move on, as they say. Or maybe not, Minogue wondered yet again. Jesus Farrell still showed up most times too, but he often spent much time on his mobile, phoning in bets. Sheehy, Plateglass Fergal Sheehy, was gone to Serious Crimes again. He had gone moderate on the jar. Minogue had heard that Sheehy wasn't happy in the job at all.

But still Minogue could feel for Kilmartin. Plainly, it was because he had the same rebel heart in his own new job himself. There had been too many days when he'd felt like a civil servant, or someone whose job was to be in meetings, or to be trapped in reports of meetings that only gave way to preparations for other meetings.

At home some evenings, Minogue's gaze stayed fixed on the page of his book without seeing a word for minutes at a time. Meanwhile his thoughts brought him to the ditches and alleys, and the small rooms where he listened and watched as someone lied or sweated more, or cried, or all three. To be hunting down a killer, to be staying awake and half-raving even, for forty hours, and to be living on yesterday's sandwiches and too much instant coffee as well as a few pints that soon soured in the gut, or to be standing in the long grass beside where a human being's body had been discarded. . . . How could any man in this day and age justify that shameful excitement to anyone, to his wife and family especially, or even to his own waking self?

"Jesus fell for the second time," Minogue thought: now he was becoming annoyed as well as a little ashamed of his wandering thoughts. He sat upright and wrote a new heading in his notes, using the most recent words to appear onscreen: "The Balkan Route." This meeting was important, he told himself, just like the other ones Lally organized. It was here for a good reason. Crime trends and developments on the continent mattered. It was very good for morale and staff development to attend these sessions, and to want more of them. Information shared was better information. No more reinventing the wheel, less time playing catch-up. This is Europe we're in; our streets have brown and black faces, and everything is on the move. Prosperity puts Ireland on the map for organized crime anywhere.

As much as he fought to stay focused, and as much as he wrote, Minogue soon felt his ra-ra efforts foundering yet again.

Whatever the merits and practical benefits of the monthly

sessions here in Garda HQ in Harcourt Square, they certainly were prized items for the Garda Press Office. There they were mined and recycled for sorely needed press releases that indicated the Guards were an up-to-the-minute, modern European police force, on top of things. The names of the organizations involved had great weight, Minogue had to admit: Europol, Interpol, US State Department.

So too did the attendees, giving the meetings an aura of well-considered and coordinated work around these meetings. "The Snowmen," the in-house nickname for the Garda Drug Squad Central, was represented by Malone now, in his second meeting. Paddy Cowan was Criminal Assets Bureau, one of "The Laundrymen." Cowan seemed to take lots of notes, but Minogue had begun to suspect he was faking it.

Minogue remembered then that the CIB's nickname was being usurped by a newer one: "The Binmen." It had come from outside the Gardai, and therefore would be slow to gain acceptance. But Minogue liked it. He liked it because of its origins, a well-publicized case where detectives had systematically robbed rubbish to gather richly incriminating evidence. That rubbish removal became the nub of a celebrated and lengthy – but failed – court case that a defendant had launched to make the detectives' gleanings inadmissible.

Turlough – "Tayto" – Collins was CDU, going back to the Old Testament. Super now too, or Inspector? Minogue couldn't remember. O'Brien . . . Donal, was it . . . ? . . . he the specky-our-eyed senior civil servant from Revenue, who apparently spoke Russian of all things, and liked to holiday in Latvia or someplace. And Larry Donohue, Immigration Bureau, next to him, all sixteen stone of him, with a humpy back that made him resemble a badly dressed bear, Larry the one-time terror at the boozing sessions in the Garda Club, but gone on the dry these years. Why didn't the Immigration Bureau have a decent nickname yet?

He'd done it again, he had. Daydreaming about *nicknames* now? "Jesus fell for the third time," he thought, savagely. He must have ADD or something.

He searched for more names to write down, and took great

care with the accents and the dots on some of the words. One word had a letter tail hanging under it. For a moment he considered sheltering behind an excuse he'd heard from Kilmartin not long ago. It was something about the projector thing being a subliminal signal thing. That, Kilmartin had announced triumphantly, was what *the* problem was with these dog-and-pony PowerPoint come-all-ye's: it tricked your brain into thinking you were going to the pictures! Relax, and enjoy the show!

He redoubled his efforts to attend to what Moser was saying and pointing to on the screen. How could he blame *Inspektor* Moser one bit for causing him to daydream? But to be fair, it had been one of Moser's phrases earlier, on the "no borders" one, on which Minogue had suddenly slid down and into the empty bog-land near Glenmalure, the Dwyer country of West Wicklow that he loved, a place of roaring wind over high boggy plateaus that seemed a million miles from Dublin. He could almost hear the grass hissing in the wind, nearly see the cloud shadows moving over the heather all about. He had been thinking a lot lately about Dwyer, the Wicklow Rebel of 1798 who had ranged here for five years before they got to his family and he was transported to New South Wales. Dwyer was forgotten, of course.

Moser caught his eye and smiled. Minogue nodded, a little pleased that his efforts to attend closely had drawn Moser's notice. He raised his eyebrows and smiled back at the genial and well-spoken visitor from Austria. He noticed that Lally was offering a smile too. Did everyone know he was adrift here? He wrote a lengthy note about some of the stats on the screen.

But as he wrote, he simply had to admit it: nothing had really changed. It was still PowerPoint hell.

His detailed and useless note finished, Minogue began to scrutinize a new map projected up on the wall. Was Romania really there? Was it always? The State Police *"Bundespolizei"* logo in the corner of the screen was the same as the one on Moser's embossed business card. Well, who needed to learn German for that one? They were changing the name soon though, he half-remembered Moser saying. There was some amalgamation of police services there, and it had a funny side to it, apparently.

The smuggling routes came back on with a mouse click. Oops, Minogue caught himself in time: *Bucharest*, not Budapest. Well, had Bulgaria moved too, changed? He felt a vague shame inch in. But for years, places like Bulgaria or Albania, or states he now couldn't list in place of where Yugoslavia had been – these places had all been map names, vaguely Iron Curtain, neither here nor there. There was a lot to learn, maybe even more to unlearn.

His mind went again to Kilmartin, delivering yet another one of his orations back after Christmas. Was it just after the funeral for Malone's brother? Yes, it was. Terry Malone had turned up dead within a week of parole, overdosed and lying on a bench in Fairview Park. That was at the New Year.

Kilmartin, then: We're in the ha'penny place compared to what I seen beyond in friggin' Amsterdam at the conference, let me tell you. A right wake-up call, oh yes.

The funeral, yes. That's when Kilmartin had been muttering away to him at the back of the church while they watched the proceedings. It wasn't just the family and relatives, and the neighbours. There had been thieves, and thugs, and Guards and priests, and social workers, and prostitutes and even a scruffy-looking teacher who had gotten Malone and his brother Terry into boxing years ago. Scattered around in the mostly empty pews toward the back, Minogue remembered a goodly number of lost-looking gougers and hollow-eyed women whom he suspected were probably living rough.

The mix of people had brought a tension to the ceremony that had only seemed to grow until it filled the church. That was until a demented man staggered in halfway through the Mass demanding to know if the circus was in town and if anyone had ever thought about what that bastard Oliver Cromwell had done to Ireland. The priest, a man with a Spanish-sounding name, had paused, smiling, and waited for the rant to run its course.

Detective Tommy Malone crying and sagging into his mother was a sight Minogue would not forget. Even Kilmartin had never spoken of it after that day. Malone, the detective who had tried to take a bullet out of his own thigh lying in a laneway in Bray while a stunned Minogue stood swaying and eyeing the delta of dark blood spreading from under the man Malone had shot dead. The same Tommy Malone, Central Drug Squad, pleading with Parole to gate his brother or he'd die. Malone thumping two dealers not a week afterwards, one into hospital, glaring morosely at Minogue over a pint that afternoon, ready to jack it in.

Minogue's mind was yanked back to the present yet again by the sight of someone stretching up ahead. Lally was taking notes still, and nodding. This was too much, really. Maybe he should just stand up, or pinch himself, or something to keep his mind on things here. Yet again he focused on the map, and studied the arrows that began appearing in quick succession there. Moser had some remote in his hand, and he never even needed to look down at it, or even to point it.

Roads appeared, routes he supposed they should be called, or arteries. Moser looked around but settled on Minogue again. Moser must be on to him now, for habitual lapses in attention.

"Is it okay if I play with the English language perhaps, just a little?"

Lally smiled and nodded.

"Actually, I should not say *play*," and Moser made air quotes. "What I am actually referring to is a word. People say 'smuggle' but we say 'traffic.' This is true, yes?"

Lally blinked and smiled again, and shrugged.

"You see, the times we have?" Moser asked. "Traffic is not cars, not only. It is drugs, it is guns, it is money, it is people. If we say 'smuggle' you think . . .?"

Ah, Minogue realized, audience involvement was being called for, and with the introvert's reflex, he shifted his eyes to his clipboard.

"Pirates, no?" said Moser, though it wasn't evident to Minogue that anything had been decided. "Things in hiding. In bags. In boxes maybe?"

Minogue began to wonder how you trafficked people. Under a lorry? Were there more of those false compartments, like the poor divils in that container in Wexford, the ones who'd died on the boat over and were left at the dock? There had been a vanload of Russians pulled in at the Lucan bypass a month or so back too. They weren't Russians at all, but Romanians and Bulgarians and people from places that Minogue didn't know. According to Kilmartin, who still heard everything and asked everything, the people in the van were being shipped out to meat processors in the midland counties where they were to work. Like slavery, he had said, paying back the smugglers – *traffickers* – for years to come.

"Well," said Moser. "Let me tell you a little about my home country. Austria."

Minogue sat back. Moser was good – he had surely sensed that it was probably more than Minogue who had been wool-gathering here.

Austria, he thought: that was a nice thought. There had to be a fair bit of yodelling, and Alpine meadows dotted with daisies, to be sure, along with cows. Plenty of them too, cows with bells. Cake of course – a lot of cake. There were surely flowers in window boxes, white walls, dark wood – and good pubs, without a doubt. Vienna was waltzes and buildings and more cake. Those leather trousers for the kids still, though? Everything seemed dainty and well made. No way were they as wound up as the Germans. Or were they? Hadn't Hitler . . .?

"My country has always been the crossroads of Europe," Moser continued. "Yes, Austria. It used to be an empire, going out into Russia, you see? But sooner or later everything moves through Austria. Everything you could imagine, and not just fine Austrian beer, I must remind you."

A few smiles came up for that. Minogue wondered if Moser wasn't playing back a little stereotype of an Irish over-fondness for the drink on him, for his postcard take on Austria some moments before. Maybe Austrian coppers read minds?

To look like he was paying attention, Minogue looked at Austria and then let his gaze drift down toward the Balkan countries. He still wasn't sure of them. He re-read names of cities there, and resolved to memorize them along with the correct names of the new states that had been Yugoslavia. Vlores, a nice-sounding name of a place in Albania: but hadn't Moser said something about it being a centre for trafficking? Well there was a name farther back toward central Europe, a name you wouldn't easily forget – Split.

"It used to be Austria was a kind of an island, you see?" Moser went on. "Of course I do not mean a real island, physically, like yours here. But I mean back with the Eastern bloc, how you say, the Iron Curtain?"

Minogue squinted at Romania. They'd shot the dictator fella there. And his wife.

"Well, my friends, if I may say, my new Irish friends – Ireland is certainly an island on the map. Obviously, you say. There is water all around it! 'You qualify' – as we say at the checkpoints on the roads when we have a man who blows over in the alcohol, you know? The alcohol?"

"Breathalyzer," said Lally and smiled. "Breathalyzer, we call it, Peter."

"Ah," said Moser rubbing his hands, and smiled. "That is the graduate course in English. For that I must study more or live here in Dublin."

A murmur ran through the thirty-odd people in the room, a few snorts of humour. Minogue sat up more and cast a quick glance back at Malone. Malone was fidgeting, and he had his mobile under his clipboard.

"What I am here to tell you, you already know," Moser said then in a low voice, and paused.

Minogue watched Moser's smile fade slowly into a kind of gentle regret. Plenty of practice with that one, Minogue was fairly sure, but still masterful enough to get all eyes on him.

"What I am here to tell you does not seem correct, by the geography you have had in your schools. No. I am telling you that Ireland is *not* an island."

It took another bout of vibrating for Minogue to realize that it was his own phone doing that against his chest. Well, he was getting better at it. It was a month now since Kathleen had stopped secretly switching it on and leaving it in his jacket pocket in the mornings. She'd shown him how to make it vibrate when there were texts too.

"As you say," Moser went on, "Or as they say in the island next door, your neighbour."

Again Moser paused for effect. Minogue kept his eyes on him while he corralled the mobile from a corner of his pocket.

"A poet, he says 'No man is an island.' Correct?"

Lally nodded. Well, Minogue thought as his fingers fastened on the phone at last, poetry, policing and PowerPoint, all in the one go. Top that.

"That was not a police officer but a poet, Mister Doan."

"Donne," Minogue said before he realized it.

"Ah," said Moser and smiled at him. "Thank you."

He met Moser's eye, for politeness, and managed a little smile.

"My friends they are true," said Moser. "My friends who visit Ireland. They tell me that everyone Irish knows the English language – and the English! – better than the English. The Island of the Saints and Scholars? No?"

No, Minogue wanted to say. Neither was in stock for some time now. The Celtic Tiger is a man-eater. It's all gone. Saints were the first.

He held the mobile up behind the chair in front of him and squinted at the text message.

NO MORE PPOINT CRAP NEED TALK U ABOUT SOMTHNG CUPPA T CALL ME OUTSIDE UKNOW STAIRS NO JOKE.

He closed the phone, but he waited awhile before looking around. Malone's baleful stare greeted his wandering gaze.

"There are no islands, anymore," said Moser. "For our purposes."

Now two photos of lorries came onscreen. They were full of packages of something. Minogue waited for Moser to finish his sweep of the room. Something was coming up. Yes, Moser had put plenty of pizzazz into this part, the finale. Moser clicked and a picture of crumpled bodies, three, in some uniform, a black stain under them, came up. Spots on the shirt of one had to be bullet wounds.

"We have left Austria," said Moser. "This is the city of Zagreb. A normal, how you say, a routine day."

Minogue glanced over at Malone again. Malone made his eyes wide. Right, Minogue understood: he had forgotten to turn his own mobile on to ring.

Moser had another picture of seized drugs, alongside what looked like assault rifles. He was piling it on, for sure. Kilmartin would be annoyed to have missed something like this.

Moser's eyes were on Minogue at the first ring. Minogue let it ring twice and put out his best half-embarrassed look.

"Sorry."

He got a dip of the head from Moser.

"Seriously?" he said into the phone. He turned away and put his finger in his other ear.

"Well . . . ," he said, a few times, skeptically, and he rolled his eyes.

Then he closed the phone, and faced the presentation again. He gave the mobile a lingering glare, while he let his face assume an air of purpose and struggle. He closed the performance with a smile of gentle contempt. He came up with a bout of minor head shaking, for the finish-up.

He stood, abashed. Moser looked like an all-knowing teacher now.

"No rest for the wicked," Minogue said. It was the best he could come up with.

He took the stairs, stopped by the window on the third floor. Two detectives passed, one with a howiya. A buddy of Murtagh's, he thought. Were the Hold-Up Squad sending people to these sessions now . . . ?

He pushed Recent and waited.

The drilling and the pounding were still going on in Harcourt Street outside. Would they never get those foundations in, and turn to just putting up bricks? He felt the drills' resonance up through the floors here at CDU. The Puzzle Palace – as nobody called it anymore. The new light rail, the Luas, was almost finished. Minogue could soon leave his arthritic Citroën, with its stealthily failing seals and incontinent sump, at home now if they took his parking away.

Buckets of rain last night had rinsed the air. Footpaths were covered with spores and small leaves, hammered down from their branches onto the footpaths.

No ring from Malone, as usual.

"Yes, sir."

"I'd like to thank the academy."

"I'm in a meeting sir, the Euro- policing one on smuggling – I mean, trafficking."

"I'd just like to say it's been an awesome experience and my costar and–"

"–Really, sir? I don't know if I can, right now."

"You're buying. Real coffee. Cake too – the whole shebang."

"Is Kearns available, sir? It's just that this meeting is going on."

"You're better than I thought. Practice, no doubt."

"I could, I suppose . . . let me see."

Minogue had already seen the stack of handouts behind Moser's table, the printouts of the presentation.

Malone put his hand over the speaker. While he waited for Malone to execute his grand spoof, Minogue eyed the pigeons resting on the parapets of the early Georgian terrace opposite. Below, the footpath was being reset, with real cut stone. Even this part of Dublin was going to be dainty soon, no doubt, as dainty as the heritage streets on the continent.

"Fifteen minutes, sir," from Malone.

He didn't miss the tone, or the paced delays in Malone's words that only amplified the subtle mockery, before the connection went.

Chapter 3

MINOGUE HALF-LISTENED to the conversation that the man waiting next to them at the pedestrian lights was having on his mobile. "But how was I to know?" the man repeated, louder. Minogue's eye went to a movement overhead then, a swivelling crane with what looked like a hopper of cement rolling out toward its tip. The lights changed. A motor-bike went through on the red, inches from a man beside Minogue still yapping intently on his mobile.

He and Malone crossed to the top of Grafton Street, and were soon enveloped in the smell of baking. He took in the dis-tant clangs of empty aluminum kegs being bounced around on the footpaths or up on the delivery lorries outside the pubs, even as their full replacements were being wrestled and rolled down. A tattooed hawker with a huge trolley of Celtic jewellery rumbled down a side street, singing.

Malone said something about PowerPoint, but half of it was lost in the start-up of a compressor outside of the soon-to-be-opened clothes shop. "Duds" sounded a bit risky for such a venture still, Minogue believed. Then again, it was a new line being sold by Sheela, lead singer of Sheela Na Gig, the toast of America since her album last year.

Malone's words came to him as the noise stopped.

". . . part of the package. Isn't it?"

"I don't know," said Minogue. They rounded a swarm of foreign students in the middle of the street. Minogue took in the unmarked Opel parked behind some bikes on South Anne Street. There were pickpocket teams coming in from Moscow even, he had heard somewhere.

"Well, you're in that line of work now yourself, aren't you," Malone said.

Minogue eyed the huge telly in the window of the Screen Shop. It was news, live, with footage from a helicopter some-where over Malahide.

"I am not," Minogue said, and stopped. "I'm not really a PowerPoint type."

"At least you switch on your mobile now," Malone said. "So I'll keep me hopes up."

The camera was zooming in on people's gardens and rooftops. There were a half-dozen cars parked in front of one house.

"What," said Malone. "Are you buying one of those, the flat-screen things?"

It zoomed in on trees, zoomed out again.

"Kilmartin bought himself one," Malone said. "Gadget Man, you know?"

The camera seemed to try again, centring on a patch of garden. Those were Guards there standing in the garden, Minogue was sure. He put his hand over his forehead and leaned in to see through the glare.

"Any invites yet?" he heard Malone say.

"What invites?"

There was a sheet there all right, out in some garden in Malahide. With the boughs intervening, the camera couldn't get a proper view,

"Kilmartin's place," Malone said. "To see his DVDs. Widescreen, mad sound. The whole bit."

"No."

"He bought all of *007* when they came out. I swear to God."

The newscaster's face looked pensively up and away, listen-ing to whatever the reporter was telling her, and then stared into the camera to say something. Stock-market numbers jumped up on the screen now.

Minogue turned away, almost colliding with an elderly woman who had slowed to look in the window too.

"I beg your pardon," he said hurriedly.

"That's a miracle," said the woman, and rearranged her bag.

"Hardly now, ma'am. I'm sorry – mere clumsiness, to be sure."

"No," she said. "That on the television. A miracle."

Minogue squinted back through the glare. A reporter was talking into a microphone on a street. Behind were two Guards, and one was talking to a man with a look of intense concentration on his face and was continually running his hand through his hair. A title came up in yellow beside the station logo. Somebody McCann.

"A miracle," she repeated. "Isn't it?"

There was something of a cat, or a nun about this woman, Minogue believed. Maybe it was the small whiskers on her upper lip, and that placid and severe calm he knew too well from his own schooldays with the nuns so long ago.

"I don't know," he tried.

"It's a visitation then," she declared. "A sign, a message to us to mend our ways here now."

She fixed Minogue with a piercing, but somehow distracted eye.

"The Almighty sent that poor man to us," she said. "He's trying to get Ireland back on track."

"I don't know what you mean, ma'am."

"The plane," she said, with a little impatience now. "A man fell out of a plane, a stowaway. A refugee. It's just like the Holy Family, don't you see?"

Minogue lined up next to Malone at the coffee counter at the back of Bewley's.

"I've heard of that kind of thing before," said Malone. "They go in a wheel well but it gets fierce cold up high, and they freeze. If the landing gear doesn't, you know . . ."

Minogue couldn't stop thinking of a body plummeting into the suburbs of Dublin.

"He'd have been, you know, before he landed, I say," said Malone. "Dead, like."

Minogue let Malone pay for the coffees and buns. He scouted out a table under the stained glass on the back wall of the restaurant. The stained glass here had the feel of a church about it, balm to the pagan Minogue, still longing for the cloths of any heaven, no matter the benedictions cast on him from the roaring, New Ireland.

Bewley's restaurant was doomed, he knew. There might be only months to go before it was closed. So many new restaurants and coffee places had opened up in the past few years, and the Bewley family that had started it themselves was gone these years. The Bewleys were Irish Quakers, and Minogue had always felt somehow obliged to them, and glad to patronize their restaurant. He never mentioned this odd duty to anyone, a duty that was actually an escape too. This was because he understood there was no exact connection between the Bewleys and the other Quakers who had kept ancestors of the now-dispersed Minogues – Minogues of Australia, and of Birmingham and Canada and Philadelphia – alive in the Famine.

But as always, the gladness began to leak into him as it always did here, just to be alive, and to be in this mad and vexing city.

There today he could see it in how a woman's head leaned in to murmur some solace, or explanation, or advice to a man in his forties. The man's eyes were huge behind his glasses, and his skin had a pink flush that seemed to go with Down's. His features were bound in an earnest attention to words that he might not grasp at all. But just to hear the voice, the tone, might be sufficient, Minogue imagined.

Farther over, an old woman was reading the paper, and beside her were two men, one with the wind-burned face of a mountaineer or a heavy drinker, and the other with a rueful and serene expression. They were talking in low tones, and only episodically, but their heads remained almost touching across the table between them. Elsewhere, somebody whistled, and there was a hiss of steamed milk, and a quick racket of plates being stacked badly. A name was called out somewhere; there was a short, rattling laugh from a waitress and she rolled her eyes.

Minogue watched Malone heading over with his tray.
Malone definitely lost a bit of weight. Gone back to the training?
Hardly: more like he'd been through the mill, with his brother
found dead of an overdose. What would it do to you to bury your
twin brother?

He wondered then what Kilmartin had said to him at the
session on Thursday, the last "Club Mad" get-together.
Kilmartin, the Tyrannosaurus from Mayo, always looking like
the suits he wore were belonging to somebody else, had his hand
on Malone's shoulder early in the session. He'd said a few words
that Malone had nodded at.

Minogue was as surprised as the others, and remembered
laughing as hard as Murtagh even, when Malone joined in bits of
Kilmartin's awful karaoke version of "Suspicious Minds" toward
the end of the night.

"Might as well tell you," Malone said, clearing the tray.
"We're not alone."

"You watch *Star Trek* now, is it?"

Malone nodded up at the railings for the mezzanine floor
that was open to the patrons here below. With its low ceiling, it
was a place of last resort for Minogue. Legs he saw between the
banister, and then the head inclining around a pillar. It was
Kilmartin giving him a solemn nod.

"What's he doing here?" Minogue said. "Are you expecting
him?"

Now Kilmartin was up, heading for the stairs.

"Tell you in a minute."

Kilmartin crossed the floor with his cup held carelessly at
the edge of the saucer. Jaunty, but like a wrestler maybe, Minogue
reflected. Marauding, scanning the faces, with a look and a walk
that said this overweight countryman was born to be a Guard and
would be so, *per omnia saecula saculorum.*

A faint smell of cigar ash wafted to Minogue as Kilmartin
sat in at the table and tugged at his shirt cuffs.

"So," said Kilmartin. "The usual suspects? You pair of
rogues here?"

"They're letting anyone in here these days," Minogue said.

"Look who's talking," Kilmartin retorted. "Now, tell me, this gig that the both of you are mitching from, this 'Policing on the Frontiers of Europe Today.'"

"How well you know all about it."

"I know everything," said Kilmartin. "So says Maura. Okay: it was right there in the newsletter, you *gamóg*. Next to the cartoons."

For a moment Minogue considered turning it on Kilmartin. It was the kind of thing he'd like to be in on almost as much as with all the tech talk he loved about his post in Procurement.

"'Basically' Lally runs those gigs, still?"

"None other," said Minogue.

"A legend entirely. But that fella, he tries too hard, if you ask me. Here, I'll let me tell you my grief with this multimedia lark. Share my pain, will you."

"You have PowerPoint in your life?" asked Malone.

"Don't talk to me about that frigging curse-of-God thing. I said to a fella – Noel Conroy, the Assistant Comm., you know him, Tipperary – Nenagh in actual fact, a brother of his in Aer Lingus? I says to Noel: 'Noel, I says, look: I'll run you up a little presentation that'll show the helicopter thing in action.' I was trying to play cute, you see – I already had a thing given to me from a fella in the States when I was over, a higher up from Washington. A CD with pictures and that."

"Do you mean a salesman?"

"Feck off. Actually a cop from Maryland or somewhere. So I says to Noel, I says, 'No bother at all. Have it for you tomorrow.' Well . . . ! Jesus wept, lads. I might as well have cut me own throat."

"It's a curse, the computer," said Minogue. "I've heard it said."

"I'm nearly destroyed with it. I had to go out and pay a fella on the QT to do it. Out of my own pocket! Worked great, says Noel. Brilliant, says I. No bother."

Kilmartin paused to take a sip from his cup.

"So Conroy knows you're the expert," said Malone. "Now you're shagged."

"Enough out of you, bucko," said Kilmartin. "And don't be vulgar."

His friend, colleague, and tormentor of twenty and more years was clearly enjoying himself, Minogue saw.

"You're in fine form, the both of you, in anyhow. I suppose I should be content with the usual barracking and bollicking I get from the pair of ye. Oh, brings back happy memories. I don't think."

Abruptly he shifted his weight and drew in his chair with his instep.

"Wait and I'll tell you, you won't believe it. You won't believe this one. This is what passes for a murder investigation these days. You won't credit your own ears."

The coffee found its way to Minogue's brain in short order. He listened at a distance to his friend's disdain. It was the old story, but just as entertaining: here again was the triumph of a Mayo man's keen intelligence, with the customary nod to a modesty Kilmartin never could carry off. Bagged the wrong shoes! Sure a tinker's horse would know better! The sheer stupidity of those detectives and they handing the defence counsel a winning ticket! And them coming in and out of the side door to the shop – exactly where the two shooters had left? Curly, Larry and Moe reporting for duty, sir!

Kilmartin sat back slowly as though to remove himself from this planet of gobshites. Minogue studied the eyebrows on the Mayo giant dancing with the scorn, the rolling eye, and the timed pause. Kilmartin began to wind down his grim oration. As usual, there were some philosophical musings on what it took to get proper police work done. There was a description of how the judge had apparently stared at the two detectives even as he told the barrister to take his client for a walk, a free man. He finished with a stoical comment on the human condition generally: Where ignorance is bliss, it was surely folly to be wise.

"So," said Kilmartin then, brightly. "Is that why they disbanded our Squad, lads? Are these the brains of the Gardai running murder cases now? Are we in safe hands?"

Minogue long knew this invitation to any reaction was already ordained futile. Worse, it was an open door for more Kilmartin. He managed a head shake. Malone had twisted the

Islandbridge

paper from his sugar into a sort of horseshoe. An American couple sat in at a table nearby. Kilmartin nodded at the man, who had loose skin and white hair.

"What's the news from beyond?" he asked Minogue. "Stateside, like."

His own son Daithi, he meant, Minogue realized.

"Same as ever. He does the emails to Kathleen mostly."

Kilmartin's eyes took on a vacant look. Minogue did not know whether he should ask his friend how the Kilmartin's own son Liam was doing.

"I hate email," said Kilmartin. "A proper letter shows, well, you know."

Kilmartin did not talk much about his young fella now. Maura Kilmartin passed on bits to Kathleen when they'd meet, which was less often now anyway. It was hardly just because the son was shacked up with a girl there, with no sign of marrying, no sign of coming home either. The last that Kilmartin had mentioned about his son was that Liam Kilmartin seemed to speak a foreign language, full of talk about start-ups, and venture capital, and breakthroughs, and alliances and cutting edge.

Nonetheless, drunk or sober, Minogue would probably never go near to hinting to his friend that you didn't have to be a detective to sense the loneliness in him, a bafflement at how America seemed to be holding his son at bay. There had been words before Liam went, Minogue had learned, a fairly considerable row. "A family matter" was all Maura Kilmartin had conceded to Kathleen. Minogue surmised that things may well have been said that had lacerated Kilmartin. Only twice in all the years Minogue had known him had Kilmartin even mentioned what he called "the adoption."

Kilmartin leaned in over the table.

"Now let's get through the James Bond stuff here," he said to Malone. "What's this gig of yours you want to talk to me – to us – about here?"

"I'll tell yous in a minute," said Malone.

"Tell me now," said Kilmartin. "I answered the call, pal. It's not every day of the week I get a personal telephone request from the Dhubbalin Man himself. There better be something to it, I say. You, Matt?"

"Oh, I'm just happy to be here, I'd like to thank the academy. . . ."

"You're a goner, there's no doubt. What gives?"

"I want you to meet a fella."

"I'm not a homo. Didn't you know that yet?"

Malone looked from Kilmartin to Minogue and back.

"All right," Kilmartin said. "Where is he?"

"He's across the way."

"Where, 'across the way'?"

"Inside in Clarendon Street Church. At the side altar."

"The church?" said Kilmartin. "Are you taking us to Mass, or something?"

Malone put on his stone-face.

"It's about Emmett Condon," he said, and he looked up vacantly along the banister that led the way up to the hidden world of Bewley's mezzanine floor. "This fella says he knows something about what happened to Condon."

Kilmartin stared at Minogue until he looked over.

"Garda Emmett Condon?" Kilmartin said in a low voice. "God rest his soul?"

Malone nodded.

Minogue struggled to remember details. Hadn't Condon's body been found back around Christmas? The rumours had started right away, he recalled, and the toxicology report seemed to confirm them. Condon had the distinction of being the first Garda ever to die of a drug overdose. It was actually Kilmartin who had mentioned something back then about a huge review of undercover operations, all the way to the top of the GNDU, the Garda National Drugs Unit, because of Condon.

Minogue found himself scanning the faces here in the restaurant anew. He felt a stirring, old reflexes announce themselves. He considered trying to ignore them, but he soon gave up. This was because he was certain he now saw in Kilmartin's face that slack, expressionless mask, one that said he too couldn't suppress the alerted hunter in himself either.

"Well now," Kilmartin said and leaned in over the table. "You have my interest here. Nothing like a botched cover-up to get that going, I can tell you. Go on, so."

"I'm going to give you the fella's name," said Malone, and eyed Kilmartin. "The reason being, is that you'll understand why I asked to meet up with you. Lawless is his name, Frank Lawless. Does that ring a bell?"

Kilmartin frowned.

"Why would it?" he asked. "There's tons by that name. Is he a gouger?"

"More of a failed one, I'd have to say," Malone replied. "His brother was, or is, the one you'd know. Tony."

"Tony Lawless? Yes. From somewhere."

Kilmartin suddenly sat upright and he looked from Malone to Minogue and back.

"Murder? About eleven or twelve years back?"

"Right," said Malone.

"You'd better explain this," said Kilmartin.

Malone hesitated and Minogue head him draw in a breath.

"He– Lawless, I mean, the fella waiting for us– he wants me to show I have some cred, you know."

"Cred?"

"That's right. See if I can get things done. Otherwise he won't tell me what he's going to tell me. It's kind of like bona fides too. Did I say that right, like a trust thing?"

Minogue nodded. A strange smile spread over Kilmartin's features.

"Are you saying that we're here for your credibility with some informant?" he said, lingering on each word.

Malone nodded.

"So this low-life is orchestrating your, what are we going to call it, your investigation here, your information?"

"Well, it's not actually an investigation," said Malone. "It just sort of came up."

Kilmartin met Minogue's eyes and raised an eyebrow.

"I'm just along for the ride, as they say," said Minogue.

Kilmartin settled his gaze on Malone again.

"It just came up?"

"Right," said Malone.

"But he's going to give you information about what happened to Emmett Condon. Information that no-one else can find. Not even the geniuses over at Internal Affairs."

"That's what I'm hoping, yeah."

"And he'll talk to us, as long as I'm here, to show him that you have cred."

"Well, not exactly," said Malone, and shifted a little in his seat. "He won't talk to you. He just wants to see you. That's all he wants in that department."

"Say that again, will you?"

"To see you. You have to know he's a bit nuts now. It's drugs, that's how it got started, right?"

"Doesn't it always?"

"What I mean is, he'll talk to me if he sees you."

Chapter 4

KILMARTIN AND MINOGUE had been waiting for nearly five minutes in the porch of Clarendon Street Church. Minogue had stepped between Kilmartin and the doors into the church proper only once yet.

Kilmartin strolled back to his spot by the holy water fount.

"A nice how-do-you-do," he whispered. "Trying to stop a man going into a chapel to say his prayers. Wait until I tell Kathleen that you came between me and God. That's a new low."

"There are plenty of other churches in Dublin, Jim."

"And how would you know?"

"Look, Tommy said the fella was jittery."

"Ah," said Kilmartin, and shook his head. "His 'informant.' You do know what this caper is taking out of me, don't you?"

Minogue nodded.

"Don't those mad plays of what's-his-name go like this?" Kilmartin asked.

"What's-his-name?"

"Beckett," said Kilmartin. "How could I forget! God almighty, Maura dragged me to one of his years ago, and it was like a fecking migraine, from start to finish. But it's this 'He'll only talk to me if he sees you' bit, I'm talking about. Christ almighty, is Malone trying to stage some kind of an I-don't-know-what, a revelation, or a miracle, or something here with this Condon shambles?"

"I'd settle on 'revelation,' Jim. Probably. But who knows."

"Well, I know," said Kilmartin. "I know this much: Malone owes me big time. And furthermore, if this turns out to be trick-acting or a con, well he'll rue the day, by God. A ridiculous set-up, this. Ridiculous."

It was, Minogue had to admit. But he had enjoyed seeing Kilmartin's reaction when Malone had tried to explain why he needed Kilmartin to come into the church when he gave the signal, and sit as faraway as possible from them but still be visible. He did not enjoy Kilmartin's extortion in return: that he be given Malone's gun for the duration, in case this was some weird set-up, a revenge thing to do with Lawless's brother.

Minogue wanted to look again at where Kilmartin's hand had stayed jammed into his pocket, holding Malone's pistol. He turned instead to watch a doubled-up old woman bless herself. A young man, tall, with a preoccupied expression, and his coat on inside out, entered as though in a trance.

The woman behind the glass where they sold Mass cards and holy pictures began rearranging papers and knick-knacks. The cards and devotional items were almost as extravagant and strange as when he was a boy. The sight of the pierced and thorn-wrapped heart outside Jesus' chest, the pillars of cloud-splitting light, the supplicant skyward eyes of saints and martyrs – all gave Minogue a secret, but embarrassing, comfort.

He liked the grime and the dim light here, the shuffling of the people, so many of them troubled. He even liked the greyed edges to everything here in the entrance, a grimy surface rubbed there by the countless people who came here, day in, day out. Most of the people were women, and they were on the home stretch too, as his father used to say.

"Jesus," murmured Kilmartin after another unkempt man had entered, stared without seeing at the three policemen, slurred something to the woman behind the glass, and left.

"Not yet," said Minogue. "He was only John the Baptist."

"Oh that's rich," said Kilmartin. "An Antichrist of the first order informing me of the ways of Our Lord. Very rich entirely."

Minogue let it go. He was fighting back his own impatience

more now, himself. He looked around the entrance again, and wondered if Kilmartin had noticed the signs about justice, and the lunches for the homeless, or the few rebel-looking Jesuses on signs in foreign languages.

Then Malone's face was in the doorway. Minogue almost laughed out loud.

Minogue shook his head. Could he ever tell Kilmartin that in this light Malone's wary, block-headed face looked like that of a monk?

"This guy's jumpy," said Malone. "So no pressure, okay?"

"Listen," said Kilmartin. "This ain't so appealing, the more I think about it."

Malone gave Minogue a look. A man came in the outer door, blinked and leered and stroked his beard, then muttered and left, awkwardly.

"That," said Kilmartin, "that is exactly what I'm alluding to, bucko. There's people coming in that door here every ten seconds, and the thing is, they're all the same. They're all head cases. Get it?"

"Look," said Malone. "It took a big job of work to get him here."

Malone headed for the candles by the side altar. Minogue followed him, taking occasional glances at the set of eyes that stayed on him from behind the wavering points of candlelight. He heard a shoe clump against a pew behind him. He guessed it was Kilmartin, making his presence felt, but he did not look around. He felt the still, scented air begin to work on his mind. It was full of burning wax and polish and incense, and generations of sweat and stains and clothes that had been slept in.

Arrayed around the walls were the expected Stations of the Cross, and then the lines of pews in the dim light, interrupted by the forms of those sitting or kneeling. A figure would stand, another kneel, another would enter the church, part of a constant eddy of people.

Malone had stopped. He turned to Kilmartin, and nodded at a pew.

"So," said Malone. "Can you wait over there?"

The candlelights glittered in Kilmartin's eyes.

"I remember Lawless now," he said. "He killed a man over a car."

Minogue saw a figure move behind the glow from the candles, a face turn his way, rapidly blinking eyes.

"Can you?" Malone repeated.

"Look, that's a monk," said Kilmartin. "I mean a friar."

"Right," said Malone. "He's part two of the deal here. You and the priest fella. So can you–"

"He's a Franciscan, right?"

"No, I think he's from Dublin," said Malone.

Minogue remembered the friar now: Coughlin, Father Larry Coughlin. He'd been on *Morning Ireland* last week. A former stockbroker in London, Coughlin now did the social work thing with addicts, as well as say Mass.

Kilmartin stepped closer to Malone. The move reminded Minogue of the exchange before the first round of a boxing match.

"Listen," said Kilmartin. "Me no likee. This could be a set-up. There could be cameras and I don't know what. I don't like this one bit."

Malone looked at Minogue.

"Jim, just a short while?" Minogue tried. "Okay?"

Kilmartin stared at the face behind the candles. His eyebrow came up, and then something close to a sneer took over his face. He broke his gaze abruptly, and muttered something about meds, and slipped into a pew.

Minogue mouthed an elaborate thank you that Kilmartin pretended to ignore, and then he followed Malone. They sat into the pew in front of Father Coughlin and Lawless. Father Coughlin grasped the long rope that hung by his side, the name of which Minogue had once been proud to know and had now forgotten, and a rosary beads he'd had somewhere, and also a bit of his robes. He got up without a word, or even a glance toward the two policemen, and knelt to Lawless's right.

"A con," said Kilmartin, and looked at his watch again. "Pure and simple. You got a twenty-minute lesson in bullshit. And I hate to say it, but . . ."

He and Minogue rounded the corner into South Anne Street. Malone had gone his own way after a phone call had interrupted their few words outside the door of the church.

"Let me guess," said Minogue. "'Tommy Malone is a desperate gobshite to go along with any of this.'"

"You too – don't forget yourself."

"Nothing personal, right?"

"Exactly."

"For encouraging him?"

"Something like that," Kilmartin agreed. "Malone needs to be reminded, but . . ."

Minogue kept working around the flow of people at the corner of Grafton Street.

"Well, at least it was interesting," he said.

"Really? But am I ever going to hear the details that the little bollocks told you two?"

"I told you everything, Jim. Lawless was repeating himself after a while. He had some talk about a Guard playing for the other team, that it's been going on a good while."

"Yes, but who? And where, and how, and when, for the love of God?"

Minogue shrugged. Was it Russian he could hear from a couple holding a street guide by the corner? His own ignorance came to him again: Serbo-Croatian, Ukrainian, why not even Polish? Ahh – he'd never keep up with this.

"He said he didn't know."

"But that this Guard feeds some of the gangs in Dublin, right?"

"According to Lawless. That's the rumour he heard from his brother in jail."

"But how did the Condon thing come up?"

"He didn't actually use Condon's name," Minogue replied. "He said that part of what his brother had told him was that some Guard, some undercover Guard, had been nosing around in this too, but then he turned up dead himself. An overdose – 'that cop they found ODed' were his words, as I recall."

Kilmartin shook his head.

"No doubt he wants a thousand million euros for this."

"He didn't say what he wanted."

"Disneyworld might buy it, tell Malone. Has Malone actually bought any of this line from that little bollocks?"

"I don't know," said Minogue. "But I got coffee and cake out of it. And I got bailed out of the PowerPoint thing too."

"Malone gets an idea into his head, bejases, and he'll sink his teeth into it like a badger, Matt. Obsessed, I call that. Don't you see?"

Minogue made a non-committal nod, and stepped up the pace. All he wanted was to be here amongst the crowds, hearing the languages, and eyeing the looming trees of St. Stephen's Green waiting for him at the top of the street.

"They tried to play Malone before," said Kilmartin. "It's the old story, isn't it? Before, they used his brother to get at him – Terry, God rest him. And now? Malone is working GNDU here, in the thick of it? The Garda National Drugs Unit . . . no wonder someone would be trying to fiddle with his head. Even just to cause trouble with his crowd, Matt. He'll always be a target for that, Malone. But he should have a bit of cop-on, for God's sake."

"Sowing the seeds of discord, is it."

"Disinformation is what it is," said Kilmartin. "Do you know what that is?"

"Of course I do. I'm a married man the same as yourself."

"You're not as funny as you think you are there, you *bostún*. Surely to God even you crowd in, ahem, International Liaison there, know there's enough of the Dublin gangbangers went big here this last while. Come on now: brazen, bigger, and bolder. Sure, they think they're running the show."

Minogue nodded.

"Remember the Egans there a while back?" Kilmartin went on, as though Minogue were still an unbeliever. "Who else is there in it? The Rynns, what's left of them? Jumbo Rynn is still in it, I hear. He's an oul lad now, he can hardly walk. Emphymesa, or something."

"'Nothing too trivial, I hope.'"

"That's not like you," said Kilmartin. "Hard talk like that."

"That was Wilde."

"Wild, is right. It just sounds odd coming from you, you oul softie."

"Ah, things are moving too fast lately," Kilmartin went on. "Waaay too fast, I'm telling you. There's fellas in town here getting into the driver's seat for gang stuff, now, fellas who have about ten words of English. Me refugee, get money, wanna drugs I get for you, friend in Moscow, let's do deals, no wanna go back there, likee here too much, lotsa stupid people I rob and cheat."

"Is that how they speak, refugees?"

"'Refugees?' Don't get holy on me, Matt. And don't be so damned naïve."

Minogue stopped by the lights, and waited. He knew that he would try to screen out what Kilmartin's remarks revealed, but it still soured him. He thought of Father Coughlin, the Franciscan sitting in the church. He had left a millionaire job in London to help drug addicts in his hometown here?

"Someone's messing with his head," Kilmartin said, over the traffic. "Mark my words, Matt. I'd be thinking Malone's losing his, what'll I call it, maybe not his *marbles* yet, but his perspective, you could call it."

"But not in a bad way," said Minogue.

"Don't be cheeky. You know what, Matt? I wouldn't put it past that bastard Lawless to hatch up a scheme to get at me – either of them. For locking up one of them. You see?"

There was a knot of people gawking into a window up ahead, and others were drifting over to catch a glimpse of whatever it was. It was another hi-fi shop, Minogue saw. There was live coverage of the event in Malahide still. The man he had seen earlier was onscreen, and he appeared to be in tears. McCourt, McCoy – no: McCann, that was his name.

"What gives here," Kilmartin said. "What am I missing?"

"I saw it earlier on. A stowaway fell out of a plane over in Malahide, apparently."

Kilmartin lingered, squinting into the window.

"A stowaway?" he said.

Someone in the small crowd turned and nodded, and said something else to Kilmartin. Minogue took a few steps to show Kilmartin he wasn't for hanging around any longer. Kilmartin exchanged a few more words with the man, stared for a while at the screen, and followed Minogue.

"Dropped in unannounced," he said to Minogue, who gave him a quick glare, and began walking faster. It took some effort from Kilmartin to catch up.

"What's your hurry?" he demanded.

"I'm trying to keep up with the coming times. Unlike some."

They had to wait a minute for botched traffic signals at the other end of the Green before they could cross and start up Harcourt Street.

"Here, I never asked you," said Kilmartin, beginning to breathe heavier from the pace. "Who are you working with now?"

"Same as before. International Liaison."

Kilmartin was like an old woman more and more, Minogue had decided. Maybe it was since the move out of the Squad that his friend had become even more of a gossip and a collector, and a cynic. But there was no-one Kilmartin didn't have a yarn about, or couldn't dig up one with a few phone calls.

"But who's your minder there, day-to-day, I mean? Your 'mentor'?"

"Tadhg Sullivan."

"Aha! I know Tadhg. Tadhg is Kerry – no prize there, with the name, I know. Fenit, is he from?"

"Worse," said Minogue. "I actually suspect he might be from Dingle."

The sun came out then, without warning. It blasted over this small part of Minogue's city, lighting up the trees and the glass. He looked up, in hope. There'd be a bit more of it, he believed, maybe even enough for him to get the last of it this evening down at Killiney Strand.

"Listen, what are you doing later on?" Kilmartin said.

"After I've concocted some excuse for getting out of the meeting?"

"This evening, I mean."

"Herself might have plans, maybe. Maybe I'll study for me French exams."

"You blackguard, you'll do no such thing. Next thing you'll try is 'herself wants the rockery rearranged.' Christ man, that rockery of yours – you must have moved it ten times."

Minogue took in the passing cars and the pedestrians as he strode along. He didn't care if this was a bit taxing for Kilmartin. He began to imagine a camera on him, someone taking notes: *"Collusion with others to leave their post. . . . Heart not in his work. . . . Appears skeptical of value of Euro-conference and intelligence-sharing, especially if presented onscreen . . . ."*

He looked over at Kilmartin, who was huffing a little now, and trying not to show it. He had gone a bit stout lately. Maybe it went with his bilious comments about foreigners that Minogue wished he hadn't heard earlier. He slowed a little.

"Look," said Kilmartin. "Will you come by the house tonight?"

"To your house?"

"Not *to* the house," said Kilmartin. "No: I have to get *out* of the damned house. It's that frigging kitchen thing of Maura's. Without a by-your-leave, she has the kip turned upside down. There's fellas working there until eight and nine at night! 'Can't get them any other way,' says she."

"What had you in mind?"

"I mean a bit of gallivanting. You go round and about some nights, don't you? A healthy stroll, and all that. Come on now. Keeps you fit, right?"

"I don't do it for that, Jim."

"Well, whatever," said Kilmartin with a touch of annoyance. "Up them lanes and hills and whatever. Let me try it out."

The irritation rose up suddenly in Minogue.

"You have plenty next door to your place, Jim. Killiney Hill there, Dalkey?"

When Kilmartin said nothing, Minogue stole a glance over.

"Fair enough," said Kilmartin then.

Chapter 5

MINOGUE HAD PICKED UP a copy of the summary from the session with Moser.

"So, was he good?" Tadhg Sullivan asked.

Minogue looked over at his colleague. Sullivan, a Kerryman, with all the Kerryman's propensities, would probably have heard about the truancy already.

"The Austrian fella's thing? Moser?"

Sullivan nodded.

"It was great," Minogue replied.

"Just great? Not brilliant, or anything?"

Minogue gave him a wary scrutiny to see any sign Sullivan was winding him up.

"He is very up on everything, Tadhg."

Sullivan flicked the pages, pausing to study some of the maps.

Minogue's thoughts began to drift back to the church, and again to Lawless's glittering eyes reflecting the candle flames, as they blinked and darted about the church. So Garda Emmett Condon had died of an overdose. Wasn't that fairly common knowledge by now? This girl that Lawless had said Condon had been been mixed up with, this foreign one that nobody knew about, well Minogue could check when he had time if there was any mention of this in the case. Or not.

The real item that Lawless wanted to use to crowbar snitch

money out of the Guards – "remuneration" Lawless had called it, in that quasi-legal wordiness so typical of a Dubliner chancer – seemed to be the story of the senior Guard on the payroll for someone big here in Dublin. Details to follow on receipt of substantial cash, no doubt. Maybe Jim Kilmartin's instincts were right on: a con.

Minogue realized that Sullivan was still hanging on the divider. He sat back and eyed him. There was always that stray cowlick of hair, a slight crossing of the front teeth, and an earnest, almost startled look to Sullivan, and his squat mesomorphic trunk seemed to insist that his shirt tails erupt out, right from the start of a workday.

"Anything we should consider using right away, Matt?"

Sullivan was talking about the presentation, of course. Minogue looked over, but could not detect any mischief. He took that to be evidence of the contrary. It would be a battle of the straight-faces then. A bit of entertainment was welcome, he decided, now that Minogue realized that part of him believed what Kilmartin had said about a con.

"Well, Tadhg. It was all fascinating entirely. The big picture, as they say?"

"Every little bit helps, I daresay," said Sullivan. "God knows, we've had it easy here long enough. With the Euro-crime I mean."

Sullivan shifted his weight. Minogue registered the bulk of the belly shift and swell the shirt over Sullivan's belt.

"How right you are, Tadhg. Part of the package. Now that we're in the big leagues."

"That's why *ich spreche Deutsch*, Matt. Goes with the territory now. By the by, how's them French lessons going?"

"*Maith go leor*," said Minogue, in the Munster Irish of his youth, fairly sure that Sullivan wouldn't miss it. *Maith go leaor*, or "good enough," was a phrase common to any dialect of Irish, alluding to a person who was plenty under the influence.

"Bet your missus has a keener interest in you now, with you enjoying that facility now."

Minogue might as well be looking at the sphinx. A true son of Kerry, this silver-tongued rogue.

"No success with the German, Tadhg?"

Sullivan scratched himself gently under the arm.

"They're not so hot on the oul pillow talk. That I know of, anyway."

Minogue looked down at the heap of files he had culled on Intermatic, a recent shell game that Revenue had come up with almost by accident. Intermatic had been a front for smuggling in dirty money that seemed to be coming in through Germany – from Thailand, of all places.

"Tadhg, tell me something. Have you got a minute?"

"Are you sure I'm not interrupting a meeting now, or a conference call with you know who?"

"Who, now?"

"Malone," said Sullivan.

"Was it that noticeable?"

Sullivan issued a wan smile.

"Matt, you were in a room full of cops. We can't all be iijits at the same time."

Minogue balanced his anniversary pen, the ten-year one that Kilmartin had paid for personally, for the Squad.

"I hear you, Tadhg. And thank you. But tell me about someone. Emmett Condon?"

Sullivan's eyes lost their glaze.

"Tell you what?"

"Well, you keep your ear to the ground."

"Why are you asking me, though?"

"Because you're a knowledgeable man."

"Is that what you're working on?"

"No. The name came up recently."

"Is this an 'I have a friend who . . .'?"

"Well, do you know anything?"

"I only know what any Guard in Dublin knows, Matt."

"Do you mean something like what I was told already, 'the Condon thing is a shambles'?"

"Couldn't have said it better myself. How bad? Well, some of that might never come out. That's all I heard."

Minogue waited. He watched Sullivan's fingers tracing something on a file folder.

"Come on. You're the one'd have the contacts, Matt. You're the Murder Squad veteran now. You and Big Jim. Glory days, were they?"

"At the time, you wouldn't think so."

"Well, how is Kilmartin getting on now, anyway? Still a character, I'll bet you."

Minogue raised an eyebrow in return for Sullivan's mischief.

"He's great. Nearly too much so."

In Sullivan's face Minogue now read the signs that he needed to plot a diversion, without delay. The topic, as so often before was: yarns of the Murder Squad, and Jim "The Killer" Kilmartin, its last and legendary section head before its honourable dissolution and folding back into the Garda Technical Bureau. Minogue had yet to hear any request for tales of the Technical Bureau. The Bureau, and the staff of the State Lab contributing to it on so many cases, was merely a body devoted to police science and procedure, a place where striding giants like James Kilmartin were seen plainly of another age. *Oisín I nidaidh na Féinne.*[1]

Minogue cast about for anything, and was relieved to remember that Sullivan had asked him about a bed-and-breakfast in Paris. Sullivan and his missus, a formidable primary school-teacher with the red hair and the face of a tinker, had never been there.

He found the address, and said he'd phone for Sullivan and sorry he'd forgotten. Sullivan asked about food, a topic close to his heart, Minogue had discovered a month back when he'd

---

[1] Literally 'Oisín seeking the Fianna,' the saying means a great longing for former times and company. This expression derives from the legends of the Fianna and its leader – and Oisín's father – Finn Mac Cumhaill. Oisín had gone to Tír na nOg with a beautiful maiden and had spent three hundred years there. Homesick, and believing he had only spent several days away, he returned to Ireland to find his friends and family long gone. He met instead a man who was struggling to lift a rock, and decided to help him. He remembered the warning that his feet must not touch the ground in Ireland or he would instantly become as old as the time that had passed in his absence from Ireland. Leaning down from his horse, a strap broke and he tumbled to the ground, immediately becoming a very old man. As in many legends reformed to suit Christian purposes in supplanting older ways, he was then baptized before he died.

started here on this, his third three-month stint working his way through the Garda sections. Sullivan left happily enough, for lunch, with a yarn that Minogue conceded about Kilmartin stepping on dogshite at a scene a few years ago, and having to put his own shoe in an evidence bag.

♣ ♣ ♣

Having his own religion, Minogue had for many years now been imposing his own penance also. Today it meant working through lunch, as repentance for slipping away from "Policing the Frontiers of the New Europe." He used the pretext of Intermatic's money-laundering trail to phone Dan Kiely in Criminal Assets, and half-enjoy a longish exploration of why Limerick city's reputation and nickname – "Stab City" – was undeserved. Then he re-read the statements that had come in this morning from Amrobank, on an island he knew was somewhere in the Caribbean, but was also the name of some kind of spirits – Curaçao.

He marvelled a lot less about the ingenuity of the laundering operation now after working on it for two days. Last week it had been a builder Mulcahy. That had been a right monkey puzzle that involved fake invoices for cement, the Cayman Islands, and the hospitalization of a foreman on a building site of the shopping centre in Baldoyle.

After a half-hour, Minogue ate a bit of a Mars bar and some crisps and he headed to the toilet. It was too early for coffee. Actually it wasn't, he reflected as he stood with his hands under the dryer, staring at his own face in the mirror, and wondering yet again how much more of this dream job he could take.

It was half past two before Malone finally phoned. Right away he wanted to know what he thought of Lawless, and what the latter had said. Minogue tried to evade him.

"Ask Jim first, why don't you," he said.

"I know what he'd think before we even went there. It's you I want to hear."

Minogue thought of the flickering candlelight on Lawless's face, his incessant blinking and his fidgetiness. Lawless had reminded him of that American actor they raved about, what was his name – of course, De Niro. He remembered that Lawless's teeth were grey, they went in, instead of out. Like a rat, maybe. Was it drugs did that?

"Look, Tommy," he said after a while. "It all means nothing. That's what I really think."

He wasn't aware of having decided to be brutal about it. Malone fell silent.

"Your informant spent a bit of time on his script, Tommy. Mr. Lawless."

"Well, what about the woman that Condon was with?"

"Supposedly with."

"You don't take even one bit of it seriously?"

"Well where is she then? I'll listen in on what she tells you, if that'll keep you happy."

"Come on," said Malone. "If I could do that, don't you think I would've already?"

Minogue pushed his chair back. Kilmartin's words came to him too, no matter what he tried, and he couldn't dislodge them from his brain: Malone was losing it.

"Listen, Tommy. Did you pass this to the people on the Condon case?"

"I won't until I figure out if it's a con or not. And anyway, that is iced. They're just going through the motions, I found out. It's pretty clear Condon was bent."

"Then just pass it on, and walk away from it. You have enough to be doing, I'm thinking."

Minogue did not like to hear silence from Malone's end again. He thought of the contented look he'd been seeing on Malone's face this past while, especially when he had met him with Sonia Chang, Malone's on-again girlfriend whose family ran a take-out in Rathmines. The flak from her family hadn't let up, flak about dating an Irish policeman, or more to the point, a Dublin Northsider who looked more like the bad guys than their idea of a cop.

"So tell me," Minogue said, brightly. "Any happy news coming our way as regards to yourself and Sonia?"

"We're doing so-so," said Malone. "But it's not Sonia I'm phoning about, is it."

There was a pause. Minogue sort of knew what was coming.

"You think I'm being pumped," Malone said. "Go on. You can say it."

"Tommy, look. Why not hand over what you have to them that can folley up on it?"

"What, a pack of amateurs, where is it, down in Kilmainham or wherever they found Condon? Six months it's been, and they haven't found the girl, you know."

"What does that tell you then?"

"I don't actually want to say it," Malone replied. "Do you? So I'm going to think, well maybe she's out there somewhere."

Malone was right, Minogue believed. He sat back.

"Look," Malone went on in a quieter voice. "If Condon really was so bent before he, well, before what happened let's say, there's people who won't want that known. People on our side, right?"

"You mean the Guards in general?"

"More than that. Like, if there are others in the same line as Condon."

"Do you believe that, Tommy?"

"If, I'm saying– if."

"That'd be part of the script from your informant, Tommy. Your Mister Lawless."

"Jaysus, give me a fair trial before the hanging here, will you?"

Minogue waited a few moments.

"I can't help but wonder," he said then, "just how much planning and conniving and rehearsing went into it. I have to say that, Tommy. Sorry."

"Don't be sorry. It's straight talk I want. So here: you and Kilmartin think Lawless came to be because of Terry. Right?"

"God rest him," said Minogue.

Immediately he wanted to give himself a right good clout for letting this reflex expression trip out of his mouth. It was another rock from his upbringing, he realized sourly, one he couldn't hope to dislodge, his pagan ways notwithstanding. For a moment he thought back again to the funeral for Malone's brother: a life so different, a life wasted in the grip of addiction.

"Right?"

"Right, Tommy."

"I do."

"Look, I *know* he's a junkie," said Malone. "I *know*. You think I don't know how junkies are? But still, I'll give the bastard ten minutes, I says to myself back when Coughlin passed on the request. The due diligence bit. You know Coughlin works with them, right?"

"Right."

"Lawless is trying to go clean. Father Larry told me that. That's what got me persuaded to listen, that monk."

"Friar, Tommy. Franciscan friar."

"Right. So Lawless is in this 3R thing of Coughlin's. Repent Rebuild Re–?"

"Renew?"

"Yeah. So I says to him after I hear him out, I says: Lawless, you just talked a load of bollocksology. That was last week. But Lawless comes back, so he does. So then I go to the next step. You know the routine: 'Are you willing to repeat what you said, to another Garda officer?' Well, he rears up a bit, but he still wants to push it. Then he lands a name on me, a 'witness,' he calls him: and up comes Kilmartin's name."

"That got you listening then, no doubt."

"Especially when he says he actually doesn't want Kilmartin in on what he says – just to see him there would be enough. So I told him I'd try but it'd be another cop would listen to what he was saying. And he wanted Father Larry there, as a ref."

Malone was waiting for some reaction.

"Tommy. Again. Hand it over to someone. Would you like me to get you a name?"

"What if Lawless is right? That no-one wants to hear what he says?"

"Let them figure it out."

He heard the breathing at Malone's end and the detached tone he'd half expected.

"I hear you," Malone said. His Dublin accent was muted

now, almost a monotone. "Loud and clear."

Minogue tried. He asked about Sonia's latest accountancy exam, and was there any sign of the parents, Mr. and Mrs. Chang, getting a bit less frosty. And were they really moving the restaurant out to Terenure?

Malone gave cursory answers. It was clear he had no inclination to talk further. Minogue felt the urge to apologize but did not. They ended the conversation with a "later." Malone didn't tell Minogue he'd be in touch.

The afternoon dragged. Minogue was soon snared in a long phone call with a woman named Finnoula Morrissey from the Director of Public Prosecutions. She tried to explain why the offshore banking records he had gone to so much trouble to get would be shaky terms to introduce. He wanted to ask how some run-of-the-mill go-boys who had bought suits and BMWs and a few accountants' crooked expertise, could pay so much money to lawyers to tie this case up for four years now, within a soft lob of being thrown out due the length of time. He didn't ask her. Instead he scribbled a to-do list on his notepad while he listened to her. All the while, Minogue still registered his own slow and steady slide from anger to annoyance and then to something approaching numbness.

Things got better late in the afternoon when *Inspektor* Moser came through the section. He was chaperoned by Basically Lally, and some others began to turn up, faces from the session in the morning. There was a bit of a catered do for him in the conference room, a lame joke from Lally about the Sacher torte, the famous Viennese cake Minogue had never heard about, and yodelling. Moser chatted about Bulgarian criminals and people from Zagreb who had even harder-to-pronounce names. He also talked about Halstadt where the Celts had a big salt mine, and also about Celtic music and how many people actually spoke Irish for real.

Soon Tadhg Sullivan tried out his Kerry-inflected German. Minogue had to turn away so no-one would see his smile. Moser was studiously polite and an earnest listener. He made no attempt to help Sullivan, or to correct his pronunciation. Soon the talk shifted to Austria and Ireland. Minogue couldn't help but admire the conversational fluency and the sheer affability of this Viennese mastercop. He liked the lilt and the changing tones in Moser's accent, and the easy humour that was never forced, or over the top: Ah, but we are all consultants now, we police officers, are we not? Ah, like you, we too have a large, careless neighbour! And of course, we in Austria have our own version of their language.

There was some fair slagging about *The Sound of Music* from a fella Minogue recognized as Serious Crimes, but couldn't put a name on. Moser smiled, but then told them that the musical was quite unknown in Austria, and how ironic that was. Sullivan got some uniquely Austrian curse words from Moser, and practised them until they met Moser's approval.

Yes, the cake was crap, and the coffee was dire, but Minogue was glad of them. He had stopped brooding about Malone, or rather what Kilmartin suspected of Malone: that he had lost it, and was now dabbling in something that would turn out to be a set-up.

Moser remembered Minogue's name when they shook hands.

"Someday you will visit Vienna?"

Minogue was caught off guard.

"Certainly," he managed.

"You are from the western county, I understand," said Moser. "The county of Clare?"

"I am, to be sure."

"The Burren, no? And the Green Roads that nobody knows about?"

Minogue had to return the smile, and the wink.

"Except you, em–"

"Peter. I wish to go back there. It is a very strange and beautiful place."

"Strange, I grant you, yes."

Had Minogue a card? Sorry. Email? Well . . . send it to the section, and it'd get to him for sure.

There was a look of polite bafflement to Moser as they parted, Minogue saw.

But then it was time to go home: transnational crooks could

breathe a sigh of relief after half five Ireland time, as Minogue left the office of International Liaison for the teeming streets of the dynamic, maddening international city of Dublin.

♣ ♣ ♣

He picked Kathleen up outside the auctioneers on Merrion Square. Waiting at the lights, he looked down the row at the Pepper Cannister Church by the canal and the clouds massing behind it. To her question, he answered that he'd had an interesting day. Not that he'd looked at the letter of resignation he kept in his drawer. Nor that he'd had a strong desire to drink ten pints at about half three. Nor that he wanted to pack a bag and head down to as remote a spot as he could find in or around the Burren for a couple of days.

Kathleen turned on the radio. They listened to someone being interviewed about the man in the garden. Already the name had stuck: The African Miracle. People had already been bringing bouquets and wreaths to lay outside the house.

"Ever since Princess Diana," said Kathleen. "I'm telling you."

"I saw a bit of it this morning. I was passing a shop and it was on."

"Well, they are sure now he fell down when the landing gear was put down," she said. "That's what I heard. He was frozen."

Then there was news of the economy overheating. He kept his eye on the clouds to the south. They finally made it through Donnybrook.

"I'm kind of concerned about Tommy Malone," he said.

Kathleen closed the magazine.

"What's it been now since the funeral?" she said. "Eight months?"

"About that."

She looked out dolefully at the traffic that sped by, released as though by catapult from the lights at Donnybrook church.

"That's not long really," she said.

They stopped at Stillorgan Shopping Centre. Minogue bought a bottle of Chilean wine along with the staples. Kathleen opted for fish.

He opened the wine immediately they got home, and he took a glass with him down the garden. There were undoubtedly the beginnings of some infestation on one of the apple trees. Painting would be needed on the garage door too, of course – and then there was the issue of windows that he'd been trying to avoid for the past few years. He looked back at the house. Sell, he wondered, and he imagined a non-existent acre in sight of the Atlantic, sheltered under the Burren heights, and an easy walk into the village. But he'd go mad for the buzz of Dublin.

Kathleen was walking slowly down the garden too now, glass in hand, taking in the progress or lack of same in the flowers and shrubs along the way.

"That was Iseult who phoned," she said. "She'll be out tomorrow."

Minogue nodded. Their daughter showed no signs of letting up on a manic schedule to finish a commissioned installation of some kind, all metal and holes so far as Minogue could see.

"Any word of Pat," he said. "Or from Pat . . . ?"

Kathleen shook her head and began to examine the small pears that were now spotted.

Minogue was sorry he'd asked.

He was able to salvage part of the day later on. He took Kathleen up to Dalkey Hill first, from the car park there. They took their time looking out over the city through the milky evening haze settling there, gazing from crane to church spire to crane again.

And instead of just driving home, he had turned down toward Killiney Strand instead.

The tide was in, as he'd hoped, and there were sizeable waves up, and Minogue had plenty of time to take in the darkening water and listen as the stones shifted and hissed at the water's edge. For a while, he watched a dog swim into the waves to bring back a stick, again and again. Two men began to take down their sea-angling rig. Soon, even the greys gave way, and the lights along the coast south began to form a line against the darkness. Kathleen had the light on in the car, and she was listening to the radio. She'd rather not stop off for a drink, thanks. He didn't mind.

Chapter 6

THE FOLLOWING MORNING involved Minogue acquiring a low-grade headache almost right away. It was something he attributed to poring over copies of bank statements and correspondence, part of the State's information being prepared on Banba Garden Supplies. Banba had shipped in vases from Poland, in containers, four of which were found to contain hashish. This was almost exactly what the Garda Liaison officer in the Europol Centre in The Hague had detailed in the series of emails from last month.

The pages were very poor photocopies, with considerable markings on them from several different sources. One of them noted the discrepancy in spelling with the company's name, another the origin of the vases from a plant that had closed the year before.

By midmorning, and a second cup of coffee, Minogue's headache had receded such that he almost forgot about it. He was even able – with Tadhg Sullivan watching and listening, a carefully guarded expression of polite interest on his face – to engage in a reasonably productive conversation with an Interpol officer in Lyon. It turned out that the officer was actually Belgian, and had visited Ireland twice.

"Them French lessons of yours must be good," said Sullivan. "Maybe I should think about trying them. Do you think I'd make a fist of it?"

Sullivan had not surrendered much of his Kerry accent in his two decades' work here in Dublin.

"Tadhg, if they can teach me, they can teach anyone."

The beginnings of a smile played around Sullivan's face, but he said nothing. Minogue saw lunch imminent: things were picking up, then. He was slipping into his jacket when his mobile went off. Kilmartin's name displayed itself, irrevocably. He considered letting it ring, but somehow his thumb found the Receive.

"I happen to be free," said Kilmartin.

"Still too dear. Free for what, exactly?"

"You don't go out for your dinner up there? Lunch, I mean? Come on now."

Minogue hemmed and hawed. He considered lying. Then the door to the hall opened up slowly, and there, looking altogether too pleased with himself was James Kilmartin. He took the mobile from his ear with a flourish, and ended the call.

"A lousy trick," Minogue said, meaning it. Kilmartin smiled.

Kilmartin's idea of an exciting lunch was still a pint and a sandwich. He ordered Minogue a pint without asking him.

"You can't beat a pub lunch," he said. "Put you in a right good humour for the rest of the day."

"It'll put me to sleep you mean."

"Stop whinging, will you? If you don't want it, leave it for me."

Kilmartin had his mind made up on Kelly's, one of the very few pubs in the area that had not been turned into an emporium.

Kilmartin drained almost a half of his beer with his first swallow. He wiped the head off his upper lip and sighed. He looked around with a satisfied air.

"One of Maura's crowd had a do here last year. They wanted somewhere centre city, somewhere old-style. There were highjinks that night, I'm telling you. But God, I suffered for it."

"You weren't alone, I'd say."

"Don't talk to me, sure it was a mob down from Longford, the half of them. My God, man, you think they'd been let out of jail or something. There were people Maura hadn't seen in years, a pal of hers from ages ago, Breda. Tons of people. A lot of scallywags entirely."

Kilmartin took another, more considered, sip from a different side of his glass while he looked up at the screen.

"Look at that," he said then. "There'll be no end to it, I'm telling you."

Minogue had been watching two men at the end of the bar start into their soup.

It was a replay of the same clip from yesterday, the helicopter view and the Garda cars on that road in Malahide.

"The plane from Spain," said Kilmartin. "The planes in Spain fall mainly – I shouldn't say that."

"Right," said Minogue. "You really shouldn't. You Mayo savage, you."

Kathleen had watched the news after Minogue had gone up to the shed for another bash at the design for the rock path. The "alien" was from Chad, she called up, before leaving for Costigans. They had found something about Chad in his pocket, a letter. Where was Chad?

Now it was live from outside the house. There were candles, and people standing about in small groups. The camera light picked up the fluorescent green on two Garda jackets farther down the street. The reporter stood aside and the camera went down to pan across flowers and a crucifix by a gate.

"Oh look," said Kilmartin. "The rosary beads are out."

A face slid into the screen now, a hefty woman of middle years. Minogue caught most of it.

"A clear sign from above," said the woman again.

"A sign," Kilmartin repeated, with a quiet, mordant glee. "A sign? What, are we back to the moving statues all over again?"

Then the camera swivelled to take in a face, a man's blotchy face. McCann again, Minogue saw, but looking very ragged entirely now.

"He's the man of the house, apparently," said Kilmartin. "Where this man just, ah, dropped in."

"Joseph McCann."

"You have a great memory. Well, I don't know any Joseph McCann."

"Maybe he's not a criminal."

The barman, no more than twenty, with a goatee like Wild Bill Hickock and a pearly stud in his nose, was looking up at the screen too.

"How are we doing on the soup and sandwiches there," Kilmartin called out.

A little startled, the barman blinked and moved off. On the screen, McCann began to cry.

"Jesus, look," said Kilmartin. "He's gone to bits. And here's the Mother Superior again."

The woman had that glint of sure knowing, Minogue saw now, the faint smile of the select believer. She said that what had happened was a revelation, a miracle.

"A revelation, now," said Kilmartin. He lost the rest of his words in a shake of his large head that bowed to the glass again.

This was a road leading to Africa, a bridge between peoples, the woman continued, an air bridge that went to heaven.

The interviewer's face took over the screen, and then the camera went back to the flowers and the cross by the gate to the McCann's house.

"I can see it now," Kilmartin said. "Pilgrimages to Malahide. Never much liked that part of the world, I'd have to say."

"You never liked any part of the whole city of Dublin."

"That's County Dublin out there, smart boy. Get your facts right, for once. And I gave that place fair go. Remember the housewarming for Hoey?"

"You trying to fix the lawnmower, after a few jars? Maybe Maura'd be better at recalling that."

Kilmartin gave him a glare.

"Leave that remark in the gutter where you found it."

Minogue watched the barman approach with the soups.

"Plant them here, boss," Kilmartin said to him. "Thanking you."

The napkins were cloth, Minogue saw. Kilmartin pushed his glass aside and leaned in over his bowl. He unrolled the napkin and placed it on his lap, and began pushing his spoon around the soup.

"Did I tell you," he said. "Maura has fellas in the kitchen, gutting the place? I come home of the Tuesday, early, and there's this van. Well, you can imagine."

Minogue held the first spoonful up: way too hot.

"I counted. It's four years and two months since she had it done before. A perfectly fine kitchen. Now do you remember what a normal kitchen was, and us young fellas? Do you?"

"You're making it up, Jim. There were no kitchens in Mayo."

But there was no energy in Kilmartin now, and his spoonful of soup stayed gently swaying over the bowl. He stared down at it for several moments.

"Middle-age crazy," he said. "Isn't that the expression? 'You're cracked, Maura,' says I."

"You might be getting off light enough with a kitchen make-over. I've heard of people buying holiday homes in South Africa."

"Well," said Kilmartin and turned to him again, "do you know, but you might be right. The thing is, everyone else is doing it. And face it, Maura's right. It's a tony area we're in, I don't mind admitting. It is, so face facts, I says to myself later on after I got me brain back, so you have to keep the value of the place up. 'It's an investment,' says she. Maura's very good with the money, always has been. And it hasn't stopped going in that agency of hers this past long while. They can't get people to work in Ireland now – Irish people, I mean. Not the menial jobs. Sure she has to go all over Europe looking for people. Visas, permits, faxes – God, you wouldn't believe it."

"You have to hand it to her," said Minogue. "She's come a long way."

"Ah, you're right. But do you know what she said to me the other day? You know how she's always asking what I'm about, and all the gossip and the backstabbing and that in the job – but she gives me a funny look. Says she: 'You should work for us, Jim. You know everybody.' 'Us' being her outfit."

Kilmartin grimaced before hoisting another spoonful of soup.

"I blew a gasket over the kitchen, I have to tell you. It's on me conscience, Matt."

"Conscience?"

The barman laid down the sandwiches.

"What are those?" Kilmartin asked.

"They're baguettes," said the barman.

The news had something about Gaza. There was a torn and burning car, people flailing and shouting, and then ads.

Minogue concentrated on finishing the soup. It wasn't bad at all. Kilmartin was ahead of him with the baguette, but he detached at least half of the bread before eating it.

"A right halla-balla yesterday," said Kilmartin between mouthfuls. "Don't you think?"

"The thing in the church, with Tommy Malone?"

"Yes. Tell me, did anything else come to you after our little chat?"

Minogue shrugged.

"You mean, do I believe it anymore, or any less?"

"Well, yes."

"Still the same, Jim. Still the same."

"Meaning?"

"Meaning I haven't got a clue."

"Have you been in touch with you-know-who, since?"

"You-know-who, who?"

"Malone."

"I did."

"And?"

"And: none of your business."

"Did I say it was? You're a bit touchy on the subject. Proves my point."

"What point?" Minogue couldn't stop himself from asking.

"What I said to you yesterday. The 'irregularity' involved. Is that a nice way to say that Malone is stepping out too far, way too far?"

When Minogue didn't answer, Kilmartin gave him a side-long look.

"And needs a wake-up call? Well?"

"There's plenty of irregular action in Tommy's line of work. That much I know."

"You didn't answer my question."

"The GNDU is its own world by times, Jim. That's all I'm saying."

"'Irregular,' is right. 'GNDU': God, I wish we could just go back to 'The Drug Squad.' Well, fair enough, you're not codding there. They have their quirks, we all know that. But what the hell exactly is going on in the man's head?"

"Phone him and ask him, why don't you."

"As if I would. Don't get me wrong. Sticking up for Malone – highly commendable and all, thanks very much now. But I know you're not a gobshite behind it all. I did my bit of research this morning, made some calls, about the business yesterday."

The pause was a signal, Minogue knew, and he also knew then that Kilmartin's lunch invitation had not been happenstance. He glanced over and made the required eye contact, the okay for Kilmartin to release the catch.

Kilmartin leaned in again.

"Emmett Condon," he murmured. "I know you said that Lawless didn't say Condon's name. What did he say again, 'the cop who ODed'?"

"That was it, all right."

"Well who else could it be. So I did a little homework."

Minogue stared at the spread napkin splayed on the countertop by Kilmartin's hand.

"Talk about in over his head, in a big way. Well Condon sure was. The whole thing was wild entirely."

Minogue nodded, and went back to the last of his soup.

Kilmartin sat back and folded his arms. He pretended a keen interest in the half-dozen new patrons who had arrived. Then he looked up at the television, while he drained his glass.

"Know what I'm saying?"

Kilmartin's effort was a poor imitation of Malone's Dublin accent.

"The whole business was a guidebook to what *not* to do."

Minogue decided against trying to finish the baguette, but he picked at the last pieces of ham. Kilmartin shifted his weight on the chair, and crossed his other leg.

"Ah," said Kilmartin, and a look of distaste took over his features. "This whole, what would you call it . . . 'Serpico Syndrome'? You know what I'm driving at?"

Minogue nodded.

"Condon got a lot of backs up. He wasn't one bit shy about letting you know that he knew the Real Deal. He put a fair number of noses out of joint."

"Did you hear talk he might have played offside?"

"He was in early on the whole international thing there. The Russian fellas in that hotel, do you remember?"

Minogue remembered something about three men in a hotel in Drogheda with a suitcase of money, some guns, and Ecstasy pills.

"Well, I also found out Condon went after stuff that he'd tell no-one about. They still can't figure the half of what he was doing. Now, that looks bad. And in his own time, even, he'd be cruising around, nosing around. Sure he didn't keep the job at the office at all. His marriage went on the rocks, and everything. Did you know?"

"Not until now."

"Well, what else could be the result of that messing around, I ask you? He showed up in hostels and the like, trying to find background to things he was following up on. But no one really knew his hobbies in that regard, no siree. So, isn't that an eye-opener?"

Minogue nodded. He fixed his friend with a glance.

"Jim, if you can't find out more, well Aughrim is lost."

"And what does that mean?"

"A Guard couldn't pick his nose without you knowing."

Kilmartin was pleased by this. As usual, he tried not to show it.

"But it's sad too," he said then. "Really now. They haven't found anything to really clear Condon. No-one can actually come out and say . . . Well, what could they say anyway? It was an accident?"

Minogue shrugged.

"There's a whole reorganization of that section done, all

because of it. It showed them up something fierce stupid, especially the command there. They let Condon off the leash, and bejases if he didn't go native, or something. You know what that means?"

"Something about west Mayo?"

"If I want clowns, I'll buy a ticket to the circus. Zero oversight, is what I'm saying. The simple fact of the matter is, no-one got to Condon in time to reel him back in and see what the hell he was into. You think they're going to open the vaults to the coppers doing the case, who are they, a few duffers out of Kilmainham Station? Robbed cars and lost dogs is all they have on their caseload there, I'm betting."

"You don't mean that in a bad way though," said Minogue.

"Of course I don't. I'm only saying it. Believe you me I take no pleasure in saying it either. It goes back to this whole decentralization crap that bulldozed the Squad. You see the consequences now, I feel like telling them. Actually, I don't feel like it."

Minogue looked down into his glass again. Kilmartin picked off a piece of crust and looked at it. Then he leaned in toward Minogue.

"They didn't even know where Condon was on any given day," he said. "Kept his cards very close to his chest, did Condon. Now you'd have to ask yourself, why would an undercover officer be doing that?"

He dropped the piece of crust.

"But my point here is this," he said. "What does it say when Malone is so keen to get himself mixed up in that kind of thing? That's what really concerns me. Right?"

Minogue had nothing to offer.

The barman changed the channels with a remote, from snooker to ads, to more ads, and then a picture of a black infant with very loose skin sitting on a dusty patch of ground. The image lingered long enough for Minogue to see that flies wouldn't give up trying to land on the child's face.

"Something else, Matt," said Kilmartin. "You won't like me telling you, I know."

Minogue knew that the odd show of reluctance on Kilmartin's part was part of the performance. He waited him out by eyeing a snooker game the barman had settled on.

"It might be wise to stay away from our friend on this issue. There's talk."

"There's always talk, Jim."

"Okay," he said. "I'm talking to the deaf here. But you know this could be some kind of a stitch being set up on Malone. Obviously, right?"

"Am I supposed to go off and give Tommy Malone some fatherly advice here?"

"Christ, no! Look, I have no axe to grind here. We want to see Malone right. But, let's face it, he has had an awful time of it this past while, with his brother dying on him."

Minogue nodded.

"And don't forget," Kilmartin went on. "Malone himself getting shot in the arse out in Bray last year, that famous visit to Bray. I mean people are finding out there is such a thing as that post-traumatic stress effort. What was the name of that place there in Bray?"

"'Wonderland.' The leg, the upper leg. I was there, remember?"

"The upper leg then. Doesn't that attach to the arse anymore? And then I hear the old love life is a bit rocky with Malone this past while. What more can go wrong?"

"You're like an old woman, Jim."

"You think I don't care about Malone, but I do. Listen, didn't Sonia's old man – Sonia's, I mean, a lovely girl to be sure – didn't he put the kibosh on the engagement? No mixee Irish, or Dublinman, with nice Chinese girl."

"Sonia's family is from Macau. That was a Portugese possession."

"From a cow?"

"Macau."

"How very not interesting," said Kilmartin. "Anyway. My advice to Malone was to go and learn some Chinese, even a few words. That'd get the Chinaman off his back."

"Tommy can barely speak English, Jim. You said so your-self."

"Ha ha ha ha! Good one. That's the style."

Then Kilmartin's face turned serious.

"All I'm saying is, watch where you put your feet. Condon was an eye-opener entirely, but that's the way things are going to go. I mean, the money in crime is gone astronomical. You get the public hearing about coppers on the take – or whatever, I'm not accusing anyone, I'm just saying – and you're in big, big trouble."

The barman asked if they wanted another pint. Certainly not, Kilmartin declared, anymore than they wanted another baguette. He asked the barman if they'd be getting sandwiches back on the menu, proper ones.

Minogue caught a glance from the barman as he picked up the change that Kilmartin was assembling on the counter. He finished the last of his lager, and looked away. For a few moments, his mind turned to a body frozen stiff and falling from a plane that was carrying hungover, sunburned Irish people home from a holiday.

Kilmartin was standing already.

"Baguettes," he muttered. "What's the point of that, I ask you."

Chapter 7

KATHLEEN MINOGUE took the ice cream out of the fridge. She stopped by the sink to get a clean spoon. Then she stood still, listening. Now Minogue too heard the little cry.

"Iseult's awake," she said. "Thank God she had that little nap, I say."

Iseult's footsteps sounded in the room upstairs. Soon they were on the stairs, pausing every few steps.

Iseult stuck her head in the doorway. She looked very pasty-faced.

"I must have nodded off," she said in a husky, sleep-clotted voice.

Minogue briefly eyed his daughter's new hair-do, or rather her hair-crop. To him it was still a stark and even brutal helmet of hair dropped on her by a cruel modernist architect. Her hands ran to her swollen stomach and she arched her back a little.

"Sit down here," he said. "Will you eat a bit?"

"Later," she said. "Thanks."

Minogue returned the look of concern from Kathleen.

"Will you consider taking the night off, love?"

Iseult shook her head and rubbed at her eyes.

"Put the feet up, slap Jude Law or one of them hunks up on the DVD maybe?"

She opened her eyes. The evening light caught the faint lines that ran from her eyes down toward the freckles still plentiful on her cheekbones. Remember not to mention Pat, he told himself yet again.

Pat the Brain had taken a small apartment in Limerick. The official version was that the commute to his lectures there from their flat in Dublin had been too much. A nice lad, always liked him, were the words that kept coming to the surface in Minogue's mind, stupidly, in the early mornings while he lay there waiting for the first light. It wasn't worry that was waking him up, he tried to persuade himself. It was more trying to figure out what he had missed, the signs that surely must have been more obvious that Iseult's marriage was not doing well at all.

"No thanks," said Iseult. "I have to get it finished."

Minogue noticed Kathleen's eye dart to his again.

"Taxi it home here afterwards, will you?"

"Ma, I'll be grand. I get my best work done at this time."

"I'm only saying, love," Kathleen said. "You'll get a better sleep here."

Minogue counted the days backward. Seven months pregnant. Iseult was unyielding about getting the welded bits on her effort before tomorrow. She had sent them some snaps of the installation she was being paid to make for a Dutch merchant bank in the Financial Centre. "HyBrasil" was her title for it. Try as he might, Minogue couldn't divine in that tangle of metal any trace of the mythical island to the west.

"Who's going to be there with you?" he asked.

"Robbie, the Eskimo."

"He's not really an Eskimo, come on."

"Of course he's not. He's from Edmonton. It has something to do with a sports team. He's being ironic."

"Do you have to pay him some of the commission?"

"No, I don't. I offered, but he won't take anything."

Minogue had yet to meet the man. Iseult's version of how he'd gotten involved was that he had seen her messing around with a blowtorch, and offered to help. He'd said it was only so she wouldn't burn the place down."

"And what does he do," Kathleen said. "This man Robbie, what else, like?"

Iseult rolled her eyes.

"He's an artist, Ma," she said. "There is no 'else.'"

Minogue took the ice cream and cut off a piece, and put it on a clean plate in front of her. She gave him a weak smile. He caught himself before the words came out, the worries he and Kathleen had about fumes and so forth, for the baby.

She picked at it, and took bigger spoonfuls. It was soon gone. She turned the spoon over before placing it in the bowl.

"Ready when you are," she said, and made an effort to smile. "I'll just take a walk up the garden to get my head back, okay?"

Gathering the dishes, Minogue caught a glimpse of Iseult before she got beyond the apple trees.

"This is her last night at it, she says," Kathleen said. "God, I hope so."

Kathleen washed, he dried, and like so many times in these past few months since they'd realized that their daughter's marriage was disintegrating, they worried separately and silently.

Soon, Iseult reappeared in the garden. Minogue did not want to be seen staring at her.

"She looks so lonely out there, Matt," said Kathleen. "So preoccupied."

He could think of nothing to say to his wife that might console her. But he, did he want to say outright that he agreed either. He draped the dishtowel over the pots, and gave her a squeeze.

Iseult was packed already. She would not let Minogue lift her carry-all.

"You have your mobile?" Kathleen asked.

"Yes, Ma."

"Be sure and switch it on, or plug it in, you hear me?"

Minogue was sure there was something strident in Kathleen's voice. She stood on the footpath until he had driven out of sight.

He slipped the Citroën easily into the traffic on the Kilmacud Road. The Citroën still floated on its pneumatic suspension as hypnotically as it did when he'd been captivated by it on a test drive all those years ago.

"Ma is such a worrier," Iseult said.

"She's not alone," he said.

"Don't guilt me, Da. I have to get it done. It's very important to me right now."

Minogue found himself whistling low.

"I know what it means," she said. "When you whistle. Bite
your tongue, right?"

"No, I don't know that tune. It's 'The Wind That Shakes the
Barley' actually."

He saw that this got a smile out of her.

She began talking about the material she'd found on the
HyBrasil legend just the other day. Minogue listened, but he imagined Iseult's words being drawn out the little gap in the back
window into the twilight air. The Citroën seemed to tunnel its
way farther through the greying streets, occasionally lightening
with the lemon sky that glowed in the gaps between the buildings.

"Any word from Daithi lately?"

"No," he said. "Divil a bit."

"God," she said. "It's the Y chromosome. All he has to do is
lift the phone."

Minogue felt the urge to defend his son to his daughter. A
very stupid notion.

"I was thinking of getting him to get in touch with Jim
Kilmartin's young lad there. Get him to phone Jim and Maura
Kilmartin. He might get the hint himself, then."

"Is he the same way, can't lift a phone or bang out an
email?"

"Yes," said Minogue. "Liam, the son and heir. And I think
he'll probably stay over there in the States."

"Huh. Not like our one – you're hoping."

He looked over, and he saw immediately she regretted the
remark.

"Hope springs infernal," he said. "But it's harder for Jim. An
only child."

"Huh," she said, not ready to give up entirely. "I got one
email at Easter from Daithi. I'll bet it was Cathy made him send
it."

"Come on now."

"It's Cathy should move here, I'm telling you. The men, sure . . ."

Minogue sped up a little, and whistled louder.

She rummaged in her bag and took out her mobile.

"Use mine," he said, and drew his out. "Do, and save your minutes. The pay-as-you-go is a killer."

"Are you sure?"

"You'd be doing me a favour, so you would."

She took it with some reluctance.

"Why don't you have it on," she said. "It doesn't cost you."

"You've nowhere to hide if it's on."

Minogue got a good run with the traffic lights coming down Georges Street. He tried, unsuccessfully, not to eavesdrop on Iseult's conversation with her friend Orla, about Orla's efforts to get an exhibition going in a new gallery near Mountjoy Square.

Soon Minogue was turning up Dame Street, and taking the turn into the Temple Bar near the quays. Iseult's studio was shared, and it had a strange schedule with a half-dozen other artists. It was in rough shape, with the owner holding out to get the permission he wanted for replacing it with apartments and a restaurant. The entrance was just before the street turned pedestrian only.

Minogue wanted to say something hopeful, to see his daughter restored to her buoyant, haughty self of old.

"Thanks," she said. "You have four messages you have. Did you know that?"

"Ah turn it off, I'll get them later."

"Honestly," she said. "Ma's right. You just refuse to move on here. It's just a *thing*, Da. It saves you time. It's just being in touch."

"I've had enough of work today, let me tell you."

"Here's two text messages from – your pal Malone. Sorry: *Garda* Malone. Will I read them out?"

She heard his intake of breath.

"Are they confidential? I forgot."

"No," he said. "Might as well now."

"First says 'phone me.' That was only a half an hour ago. Got that?"

"I did."

"Phone me – again. Ten minutes ago is the time for that, and . . . oh dear. Guards using bad language?"

"What?"

"Can I say it? It starts with a b and ends in t. There's a male cow in it."

"Go ahead."

"'Condon bullshit,' it says. Did I say it right? And it says urgent. Is it urgent? Bullshit? Urgent bullshit? What's Condon?"

"Enough," he said. "Thanks."

He watched while she undid the locks on the galvanized door.

"It's all right, Da. There's no one here."

"That's what I'm concerned about. I wish there were someone."

"There will be – I'll have my Canadian conceptual artist welder here in a while."

She undid the last lock. He looked up and down the laneway. There was always the reek of urine here from the boozers who came through from the Temple Bar. He looked in the darker shadows by the doorways for a glint from a syringe.

"Are you sure you have enough minutes on your phone?"

"Yes, I do. Really. Now go on, will you?"

"You'll get a few hours of a nap, won't you? That old couch thing . . . ?"

He gave her a hug, and slid the two fifty-euro notes into her cloth shoulder bag from Peru. She had spotted the move.

"No," he said. "Don't be fighting me. Order a pizza or something."

He suspected he heard a sob from her, but he didn't want to find out. She waved, but said nothing, and he saw her hand go to her face afterwards. He wanted to stop then, right in the middle of the street, and rush back and carry her off back to the home she had grown up in. He was angrier than he expected now, and he continued to swear calmly and methodically as he piloted the car over the cobblestones and toward the quays. The sharp trill from his phone stopped him. He picked it up from the seat where she had left it, and saw that it was Malone.

He braked and stopped by the curb. For a moment he considered leaping out of the car and running to the quays, and flinging the phone as far as he could, and watching it splash and sink like a stone into the greasy swell of the River Liffey.

Chapter 8

MALONE HAD A SPOT near the door to the restaurant kitchen. He had a bottle of Chinese beer going. Minogue suspected it wasn't his first. Mr. Chang was working the cash mostly. His spare words and slow way of moving reminded Minogue of a reptile, but of course he could never say it.

Never effusive, seldom with sentences, Chang seemed to have registered Minogue as respectable. Malone was a different matter of course, and Chang managed with nods and quiet, sparing words. No quitter, Malone continued to patronize the restaurant at least once a week. He had told Minogue that he was working on wearing Chang down, just by enjoying the food. Sooner or later, Sonia Chang's old man would see that he should change his mind about Thomas Malone, and give his blessing to Malone's engagement to Sonia. Malone turned up at the restaurant whether Sonia was working there or not, as she still did, fitting in her obligations along with night courses.

"How are you," said Malone. "Want one of these?"

Minogue eyed him.

"No thanks."

"I'm ordering a take-out. Want some of that then?"

Minogue shook his head.

"First thing is this," he said. "Are you going to pass on this tip you told me about on the phone, the way you should?"

"Wait and we'll see. It's not a tip yet. It's only a hunch."

"Tell me what you want to tell me," Minogue said then. "And it better be good."

"Okay," Malone said. "I'm going to start by asking you a question. How many times have you been down the Naas Road? The N7, like? On your way down the country, like."

"Is this a *Gobán Saor* story, Tommy?"

"What's a Gubawn Sare? Is it a curse word?"

Minogue shook his head. He eyed the Chinese beer again, but decided against it. He brooded a few moments on the loss of the stories of Gobán Saor, literally the journeyman mason. Long a relic of primary schoolteachers in the country in a different age, the stories of the Gobán Saor had no chance these years, really. They would never show up in *Riverdance*, and that was a fact. What use could anyone here have for those instructive yarns of wit, wisdom, and correct behaviour from a Gaelic Ireland? That Ireland midwifed by spittle-flecked schoolmasters pressing their frightened students into the service of the Great Ireland Nation had disappeared for decades now.

"How many times?" Malone asked again.

"A million times. I don't count. Why do you want to know?"

"Did you ever stop in one of the places there, you know, the pubs or eating houses? All them new places sprouting up out there . . . ?"

"Never. Wait – one of the kids had a bad stomach years ago and we were stopping every ten miles or so. I forgot. Some pub. The Red Cow maybe."

"Seen the place recently?"

"Well yes. But I don't be stopping in. It's only a few miles out of Dublin."

"So then you don't know the likes of what goes on there, do you?"

"Not much, happily. But I hear the stories."

"The knocking shops, and all that?"

Minogue watched Malone pouring the last of the beer.

"All the truckers and the salesmen . . . ? The chancers and the skangers? The dealers and the fences and the tinkers and the thieves? Have I left out anyone?"

Sonia appeared from the kitchen and laid a tray on a table where two young couples sat. She did not look over toward Malone. Minogue wondered how many hours a week she logged in, between helping here, and her studies, and her bookkeeping work.

"I don't know, Tommy," he said. "That's not my end of the patch, that stuff."

"A lot goes on out there, I can tell you."

Minogue watched the couple launch into a bowl of something, with chopsticks. Then he turned to Malone.

"Do I get to say something now?" he asked him.

Malone took another swallow of beer.

"Only if you like," Malone replied.

"All right so," he said then. "You're going off your patch here with this. Have you noticed?"

Malone's eyelids slid down a little.

"How do you mean?"

"Aren't you coming in sideways on someone else's case, without telling them?"

"The Condon thing? When I have something, I'll put it out for them. I didn't expect this stuff at all, remember I was telling you and Kilmartin the other day? I only went to Lawless on another thing, a heroin ring, the ones getting in stuff off boats down in Waterford and Cork, and that. I wasn't expecting him to spin out any stuff about Condon, or Guards on the take, or that. I go where the information leads."

"The fact is, you should be talking to the ones doing the Condon investigation."

"I will, I will. Just as soon as I check out this tip tonight. Won't take long – but the minute you leave Dublin, well anything's liable to happen."

"What are you on about, 'leave Dublin'?"

"There's someone I want to talk to, and I have to drive a bit out of town to do it."

"Who?"

"Condon's girl," said Malone, in a voice little above a murmur.

"You found her?"

"Not exactly. But maybe someone who'd know where she is."

"What's the name?"

"I don't actually have a name, a proper name. It changes, I think."

"No name? Changing name? Is she visible, or maybe invisible?"

"If I knew I'd tell you, wouldn't I?"

"Tommy, think about this, will you. Think about what I'm thinking about, when I hear you talk like this."

"It's the best I can do," said Malone. "I heard 'Marina' but the illegals here move names around, and go under different names. She's a foreigner though, for sure. Not much English, I was told – and she's from someplace the far side of all them other places. Way over in there, you know what I'm saying?"

Minogue shook his head. But Malone eyes rested on someplace on the wall of the restaurant where a portrait of a dragon hung.

"Moldova," said Malone. "Yeah, that's it. Thank God I didn't mind Geography. Moldova."

"Moldova," said Minogue. He noticed Malone's eyes were not focused at all.

"Yeah," said Malone. "But I'm not actually *going* to Moldova, am I."

"Where are you thinking of going, then?"

"Oh, me and me take-out are going out into the car now in a minute, and we're going off down the Naas Road."

"What's there?"

"The story I got is that she's maybe part of that scene. The after-dark scene or the 'late lunch' crowd. You know?"

Malone's order was ready. Minogue watched Mr. Chang's appraising eye linger on Malone, and then return to taking down an order on the phone. Was it Kilmartin who had told him that more of the hotel rooms along the Naas Road were actually booked during the day than in the evenings?

"So?" Malone asked him.

Minogue couldn't persuade himself that he hadn't seen it coming. It did not stop his irritation turning to anger, however. He glared up at Malone, but he knew immediately that the game had moved on.

♣ ♣ ♣

"Just get me back to me car there in good time so's I can go home at a decent hour," Minogue said.

Malone shrugged, pulled at his nose, and pushed his Fiat into fifth. There was just one more junction before they'd get a clear run at the Naas Road.

Minogue made sure the power was off on the mobile. The smell of the Chinese food had made him hungry now.

The traffic coming into Dublin gathered in slow sullen herds at the traffic lights. Minogue eyed the aluminum plate that Malone had been forking noodles from while they talked. Malone made a face and swallowed slowly.

"Sonia's oul lad must have put frigging rat poison in that noodle thing."

Minogue spotted the building coming at them in the distance.

"Is this where we're meeting this fella," Minogue asked. "Paddy Bang Bang?"

"Not this gaff coming up, no," Malone replied. "We're going to the next one, The Roadhouse."

"Look," he said after a few moments. "Just call him Paddy, or Mr. Finnegan, will you? The Bang Bang's what got him into trouble in the first place. Okay?"

Minogue said nothing, but turned instead to look at the full car park as they passed a place called Highway 66. There was a separate place for the transports and buses the far side of the sign. The sign was enormous, a composite of American highway signs, cowboy hats, and lariats next to some kind of an older-style American car.

"Yeah," Malone went on. "Paddy had a short fuse. This was back in primary school even. He used to get slagged something fierce, I'm telling you. No 'special education' them days. So one day, Paddy had enough. Scrawny fella he was then but wiry, like a monkey. Anyway. Out of nowhere, he came at one of the worst of them, a fella in fifth class, fancied himself I suppose. Up jumps Paddy, gives him one in the snot. Bang, he put him away."

"'Bang?'"

"A puck in the snot. Not a gun. God, what are you thinking there, a gun in primary school, in Crumlin?"

"Maybe I was thinking of secondary."

"Paddy quietened down a good bit when he moved school. They found out he couldn't read. Dy-dy– no, it's not diarrhea. It's where you can't read."

Minogue nodded, but didn't supply the word.

"So someone called him Paddy Bang Bang and that was it?"

"God, no. That was only a while ago that happened. You see, Paddy was never one of the crowd. For one thing he always liked farming and the woods and that. Growing up in Crumlin, yeah, I know what you're thinking. But he had people out in Kildare. That was the saving of him really. Funny thing was, he got into the fishin' and shootin' you know, the rod and gun crowd. Of all things."

"With a temper like that?"

"Ah, now. He did great – compared to what could've happened. He's very handy, great carpenter. Didn't he fall for this girl over visiting from, are you ready for it – Brazil. Where they make the nuts, right?"

"I never knew that."

"It's true. In the heel of the reel she came here to live and they have a place, a few acres not far off here. Still goes out with a gun but only on contract. There's a ton of deer now, I swear to God, and there's farmers are paying him to take a few. Paddy goes out lamping. It's a bit pathetic, he says. The deer, they just look into the torch and he shoots them. Then he eats them. Honest to God. He even uses the fur."

"The hide."

"That's right. He waits in a place he knows they're likely to be. All night sometimes. He's happy enough, he says, sitting in a ditch, in the rain. Snow, even. Does a lot of thinking on the job, he says."

"Then shooting."

"Not so much. 'It might sound cruel,' says he, 'the lamping. But it's not. They just freeze, so you get to shoot right.'"

"Hence the bang bang."

"No. And will you stop interrupting me? That was remarks passed about his missus. You know the kind of music they do like over in them places, Brazil and that? It's very, you know, cha-cha and all that. Dance stuff, right? So there were jokes going around, you know, the hot-blooded people and the topless beach thing in Rio. The 'bang bang' thing. So of course that sort of attaches itself to his missus. Slagging, like? They were jealous of him, the locals. I mean, I hear she's gorgeous. So Paddy hears about it, one particular fella, and he, well, he . . ."

"Shoots him?"

"Christ, no. He loosened his joints for him one night. I think there was some dentistry involved, orthodontic things. Is that the right word? Teeth. Whatever. So that's how I got back in touch with him. It was his ma actually, she phoned my ma. Could I help out, etc.? So I did – only after I found out if he was on the level. He was. The other fella was a go-boy. He had paper on him, in actual fact. So I had a word with this fella's ma, who had a word with him. And so forth. You know what I'm saying."

"Dropped the charges?"

"Yep. I told Paddy it was only right he footed the bill for your man's orthodintec– dentistry, whatever. So, it's a favour back. I know it's a long shot, but I was thinking, where would this girl of Condon't be likely to be, if she, well, you know. If she hadn't been . . . You know?"

Two cars came up quickly behind and flew by. The second, a black Porsche, Minogue registered, was chasing a silvery Lexus.

Minogue turned to watch the lights appear through the hedges and the trees only to be swallowed up again. Small farms here in this horsey part of Kildare had suddenly been selling for a few million euros. There were sheiks with helicopters, film stars, talk of the Rolling Stones.

"Here we are," said Malone.

He took the Fiat too fast into the bend as they left the motorway.

Minogue hadn't really seen this place at night for a long time. Even a few years ago, when it was still Shannon's, The Roadhouse had been a big barn of a place, complete with flood-lights and flags and planters and metal lawn furniture of the friendly Ireland. But now there was a big restaurant out the front, with tons of plate glass and an outdoor sheltered trattoria. He spotted several of those propane heaters that were capped with shiny saucers glowing amidst the candlelit tables and Singapore-style umbrellas. Ireland, *al fresco*.

"Was that always there?" he asked Malone, craning his neck to see how high the beam of light went.

"The *Star Trek* thing, that searchlight? This year. But Dublin Airport is getting them to shut it down, I hear. Plus, it's attracting too many aliens."

"How would anyone know that, in Kildare?"

Malone began trolling the car park for a spot.

"Tommy."

"Go ahead."

"Say you do find this woman, this ex of Emmett Condon's."

"Yeah."

"That'd be something the team working on Condon could-n't do in all this time."

"I know, I know. Didn't I just tell you it was a long shot?"

"Okay, but what would you do with that information?"

"Listen," said Malone, "before I even think of giving you an answer to that. Do you think they wanted to find her? Do you think they even believe, or they even care, whether she exists or not?"

"You're dodging it."

"Am I? Aren't they, you mean? They don't even call it murder, did you know that? There's wraps all over the case, you know that. Blake and them want it that way."

"How do you know?"

"You're asking me? You should know what a murder investigation looks like. Have you seen one, heard of one, a murder investigation on Emmett Condon?"

Minogue said nothing. Malone coasted down the next row of cars. There were enough Range Rovers and BMWs here to make an ad, Minogue thought.

"Look, I'm just curious, okay? There's lots of action out here. Condon seems to have been out here a fair bit – yeah, I found that out. There's people out here with foreign accents, girls. That's why I phoned Paddy. It was him that told me that before. He says he thinks there's people here, a barman he knows remarked about some geezer with an accent and a girl on his arm, looked like, well – fella said he thought the guy was trying to pimp the girl. They move around, those people. Yes, prostitutes. You know what I'm saying?"

"Blake's crowd should be in the picture, Tommy. Especially now."

Malone gave him a quizzical, sidelong look.

"Can you imagine Blake's gobshites barging in here?" Malone asked quietly. "With their big feet and their tough-guy talk? I know this much: the likes of Paddy Bang Bang wouldn't talk to them. And it's like Paddy says. People in this game move around. They fade. This is the place they're working here this past while. They'll move on."

Malone found a spot directly under a light. He turned off the ignition.

"So no guarantees," he said. "Okay?"

Chapter 9

HOW COULD THERE BE so many people in one pub – not a pub, a complex, a shopping centre, no, a theme park . . . ? It was the second time that Minogue had been thinking out loud.

Malone kept eyeing the tables, but stayed standing by the bar. Minogue half-sat on a stool next to him.

"Well, it gets hairy on the weekends," Malone said. "This is nothing."

The barwoman looked like a rock star too but Minogue hadn't a clue who or even why he thought that. The T-shirt she wore was one of those ones for sale by the entrance.

"Seafood," said Minogue. "Look."

"Well, yeah. Like, what about it? We're on an island. Right?"

Minogue already felt light-headed, overloaded with the light and the smells and the music.

The barwoman was very friendly. Minogue tried not to watch her balletic motion too closely, the fluid transits she made with bottles, ice, and glass, the sweep of her arm and the bright look she could throw at each customer. She had a flourish to spare for the cash register and even for when she slid the dishwasher thing home.

"There's Paddy," said Malone, and half raised his arm.

He needn't have, Minogue sensed right away. He watched

Paddy Bang Bang in the mirror – watching Inspector Minogue in return – as he sidled up to the bar. The jean jacket and the 1970s moustache put Minogue in mind of a cowboy. He had the look of a man who worked outside, a wind-buffed face, and eyes that seemed ill at ease indoors.

"Is there any more of yous?" Finnegan asked.

"Only the SWAT team, Paddy," said Malone.

Minogue looked for signs of temper on Finnegan's face, but found only the mask of insouciant indifference that Malone shared, along with other Dubliners of a certain disposition. His hands still stayed in his pockets.

"I had a gander on me way in," said Finnegan. "No sign of them."

"Do they be here every day?"

Finnegan hesitated before answering Minogue.

"I don't know. But I know that I don't be here every day. So maybe they are. But I don't know. You know?"

Finnegan was drinking Coke. Malone ordered a round. He got Finnegan started on talking about deer.

"I don't like doing it," Finnegan said. "Pulling the trigger, I mean."

"Bambi," said Malone. "I was always fond of Bambi."

Finnegan wasn't going to relax. He looked around the pub, even standing for a moment on one foot to see around a partition.

"Bambi can eat your dinner," said Finnegan. "If you're a farmer. And then the same Bambi can walk out in front of a car and kill you, too."

"They come out on the roads?"

"They certainly do. I mean everyone has issues, the wildlife, the environment, all that. I'm all for that. But there's an explosion of deer going on. Foxes too."

"Hard to believe," said Minogue, thinking of deer flying up into the sky.

"Only if you never stray out of Dublin," said Finnegan. "Tell you what. I'm going to look around the place again. I'll be back."

Minogue followed him in the mirror until he was lost in the

thick of foliage and raised seating.

"Touchy," said Malone.

Minogue thought of Finnegan sitting in a ditch at night, waiting for a deer to pass.

"How do you want to go at it, if this woman really turns up here?"

Malone scratched his head.

"Well, we have cause on her," he said. "We could pull an Immigration, and bring her in on that. If I had to, I suppose."

"You're not going to pass it on to . . .?"

"Like who? The ones working on Condon? Blake and his mob?"

"You plan to just sit on this, then?"

"Well, I'm not doing Blake's dirty work for him," said Malone. "Right now, anyway. Look, aren't we getting ahead of ourselves here? Let's just see what comes up here now."

We, Minogue repeated in his mind, and his misgivings returned stronger.

He sipped at his pint when it came, and he tried to ignore the music. Willie Nelson, for the love of God. He also tried to read the frothing head remaining on the Guinness for a face, for words. Was that a map of Africa on it? He closed his eyes, and rubbed them. When he looked again, there was no sign of it. Malone looked at his wristwatch and scowled. Finnegan was gone five minutes now.

A loose and medium raucous group of three couples came in and stood near them. One of the men, a rugger-bugger, eyed Minogue over the bare shoulder of his companion, a very animated woman with a fairly daring halter-top. Minogue listened to the talk about what had happened on someone's holiday in Corfu, and then somebody else called Dermot who had written off a new Infiniti, but had walked away from it.

Ten minutes. He caught Malone's eye, but Malone merely rolled his eyes and let his gaze return to its drift around the pub again. They couldn't be more than twenty miles from the middle of Dublin here, Minogue began to reflect, here in the well-tended monotony of the rich lands of Kildare and the midlands beyond.

For a while he imagined walking out to the car, Malone's lousy and much-abused Fiat, and driving it himself out onto the Naas Road again. He would not point it back toward the city, however, but toward the southwest instead, to the farthest tip of Kerry, where the hills ended in cliffs over the Atlantic.

The Guinness had a predictable effect, and it was one he didn't much like, but was used to. While his waking brain continued to eye the patrons and look for Paddy Bang Bang, and half-listen to these new Irelanders and even make guesses at their jobs and their homes and their habits, Minogue was inexplicably back in that dusty afternoon schoolroom with the Christian Brothers, and their *Gobán Saor*, and their poems that no-one cared about anymore.

> *Tháinig long ó Valparaiso*
> *Scaoileach téad a seol sa chuan*
> *Chuir a hainm dom i gcuimhne*
> *Ríocht na greine, tír na mbua*[2]

"Jesus," he heard Malone say. "It's going to take over the whole street."

The couples had stopped yammering. They too stared at the television. Minogue turned toward the television. The footpath by the McCann house in Malahide was completely full. A Guard was directing traffic. Some woman was lighting a candle, another rearranging wreaths. There were rosary beads, cards, even a doll.

"The place is gone mad," said Malone.

Minogue looked at the couples who were still entranced by what they were watching. He wondered if the glow on their upturned faces and the little splinters of light on their eyes from the television did not, for a few moments at most, remind him of an adoration scene in a holy picture.

The barwoman broke the trance when she turned on an

---

2 A ship arrived from Valparaiso,
   Dropped its anchor in the bay,
   Her name reminded me of kingdoms,
   Sunlit countries far away.

electric mixer. Cocktails, Minogue thought: cocktails on the Naas Road? But why not?

"Malahide," said Malone. "Hoey's out there. With his lawn and his garden shed and all that. No way I'd go out there. No way."

"It's another continent for you, is it."

"Hoey told me all the kids are called Chloe out there," Malone said.

Then Minogue caught sight of Finnegan coming around a fake tree. Finnegan didn't look at them when he spoke.

"There's a fella over there, in the Paddock. I think it's him."

"You *think*?" said Malone. "We need better than think here, Paddy."

"It's the best I can do, man. What do you want me to do, lie?"

"What's the Paddock?" Minogue asked.

"It's one of the rooms here," said Finnegan. "Just look for horsey shite up the walls."

"Okay," said Malone. "Who is this fella?"

Finnegan gave Malone a hard look.

"I don't know, do I?" he retorted. "Look, didn't I tell you I only heard stuff, from other lads? I don't do this type of stuff. I'm a married man, you know that. Okay?"

"Is there a woman with him?" Minogue asked.

Finnegan shook his head.

"But the way this caper works – if we're on the right track, *if* – is that she could be in the vicinity. At her work, if you get my drift."

"What's he look like?"

"He's like what a mate described, in actual fact. The dark hair, white shirt, open-necked. Big lad. He has a bit of flash metal, the rings and that. Tom Jones, you'd think maybe."

"Tom Jones the singer? Jesus, sure he's ninety if he's a day."

There was no budging Finnegan from his solemnity, but now Minogue began to see it as worry.

"Well, what's his name?"

"Are you deaf? No offence. I don't know his name. I don't know the guy at all."

"Ah Jaysus Paddy, come on. I mean, give-and-take here now. Didn't your mate have a name for him? Let me talk to your mate then, what's his number?"

Finnegan gave him a glare.

"Look, he's not one of us. I mean he has an accent. That'll have to do. Okay? So this is where I get off. That was the deal. You experts take over from now."

"If I have more questions, I'll drop by the house then, will I?" Malone asked.

"Don't bother," said Finnegan, and his gaze bored back into Malone's. "I'll be out, working. Putting down vermin, yeah? That's what the farmers consider foxes you know, still. Maybe some of your crowd would like to try that job for a while."

Minogue watched Finnegan leave.

"Thanks," said Malone.

♣ ♣ ♣

Minogue let his eyelids slide down, almost closed, and gave the man a leering smile. The man smiled back briefly, and then he looked to Malone.

"Well, I think your friend has played a trick on you," he said.

Malone leaned in over the table between them and winked.

"Ah come on now, George, is it . . . ?"

"Yes, George is okay."

Minogue was well into his role now. He pivoted toward the bar, and tottered a little before steadying himself against the counter.

"What does a man have to do to get any drink in this place," he called out.

"People, they like to joke," said George. "How you say, take the piss?"

"Ah no," said Malone. "He's well able to pay, now. My friend here, he just got a bit of good news, businesswise, you know? He's in the humour of celebrating, oh yes."

George's smile stayed fixed.

"It must be someone else," he said. "A trick. Who is this, your friend who tells you this thing?"

"Ah go on," said Malone. "We only want a bit of fun."

Minogue put more effort into his wavering and he called out to the barwoman again.

"Your friend, he's drinking a lot," George said. "He should maybe go home?"

"Oh he's the happy man," said Malone, and leaned in toward George, his hand cupped to his mouth. Minogue watched the hands go to his chain again.

Whatever Malone said seemed to work. George's smile faded a little, and a look of baffled amusement took its place. He eyed Minogue again and muttered something to Malone. Malone took out his wallet. George finished his drink.

Malone counted out three twenties, four. George frowned and flicked his head toward the door when Malone offered the notes. Then he held up his hand, open, toward Minogue.

"Your friend, he waits here."

Malone stood slowly.

"Well, where's he going to, you know?"

"It'll be okay. Don't worry."

"I'll go with you."

"Is not necessary. No."

"Ah, now. Maybe it'll be the both of us, know what I'm saying? I'll pay, oh yes, God, yes."

Minogue didn't know what to make of the hesitation and the look from George.

"Ah, Jesus George," Malone said, and put his arm around George's shoulders. "We're pals now, aren't we? Come on, now. I'm getting fierce interested now myself. I'll go out with you."

He turned to Minogue.

"Wait there Pat, wait. We'll be back in no time now. I'll make sure you don't get a wagon. All right?"

"Swedish," Minogue said. "I want Swedish."

"No bother," said Malone and winked at George.

"What is your friend saying?"

"Swedish," said Malone, with an added *sh*. "What he means is blonde."

"Swedish, you hear," Minogue said, louder.

"Calm down a minute," Malone said. "Will you? Me and me George can organize that, can't we George?"

"And what is 'wagon'?"

"Wagon," asked Malone, and laughed. "You must know a wagon. How long are you with us, George? From Turkey is it, am I guessing right, am I? Am I, George?"

There was a change in the man now, Minogue saw.

"A wagon? Is it a car you drive?"

"Ha ha ha. No, no – a wagon is an ugly one. One ugly woman. You get it?"

George looked toward the bar.

"I get it," he said. "I get for you. No problem."

He mimicked a phone to his ear.

"Grand," said Malone. "Phone away."

George slipped out a mobile and flicked it open, and he began to walk away.

"Ah now, don't be standing us up, George. Here, is it the money? Go on, here's half of it. Go on."

George looked down at the bills.

"No," he said.

But Malone had chosen a spot between George and the entrance. He put on his sleepy-eyed leer again.

"Ah George, come on. We're burning up here, man."

George smiled briefly then and let his head go slowly from one side to the other. Was he Italian, Minogue wondered. Greek? George used the mobile to point to the toilets and wrinkled his nose. Malone turned with George to head for the toilets.

"Swedish," Minogue said. "You hear?"

A server he hadn't seen before, a youth with some powdery stuff over his acne, came over with his tray held over his chest.

"About time," said Minogue.

"I'm sorry, sir," he said and swallowed, his Adam's apple flying up and down. "But the management . . ."

"Arra go on now. Don't mind the management."

"The management says I'm not to serve you, sir, I'm sorry."

Minogue looked around the table. George's pint was nearly gone, Malone's too.

"You are out of your mind there."

The lounge boy picked at the back of his neck and looked back to the bar.

"I'll be back from the jacks in a minute," said Minogue. "There better be a change of heart here, young fella."

The lounge boy took a step back.

"I'm sorry sir, it's the management."

Something in the kid's face, the line of worry between the eyebrows maybe, awakened something in Minogue.

"Is this the only toilet for the whole pub here?"

"Yes," said the lounge boy, clearing his throat. "But it's big. There's different doors."

Minogue brushed by him; smelled the overdone cologne; felt sorry for the poor repairs the boy had tried on the raw acne he couldn't help picking; cursed himself for not acting on what his gut had been telling him.

He hammered open the door, barely breaking his stride, and made a run at the man who was standing over Malone. The man yelled something and jumped back. It wasn't George. Malone's legs were drawn up and moving slowly, and he was clutching his head. There were lines of blood coming through the fingers of both hands.

"I just got here," he heard the man say, "I didn't do anything, I swear to God!"

Minogue's kneecap ground into the grouting as he knelt. Through his fingers he saw Malone's eyes and the lines cut into his forehead from pain.

"He had something in his hand," Malone wheezed. "I didn't see it coming."

"Is it just your head?"

"He gave me a dig in the ribs too, a kick."

He took down one hand.

"Don't call an ambulance," he said. "Don't, it's okay."

Minogue stared at the raw, torn flesh on Malone's cheekbone.

"You're hurt," was all he could say.

"No. I'm okay, I mean I'm going to be okay. There's nothing broke, I'd know. Really. Believe me."

Minogue looked up at the man who was now by the door.

"Who was here when you came in?"

"Just this man here, on the floor. Your friend? I swear? A fella left as I was almost coming in – in a bit of a hurry."

"What about him? A big fella, was it?"

The man hesitated.

"I'm a Guard," said Minogue. "Tell me about this fella. Was he big, black hair?"

The man nodded.

"Chain around his neck, rings . . . ?"

He began to shake his head. Minogue got up.

"Go get some clean paper towels for this man. Don't be gawking – get going."

"Don't budge, Tommy. I'll be back in a minute."

Behind him he heard the sharp crack of the door hitting the wall, and the night air flowed around his chest. There were couples coming in from the car park, sounds of idling transports in the distance. He ran to a man closing a car door.

"A big fella, chain around his neck, black hair, did you see him?"

He stood amidst the cars, listened for running footsteps, a car starting up. To his dismay, he caught sight of more cars parked beyond a corner of the Roadhouse. He slowed and tried to see through the gauzy beam of light flung down by the quartz lamps clustered overhead.

A glint from a car door closing caught his eye and he began to run toward it. There was more noise around here, a rumbling hiss from the traffic out on the main road. He kept his eye on the car but it reversed out, rocking as the brakes were applied at the end of a short arc.

The car's lights stayed off. He heard a wirp from the tires as the car shot forward and the lights ran along the side panels. He listened for clues, the burr of a six-cylinder engine, a diesel clanking maybe, an exhaust note. A Passat he thought, dark, or maybe a Primera – no, the new Mondeo. He gave up on names: he hadn't a hope in hell of seeing this.

He slowed, stared at the roof of the car, itself almost floating over the roofs of the parked cars before it hit an open spot. A manual gearbox anyway, he heard, and he watched the brake light glow and the bonnet drip when the driver pulled it through the curve that led out onto the N7.

"You're a bastard," he said, panting, as the worry of his thumping you're-too-old-for-this-caper heart took over.

"But I'll have you for this, George, or whoever the hell you are. I'll have you."

Chapter 10

SLEEP, EVEN WHEN it finally arrived last night, long after the one o'clock when Minogue had sneaked into bed, had been a wild caravanserai – a marathon entirely. He saw their neighbour, the Costigans' eldest, a harmless lad really, who never got a niche in adult life, hanging himself in the garage two years ago. There was that day in Virginia with Daithi and Cathy, a day as hot as the hob of hell, staggering through that Jamestown Settlement place, at once interested and vaguely repelled too. Several times his dreams took him to the sea, by Killiney he thought, but then suddenly right across the country to Lahinch with huge rollers almost sweeping away an adult Iseult, who then became a baby somehow, and later a seal too.

Then it was Kathleen, and mad sex, until he was suddenly abandoned, and he was alone somewhere in an empty spot full of roaring wind and frightening clouds. There were narrow empty laneways in Paris somewhere, and a body shifting with feasting maggots and Malone cursing somewhere nearby, but he couldn't see him.

It was barely light when Minogue willed himself awake, or so he thought. He lay there as unmoving as he could, staring at the glowing imminence on the curtains. It felt like he had barely slept. The whiskey he had drunk later on, as he pressed one on Malone too, hadn't helped.

He thought back again to the end of their adventure last

night. He had interviewed, or tried to interview, some staff, but beyond a weak acknowledgment from one barman who thought he might have seen this George a few days back. He remembered Malone slowly sipping whiskey, and glowering around the pub and returning the uneasy looks from anyone who dared to meet his eyes or even look at the stains on his shirt and jacket, for even a moment.

It had been half past eleven or so when they had finally left the Roadhouse place. As Malone had dropped him off by his car, Minogue had tried one more time to persuade him to go for an X-ray. No go: it was nothing more than a scrappy fight, Malone assured him, where a boxing opponent had landed a few good ones.

A flood of morning light hit him from the open door of Iseult's room. The garden had been rinsed by the light, and there was a soft glow over the grass. He plugged in the kettle, and took down the filters. It would be a long day.

Malone phoned him at half nine.

"So there," said Malone. "Just to keep you in the picture. I'm going to look through the database at Joe Sinnott's, an aliens list they keep there. It's something, anyway. Joe'll do it handy enough."

"Any more give out of your man, Paddy Bang Bang?" Minogue asked.

"You mean Paddy 'I-never-met-the-man,' Paddy 'I-don't-know-nuttin'?"

"You have no way to improve his memory?"

"Don't talk to me about that iijit," said Malone. "Yeah, I phoned him first thing. I put the heavy word on him too. But in the end, you know, I have to believe him."

Minogue waited.

"It was a tip from a mate of his, that's all," Malone went on. "I got the mate's name out of him finally, and I even got a hold of the mate late last night. Nothing. He heard it 'from another fella.' The usual. Everyone has Alzheimers, apparently. They want to stay well clear of anything."

"Did you try the local Guards yet?"

"Not yet," said Malone. "No hurry. But it's a weird place out there, I'm telling you, isn't it? Tons of money sloshing around, you know, farms going for millions, all that. The horsey set are all over the place too, and a lot of passing trade. Strange."

"I suppose," said Minogue and yawned. "But if you're asking me, my advice is still the same: hand on what you have now. Now more than ever."

"Listen, I'm not hiding under the bed after this. No way. I'm going to find that girl, you know. I am. And I don't care who likes it or . . . Wait a minute, there's somebody wants to talk to me here."

Minogue didn't want to think of the girl, or what could've have happened to her. He heard Malone's fingers move over the speaker, and voices behind.

Tadhg Sullivan was on his way over. He stopped at the entrance to Minogue's cubicle. His eyes bulged, and he flicked his head in the direction of the passageway. Minogue showed him the phone. Sullivan nodded, but pointed his finger at Minogue, and then back toward the passageway, and he nodded portentously.

"I have to go myself," Minogue said into the phone, not sure that Malone was yet listening. He hung up.

"You have someone waiting on you outside by the front desk," said Sullivan.

Minogue studied Sullivan's expression for several moments. Then Sullivan looked to the ceiling, and jabbed his finger skywards.

"Who?"

"I'm not certain," Sullivan whispered. "But I think it's one of Blake's crowd."

Blake, Minogue thought: Blake?

"Internal Affairs," said Sullivan, and his eyes grew big again. "I think."

♣ ♣ ♣

Minogue was ushered out of the lift by the detective who had called to the section.

"Straight down here."

They filed down a hallway and came to a small, open area. A woman sitting in front of a monitor there glanced at Minogue, and called out "Paul?" and went back to something on the screen.

A fortyish detective with a moustache and a phone to his ear looked around the corner and met Minogue's eye. He held up his first finger, and nodded, and disappeared again. There were no glass panels in the doors here, Minogue noticed. From down a short hallway came the muffled sound of a phone ringing. Someone had made tea nearby.

The detective reappeared and made his way over.

"Inspector Minogue?"

Minogue nodded. There was no offering of a name in return.

"Come on down here with me."

Minogue eyed the smattering of dandruff on the collar of Moustache Guard Paul ahead, and thinning hair atop.

Garda Moustache tapped at a door, and opened it.

The man inside was Superintendent Eamonn Blake, the head of section for Internal Affairs. He was on his mobile.

Minogue scrambled to try to recall how or why Blake had gotten his nickname of Earthquake Blake. He vaguely remembered that it had something to do with an article in the *Irish Times*, just after Blake had been given the job. It was when there had been a big fuss for years about the backlog of complaints against the Guards. Yes – he had it now: it was the phrase from the newspaper, something about a seismic shift in Garda accountability.

Blake waved Minogue in. Moustache Guard pointed to a cloth-covered seat at the table, and closed the door again. He sat at a separate chair close to the door.

Blake said "fine" and put down the phone, and scribbled something.

Minogue refused to look over, but instead kept his eyes on the noticeboard where someone had pinned printouts of Web pages he couldn't read from here.

"How're you, Matt?"

"So-so," he said. "But I have questions."

"I see," Blake said. "Always a good sign. Give me your first one."

Minogue looked at the veneer on the table for a moment and then turned to Blake. He hoped Blake couldn't hear his heart hammering away, like he could.

"I went to bed last night an Inspector. Did I wake up a suspect in something?"

"A suspect in what, now?"

"I think that's my line."

"I see," said Blake again. "But you're nervous, are you? Why is that, now?"

"Well, why am I here?"

"You're here because of your involvement in something recently."

Blake began tugging at his watchstrap.

"Recently? What happened?"

"Well, that's what we're trying to find out."

"Tell me," Minogue said. "Am I the only one you're talking to about this?"

"Well, who should I be talking to then, Matt?"

"Maybe you're making this up as you go along. Are you?"

"Ah, I see. A bit contrary, are we?"

"Me? We could play the man from UNCLE some other time, I'm thinking."

Blake seemed almost indifferent to the remark. Minogue imagined a tape turning on a spool somewhere. But no, he thought, it'd be all digital now. He glared at the one-way glass covering the camera slot in the ceiling tile. Blake shifted in his seat.

"I was down in New Quay over the summer," Blake said, as though it were a question. "New Quay, County Clare. And I spent a fair bit of time in the hinterland."

Minogue studied how Blake was now turning his watch around and around on his wrist.

"There's a ton of McNamaras there," added Blake. "Am I right?"

"There'd be plenty, probably. Too many, maybe."

"Great Clare name, McNamara. My wife's a McNamara.

She tells me McMahon would be top of the list for names in Clare though."

"We disagree. But McNamara says it all. How you roll the R, is what counts"

"I see. Kings of the Burren, they say. Or was it the Davorens?"

"Neither. Look, why are we talking about this?"

Blake paused in his detailed calibration of where his watchstrap might settle. Then he went back to turning it again, with minute tugs.

"Just waiting for someone," he said. "A person wants to join us."

"Someone," said Minogue. "Now who would that someone be?"

Blake looked up.

"The Commissioner," he said, brightly. "He's running a bit late."

The door opened. The woman Minogue had seen earlier had a manila envelope, and a lidded, but steaming, Styrofoam cup.

"Thanks," said Blake and read something on the back of the envelope. He pushed back his chair and got up.

"Have a look at these while you're waiting, why don't you," he said.

He tilted the envelope and spilled out the 8 by 10s. Their fresh emulsion scent came to Minogue almost immediately.

The red was almost ruby, and it led in jagged streaks up to the body. There was a moist glistening from the flash in the dark blood matted on the hair.

"What's this," Minogue said. "Give these to one of those new Site manager fellas, over at the Technical Bureau. I'm a suit now, remember?"

"There's a French expression for this, I think," Blake said. "What was done to him, I mean. *Coup de grâce*, is it?"

Minogue stared at him.

"But poor Lawless didn't speak much French, I'll wager," Blake said.

Minogue looked back down at the photos. They had none front-on.

Minogue's mouth was dry when he went to speak now.

"Prove what you just said."

Blake began to uncap the coffee, and he blew into the cup.

"You mean you don't remember what Lawless looked like the other day, when you saw him?"

Minogue looked at the photos again. There was no way to be sure.

"No trick-acting now, if you please," said Blake. "Yes or no?"

Minogue was aware of the detective with the moustache staring at him. Still he studied what he could, trying to ignore the lines of blood that had come down over the face.

"I don't know," he said to Blake. "It could be. Is it?"

There was a knock at the door. Blake nodded at the detective, and he stood slowly and opened the door. Minogue tried not to look surprised to spot Brendan O'Leary, sergeant and also the Garda Commisioner's Sancho Panza, perched on the desk glancing in.

O'Leary's perpetually wary look did not change, nor did he so much as nod.

Blake slid the photos into the envelope, and pushed back his chair.

"Okay," said Blake. "We can start."

Minogue kept his eyes on the bin by the wall. The tension he'd been holding in his shoulders had turned to an ache. He looked back when he heard the footsteps enter.

Commissioner Tynan's eyes were baggy. Minogue couldn't decide if his hair had gone greyer or a haircut had made it look that way. Ruth, his wife, had been wearing a wig when Minogue and Kathleen had bumped into them on Dun Laoghaire Pier in June.

"So you've seen the photos," Tynan said.

"I have," said Minogue.

"You had a chance to pass on proper advice to Malone, then."

Minogue hesitated. He wondered if Malone was here in a room on the same floor even now – or even Kilmartin.

"Right," said Minogue.

"And you did, it's fair to say?"

Minogue looked at Blake for any clues, but saw none.

"That doesn't change what happened," said Tynan. "Does it?"

"If I had even a tiny suspicion," Minogue started to say. Something in Tynan's gaze made him stop. Blake made some hurried note.

Though he couldn't be sure, Minogue thought he heard a faint snort from Tynan.

"No," said Blake, with enough irony for Minogue to look over. "You're taken care of only well in that department."

"So . . . ?" was as far as Minogue got.

"Your session last night down on the Naas Road was verified already," said Tynan. "There are two staff there who remember you and Malone a bit too well, it seems."

"But why all the secretiveness?" Blake asked.

"It wasn't meant to be," said Minogue.

"Well, maybe," said Blake. "Malone backs you up on that aspect, you telling him he should be passing on his leads and his information. Fair enough. But at what point would you have stopped advising him, and actually made him contact us, or done so yourself?"

"I'm at a bit of a loss to explain that one," said Minogue quietly.

"Leave that for a minute," said Tynan. "And tell us what exactly the pair of you were up to in that place last night. Apparently there was a bit of a row."

"We were looking for someone. Tommy thought he might have a lead on a woman, one that supposedly was with Emmett Condon."

"'With,'" said Tynan. "The late Garda Condon's girlfriend, I believe you're saying?"

"That was what was described to me, yes."

"You know Garda Condon was married," said Tynan. "Don't you?"

"I do," Minogue replied. "I'd heard that, I mean. But if she could be found, well, we'd all be back in the game then."

"Were she to be found alive," Blake said.

"There's been no trace of her since it happened," Tynan said. "Right, Eamonn?" Blake nodded. The word "alive" kept circling in Minogue's mind.

"Remember now," Tynan said, "this young woman has been sought for, what, six months now? There are several possibilities, as I understand them. She's left the country. Or she's hiding out here somewhere, under one of several identities, or being sheltered by persons as yet unknown. The other possibility is that she may be dead."

Minogue watched Blake turn his pencil over and over again, tapping its ends slowly and gently on his notepad.

"But evidently Garda Malone has such contacts that he can turn his head and instantly, he has a tip to this Roadhouse place out on the Naas Road. Does your visit there last night throw any light on this?"

"Well the lug who walloped Tommy and ran . . . ," said Minogue, "he goes by 'George.' He had an accent."

Tynan looked over at Blake.

"That name hasn't come up," Blake said.

"He might have nothing to do with this at all," said Minogue. "It's a bit out there, the tip that Tommy was working on."

"Really," said Blake. "How far out?"

"Apparently there's prostitution and the like out there, and he thought maybe the girl was mixed up in it. Being an illegal, I think, that was the logic."

Tynan seemed to consider this for a while.

"Okay," Tynan said then. "But let's go back to Lawless for a minute here. Father Coughlin tells me he finished the session abruptly."

Minogue nodded.

"Father Coughlin and I, we know one another," said Tynan. "He says that Lawless was very shaky that day. Nervous, agitated. What was your take on him?"

"Maybe both. I couldn't tell the difference. He might have been climbing the walls. Maybe he wanted a fix. I don't know."

"You think he had more to tell than he did?"

"I got the impression pretty quickly that he wanted money before he'd come up with anything more specific. But as to whether he was spinning us one . . ."

Blake paused in his notes.

"Yes," he said. "But you're in no doubt he referred to 'Garda higher-ups'?"

"That's right," Minogue replied. "What I heard was, on one of his visits to his brother in jail, Lawless's brother told him that he'd heard about criminals being so well set up now that they had Guards in their pocket. 'Even higher-ups' he'd heard, and it had gone on a while. For years, he said."

"Did nobody push him for details on that?" Blake asked.

"Of course we did. Tommy asked a few times. But he wasn't forthcoming. He'd always go back saying there'd have to be arrangements made if we wanted to go ahead."

"'Arrangements,'" said Tynan. "Was he specific on what he wanted?"

"No."

"And when exactly did he bring the name Emmett Condon, up?"

Minogue wanted to ask them what Malone had said.

"He didn't," he said instead. "What I mean is he never mentioned the name. He just said, 'that Guard with the overdose, the one they found a while back.'"

Blake cleared his throat with a single, soft cough.

"Specifically . . .?"

"That Condon's death was 'down to them.'"

"'Them' being . . . ?"

Minogue shook his head.

"That's the problem," he said. "It was 'they can do this,' 'they can do that.'"

"What else did Lawless have to offer, then?"

"Well he did a bit of rabbiting-on about gangs and the likes in Dublin, especially, and how the bad guys from the continent are setting up here, bit by bit."

"Specifics? Names? Places? Dates?"

"Very slim," Minogue said. "Very slim entirely. It's only

what you'd read in the newspapers, to be honest."

He met Blake's eyes for a few moments.

"That's partly why I didn't push Tommy more to contact the investigation team on Condon."

"I see," said Blake. "But at the time, did you think Lawless was on the level?"

"At the time, I couldn't figure it out one way or the other. But tending toward the skeptical."

"And later on?"

"Closer to disbelieving. Much closer."

Tynan looked down at his mobile, frowned while he twisted his wedding ring slowly around his finger once, and then back. Tynan never had idle thoughts, Minogue had learned a long time ago. He glanced at the Commissioner's hat, the braiding.

"All right," Tynan said then. He exchanged a glance with Blake. Blake nodded, and then gathered himself more over his notepad. He looked across at Minogue as though for the first time he had met him.

"I have a question for you now," Blake said. "And I don't want you to feel you have to answer it right away. But just consider it, and when you're ready, you know?"

Tynan had begun a scrutiny of the cabinets along the wall.

"Fair enough," Minogue said.

"Did you consider the possibility," Blake paused, as though to allow Minogue to reflect more deeply, "did you consider that something else was perhaps going on in that meeting you had in Clarendon Street Church the other day?"

Minogue searched Blake's face for a clue.

"I don't know," he said. "I don't know what you're getting at."

"I see," said Blake. "Now you are aware of Detective Malone's family, of his brother Terry and his situation?"

"I was at his funeral. Is that what you're asking?"

Blake returned a cool stare of his own.

"So you know the circumstances that led to his unfortunate death?"

Minogue nodded.

"Did you make any connection, or even wonder about one

perhaps, with Mr. Lawless and the late Mr. Malone? Mr. Terence Malone?"

"I suppose I might have," said Minogue. "Fleetingly, can I say?"

"Fleetingly?"

"Lawless is, or was, an addict, wasn't he? Father Coughlin's group thing?"

Tynan sat up abruptly.

"Eamonn," he said. "I wonder if I might ask you to give us a minute here, please?"

Blake showed no surprise at the request, and he rose and took his cup of coffee with him. They had prearranged this session, the pair of them, Minogue was sure now.

Tynan waited for Blake to close the door.

"I have to go in a minute," he said. "So I'll get to the point here a bit sooner than I would have liked."

Minogue sat up.

"Well, before you go," he said, "can I get a word in?"

"Has anyone tried to prevent you getting a word in, up to now?"

"Why is Blake trying to hang something on Tommy Malone?"

"He's asking a question that any policeman would ask," said Tynan. "It's because we take seriously the fact that a man, an informant, who talks to some policemen in the safety of the church, ends up shot to death soon afterwards. We need to give this a hard look, a very hard look. You can understand that, can't you?"

"But why the eye on Tommy Malone then? It's still basic police work to challenge an informant to repeat what he's saying to another Guard, isn't it?"

"I don't disagree. But Malone should have passed this one upstairs right away."

With that, Tynan lifted one finger, then another, and slowly he let each one in turn back on the table again.

"But what I want to tell you here is this," he went on, in a lower voice. "If this murder really does have any bearing on

Emmett Condon, then what a number of very skilled, very astute, very experienced Garda, high and low, have been intimating to me on the quiet for some time, is true. When I hear one of them whispering to me that it looks bad, do you know what they mean by 'bad'?"

Minogue shook his head.

"They're telling me that Garda Condon was a criminal," Tynan continued. "Pure and simple. That he had gone over. They're also suggesting that he may not have been the only one."

He fixed Minogue with a glance for several moments.

"Garda Condon's death left a lot of unanswered questions, a lot of damage in his section. In our whole service, in fact. Here was a detective who used unorthodox, and unapproved, methods. 'Undercover' is one thing, but running your own show is quite another. From what we now know of Garda Condon's last weeks and months, we should have seen a pattern. Poor judgment, impatience. Not documenting his contacts and leads, being out of sight of his colleagues and unit commander for days. His parents have said to me, through their lawyer, I better add, that we were negligent in supervision. We did not take proper care of a Garda detective doing dangerous work in a dangerous environment. That we gave him enough rope, you might say."

"There are not too many to stand by him," said Minogue. "Are there?"

"Correct. But now we have Malone coming in sideways with this, and dragging you in with him. And look what's happened."

"Are you saying, drop the matter?"

"No, I'm not. I'm saying something quite different."

Minogue felt a slow eddy of excitement work its way up into his chest.

"I am saying that Eamonn Blake and myself are not at all convinced by what's come up to the surface here."

"That . . . ?"

Tynan nodded.

"That Emmett Condon went to the bad. I'm not saying it won't turn out otherwise. But it seems to me that six months of work on the case should have, could have, turned up at least something not so damning."

"Too easy, you're saying?"

"It has that feel, all right. I met his wife, his widow. I met his parents. I thought about them for a long, long time. The kind of people they are, how absolutely . . . crushed is the word, I suppose. So I want another look at this. I talked to Eamonn Blake, and he's okay with it."

"So he'll get someone then."

"No. You're going to do it."

Minogue frowned at him.

"You're going to round up Malone and go visit the team who first did the work on Emmett Condon."

"Malone," was all Minogue could think to say back to Tynan's stare.

"Malone seems to be able to find people, or leads, in one day. I want to run with that, see how far it can go. So work it through again, see what might have been missed."

"Treat it as a pending, do the review . . .?"

"That's right. We need to find out if this Lawless story holds any water at all."

"Well, my head of section will be wondering."

"Not so much now," said Tynan, rising from his chair. "I briefed him on it just before we started here."

Tynan opened his briefcase folder and slid a stapled set of pages over.

"Start with that. Then get Detective Malone to read it."

Minogue glanced at the PM summary, the State Pathologist's runaway signature.

Toxic, he read, arrest, coma, before Tynan began speaking to him again.

"You report to me, and I'll be consulting with Eamonn Blake. As for the team who carried this case, you can tell them it's just a routine once-over before it's put back in the long-term basket."

Minogue let the cover page fall down over the booklet again.

"I'm to work with Tommy Malone on this," he said. "Did I get that right?"

Tynan made no reply.

"It's not for me to be inquiring further as yet, is it?" he asked.

"Exactly," said Tynan. "But I know that you will exercise good oversight with Detective Garda Malone."

Minogue felt the chill settle in his stomach now. He suddenly wanted to say something about forty pieces of silver.

"And you will phone me if you see the need," said Tynan. "In the light of what we have discussed earlier concerning the matter."

"You're asking me to," Minogue began to say, but stopped. Tynan's stare was not intense, but there was something sombre about it. It was enough to persuade Minogue to leave the words unsaid.

Tynan grasped his hat and settled the brim low on his forehead. He eyed Minogue before pulling open the door.

"I don't expect any PowerPoint shows when you have something to tell me either."

Chapter 11

September 22, 1984

EIMEAR KELLY LAY AWAKE at the usual hour. She didn't bother with the light. It had been a few days now since she'd stopped, or maybe forgotten about, the thoughts about the car in the garage. It would be easy and painless; there'd be no mess, no melodrama to it at all. She used to imagine the carbon monoxide like a rising pool creeping up the stairs, like a fog or a mist, across the carpet and up the legs of the bed. She wouldn't smell it, and she wouldn't see it. Oddly, she'd prefer to.

And that was probably why she was never alone now. Her mother was coming Thursday, to take over from her sister Róisín whose whistling breath she could hear through the open door of the second bedroom. Róisín had always slept on her back, even as a little child. Róisín had cried a lot since that night, something she hadn't done much as a child, a tomboy, and now as a civil servant clerk just starting out in Social Welfare on Pearse Street. She had heard that Mam had gotten the local TD at home to pull strings with the civil service so's Róisín had time off.

Mam. Well Mam was a tough one, so she was. She was like a colonel now, grim and determined. She'd do her crying in private, or at least away from her daughter. Her daughter the widow: there — she'd said it, in her mind at least. What a terrible, ordinary, damning, unbearable, simple word.

Eimear knew, with that peculiar knowing that seemed to come from a long distance away, that Mam believed she was fighting for her own daughter's life now, and her grandchild to be. How angry she had been, Mam, how stricken, when Eimear had stumbled in on her crying helplessly into a cushion downstairs. A stronger sleeping pill, she'd heard Mam telling the nurse, and seen her eyes flashing when the nurse had tried to whisper about the baby.

Four. Then it'd be a quarter after. Then half. On to five and then six, and all hands ticking and shuddering as they jerked from second to second. If she kept her eye on the clock on the mantelpiece below she could see the minute hand more. She ran her hand under her breast, held it there for a moment to see if her fingers still caught under it. Then her belly; it was like a drum. The baby had been active enough in the evening.

She rested her hand on her belly now, and she imagined a hand within, reaching to touch hers. Surrounded, floating no longer but curled and tight, needing to stretch. Eyes like an old man. The fears she'd had, the shiver at the thought of that cut and the blood, they'd faded. Now she just registered them, wondered, moved on.

Praying was useless. All she had wanted to pray for anyway was that what had happened wouldn't affect the baby, and then she didn't want to pray for that. That had been a shock, but it too, like everything else, had faded into what used to be. Work, she could be at work, like Maureen what's her married name in Collections, who went straight to the delivery room from her desk last June. Maureen was a jogger, she was always going somewhere.

She stared at the picture of the River Shannon over the chest of drawers, the wedding present from her aunt in Portumna. For a while she thought back to the summer holidays there by the banks of the river, the warnings not to stray into the water or the reeds where there was muck that'd draw you in, hold you, and drown you. She and Róisín had gone lots of times, even put their bare feet into the mud, to feel the malevolent power they imagined.

It disappeared, as her eyes left the picture, and she stared at the dark corner above the door, willing it to turn to some picture she could see, or at least to make her eyes so tired she could close them. It was like being on life-support or something. She'd just drift away; it didn't matter much one way or another.

The anger had been sometimes pure rage, so much that she thought she'd burst or jump or do something in an uncontrollable spasm. She couldn't cry now, that had all stopped. Everyone else was in bits still, Mam even, and they all were telling her to cry, to say her feelings. She couldn't say her feelings because she couldn't find them now. And they said that the women were the emotional ones. Yes she felt like someone had gutted every organ out of her, and that inside her was not their baby, but clouds, air and empty, empty space. That the baby, hers and Declan's, was part of her own body and then not there at all. That was mad enough to think, she knew, much less to say. They'd bring her into hospital for that, for sure.

Declan's side of the bed would always be cold, and the clothes there always unruffled. She wished she had told him how she looked at the stains on the sheet from his side, and the other secrets she had been too sparing with. His belly and his hair there, how he frowned in his sleep sometimes.

All in the long ago, as Nana used to say. She had to pee. She wondered again while she pushed herself upright if they had been putting something in her drink to keep her like this. Probably not: they all knew you could harm the baby.

She held her stomach again, felt the shifting weight settle, thought of how it was possible this baby could grow to be an adult. It held none of the wonder for her now. Like everything else, that had faded and fallen away somewhere, and on she went, a familiar enough figure in a familiar place but not trying much to figure out why this all seemed to be happening to someone else. It was someone she knew, yes, and was on good terms with, but still a stranger in many respects, someone else.

This had frightened her the most. It was losing your mind, she believed. People went mad like this when they shed themselves of who they were, or had been. She got used to it, even remembered the details of where she was when it first happened. It was like a sudden, silent snap, and immediately she was cold and terrified. They expected her to be numb, she realized later, the lines and lines of Guards at the funeral, the Superintendents and even the Commissioner she'd heard but couldn't tell which one he was in that daze of strange hand-holding and hand-shaking and hand-patting.

Disconnected, that was all. You lift a receiver; expect tone, a voice, an engaged burr. But there's nothing, and there never would be.

Her legs were swollen a long while now. Her ankles felt they'd give way easily. She threw a cardigan on and headed out into the landing.

Róisín, God love her, was awake before she even crossed the threshold. Going to the toilet only, she told her.

She pulled the cord for the little tube light over the mirror and backed onto the seat, her spine as straight as a board. "Are you all right?" from Róisín. "Will I come in?"

She told her she was. The cabinet still held Declan's stuff and it probably always would. She shuddered when the thought came to her about his toothbrush, and how a person could need one, and use one, one minute and then never again. No more shaving foam needed, or an Elastoplast for a cut. The vitamins she'd made him take were still untouched in their bottles by the cooker.

She looked down at her knees, almost hidden by her stomach. A part of her knew that this was dangerous, to be thinking you were gone and that this was someone else here in your place, but it no longer scared her now. She had been able to let her mind go to the hospital room where they'd brought Declan, and where she'd looked at his unmarked face.

Yes, he had let her down, by keeping things secret. Yes, she should have sensed it, with the arguments about emigrating. "Trying it for a little while," was Declan's way of getting it out. Then it was how lousy Dublin was, and how Guards weren't likely to get proper pay for a long time.

Money: the anger she'd felt as she took the envelope he'd covered in cello tape, and the letter, from the tin had shamed her and made her want to just end things when the two Guards had come out to the house, O'Keefe and the sergeant, only an hour after she'd come home furious with the insult of waiting in the hairdresser's. She had been crying with the anger all the way back, hoping Declan would be at home already, knowing that it was impossible somehow, so she could lay into him.

Declan had lied. There was no other way to say it. And he had stolen. Or taken a bribe, if that's what you wanted to call it. All the should-haves that raced and collided in her head since: should have gone to O'Keefe, should have gone to her, should have gone to his sergeant – to anyone, right away.

She herself should have said nothing about the tin or the money. But they had gotten her in a weak moment. All very gentle and polite, of course, but they must have known. Declan had been seen with this Rynn man. What did she know about that, they had been asking.

"Are you coming out?"

It was Róisín wanted to know.

She considered the anxiety in her sister's tone. How they all must worry, she thought. How strange it had been to see the same pinched wary look on Róisín's face that she had seen on the detectives' faces, the ones who had asked her about the money. Were they afraid for her, as well as of her? She was set aside from them now, a different person. How useless and maddening to her the phrase going around her head for so long now: there's no going back.

"Are you?" from Róisín.

"I am. Go back to bed. I'm grand."

Her thoughts vanished then, and she was left with a sudden clarity. The Guards wanted this wrapped up. They didn't believe her. That Superintendent who'd come out to the house on his own a fortnight ago, he'd been sent as a last chance, she decided later on. He sat in her kitchen and told her that they could not get a case on Rynn for this, no matter what was in the letter Declan had written. That was unless she could tell him anything about the matter, that she had maybe forgotten to tell the other Guards . . . ? "Forgotten?" Well, had Declan never once mentioned this matter to her? Not once . . .?

The look on that Superintendent's face, she'd never forget. The grey uniform, the gold braid on his collar. Did they think that would impress her, frighten her, or something? They had gone through the house for Declan's things, twice.

She had his pay stubs, his membership at the rowing club, old notebooks, patches from American police that were to start a collection, all the birth and baptismal stuff, the insurance and bank books, the second set of keys for his drawer.

Had they really needed to take away even his work shirts?

Later, the Superintendent's quiet voice that reminded her of a teacher discussing something you'd done with your parents sitting next to you: no, she could not have the letter back. No "sorry, but . . ."; no "in due course"; not even an "at the present time." But it was addressed to her, she remembered telling him. Not the money, of course not – just the letter. She'd wished she had asked him directly: do you think I knew about this? That I was in on it? Is that why you have that look on your face?

The radiator sighed. She ran her finger along its edges. She'd heard it in the mornings as the water would heat up and begin to move through the pipes. The timer would click or do whatever it would do, the flame would light up and the water would start to flow. The Gas Company man would come by and read the meter, some electronic signal would be sent, the bank's computer would signal back. The summer would come and the heating would be off. Then one night, probably in late September, there'd be a cool evening and someone would say that it'd be no harm if the heating was on tonight. Just for the present time. And it'd start again. Things just went on, with or without you.

She stared hard and unseeing at the row of tiles. Declan had tiled it with the ones she had picked out. He had used little matchsticks to keep them apart until the cement set and he could put on the grout. Declan was full of little tricks like that.

Some days still, it was like she was dead, herself. Was that a bad thing to think, as bad as thinking nothing could ever get better? In the first few days, and weeks, she'd thought she wouldn't get to Christmas, much less to the due date.

She hadn't seen the other part coming at all, with her parents.

She'd turned to her father for advice about how to deal with what the Guards were doing, what they were insinuating. She had first gotten only the wait-and-see line, and somehow she'd managed to swallow that. But not long afterwards her father had been more direct. He was frightened and angry too as much as worried about her, she could see then. This time it was: let them do it their way, we'll see. And when she pressed him, he was direct, with that odd mixture of apology and annoyance that he tried to make up for later: let it rest awhile, it would only be worse if it got public. Focus on your health, on rest, on the baby.

She was too exhausted to understand that, or go back at them, any of them, then. How could it be that everyone had gone against her on this? How did that start? She had put it away somewhere, thinking about it every day, but all the time aware of it slipping into that other place like everything else had.

"Can you sleep?" came Róisín's voice.

There was a pleading in her voice. For the first time she could remember, Eimear Kelly wanted to smile. It was Róisín herself who'd conk out at the drop of a hat.

"Of course I can," she lied. She actually didn't mind lying there a couple of hours. She could replay the words and the faces and the memories; maybe cry awhile; think.

She let herself down on the bed, turned, and lay down. The baby stirred, stretched, reached out. She placed her hands on her stomach again and let her eyes grow used to the near dark again. A lot of the time she had imagined that the ceiling and roof would disappear and she could be looking up at the night sky where Declan might appear, in a way you couldn't see him, but there all the same, floating over her. There were the stabs in her throat and chest as the grief flooded over her, but tears didn't follow.

When it passed, she was back to thinking about that Superintendent again, and how his face had told her more than anything else that he wanted this out of the way, and over. They'd be looking into the widow's pension, of course, and to see what could be done. Et cetera, et cetera. How could she not notice the hint? No, no-one had to say "scandal" or "disgrace" or "best not to bring it up."

It took an effort to find something else to think about, but she did it. The man she'd gone to see, the Dr. Herlighy that worked with Guards, had been nice. He'd told her she'd feel alone, no matter how kind and loving people were. He had a nice smile, the look of a man who had come through some bad times or illness himself. The words he had used had stayed with her.

She thought for a while that he must have hypnotized her. Then later she didn't care. Even with the baby, she'd feel alone, he'd said, adrift. Other words he had used too, she remembered how true it was, that feeling of floating. Unmoored, he'd said; offshore. Stranded. Maybe he was big on the sea or something.

Now she heard the low steady breathing from Róisín. There was almost a whistle in it when she was deep asleep. Her mind went to the times they'd shared in the Gaeltacht, and their brothers Conor and Liam too, supposed to be learning Irish. Declan had been in the same village before, but a different year. Then she saw Róisín coming up to the flat to visit them; going in to work with her, acting as if her new Junior Ex position in Foreign Affairs must be the most glamorous thing in the entire world. But Declan appeared again now, coming into the office in uniform to pick her up those evenings before they got engaged. She enjoyed the looks he got, but he laughed about it.

Everyone wants the best for you, Eimear: Herlighy's voice, it was. They want you to return to them; they want your suffering and pain to lessen. They want you to be healthy and well, to come back to life fully, the best you can, bit by bit. They want you to turn toward the sun–

Turn toward the sun?

She opened her eyes wide: he had hypnotized her, that Herlighy. How else could she be replaying words like that over and over again. They were like a spell, or a poem. The bugger, she thought. But it seemed to have done something for her.

Still, nobody could really see into her mind or read her thoughts. She was certain of that. She knew she could continue to keep this to herself, the rage at how everything had changed so fast, at how everything had been ripped from her. It was the Guards who had stripped her of pieces of Declan while they made out to honour him in their salutes and cortege and prayers. The man who'd been driving the car that evening without his lights on yet. Her own family, she'd had to admit, for all their love: they were ashamed in some way they might never say. Still she knew, just as she knew what was going on in that Superintendent's head.

A coldness came over her then when her thoughts fixed on the other one, the man she didn't like to think of, whose name she fought not to say in her mind even lest she scream it out loud: Rynn.

She wrenched her thoughts away, fled to her childhood and school, to work, to the holidays on her aunt's farm. Soon she stopped, and her mind settled back on Declan. She had even thought the impossible, and it didn't terrify her now: Declan had let her down. Declan, with his stubbornness and his loyalty all mixed up, had brought this on too. It was no use saying bad luck over and over again, or that something in Declan had been broken that night so that a part of his mind, his judgment maybe, had given way.

He had been working away secretly, planning for weeks or even months. He had even bought the tickets to New York. They had asked her about that every time they'd come out, the detectives, and later that bastard Superintendent. Maybe they had run out of ideas and had sent him out in uniform to impress her, or to frighten her.

If only Declan had said one word, she would have known. One word.

She felt that numb weariness that she had come to dread was close now, and she seemed to be sinking through the mattress further, into that pit as she'd called it, in the sessions with the psychiatrist. If she came out of this, and somebody asked her what it was like, she wouldn't say what she'd heard and read other people said, like "nightmare" or that. She'd remember the blinding pain in her heart as much as the numbness after, the indifferent wondering if she'd make it at all, or even want to make it.

She wouldn't hold back telling about the thoughts of killing herself, and the worrying if she was damaging her baby with that thinking, if he could pick it up from her. She'd say how everything normal had been completely turned into something else, often frightening and loaded with a dread: a chair where Declan had sat, a word someone used. She wouldn't forget to tell them of the sudden, overwhelming hatred of things, of people – complete strangers even; of the way things were, and couldn't be changed; the blame she wanted so much to pin on someone.

Her own shallow breathing alternated with Róisín's down the hall. The baby gave a stir, a stretch. She had come to believe that the baby seemed to know what she was thinking. "The baby," why didn't she just call it "he"? Declan liked the name John, after his mother's uncle who had died young. But they had both liked the name Liam.

Liam: how many times had she seen Declan and herself in the house here after Liam would be born: in Declan's arms, or sleeping beside them; feedings, playing, the soothing to sleep, the night waking. Everyone just assumed she'd move back home for a while after the baby was born. Would she? She wondered if she'd ever have a man again, even to talk with, to sit next to in the car, to hold on to at night. There was nothing wrong with that, she now believed; that wasn't betrayal.

Chapter 12

MALONE PICKED UP MINOGUE just after two o'clock. Malone had corralled his work car, the Nissan. It smelled of McDonald's again.

"My head's still spinning," said Malone. "But I'll go with it. How about yourself? Like old times, isn't it?"

"I suppose."

"They came for me at the exact same time," Malone went on. "Remember I was talking to you, and I says, 'Hold on?' And then when I go to say something to you, you're gone already?"

"Indeed."

"'Indeed'? Didn't it kind of freak you out? But wait, you got the big wigs, didn't you. I had two normal fellas shooting questions at me."

Minogue's arms went out reflexively as Malone threw the Nissan into the curve that led through Kevin Street. A car horn faded behind.

"It doesn't seem to have taken much out of you."

"Ah, come on. They knew I couldn't have had anything to do with Lawless getting murdered. They just wanted to know how I'd gotten involved in the thing in the first place."

From somewhere under, or by the seat, Malone drew up a half-finished bag of chips. Minogue looked at the bruise on Malone's cheekbone. It had spread.

"I didn't hold back anything from last night either," said Malone. "Did you?"

"Not a bit."

"They showed you pictures? Lawless . . . ?"

"They sure did."

"I heard that Lawless was done yesterday evening. Someone saw him last around seven or so. And then he's spotted lying there on the steps at eight o'clock. That's when that priest got called, Father Coughlin. He must have told someone about our little get-together at the church the other day."

Minogue yawned again.

"Dear Diary," Malone started out. "I am going down to my colleagues in Kilmainham Garda station to see what a bollocks they made out of the Emmett Condon case."

"That'll go over well there, that approach. You'd have a matching clout on the other side of that thick head of yours, I'd be thinking."

The Nissan was not designed for what Malone seemed to want to do in his detours through the laneways and cramped streets behind Thomas Street.

"What's your hurry, Tommy? Slow down, will you."

Malone crumpled the empty bag and tossed it into the back.

"Easy knowing you didn't get battered last night."

"This isn't about settling scores with some George character. This is about us looking over the case files asking a few polite questions – watch that van, will you."

"So," said Malone. "He'll show up along the way. I'll bet you anything."

"And you'll do what if he does?"

Malone looked over for long enough to get a rise out of Minogue.

Minogue looked back at the report to check the detectives' names again. Fintan Donnelly was supposed to be waiting for them at Kilmainham Station to give them the rundown. Never heard of him. He wondered if Donnelly was newer, or if he and Malone would be facing a veteran who'd be only as helpful as his orders had told him.

Malone got them back out onto James's Street just before the road forked. He accelerated through the light at the stop of Stevens' Lane, the road that Minogue had taken hundreds of times before on his way to work in the Murder Squad, across from Kingsbridge, or Heuston Station as he refused to call it for decades now.

"Where the legend began," said Malone. He looked over.

"Do you miss it?" he asked Minogue. "The Squad?"

"For all the wrong reasons."

"You don't fit parlez-vous and all that, the nine-to-five?"

Minogue knew from the voice that Malone was slagging.

"'Ah by jayses, they'll rue the shagging day they ever broke up the Squad, so they will!'" Malone said. It wasn't the worst take on Kilmartin's accent he'd heard from Malone. "'The so-called experts will be begging to put it back together, and they should kick the arses of every lousy, jumped-up Superintendent that moaned and whinged until they finally dragged us down! The jackals!'"

"Dingoes, he called them too," said Minogue.

"'The fecking dingoes! They couldn't fault us for our record! No! So they had the nerve to persuade the boss that they had staff trained *too* fecking well already! By who?!'"

"–By whom–"

"'–By the very Squad they want to drag down to their level! All in the name of some fecking decentralization fad that'll blow up in their won snots in short order . . . ! The *bashtards!*'"

"Not bad," Minogue said. "But he does a good one of you too."

The Nissan made its way with much less urging from Malone, to within sight of the lights at South Circular Road, before Malone turned it onto Kilmainham Lane.

There were two squad cars parked by the door in from the yard. Four Guards, the whole complement of both cars, were in a bunch holding a very fat man. They carried him sideways through the staff door. There was no fight in this client. His shirt had gone up to his chest and his one shoe was unlaced. To Minogue, he looked relaxed and even happy, like a child being brought to bed.

JOHN BRADY

The air held a dank staleness. The River Liffey, Minogue decided, with that faint, malty scent that was actually hops. It was the same smell he'd noticed the first time he'd ever visited Dublin, carried up through the city from Guinness's brewery from nearby Islandbridge.

They were let in through to the staff office crowded with furniture. There they waited by a desk, in two chairs that a Guard found for them.

Donnelly was all business, so much so that he'd skipped upstairs two steps at a time ahead of Minogue, and waited there to usher the two detectives into a smallish, cluttered room that seemed to do treble duty as storage room, cloak room, and place to hide in. There was a bockety table, probably saved form the scrap heap Minogue decided, and creaking foldaway chairs that Donnelly ripped from a stack.

"Well, Fintan," Minogue said. "Thanks very much now. Sorry about the short notice and all."

"No bother," Donnelly replied, a little too quickly.

Minogue looked down at the box Donnelly had brought with him.

"Hurling?" Donnelly asked Malone, who didn't get the connection until Donnelly touched his own cheek.

"God no," said Malone. "I got it going to the toilet."

Minogue flipped through the pages. The colour photocopies were improving by the day. Then he smiled up at Donnelly.

"Could we maybe take these with us, Fintan? We'd bring them back, to be sure."

"Fire away. You know Internal Affairs have copies of everything?"

Minogue nodded, to avoid a fib outright. He had a smile ready.

"Was there mention of a girl somewhere along the line?"

Donnelly had found something on a wall to concentrate on for several moments.

"There was," he said then, and Minogue knew the tone had changed. "One of the blokes said she was maybe Russian."

"Any way of verifying that?"

198

"Verifying the fella told us?"

"No, I mean if what came of an interview with her."

"Nothing did."

Before Minogue could say anything, Donnelly broke in.

"'Cause there was no interview. 'Cause we haven't come across her."

"Are you concerned maybe she's, well, let's say prevented from speaking with you?"

"Like you mean maybe dead?"

Minogue raised an eyebrow and watched to see if Donnelly read his lack of immediate reply right. He saw that Donnelly was no gom in that department, but the same Donnelly wasn't going to pass the ball without lobbing a few more at these two fly-ins.

"Who's the source on this woman, this girlfriend?" Malone asked.

"It came from a fella knew Condon off the street, a right louser the name of McHugh. An addict – in and out of prison. All he had was something about Condon and a foreign bird."

"McHugh's term?"

"More or less. The transcript is there, I think?"

"People still say 'bird' in this day and age? For a girl?"

"It's back," said Donnelly. "You hear it a fair bit. It's a sixties thing, the 'lad' bit."

"Well, did he ever see her, meet her?"

"He says he saw her once, but it was across the street. . . . He can't remember which street. He can't remember when. But he took two hours with the Ident man jigsawing that composite. Your man had to give up with him after the two hours I heard."

"Is he the only source for the composite that Missing Persons used?"

Donnelly nodded slowly for ironic emphasis.

"Jesus," Minogue heard Malone mutter.

"The way he is, I'm surprised he could describe his own mother. Much less see her."

After a few moments, Donnelly seemd to think better of what he had said.

"Ah who knows, maybe I'm wronging him."

"How so?" from Malone.

"Well, maybe he was a pal of Condon's, some might say."

Malone sat back and gave Donnelly a long, neutral look.

"Which would you say?" Minogue asked.

"Couldn't say really."

Minogue was beginning to seriously dislike this detective. Eight or ten years in, Minogue decided, and probably half that in plainclothes. Long enough to be brazen. Again he wondered if the rest of the Guards who'd worked this case had talked it over about how to treat himself and Malone. "A Sergeant Daly was lead. John Daly?"

Donnelly nodded. "John's out."

Minogue let the brittle silence last a while. He pretended to read a Statement Summary from Mr. Edward McHugh, source of the "foreign bird." A total of eight years and some months of McHugh's twenty-six years on the Emerald Island had been in the custody of the State.

"So I'll leave you to it then," Donnelly said.

"Where will you be if we need a bit of elucidation?"

"Well, there's Dispatch, I suppose, if I'm gone out."

Minogue wanted to ask him if everyone who'd worked on the case was similarly hard to meet with. Instead he watched the door close behind him.

Malone stretched and pressed his bruise delicately.

"There's a prize bollocks for you," he said. "No prize to you, but, for guessing his take on all this. And the rest of his crew."

In the hour that followed, Minogue read and made notes. He mostly ignored Malone's low humming and scratching as he read also. Finally he stood up to stretch.

"The Naas Road," he said to Malone. "Did you get that?"

"Yep. Interesting. I'm betting he was in that Roadhouse place too."

Minogue looked at the window.

"What?" said Malone.

"Did you ever think maybe Condon was looking for this woman too? That maybe she left town on him, or the like?"

Malone rubbed gingerly at his bruise. Minogue imagined

Condon arguing with a woman, her storming out, shouts.

"But nasty company Condon kept," Malone murmured after a while. "I can say that for him. That's the job though, isn't it. You get your grasses and your snitches, the more, the better."

Minogue turned over the pages to get back to the composite they'd made of the woman's face. He paused at the Scenes pictures. Condon had been found under a bridge. The flash showed blackened cement supports in the background. All about him had been the detritus of fires and half-burned clothes, sticks and tins and bits of cement blocks and plastic bags.

The lab work on all the debris was a dizzying amount of baffling inconsequence. You could guess from the pictures even that people had their fixes there, gotten drunk there. They had eaten and opened their bowels there, by choice or necessity. No doubt they'd probably fought there, passed out, beat others, and probably even raped there. And there was Emmett Condon's body, with an arm under him, his head twisted toward the darkness higher up where the bridge joined the earth again.

He went on to the composite of the woman. Malone looked over.

"If that's the best they can do with their fancy computers over in Ident, I'll stick to me PlayStation."

Minogue went back to the transactions on Condon's cards and his mobile record. He'd bought a stereo a week before he'd died. He'd paid for petrol down by Clondalkin, a hotel room at the West Land Hotel out on the N11. He found the report from a Garda Tracey who'd followed up: no additional info. There was a chambermaid with a Spanish-sounding name.

His mobile had placed calls to his ex-wife – a long conversation in two of them – a garage, three people, one of whom was found to be an informer for a detective working out of Kildare, and the others with criminal records. Their alibis were holding up so far.

Malone stretched.

"You have to be bloody good at reading between the lines here," he said, and groaned and yawned at the same time. "I'm going down and beat a cup of tea out of them. You want one?"

Minogue said he did. He took up what Malone had been reading.

Condon's section head, one Mick O'Toole, had spoken to him twice in one month. He'd told Condon one of the detectives on the unit had complained about him. There had been lousy paperwork from Condon, even no paperwork. One incident had made O'Toole suspicious, according to what he told them. Bait money – the money they'd used to get or pay informants – didn't get due authority several times. Condon had not made satisfactory representations to him on at least one of them, according to O'Toole. And here was something to stand out from the oddly muted summary, beyond the cover-your-arse descant: O'Toole said that he would have moved sooner had he not been overloaded with other casework. Did O'Toole mean Condon's removal, Minogue wondered, or a disciplinary charge? He scribbled down a memo to phone O'Toole.

A rain shower lashed the window now. Minogue stopped reading to study the patterns that were slowly spreading and twisting on the glass. A minute passed, and his mind stayed on hold to the sounds of the rain. Footsteps in the hall outside and a raised voice, a man's, brought him back. Minogue realized that he had been thinking again about this woman. He found the page with her composite on it. It still looked like a weird cross between a Barbie ad, and one of those old science-fiction puppets on the telly.

But Daly had gone by the book, sending out the composite to Missing Persons the second day of the investigation, after a day's search in Immigration. All the eleven Missing Person contacts had been duds. Russian, Bulgarian, Romanian – no-one knew which the woman could be. Somebody McHugh, listed as an informant to Condon, couldn't offer more than "He was involved with some foreign bird."

Minogue couldn't conclude otherwise really – this case had cooled pretty quickly. The immigration and work-permit search had been finished two days after the request. An aid organization for foreign workers had been tried, three charities too. A copy of the composite sent to Europol, even. This was solid work from the currently unavailable Daly, right down to door-to-doors where Condon's flat was, to see if any girl had shown.

There had been no paraphernalia in the flat. A search on floors and ceilings had been done. "No items of female apparel or effects." Mira, Marina, Maria: Mary? Where did that name start anyway? Minogue had almost forgotten – McHugh again. Not for the first time, Minogue began to weigh more heavily a suspicion that McHugh might not be as stupid, or as addled as he'd let on. McHugh's information amounted to nothing much, a nuisance maybe. A diversion, though?

Minogue began to remember the bumblers and the gobdaws he'd dealt with over the years. There were hangers-on with a slim enough grasp of things, and plenty of others who were half-cracked or just simple-minded, but driven to believe they could help. Help? They weren't lying, many of them, he'd learned. They wanted just to be listened to, to be part of some excitement, to be part of the story, to be in the light.

His midafternoon, caffeine-starved brain lurched back to Lawless. The man's words played back to Minogue, in no order: higher-up in the Guards; for years now; getting the lowdown on what the Guards were up to; know when the Guards were coming down on someone. Lawless swearing that his brother wasn't lying, but had been hearing about this for a while in jail, and why would he lie, and what could be done for his brother now that he had provided such important information, and here they were trying to help the Guards, and he was taking risks passing this on, and why were they suspicious of him, and didn't he have Father Coughlin here believing in him, and he trying to rehabilitate himself, and . . .

Chapter 13

MINOGUE STARTED WHEN the foot-tapping at the bottom door began, and his heart raced. He must have actually dozed off. It was Malone at the door, and his hands were full. He had foraged well enough to land some Coconut Creams.

"Are you okay?" Malone asked. "Something happen?"

Minogue shook his head and heeled the door closed behind him.

"Did you check they're not poisoned?"

"No way. I rob – I got them out of a package."

"Who did you have to fight for them?"

"It's self-serve here, I think."

Minogue ignored the dull film on the spoon. He pressed the pad of thick creme attached to the biscuit below, fought again to rid his mind of the photos from where Lawless had been murdered. The smell of tea began to win over the room.

"*Jayzuz!*" cried Malone, and held out the cup. "The tap water here must be from Liffey or something! Straight from Islandbridge or somewhere – *poxy*. But I'll drink it."

Minogue blew on his tea. Neither man spoke until they had half a cup and three of four biscuits gone. Minogue listened to the varying hush of the rain still landing on the glass. He believed it was easing.

"Tommy. About Lawless."

Malone looked over.

"Is there any word on what they've found?"

"Shot three times," said Malone. "The back of the place where he had a flat. No witnesses yet."

"Not a single one?"

"Last I heard, no. Nobody heard anything. There's no casings at the scene either. I talked to one of the team there, he told me someone waited for him there. They – he – knew Lawless's moves, his habits."

"Was it really Coughlin, sorry, Father Coughlin, found him?"

"It's true," said Malone. "When he didn't show for his group thing . . ."

Malone shrugged and took a sip of tea, and grimaced.

"Coughlin is bulling mad, I hear," he said. "Livid. He went straight to Tynan."

Minogue watched Malone detach a biscuit.

"I wish I'd actually written down the exact words Lawless used there in the church, Tommy. How's your recollection there? It was the second time around for you, right?"

Malone looked up toward the ceiling.

"Okay," he murmured. "Here it is. There was 'higher-up in the Guards, for years now.'"

"'Years'? How many? Did he say?"

Malone shook his head.

"And he said 'Getting the lowdown on what the Guards were doing.' He said that they would know ahead of time from this 'insider' if the Guards were coming down on someone."

"Right," Minogue said. "I remember that. That was it, though?"

Malone shrugged.

"That's it," said Malone. "What are you thinking?"

Minogue remembered Tynan's unspoken suspicions.

"I don't know," he said after several moments. "But whatever Emmett Condon was into, people don't want it sticking to them."

"The fellas he worked with, you mean?"

"Everybody. Maybe even his family. They're circling the

wagons a bit, if you read through their statements. Emmett Condon's father is a retired Guard, you know."

"Ouch."

"Ouch, is right. I think maybe someone got to them, like a senior fella. Maybe O'Toole, the head of Condon's section. Gave them the bad news early."

"Let on like Condon had done the dirty? Best not to dig too deep?"

"I am wondering that self-same thing, if something like that happened."

Minogue sipped at the tea again. The metallic aftertaste wasn't getting better. He became aware that Malone was looking at him.

"What?"

"Condon really was bent," said Malone. "Wasn't he?"

The question hung in the air. Minogue kept at the tea, listening to the rain. He reached for another Coconut Cream.

"Well? Do you?"

He wanted to tell Malone to go find some course on etiquette, or diplomacy, or tact or something. A Guard had died, he wanted to say, doing the dirty work on the front lines. He looked away toward the papers strewn across the table instead.

"He could well have been," he muttered.

♣ ♣ ♣

Four o'clock came but the minute hand seemed to get jammed before the twelve. Minogue got up and went to the window.

The rain had moved off a half-hour ago. It had been quickly replaced by a steely brightness that glowed more and more, until finally the sun broke through. It blazed on the leaves and patches of grass, and glared back from puddles and glass and metal into the clear air. The more ragged and torn clouds retreated far off, beyond the trees that rose over the rooftops between the Garda Station and the Liffey, and the infinite acres of the Phoenix Park beyond. The river would be brown in the sunlight now, Minogue knew, and remembered even seeing the turbid rain-swollen waters a weird azure under O Connell Bridge not long ago.

He studied the blues and greys that had been deepened by the rain. Off over the city, the little bit of the city left to see here, he believed there was a softer light already. It was the pearly tint that he'd had to concede was apricot, one day in a roistering argument with Iseult. His eye roved from rooftop to chimney across the horizon, and he wondered what his daughter was up to at the present time. Welding was only the latest. Her intent, said she, with a glitter in her eye, was to make that iron contraption float in the air. HyBrasil, he whispered: The Isle of the Blest, indeed. For a moment he tried to remember the Magrittes, the ones where the boulders floated over the seascape. Seven months' pregnant, her marriage adrift, working through the night. Contrary is as contrary does, to be sure.

"What?" Malone asked.

"I didn't say anything, Tommy."

"You were muttering."

Minogue looked over.

"I always mutter."

He returned to his idle stare, this time toward the Phoenix Park.

"Did you read his missus' statements yet?" Malone asked. "Condon's? Jaysus, but she's bitter."

They had finished the summaries an hour ago. They had been passing the transcripts and statements between them.

"I did," said Minogue. He heard Malone yawn and turn pages.

A sharp and pleasant glow came to him then when he realized that it might be sunny like this at Killiney this evening. He'd phone Kathleen, warn her. She was usually good for five or ten minutes down on the beach, at the water's edge. For himself, he didn't want to do much there except stand around and gawk at the water again. As had become a habit in recent times, she would leave her culchie husband to his thoughts and go back and sit in the car overlooking the beach. Now Kathleen had a mobile, he often returned to the car to hear her gostering away on the phone.

Yes, he thought: skipping stones out over the waves at Killiney tonight, the rolling waters he depended on, would be where he would wash away the feeling of being tainted by what he was coming to believe about Emmett Condon.

"Separated a year," said Malone and got up with a grunt. Minogue heard the floor give as Malone walked slowly to the window.

"What are you looking at?"

"My escape route," Minogue said.

"Huh."

"How many deer are there in the Phoenix Park?"

"How would I know? How would anybody know? Why are you asking?"

Kilmainham, and the area next to it, Islandbridge, would always be grimy parts of old Dublin to Minogue. No amount of film studios or cappuccino bars would fix it. But they'd said that about the Temple Bar even, hadn't they?

"You know," said Malone, "I have a lousy feeling about this business. That girl? The one supposed to be something to Condon?"

"If she's not a figment of this fella McHugh's half-cooked brain, you should be saying first."

"I got that earlier, okay? If she's not here legally, well . . ."

Minogue turned to him.

"Okay," said Malone. "She doesn't show up, so (A) She doesn't exist; (B) She does and she's done a bunk, under whatever papers she has, probably fake anyway – out of the country; or (C) She's gone under a new name, moved to, I don't know, Cahirciveen, Ballygobackwards."

"Do we have an embassy in Ballygobackwards?"

"There's thousands – tens of thousands – of them people here now. They get a one-year permit, crap jobs, pay's not great. That's bad enough, right? But if she was illegal in the first place, well, who's going to help her out in a thing like this?"

Minogue nodded.

"I mean, she'll know she'd better take a dive somewhere after Condon turns up dead. Because that is serious. Right?"

"Would she leave the country then? Go home?" Minogue asked.

"What if she can't?"

"Why 'can't'? She hasn't the fare?"

"How about because she's going to get in worse trouble if she tried that?"

Minogue began to get it now.

"Her– what am I going to call it– her manager here?" he asked.

"Pimp," said Malone. "Whatever. Let's say he holds her papers, and she can't travel. Or he threatens her family. Or threatens to tell them what she does here. That goes on, you know."

"I've heard of them owing money they can't pay back."

Malone nodded.

"Our best hope is that she's lying low here, maybe under another name."

"Wouldn't she turn up somehow though?" Minogue tried.

"Like how – with that lousy dot-to-dot I-don't-know-what-kind-of-a-thing, of a face their computer spat up for Missing Persons? Hah. Like I said. I've seen PlayStation One games with better faces than that."

Minogue's thoughts drifted to the presentation yesterday. There had been countries he'd heard of but didn't know whether they were parts of Russia or floating somewhere the far side of Berlin, or Vienna or somewhere.

"I don't know," he said. "There's just so much we don't know here."

"Well, I do know a few things," Malone said. "And one of them is this. A lot of the people they're working for here in Ireland are no angels. And it's Irish people I'm talking about who are doing the gouging and the under-the-table stuff. Fellas in Immigration there, they could tell you stories."

Minogue headed back to the cluttered table. He looked at the picture again.

"Sometimes I wonder," Malone began. "Are we doing to people what was done to us?"

"That bad, do you think?"

"Them people who are cleaning toilets and cleaning offices in the middle of the night. And then, bejases, we turn around and tell them their time is up and they can go home. Home to what?"

"You and Karl Marx, Tommy. I never knew."

"Ah now. It sucks. It's not right. Anyway, what I'm saying is, she'd be doing her best to stay away from any of us. But I don't want to push that any further now."

"Push it," Minogue said. "It's all you're good for sometimes."

Malone let out a breath.

"Well, we better face up to it at some point," he said, and he scratched his head hard. "We keep on coming back to it, don't we? Maybe what happened to Condon . . .?"

Malone turned quickly from the window.

"Happened to her as well?"

Chapter 14

October 15, 1985

E IMEAR KELLY COULDN'T BEAR to do the paperwork. "Widow": she couldn't bear to read it, much less say it: even think it. So, in the end it was Breda who came through. Now Breda herself was getting married in a few months. She had been in insurance since she'd come up to Dublin. Breda smoothed it all out, made the phone calls, brought the forms out to the house. But the same Breda had broken down in tears just after starting. She'd kept apologizing for it. Before she left, she even apologized for telling her there was a ray of light in this, and that Declan would have been happy for her. It was such a stupid thing to say, and it had just come out of her and she didn't know how or why. Still, the house was hers now, mortgage-free, wasn't it? And there'd be payments coming in each month, if all went well with the Garda Pension and Benefits crowd. And God help them if they didn't hurry up! Then she cried again, for nearly a half-hour.

She remembered Breda's reaction that night, the night when she'd told her about her plans. The bewilderment on Breda's face, she remembered, and the anxiety too. Breda wore her heart on her sleeve – always had – and she said things on the spur of the moment, often laughing or apologizing later on. It was actually endearing. But even if she'd tried her best that night, Breda couldn't have held back that look. It was a kind of a pained frown, and she had sat there completely still, trying to smile or something, but obviously thinking the unthinkable. It was the was-Eimear-mad look.

That reaction, from her oldest friend from primary school, had stayed with Eimear, and she knew she would never again try to explain it to anyone. She couldn't tell anyone how it felt, like she was away from everything but surrounded by it too. To be floating here amongst people, able to do and say the normal things, but to feel it was someone else they were talking to. A ghost really, some sort of a living ghost.

Breda was logical though, as well as everything else.

"Eimear," she'd said. "Maybe it's the tablets they gave you, that treatment? Maybe it's time to stop. I heard they change you. That you get used to them."

"No," she remembered replying, and she was astonished at the words that came out of her own mouth then. How calm she had sounded, how reasonable.

"I've thought about it a lot. It's the only way, Breda. I can't go on like this, it's like I'm sleepwalking or something. I won't."

That part had definitely freaked Breda. She could tell straight-away, because Breda tried to change the subject. Still, she was drawn back into asking her things that led into what Eimear had told her. Was she eating right? Had she been able to get a few hours' solid sleep? Was the breastfeeding wearing her down or something? "Wanting to start over, well great," Breda had said after. "But changing your name? You mean back to your maiden name?"

"I do, yes."

"Do Declan's parents know?"

"Why do they need to know?"

Breda hesitated.

"They might think," she began. "Well, you know."

"I know they're worried, I know. We're all worried. But in the end of the day, it's up to me to do something. I'm not trying to hurt anyone."

"You mean it, really, don't you?"

"I do."

"But why, Eimear? You sound like it's part of some plan you've come up with?"

"It's not a plan really. It's just that I'm so tired, it's like I'm carrying this huge something. I want to be a different person, somebody new – or I want to get my old self back. I can't explain it totally."

"But what will you do?"

"I don't mean a big rigmarole. Just something simple. I'll get a job, maybe back in the insurance business, and see where that'll go. I'm going to use my middle name as well. Remember I used to do that, back in school, after Confirmation?"

"But that was a lark, Eimear! That was our Hollywood-star stuff. Come on!"

"I'd still be *me*. I just want another start. That's not a bad thing to want, is it?"

Breda's look stayed with her over the years. That effort of trying not to stare, but with still a stricken look on her face that she couldn't hide. It felt like Breda had actually shrunk, shrunk physically, in front of her. It saddened her, but in a strange way it also gave her a hope, that Breda would probably never come around to accepting this.

"Eimear, have you talked it over with anyone?"

She understood the tone as much as the words her friend used, and knew then that she wouldn't be able to go on with trying to persuade her. It was just another thing to let go of, she thought. Sadness certainly, and she had felt herself want to cry then and there, but it was just another stage, she knew, and it had to be endured. Breda asked her something about a doctor talking to her about postpartum, or that sort of thing?

She listened, and she went through the motions. It didn't shock her anymore to see how quickly things changed, even in moments. It was another veil lifted, she understood. Whether you liked things the way they were, whether you feared them, or whether you wanted to change them, none of that mattered. There was no going back. The panics that came suddenly, like the one the other day in the supermarket, and the feeling of falling into something that would not let her out again – those might never go away. There'd always be the anxious looks on her family's faces, the smiles that were too watchful, and the kindly, distant looks from the doctor murmuring questions and advice.

"Will you go back and see that, em, doctor?"

"The psychiatrist? No, I don't think so."

Breda had looked around the kitchen, biting her lip. Eimear knew she was trying not to cry again.

"Rent this house out, Eimear, and you could go home awhile. That's found money, and you'd have, you know– Look, how about a girl from down her way, one coming up to study in Dublin? Babysitting, all that . . .?

Breda's words trailed off. She began to shake. Maybe it had been seeing the baby things around the counter, the toys, that had put her over the edge, Eimear thought, while she held her.

Breda hugged her long and hard in the hallway again later.

"Oh, Eimear. I'm sorry, I'm so sorry. I wish, oh, I don't know how to help."

Sorry for what, she thought, and looked back into her friend's streaming eyes. She wanted Breda to leave here thinking she'd done good.

Later, in the early hours, she realized that Breda had joined that group of people she knew she'd keep things from. The family things, she meant. It would have happened anyway, probably, once married life started for Breda. It was just another milestone.

She heard the baby stirring, a small cry. At least her mother had gone back home now for a week at a time. She didn't have to feel her mother's worry too, how she watched her with her baby. Around her, everyone worried and cried and talked amongst themselves. What'll we do about Eimear? She's depressed. It's the medication. She should try something else. She won't go to the psychiatrist anymore. She never cries now. She needs to get it out of her. Will she harm the baby? Soon it'd be: why does she want to get a job now, a new job? Doesn't the baby need her? And on, and on.

The sniffling would turn to those little gasps soon. She'd wait, and let him have his say. Declan would have gotten up; that was the way he was. Everyone expected women to be soft, to fall apart, she had learned. It gave her no satisfaction to know it now, this knowing that she'd never get over this, but that she'd just go on.

She sat up and reached for her dressing gown. The baby was in his own room now, and down to just one bottle at night. Had he sensed her calmness, the very thing that her own family were agitated about, and Breda, not four hours ago. He was a good sleeper. She loved him; it was as simple as that.

The carpet was cold. She reached out her toes for a slipper, and the sharp sting of what she had learned came to her unexpectedly. She stood there to let it sink in.

It wasn't just Breda, no: they were all of one mind. Eimear was to be pitied, fretted over. Only nice things would be said, and the awkward things let slip away, forever, if possible. But she would never forget what she'd seen in that Superintendent's eyes that day he'd come out. He couldn't wholly hide his true belief about Declan.

Nor could they. Even under the gentle talk and the hugs and the telephone calls, and the endless things they brought, she'd seen it, and she'd known it: Declan was not one of them anymore. He'd never say it outright, any more than the people close to her would say it, that it was good that Declan was gone.

She found the other slipper. The air in the baby's room was close, and tangy from the used nappies in the bin. She listened to see if he had heard her, but the small coughing cries did not slow.

"It's all right, love," she said. "Here I am . . ."

♣ ♣ ♣

March 28, 1986

There was a spell of warm weather early that spring. Eimear spent a lot of time in the park, Marley Grange, with Róisín and the baby. Sometimes, too, it was with their mother, or Breda, or Declan's sisters Bridget and Anne. There was a good view over the city in many places in the park. The mountains and Pine Forest were close behind.

Doctor Dempsey changed her tablets. For a while she noticed the change, but then things went back to being the same. She didn't like anybody asking her how she felt, or how it was going, no matter how much they cared or wanted the best for her.

The baby: for some reason, it bothered her mother the most that Eimear still called him "the baby." She told Róisín, who told her. Then Eimear told Róisín to tell their mother back that it was just words. Couldn't they see she did love "the baby," and was taking the best care of "the baby," and not to say things like that again because it upset her to hear them secondhand? She was satisfied, and not too guilty, when she head later that her mother was mortified for days.

It was actually funny, she knew, but only for someone who could laugh.

Everything was too easy sometimes, on the outside, in that world, and that alarmed her. Dinners made, the shopping done, the bills paid. She was regular again and her breasts weren't sore anymore. The stitches were long gone.

After the episode where she'd told Breda she wanted to change her name, to be someone else, there was always someone calling to the house. It had taken her a while to catch on. She thought that Dempsey had given her different tablets for a while. From time to time she began to skip the tablets. All she noticed was a bit more energy or interest, and a feeling of being very heavy too though, along with a frightening feeling that she was not far from panic over simple things.

She looked over at her baby cradled in Róisín's arms, and Róisín talking and cooing as she set the swing to a gentle glide with her feet. If she ever told Róisín to keep him because she loved this nephew so much – even as a joke – that'd have them all on her again.

They were keeping some things from her. She didn't mind. She didn't want to know anything about the Guards, even Declan's pals. But she had heard Breda and Róisín talking about something to do with the Guards, how they were all like that, or something.

Was it for her sake they had not fought to get proper benefits from the Guards? Maybe they had no heart to, because they wanted her to be as far as possible, forever probably, from the Guards.

Róisín lifted the baby and laughed. There, she had heard a

little something, a gurgle of pleasure. Eimear felt that she was surrounded by love, and such concern and minding. She sometimes thought she should say it out loud, how grateful she was. Something stopped her at those times, and it had disturbed her. She should never, ever say to one of them that sometimes she felt suffocated by it all.

What nobody had said, or hinted at, would never be said to her now either: that she had brought this on. It wasn't about how Declan wanted to emigrate, and her so against it, not knowing. It was the stupid belief she had, and in her addled state couldn't possibly have thought it out. She had shown them Declan's letter from the tin. She remembered one of the two detectives, the man, asking for the loan of a spade.

She'd sat with the woman, Marie, who turned out to be a sergeant, looking out the kitchen window, as a small mound grew bigger. Marie smiling, reaching out to pat her hand when she'd keep coming back to it: there was no other tin, just the one. The next day there had been a half-dozen men out digging. Still, even then as they dug up every square inch, she kept on thinking all the while that somehow, this would help.

Weeks later, that Superintendent sitting across from her in the kitchen, asking her again; almost accusing her. What did they think? There was nothing she could say that'd persuade them. You can never prove you didn't, she had realized. And in a smaller way, it would be the same with even her own. They wanted it behind them, to just move on. Proof of that, she supposed, was that her mother hadn't been asking her why she wanted to go out and apply for a job now. Maybe she understood now, the need to change in Eimear, to reach toward a new start.

She wondered again about the name. Surely to God they'd know now that she wasn't trying to disown them or anything, or that she wasn't gone cracked. It was the name she'd used when she was a little girl, for heaven's sake – they'd remember that, at least. Symbolic, that was the proper word: that's what she'd say.

The baby's giggles drew her out of her brooding. Róisín had a way with little ones and that was obvious: a real gift. Here she was now, with the baby and him laughing nearly, sputtering away.

She smiled and held her arms out. For a moment it felt as if she were holding them out to the fields and woods, the hills and sky.

"Here she is, your mammy," cooed Róisín. "It's your mammy. Isn't she gorgeous, isn't she?"

He was gurgling with excitement, she saw. Róisín's teeth gleamed as she laughed herself, and she brought him in a slow swing to her arms.

"Here's your mammy, Liam."

Chapter 15

MALONE TOOK A CALL on his mobile at around four. Soon after, he gave the caller a howiya, he began to look Minogue's way. He pointed to the phone with his other hand and lifted his eyebrows. Soon, his eyes glazed over.

Minogue had been ready for some time to bale out of the interviews with Catherine Condon. Some of it was beyond depressing. Her regrets, her anger coursed through it all.

"Thanks," Malone said to his caller. "Listen. I'm sorry I said that about your sister. No hard feelings."

The occasional flicker at the edges of Malone's mouth didn't survive to become anything close to what Minogue could call a smile.

Malone closed the phone, flipped open his notepad and scribbled a name, a number.

"Joe Sinnott," he said. "Immigration Bureau."

"Well, I didn't see any Sinnott in the case files," Minogue said. "Did I?"

Malone looked over with a half-hearted scowl.

"Well, do I really need to say it?"

"If it makes you feel better."

"Okay then," said Malone. "Someone should have bloody well talked to Joe Sinnott earlier, shouldn't they?"

"If they were serious about finding this woman at all, you're telling me."

"Well, duh," Malone said. He studied the name he had written for a few moments.

"Anyway. It looks like we're going to get fierce holy out of all this anyway."

"Father Coughlin? Is he back in the picture?"

"Sister Foran. You know her? She's a nun, like."

Minogue shook his head.

"I thought all of yous country people knew every priest or nun from one end of the kip to another. She runs an outfit called Settlement House."

Minogue searched his foggy mind again, found something.

"She was on the telly – no, the radio, a while ago?"

"She does work with aliens and that. Immigrants, those people."

Minogue had never figured out why the civil service had ever aped the American lingo so many years ago when the Aliens Office had been set up

"Joe says she's the business," said Malone. "And he got us in there too. She says come over. She doesn't do phone interviews with Guards. How do you like that?"

"Don't mess with nuns, Tommy. That's all I know."

♣ ♣ ♣

It was Malone who found the small sign, the size of a business card, taped to the inside of a window on Pearse Street.

They had driven by in both directions, twice, without spotting numbers or names. Malone was working through his second layer of bad language by the time Minogue parked. They would walk this part of never-ending Pearse Street, starting at Grand Canal Street.

"You would think the fu–"

Then Malone spotted the small, grimy window by the electrical wholesalers.

He hit a buzzer by a dented grille that covered a speaker.

"Translate that thing, will you," Malone muttered.

"Why don't you know your native language?"

"Amnesia. I never thought much of a language being beat into me."

"All right. Teach Chúram."

"Say it again?"

"Pronounce it Chock. Chock Coor-om."

"What's it mean?"

"It means Dublin people are wicked ignorant."

"Give over, will you."

"House of Care. House of taking care, I suppose."

Malone stuck his nose to the window and tried to look in. Then he stood back and looked up at the windows above.

"Teacher's pet," he murmured. "That's how you know that Irish stuff."

"*Mallacht ort, a claidhaire*," said Minogue.[3]

"Yeah, yeah. Look up there. Smile"

It wasn't the box for an alarm system that Minogue's eye first assumed.

As Minogue eyed the closed-circuit camera, the speaker poured out a crackly woman's voice. It was propelled by a strong country accent. It sounded like an invitation to dispute something, but also to be ready to get steamrolled trying.

Malone announced they were Guards.

"Joe Sinnott?"

"A friend of his," said Malone. The door release buzzed after several moments.

There was a smell of soup, and some kind of vegetable. It grew stronger the moment they opened the second door. Cauliflower, Minogue realized, and it drew him back to childhood, and a Sunday dinner.

Awaiting them was a woman who was taller than Minogue. Her steel-grey hair was cropped short. Her waistcoat and purple gansey underneath called up wise woman/whole health/vegetarian/tree lover/feminist to Minogue. Sure enough, there were sandals and slacks. He almost missed the small silver crucifix near her throat.

Malone seemed to be paralyzed.

---

[3] A curse on you, you fool.

"What," the woman said. "Have you never seen someone tall before?"

Minogue was first to shake hands. Bony, he registered, and with bumps where they shouldn't be. He put Sister Imelda Foran at over sixty. Arthritic; regal. A bit of a witch into the bargain.

"Come in, sit down," she said.

They passed a kitchen that also had two battered sofas and tourist posters with writing Minogue couldn't figure out. Sister Foran's office was tiny but organized enough for three chairs. Minogue caught a glimpse of a screen saver with mention of God at the bottom of sea views and foresty scenes. He only managed a glance at the spines of some of the books. Merton, he saw, an Elaine Pagels book. And Germaine Greer?

"So ye're not in the same line as Joe," she began. Minogue hadn't missed her grimace as she sat.

"No, Sister."

"No Sistering if you don't mind. Imelda."

"Grand," said Malone. "Yes. I mean no."

Imelda Foran leaned over the desk and fixed Malone with a stare.

"Are you all right there?"

"Tommy, Sis – Tommy Malone. Yes. I am. Thanks very much."

Minogue couldn't remember seeing Tommy Malone like this.

"I'm Matt Minogue."

He held out his card but she looked away.

"Tell me, then, are ye going to be investigating the poor man who tried to immigrate the other day? The man in the plane?"

Minogue doubted she was being sarcastic. It dawned on him that some of Malone's unease had worked its way into him too.

"We're trying to locate a woman, Sister."

"Imelda. Yes, Joe told me. But he didn't tell me much. Joe's good fun you know, but he's still a Guard. Plays his cards right close to his chest."

"A busy man," said Minogue.

"As are we all. Why do you want to locate her?"

Minogue made a fair effort to return her gaze. He decided she must have been a principal. He recalled from childhood one of these severe faces, boxed in with the huge nun's hat like some mad, white bird of prey.

"She may be able to assist us in our investigations."

At this, Sister Imelda raised an eyebrow and then sat back.

"And if she can do so, or after she has done so, what would happen to her?"

"I don't follow," said Minogue.

"You're here to see me as a last resort. If I am to help you, if she is to help you, then you'd be able to see her status here. Whether she has a permit and that. What if she were here without that?"

"I don't think that concerns us, er . . ."

"Well, it concerns me."

And there it was, Minogue saw. This lioness had flexed.

"If she needs protection, we're here to help her."

"Protection, fine. Do you mean condoms, is it?"

Minogue sat back then.

"Don't be upset," said Sister Imelda. "You'll appreciate the world I work in. The niceties don't often apply."

Minogue saw that she was fingering her chain now. He couldn't remember what the books on body language said about that, but there was probably zero about how she stopped at the crucifix and held it.

"You'll excuse me so," she said. "But I'm expecting some people."

"Look, Sister. I can't break the laws of the land here."

"What land is that? Brussels, is it? I respect the law now – Mike–"

"Matt."

"But there are human needs that cry out for justice."

"Break the law to uphold the law, is it?"

She didn't answer but looked over at Malone instead.

"Do I know you?"

Malone nodded.

"Aren't you . . . ? Wait a minute, it couldn't be."

Malone didn't look up when he spoke.

"It was my brother," he said.

"Sister Imelda," said Minogue after a mouthful of tea, "you should have been a Guard."

"My father was, God rest him. No, I got the vocation. Little did I know then it'd get me into such trouble."

She looked up from the drawer of her desk.

"I was a right blackguard growing up," she said. "I don't mind telling you."

"Fond memories," said Minogue.

"Well, I'll tell you one thing: it made me well able to hold me own in the dealings I've been in. Sure my God, the nuns were nothing like this when I joined up."

"How did ye manage to terrify half the country, so?"

She made a small, conciliatory smile.

"Well, you might have something there. All I know is this: God is everywhere – just like we used to believe before. . . . Well, I supposed I'd better be delicate here."

"Before the Roman . . . ?"

She winked back at him. He offered his own smile now.

"It's the men," he said. "We're great for handing out orders, I suppose."

"You're a blackguard yourself," she said. "You should come and work for us."

She pulled open a drawer and drew out three manila file folders.

"These are my only chances," she said. Minogue didn't get a chance to ask her what that meant. There was a knock on the door and it opened.

"Come in, Charity, come in."

The lustrous eyes against the dark skin were not as striking to Minogue as the teeth that appeared when the arrival smiled.

"I am sorry, Imelda."

"Don't be sorry. They're only Guards. Harmless, they are. I hope. Charity Nkeme, meet Mike and Terry."

"Matt."

"Tommy."

"That's right," said Sister Imelda. She took another envelope from her drawer.

"Charity is from Botswana. And her sister is with us.
Patience."

Sister Imelda looked up.

"God, I love saying those names of yours, Charity. It puts
me in a right good frame of mind."

The women enjoyed this greatly. Do all Africans, black
Africans, laugh this way Minogue wondered, and he replayed
Charity Nkeme's pronunciations again. Ee Meldah. Soh-rree.

"Missionary nuns to Ireland," said Sister Imelda as the
other closed the door behind her. "Just in the nick of time in this
godless island, I'm thinking some days."

Her eyes blazed with a sudden zeal.

"Those two women, those sisters – they'll save Ireland.
Mark my words. And what sweet justice that'll be. Maybe this
poor man up in Malahide will save us too."

Minogue remembered the shrine on the street there, from
the television news.

"Now, these are my files," she went on. "They stay with
me. So before I answer any of your questions I want your word
that you'll do no harm to any girl, any woman, who might appear
out of this."

"Harm, sister?"

"I'm going to give you back something you fired at me a
minute ago: Don't break my law to keep your law. Do we understand one another, Mick?"

Minogue nodded.

"Okay, first the bad news. 'Marina' doesn't mean much. It's
like 'Paddy,' the way they'd use it in England."

"Not her name?"

"You can find that out yourselves. If she is trying to avoid
deportation, if she is Russian or Ukrainian or Bulgarian or
Moldovan or Byelorussian or Romanian or – you pick: it's all
'Russian' here. That's the first injury to these beautiful girls.
Their names, their pasts, are all disregarded. They become a

'Marina' or 'Natasha' when they go into that world where they
are injured each and every day. Injured in ways that should haunt
you. Do you think it can't happen in Ireland, our Island of Saints
and Scholars?"

"Well, a man told me not long ago that Ireland's not an
island at all."

"Right!" said Sister Imelda. "Good! Was it a priest said
that?"

"A cop. Sorry."

"Well, I don't know what that means to you, but I'll tell you
what it means to us here. We build bridges. Do you know what I
mean?"

Minogue didn't want to voice his weary contempt of clichés
like this. They came out of every face on television these days.
They were always a bit behind in the religion department, and
then they thrashed things to death. Everyone was special now; it
was all about sharing and validating, feeling comfortable, in the
church stuff that Kathleen Minogue brought out from Mass to
leave for her pagan husband to read. He hadn't found a way to tell
her that this only stoked his aversion.

"That's my vow: to help the Holy Family, however they
appear. They were refugees, you know."

"Flea to Iijit, I thought they said when I was small," said
Minogue. "The way you learn words, you know?"

"No harm," said Sister Imelda. "Look. I spent a few years in
a sister house in California years ago, trying to get over arthritis.
I came back from there on fire. What I saw there. The money. The
hate. And now we could end up like that here if we close our
hearts, if we burn our bridges. So that's my vow – did you ever
play hurling? Do you know what camogie is?"

"I have a fierce interest in hurling," said Minogue. "As it
relates to County Clare. But I have a sister played a lot of camogie."

"Well, now. It's all gone to hockey now, the girls. At any
rate, I brought my old camogie stick out to Tiburon with me. For
luck. But do you see it up on the wall behind me?"

"Hard to miss," said Malone.

"Ah, you woke up there. It's here on account of our work and a second vow."

She looked over at Malone, now pretending to be checking something in his notebook. He looked up finally.

"I made a vow that I'd use my camogie stick to beat the living hell out of any man – anyone, I should say – who would cause hurt to the Holy Families, everywhere. Dublin, Wicklow, Tiburon, Seattle. Wherever I live. So, have we an understanding, Mike?"

"Have you had to use it yet?"

She gave him a cool appraisal. Another warrior, Minogue thought, and smiled, more at Malone's discomfort than at this happy scrapper disguised as a nun.

"Here's one," Sister Imelda began. "It's her real name. She came here on a one-year permit and got work at a hotel. Marina – she's twenty-two now. She's from the Ukraine – no, Moldova. Sorry, I haven't got them completely sorted in my head yet. She lived then – before the nightmare started for her, I mean – at a flat on Dorset Street."

Minogue glanced over at Malone.

"How does she come to be here," he said, then. "In your files, like?"

She looked at the two men as though they had landed from a spacecraft.

"Did Garda Sinnott not tell you what we do here? Why we do it?"

Minogue could guess. In a few seconds, she had become a different person. Was it being police, he wondered, or merely men.

"Well, I'll tell you. I'll keep it as succinct as I can."

Chapter 16

MINOGUE SAT IN beside Malone and pulled the car door closed. There was little energy left in him. He looked down Pearse Street toward Ringsend, and he imagined going straight out beyond the chimneys there, out to Poolbeg. There he'd park at the beginning of the South Bull, and he'd start out along the pier of quarried stones that cut through the estuary waters and led out into the middle of Dublin Bay. He'd take his sweet time walking out to the lighthouse there, his only task to move his feet, and to let the rolling seawater, and the Wicklow Mountains across the bay to the south, put his head to rights.

He heard Malone turn the pages of his notebook. He guessed Malone had been shaken too. A bus passed and let him see again the bridge over the canal quay in the distance, the gentle rise in the road that then led down to Ringsend and the bay.

"Jesus," Malone said. "I thought I'd heard everything."

Minogue said nothing. He still didn't open his own notebook, but let his gaze rest on the street. His mind wasn't going to just surrender this escape. It took him by the beaches at Shellybanks and up the side of the power station to the beginning of the Bull Wall. Bligh, that tyrant and navigation genius, had mapped Dublin Bay in preparation for this Wall, he'd read some time back. This was the self-same Bligh that had later locked up Michael Dwyer, the Wicklow Rebel, in Australia.

"I thought that sort of thing only happened in, well, I don't know where, in actual fact," Malone murmured. "Eastern Europe maybe."

Minogue kept fighting to hold onto his piece of fallen Eden out over the water. Surrounded by water except for the line of the pier back, he could sit and study Howth and the Wicklow hills across the bay.

"I wonder," said Malone, and this broke the spell on Minogue. "I wonder if people know about this."

He was looking over at Minogue.

"Or if they're doing anything about it? Us Guards, I mean."

Minogue didn't want to talk about it. It would lead him to absorb some of the pain and fear he imagined in those lives.

"If that's what this woman is caught up in . . ."

Minogue opened his notebook. He looked over at Malone's. Seven names, three of them actual Marinas; four that could be leads.

"Even if she has nothing on Condon . . ."

Again Malone's words tapered off.

"We'll do our best to find her, Tommy. It's about her for now, I'm thinking."

"If Condon really was with a girl like this, well, like . . . ?"

Like this, Minogue heard repeated in his head. As if they were interchangeable, just as Sister Imelda had said. He looked at the names he had underlined, the four of the seven that had made contact with the Teach Chúram, but had not been heard from again.

"I must be a complete iijit," said Malone. "Not to have known this. Maybe I couldn't imagine it in Ireland. Jaysus, I'm in the game long enough. I mean, I've been around. But this? How could somebody Irish do this? Make money out of this? I mean it's one thing to be gouging people in their pay in some factory or meatpackers, but then to be in on this blackmail thing? I mean that's – well you know what that is."

"Slavery, I'd have to say," Minogue said. "Is there another word for it?"

"Look, I'm going to phone Sinnott and see who takes this stuff on."

Minogue half listened while Malone talked with, and half argued with, Sinnott. He watched Malone scribble and tried to decipher the writing. Malone wrote some words carefully, and eyed Minogue after, tapping on the page with his Biro. Temple, Bar, Bistro Seven Oh. Sweeney Meat Packers, Clonmel. The Grange Hotel, a Hotel Aisling. Another hotel, The Strand.

When the call was over Malone made a few changes to what he had written. Then he shook his head.

"Well?"

"Everything from cleaners to waitresses," Malone said. "'Modelling.' I mean what girl would fall for the 'modelling' bit?"

Anyone desperate enough: Minogue didn't say it aloud. He thought of Moser and his maps, the little arrows swooping in with a little peal of bells, colours and lines that shone and moved on the screen.

"There are places you can go, says Sinnott. Massages that turn into other events, for a price. There's apartments in Dublin they move around people in. There's escorts. The most of it is done by phone. You get a name, you phone him. The next week it is a different name, a new number, but the same story. You can add in whatever you like, Sinnott hears. If you like gambling; if you want cocaine. Even fencing stuff goes on."

Minogue eyed his list.

"The girls get threatened," said Malone. "They use their families back home on them. There's these 'fees' they're made to pay. And then the places they get the permits for, they'll hold back pay. If one of them complains, the employer can pull the rug out from under their feet with immigration. Ident – what's that word, like slaves? Sister Imelda said it."

"Indentured?"

"That's it."

Malone took a deep breath and let his notebook close. At the mention of Sister Imelda's name, a small glow started in Minogue.

"She certainly had the measure of you," he said to Malone. "Did she frighten you?"

Malone looked over with a serious expression.

"Easy for you," he said. "She's a culchie, like you. Yous have your own thing."

"There was more than that to it. She stared at you plenty of times. I saw it. What did she have on you?"

"Nothing on me," Malone said. "But she used to do prison visits. To the men, if you don't mind. She might have met Terry. That's what was going through my head."

Minogue waited. Malone's eyes had slipped away down the street now. Minogue tried to remember what physical feature distinguished Malone from his twin brother, Terry. Was it the hair? Or some scar on his thumb?

"She's only half a nun," said Malone. "Or something, according to the story."

"What story, now."

"On account of she gave someone a hiding a while ago. A priest, was the story, but, er, off-duty. She gave him a semi-serious dig in the snot, is what I remember."

Malone shook himself then and turned the ignition. Minogue was storing away the yarn, imagining the glee that his telling it to Iseult would bring her.

"George," he said. "He'd be the one, more than ever. Right?"

Minogue remembered Sister Imelda talking about how a woman who had told her of a man here, her "driver" she had called him, who could speak Serbo-Croatian.

"Where to start," Malone murmured. Minogue looked at his watch

"Cup of tea and a bun."

"Well, I know a great place and all," said Malone. "Yes I do."

"Not McDonald's. No way."

"Temple Bar," said Malone. "Let's try some of those places Sinnott mentioned, those bistro-type places. You'd be up on that, monsieur. All that dainty French stuff."

Minogue took up his customary sentry duty, watching for traffic that Malone didn't care about, and had too often ignored, in the Malone School of Motoring.

"It's pronounced Muh sieuh. Okay?"

"Have it your way," said Malone. "If it's that important to you."

Temple Bar had been the old new Dublin for a good while now. It had been a decade and more since the dreary boarded-up buildings, the cramped lanes and the mean little doorways that did nothing but collected decades of soot and dirt, had had their deliverance. In Minogue's mind, he took the area to be a way to measure how long it had been since the Celtic Tiger had announced the end of the Sinai years of the Irish search for prosperity itself.

The only legit parking Malone finally found was all the way up by Christchurch. Minogue didn't complain. It was a chance to walk, to take in the doings, on their walk back down toward the Temple Bar, time to figure out a sensible way to go about their search there.

The two policemen then began to thread their way through the late-afternoon groups that were beginning to gather by the traffic lights and the bus stops. They crossed Dame Street and headed down the lane toward the back of the Clarence Hotel, where Temple Bar really began.

Malone remembered Iseult's old studio. He asked Minogue if she was there now.

"No. She's gone out of that one. Since Christmas."

"One step ahead of the shapers, no doubt."

"Shapers" was a few years stale, Minogue knew. He was sure Malone knew too, even more so, but he dimly understood Malone's reluctance to give up this one. It covered so much here in Dublin now, and it fitted Iseult's situation. Like a guerrilla ceding positions bit by bit in a door-to-door running fight, Iseult had fought to keep some toehold here for years. Her best hope would be to parley with the winning side in this battle between Art and Commerce, and sell them her art. But then she'd be one of them, she had protested, making Celtic-pattern dinner plates up in the Kilkenny Design shop.

"What?" Malone asked.

"What, what?"

"You said something. Harry Veest?"

"*Arriviste*? Did I say it out loud?"

"Yeah, you said it. You're talking to yourself again. What is it anyway, French?"

"It's French, yes."

"French for what?"

"French for a certain class of person."

"I don't believe you."

They paused at a restaurant Minogue didn't remember seeing before.

"Do we have a system here?"

"No," said Malone. "I'll go in this one."

Minogue watched him through the window, talking to a man with violent red tinker hair behind a counter. With the first head shake, Minogue turned away. He studied the parked cars and the few that drifted in from the quays, cars who'd have to make do with lots of tight reverses and delivering vans half blocking the street ahead. It was a pedestrian-only zone just around the corner.

"No," said Malone. "No waitresses, dishwashers or the like. Let's head on toward that bistro place. Oh Seven?"

Minogue considered dodging into the Clarence Hotel and checking staff there. A huge headache, with shifts and the like. If they let him look the records over without paper to back it up, that is.

They stopped at a bollard that marked the beginning of the pedestrian area.

"This is not what you'd call police science, is it," he said to Malone.

"Just for an hour or two," said Malone. "Just to see. Okay?"

Mostly the people in the restaurants and pubs were helpful enough. Only one – an annoyed, flustered man trying to juggle a delivery and a broken tap – wanted to see a warrant. Malone told him it was only on the television they used warrants.

Four Englishmen gave them minor grief in one pub. They were at the start of a pub crawl, Minogue believed, more mischievous than aggressive for the moment. They were eerily similar to one another, with the regulation sunglasses stuck on their cropped and gelled hair, and the open shirts with the tails out. One with bleached hair and a ringed nose must have overheard part of his conversation with a barman. "Do you have detectives here in Ireland?" he asked Minogue on the way by.

Minogue took in the cluster of glasses on the table, and the brazen, reddening eyes. It was considerable work to squelch his reflexive distaste at the man's accent, and the beefy face of The Ancient Enemy here amongst them again

"Hello," he said. "You're enjoying your visit, I hope."

"We're here for some craic," said another.

"Oh you'll get plenty of craic," said Minogue. "You're in the right place for that."

"You're looking for a baddie, are you then, officer?"

It was the bleached one again. Cheeky from birth maybe.

"In a manner of speaking, yes."

"Well, no-one here's like that, are we lads?"

"Not yet we're not," said another. Laughter followed.

The urge to mischief came to Minogue quickly, along with his annoyance.

"Maybe you might know this person though?"

"Sure! Glad to be of assistance! Go ahead. Officer."

"We're looking for two actually. They may be travelling together. I think they're from your part of the world, maybe?"

"Only too happy to oblige. Aren't we, lads?"

"Great. One is Jane Austen. Travels with another woman, let me think. Charlotte Brontë. They're getting on in years now – you'd notice them right away."

Minogue saw that only one of them had doubts right away. It looked like the barman, a young fella, had twigged though.

"Can't say as I do," the bleached one said. "How about it, lads?"

Minogue nodded at the one who was giving him a serious look now.

"I think he might know them," he said. "They went missing from the Penguin Library a while back."

He gave one of his cards to the barman. Malone was by the window outside now.

"Maria?" said the barman. "Marina?"

"Something like that. And there might be the big fella, the man. Goes under the name of George – an accent. A right big fella."

The barman nodded. Minogue considered using Malone's line about George speaking with a Transylvanian accent. Instead he thanked the barman and headed for the street.

"See you around then, Shamus. Pip-pip, right?"

Minogue stopped and turned to the group.

"Shamus? Are you referring to me?"

Most of them had their faces well under control, but one gave way. The bleached one was not fazed. Minogue gave him a hard look.

Malone had come in now and he was holding the door.

"Can't take a joke? Dish it out but can't take it, right?"

Roigh, Minogue repeated within. He continued to study the face. Puffy, designer stubble, bad eyes. Malone had read the situation, and had come over now.

"This would be a grand opportunity for you to say nothing further," he said.

"It's a free country, isn't it?"

Innit, Minogue heard, and he didn't resist the surge of anger. It must be in the genes, all those centuries: just the accent set him on edge, instantly.

"It's a chance you shouldn't pass up now, Nigel."

"Who are you?" the bleached man asked Malone.

"I'm Bono," Malone said. "Who are you? And what's your problem exactly?"

"Are you an officer of the law too, then?"

Minogue saw with some satisfaction that the smiles had faded. Malone held up his photocard. Bleached man made a thing about comparing it with the live specimen.

"Doesn't look like you though."

"Seems to me you're under the influence there," Malone said. "If you can't see something in front of your nose."

"Are you going home in the near future?" Minogue asked. "Back to the motherland?"

"Since when do I need to answer any of your questions?"

"Since you fit the description of an alien. Have you registered yourself as a resident?"

"Don't be ridiculous. I'm here with me mates, for a couple of days. We're here for the craic, like I said. See, I know what craic is?"

"United fan, are you?" Malone asked.

"As a matter of fact, I am."

"Curry and chips? Watch the telly, point a bittah? Oi, oi. Right?"

"What are you getting at?"

"I'm going to give you the benefit of the doubt," said Minogue. "And assume you have a return ticket to Great Britain."

He looked around at the group.

"Safe home now."

He eyed the barman.

"If Nigel here and his mates call for a Black and Tan, phone me. All right?"

"Still fighting the War of Independence," Malone said outside. "Are you?"

A little ashamed now, Minogue resisted mentioning his granduncle who'd been shot, or some ancient Connole relations, from his mother's side, who'd been transported in 1848.

"Better go with you from now on," Malone said. "If you're going to be like that."

Chapter 17

April 16, 1987

EIMEAR KELLY HAD the painters in for a fortnight before she actually put the house up for sale. They made a fuss over Liam, and it was lovely to see. The boss, or foreman, Danny, wasn't fifty yet himself, but he already had grandchildren of his own. He let Liam watch them, and finally got a few words out of him. The very next day, he'd persuaded Liam to pick up a brush. The others followed suit, even the young fella who seemed to be hungover every day.

It was Danny, the chain-smoking, grizzle-headed Dubliner who always appeared in a boiler suit, it was he who persuaded her that her future was Dublin. He'd never know, she thought. What won her over was his bluntness: Missus, this house is new. You don't need to paint anything. You'd be wasting your money.

It was also the friendliness that evaporated all of the Dublin sarcasm she had grown inured to since she had started here. She'd never say that to Danny, of course, that he'd convinced her. He probably hadn't an iota of a clue what effect he'd had on her. And he had never once let on that he might know her circumstances, being as there was no man about the house. The nearest he got was a polite question about Declan's picture in the hall, as he was taking it down. My husband, was all she told him. She left it under the stairs afterwards.

On the last day of the job, Danny brought a cake. He also brought a present for Liam, a lorry that had things in it. They sat in the kitchen, the two of them, with Liam having a late snooze in his playpen, while the other workmen gathered stuff they'd stored in the garage and upstairs.

"A grand house," said Danny. "It'll go like a flash."

Around the house came the sounds of whistling, plastic sheets being put away or crushed, tins being hit.

"Where'll you go then?"

"I'm not sure," she said.

"You can leave Liam with me. I'll put him on the team."

As if hearing those words, Liam stirred in the playpen, groaned, and then went back to sleep.

"I'll paint the new place for you. How about that?"

She told him she'd take him up on it if only she knew where she'd be. He smiled and poured more tea.

"Your fella's not telling you, is it?"

She looked down toward where he had nodded, said nothing. The engagement ring: she had forgotten. His voice dropped when he spoke again.

"I know what happened," he said.

She heard him sipping at his tea, and it reminded her of growing up, with her father in from the fields or the barn or the milking, mad for a cup of tea.

"Sorry if I'm butting in, now."

"It's all right," she said. "You've a good eye for things that men don't notice."

He gave her a pirate's wink, and he sat back.

"Engagement rings are nothing to me," he said. "I'm nearly allergic to them at this stage. Sure, I have three daughters."

The sounds from the hall and the clumping upstairs had died down now.

"I hope you don't mind me saying that now."

She shook her head.

"A person has to keep going, don't they?"

"They do," she agreed.

"A nephew of mine, a terrible thing, a few years back. He was knocked down and killed by a car. His wife, sure she'll never be over it. I says to her a while ago, 'Helen,' I says. 'Helen, will you pay no heed to them what'd be telling you what you can or can't do. Find a fella, get married.' And tell them I sent you."

"How did that go over?"

He sucked in his breath, and shook his head once.

"Oh I got a fair raking over the coals for that one. But I didn't care. That's the way I am, I speak my mind. And didn't she do it? A grand fella, very quiet and good living – but like I said, she'll never be over Gerry, the first one. The thing is, she doesn't have to get over anything. She figured it out, you see? You can't get over anything. You only carry things. Am I right?"

She nodded.

"It's asking too much, I'm telling you. But now, sure, Helen she has company and someone to carry her over the bad parts. So it gets easier. Things fall into place."

He suddenly scratched the back of his head and gave a little snort.

"Declare to God, her new husband's quiet and decent, but he's a quick worker. They have two youngsters – already."

A frown descended on his face then, taking away the smile. He blinked and looked away. He thinks he has said too much, Eimear believed.

"Well, I'm lucky," he said. "Sheila tells me to mind me own business. She's right. Sometimes, only."

She finished her own tea and watched Liam squirm and grimace as he began to surface from his sleep. His hair had come in even fairer than she'd expected.

She was aware that Danny was looking at her again. She looked back into his quizzical, half-smiling face.

"Watch for the quiet ones," he said. "Like Helen's one. I'm telling you."

"Oh he's far from quiet," she said. "He's loud and he's big."

"A Guard?"

She nodded.

That seemed to change something. Danny was soon up, putting the cups and saucers by the sink.

"Well good luck to you now, Eimear."

"Thanks," she said. "It won't be Eimear long."

He smiled warily.

"I'm going to go with my middle name from now on. I actually prefer it."

"Well good luck in the new job," he said. "Before I forget."

"Thanks," she said. It was one of the few things she'd noticed, and it still disturbed her a bit since coming off the sedatives. Sometimes she wasn't sure if she had told someone something, or only thought she might tell them.

"Personnel, right? People? That's great. That's the future, no doubt – if this bloody country ever gets off its hind legs and there's jobs to be had. What are we now, nineteen and eighty-five? Sure the Common Market thing, that's been ten or fifteen years now. Another cod, I say. I just hope my ones don't end up taking the boat too."

He called her Eimear again as they shook hands but she said nothing. One by one the other three shook hands with her. There was something solemn and too respectful in it, she reflected later. Danny must have told them of her troubles.

Liam was fierce cranky waking up. Maybe the fumes from the paints or wallpaper were getting to him. She changed him and cut up some banana and gave him warm milk in his Duck mug. Still he was clingy and hot. She looked at his gums again. She carried him around to show him the furniture back in the place and pictures hung, and then upstairs to look out the windows to see the birds in the shrubs opposite. Auntie Róisín would be coming for tea, she told him.

Below, in the driveway, was her car. The house was hers. The Guards union, the Representative Body, had pushed her case to the forefront, and the widows' pension would be getting an increment before the end of the year. Falling into place, that was the expression Danny the painter had used. But of course, not without help. So much she owed them: Róisín and her mother – her father, even, in spite of his quietly sly hints that she should move on, and away from this disgrace that Declan had gotten them into. Declan's family, yes, Breda . . . for all her crying.

But still she felt that peculiar weight on her, and that sense something was always following her around. Well, the psychiatrist wasn't going to be the one to put names on things for her – she'd found that out quick enough – but had coaxed, or goaded, her into thinking out loud, and trying to say things. Maybe it was all the what-could-have-beens following her around, or her own remorse at not giving Declan the chance to leave. Anger, of course, that Declan had bottled it all up, like men do, and then let it build up until that day. Shift work, the baby, she had decided, when she'd noticed his moods and sleeplessness.

She couldn't sit here and fall into brooding. She got up from the chair, hefted Liam on her hip again. He laid his cheek on her shoulder. She heard a little rasp somewhere in his breathing. She began to hum to him, and he tried to join her. Together they walked and swayed around the kitchen, out into the hall, and back.

She had her wits about her from early on, it had to be said. Was it just some survival thing, a new mother's instincts taking over? No, she had decided, and she had grown proud of how she had managed it all – them all – her mother and father, Róisín and Breda, the Guards, everyone – as they had swarmed around her in those first few terrible weeks. No, not a swarm: it was more like being in the middle of a stampede. Even in that half-waking, half-dreaming state the damned medication had left her, she had come through, kept herself in one piece.

Still, the hard part now was that she wanted to tell someone, just one person, what she wanted in the future, where she wanted to go. The only trouble was, she didn't have the words. Something had been stolen from her, left unfinished. There was a huge hole. It wasn't revenge she wanted, no.

"Wook!" said Liam, suddenly lifting his head.

There was Theresa Murphy working in her garden opposite.

"Do you want to go out in the garden?"

He began to buck in her arms, and then lay down on her shoulder again.

"Soon," she said. "When you're really awake, right?"

She resumed her walk, through the sitting room, into the dining room, and back into the hall, listening to Liam's gurgled words. Theresa was going goodo with planting some shrubs, she saw, when they came back to the kitchen window.

The road was already taking on more of a lived-in look, after just two years. It would be so easy to just stay. She was house proud, with all her flowers and shrubs, and she was not afraid to admit it. For all his talk about dirty Dublin, her new husband would fit in here just grand. So what if anyone wondered at her remarrying only a couple of years after Declan.

He was old-fashioned, and it was good enough for her. For all his big talk, he was a softie. He had that protective attitude, wanting to look after her. It was sweet, and sincere. He was dependable. Yes, a Guard, but he was very ambitious. It was only an odd time she wondered if he'd become like these other ones, the ones who'd talked to her about Declan. Would he ever lose that boyish sweetness, the longer he'd be in the job, or the higher he'd rise up the ranks of the Gardai?

She recalled the Guards who had talked to her about Declan, their vague, condescending answers and their looks that said damaged goods, all the while coming up with their hypocritical words of sympathy. Surely in some part of them, one of them even, they'd know that Declan's last tortured months had been down to them as much as that bastard Rynn. They couldn't have protected him from Rynn and his people. They probably would have pushed Declan back in, to play him to Rynn so they could use him too.

The fact was, they'd looked at her as an accomplice: it was as simple and as brutal as that. They didn't believe her, any more than they'd have believed Declan. And Declan had known that too, all too well: that's why he was backed into a corner. The last straw had to have been the humming and hawing when the issue of the widow's pension came up. She was certain right from the start that they weren't above using it as leverage. When she'd finally gotten it settled – and then only through some influence and pleading through a local councillor friend of her mother's – she had been as much as told that from then on, the best she could expect from them was to be forgotten about.

Liam was restless. His cheeks were rosy still, but she could-n't be sure it wasn't from lying on her shoulder. She tried to look at his gums again, but this time he wouldn't have any of it. She didn't push it. She'd humour him a bit longer.

She walked from room to room upstairs, listened to him saying things. Then he grew quiet again, and held her shoulder, reaching out sometimes to touch the mobile that circled over the bed. She stood by the window awhile. Theresa had two big shrubs in. Digging away, like a farmer. The back gardens were dotted with sheds now, and vegetable patches. There were swings and balls and bikes all over. Soon the trees and bushes would hide the walls. Here, on this road, with a good number of couples their age, was the future she and Liam had planned. Maybe assumed, was the better word.

The woman from the estate agent had told her she'd get what she paid but the market was flat. If she did a proper paint job – not just the original stuff – and showed up the kitchen more, it'd sell quicker anyway.

She looked across the rooftops in the direction of the city, and she wondered what it'd be like when she was full-time at the new job. What would it be like in the mornings, having to leave the baby at a minders, would he cry his eyes out? Would she, and would she be worrying all day? And would they let her go early some days, or give her time, if Liam got sick?

Maybe she should wait. But they were expecting her, her mother said. It was her mother had contacted a man from home who knew the owner, and it was the owner alone, Michael, who had interviewed her. The typing and filing was all she'd expected, just like in the civil service. Michael said he'd hoped she'd try more, when she was ready. A nice enough man, but the phrase told her that he'd give her a start based on sympathy and pull from her family, that he wasn't expecting much.

At least her mother and father had moved more her way, she recognized. They'd realized she wouldn't be swayed by their appeals to move home or at least out of Dublin, where this awful thing had happened. Well, she wasn't going to just get up and move. She'd show them what she was able to do, all of them.

Mitchell Personnel, her own family too. Most of all, she'd show those Guards at the meetings she'd had to go to, with their dull eyes and their sparing, barren words.

Chapter 18

PECKISH NOW, AND FRUSTRATED by this clumsy, half-arsed, door-to-door effort they were doing, Minogue was still managing to bite back his complaints. He followed Malone into a place called the Orient Express. He sort of remembered Iseult saying it was good, but dear.

The woman adding up something on a pad of paper looked like someone famous, but he couldn't remember who. A very skinny waiter was walking between the tables, fixing napkins or something. Minogue saw from his backward reading of the sign pasted to the window that it had only just opened for the day.

He kept his card ready but let Malone do the talking. The woman had a country accent that she hadn't troubled much to tame for the cosmopolitan Dubliners she now fed and profited from. Handsomely too, Minogue was certain, and he turned the last page of the menu to see if the wine, even, wasn't priced as extraterrestrially as the food. It was worse than he had expected. He closed it.

"We do go through an employment agency," she said.

The "do go" counted for a lot with Clareman-in-exile Minogue. This was all the more so, he knew, because his recall of the English Lagerlout Touring Team episode was still circling in his mind.

"It's hard to get people," she said. "For the jobs in the back especially."

"Marina, we believe," said Malone. The woman seemed to consider it, but then shook her head.

She might have been seen with a fella," Minogue said then. "A great big lad. Foreign accent but has the English no bother."

She made a vague smile and looked up and out the window into the now greying afternoon sky over Dublin and then shook her head.

"There's a wojous lot of foreign accents now," she said.

"Wojus . . . ?" asked Malone.

"A hell of a lot," said Minogue. "That is to say. An expression from God's country."

Who had she now working in the kitchen, Malone asked. She laughed.

"My sister's two young ones, up from Bandon. It's only for a month and then I'll have to find someone. Go to an agency, I suppose. But that's the way things are nowadays."

Minogue waited for Malone to try his last-chancers. It went on more than he expected when Malone got sidetracked into talking about woks. He watched the passersby, and cast an eye up. That light was deceptive, he was beginning to think. There could well be rain before the day was out.

He was ready to jack it in now. They should work out a way to get proper manpower from Tynan to canvass the place properly, not this hit and miss.

He left a card on the glass beside her pad, and thanked her. Iseult, he thought of then, a future treat here?

"When's your busy time here?"

"We open at five. It's go go go from about the half-five mark, I'd have to say. Until eleven, sometimes midnight."

That was just when night-owl artist and dangerous welder Iseult Minogue, almost a single mother now, would be getting started.

A teenager passed the windows, and the light caught the glint of a chain around his neck.

"This man that might be with her sometimes," Minogue said. "He likes his rings and things. Not that hip-hop hobo going by now, but a chain. Big lad."

"Yeah," said Malone. "Like Tom Jones, but without the wrinkles."

She made to smile and stopped. She looked out again.

"You know now, there was a man . . ."

Minogue waited. She turned to catch his eye.

"A big man, but a black shirt – not a polo. Had a nice chain, I remember eyeing it and thinking I'd like one. Had big hairy arms, with a big watch. Rings too, yes."

"An accent maybe?"

"Well now. I remember he laughed."

"Who was he with?"

She frowned and shook her head slowly.

"This is a while back," she said.

"A long while, was it?"

He saw her draw a breath before replying.

"I don't remember. Sorry."

The tight, business smile she offered now said goodbye, and be quick about it, thank you very much.

"Maybe someone else on your staff might?"

"Hardly," she said.

"But you remember something . . ."

"Look, I'll tell you something," she said. "I don't do scratch-your-back for anyone, even the Guards."

"Do you mean, especially Guards?" Minogue asked.

She started gathering menus. Minogue waited.

"It concerns a matter relating to people being mistreated," Minogue said. "Particularly girls, women, we think, from over that way."

She was about to say something but decided not to.

"We're real Guards," said Malone, "we're not iijits, you know."

"Are you not, now. What happened with your face, do you mind me asking?"

"He had a contretemps with an alien, we think," said Minogue. "He's one of the people we're looking for."

"An alien."

"That's their official name here. Russian, Turkish – we don't know."

She looked toward Malone again.

"Here's what I'll do. I'll keep your number here and maybe I can phone you if this man comes by here."

Minogue gave her a few moments.

"This whole place has come a long way, hasn't it," he said. She looked up from the card. Minogue was sure she was holding back something now.

"Not just this lovely place, the food and all," he went on. "Not even the whole Temple Bar thing – not even Dublin, actually."

"What are you getting at?"

"I meant how a citizen can say that to a Guard, she might help. If it suits her."

Her eyes lost any warmth.

"We do criminal investigations, did you know that? Real policemen, yes."

"Are you trying to insinuate something?"

"Know what Moldova is?"

"It's a place, I think."

"You're right. It's a country that doesn't have much of anything like we have here now. It has lots of misery though, and crime, and girls who are desperate and gullible and vulnerable and probably not half as educated as to the wider world now as we are."

Again she looked over at Malone.

"He does this every now and then," said Malone. "Gets fired up, like. Thing is he means it."

"So we have aliens amongst us," said Minogue. "Do you know where this is going?"

Her face changed.

"I want to tell you something," she said. "Come here. Only you – leave Scarface over there. You're senior, I take it?"

Minogue followed her to the back of the restaurant. She sat and placed her hands flat on the tablecloth there.

"You don't know the half of what goes on here."

"What, in your restaurant? Tell me, so."

She stared at him.

"Okay," Minogue said after a count of five. "Okay. I'll back off."

She spoke in a low voice, her eyes on the door.

"After I tell you, I want you to do something. Ready?"

Minogue nodded.

"I want you to keep this to yourself, what I tell you. More than that, I want you and your mate to leave."

"Tell me why."

"I have a business to run. I can't control who my customers are. I just make great meals, offer the best service I can, and I can't think about the rest of it."

"Taxes . . . ? I hope you're not one of them–"

"–Don't even think about it. I do everything by the book. Check it out. I'm a model for it."

"Are you paying to keep your windows in?"

A look crossed her face.

"I mean protection money," he said.

Three women came in and she waved at them.

"I've got to go. You do too."

"You didn't answer my question."

"Listen. This is what I want you to know. Do you know names in Dublin, like the other side from you?"

"Criminals?"

"Yes. You know the Rynns?"

"Heard of them, yes."

"Good. He came in here one night a while back with another man. It was a man like you're describing."

Minogue squinted at her.

"He's old, and he didn't touch much of what the other one ordered. The big one, he knew his food here. He had an accent. He wasn't showy or loud or anything."

"When?"

"I don't remember, I told you."

"More than a month? Less than a month?"

She shook her head.

"A month then, say," she said and she stood. "You need to go now."

Minogue watched and marvelled and later tried in vain to describe to Malone as they walked slowly down the lane, how her face changed into the perfect maître d' – or was it madame d'? – as she went to the table where the three women had chosen.

"Rynn," said Malone. "The old maestro himself. He's a right, rotten, conniving old bastard. A long, long time, he's been on the job. I could never figure that out about him, you know? Bulletproof, or something. Walking the streets still."

They stopped outside another restaurant. Minogue held up his hand against the glass to see in. The place was half full already.

"But Rynn's ancient," Malone said. "And I don't see him eating goat or whatever she has on the menu."

It was decision time, Minogue knew: jack it in for the day, and go home, or . . . Malone was reading minds.

"Come on," he said to Minogue. "I'll buy you a burger and we'll come back here in an hour. There'll be more staff in, the busy time . . . ?"

"A burger."

"What's wrong with a burger?"

"Have you ever actually eaten at one of these places, Tommy?"

Malone shook his head.

"I had a kebab and something once."

"But you prefer a burger."

"I'll buy it for you. Jesus, you'd think I was trying to propose to you."

"Fries," said Minogue. "That's all I want for now."

They went under the Central Bank and crossed Dame Street. The rush hour was started in earnest. He followed Malone along Andrew Street, watched how he took in everything. The faces that passed included two black women, laughing and carrying books. An Asian man of middle years was taking a call in the doorway next to a sports shop. One head-scarfed young woman, again with a schoolbag and an intent expression. A drunken pensioner was weaving about at the foot of Grafton Street where the traffic was locked in place indefinitely.

McDonald's was mad entirely. Minogue decided he wouldn't let on he was enjoying this. He was quick enough to nab two stools near the door, and hold them. He looked out at the river of people passing, hoped for a familiar face.

Malone delivered a Big Mac and a steamy smell of grease along with the fries.

"I know better than to even ask if you want coffee here, at least."

Minogue didn't mind the fries. He'd keep that to himself though. He certainly didn't want to watch Malone wolfing down his burger. He wondered what Kathleen would have for her tea at home; if what's-his-name at her work had given her a lift. He kept his eyes on the crowds outside.

Malone found pieces of a newspaper. Minogue looked over.

"Your man, they found his family," Malone said.

Minogue tried to read sideways but Malone turned the paper for him. The man who'd fallen to earth, the African Miracle, was from Chad. Some organization was saying they'd pay for his widow and kids to come and live in Ireland.

"What language do they speak–" was as far as Malone got before Minogue's mobile went off.

Chapter 19

September 6, 1993

S HE'D NEVER FORGET THIS YEAR. Too much happened. There was no reason, no logic in the wide world, as to why it should also be the hardest since the time after Declan's death. The hardest part wasn't that it was unfair, or undeserved, or even cruel. It was because it was so unexpected.

For weeks, she'd felt the signs. The old, cold dread had been leaking back into her, more each day. Things had started to lose their colour and often there was a foreign look to them too.

She'd fought back: she'd had no choice. Work was busy, busier each passing day, but that was supposed to be good. As if by some kind of weird magic, changing the name of "Personnel" to "Human Resources" seemed to result in a steady growth in the business. Even by the summer, people were saying that things seemed to be taking off in Ireland, but could it last? How little they'd known then.

That was the beginning of the crazy hours that descended on the office. Almost overnight, she found herself running an office with five recruiters, standing in a hurricane of paper, and calls, and interviews, and requests, and meetings, and travel that roared through the office. The agency started dealing with work permits coming in from the continent. It wasn't just the odd student working behind a bar in Dublin anymore – it was factories and hotels looking for staff. Soon there were people with accents showing up in the agency, almost all of them armed with their work permits, laboriously learned but hesitant English, and keen for work. In only a few weeks, it seemed in retrospect, her agency had become a place for a half-dozen employers to find cleaners, assemblers, and hotel staff.

She kept her eye on the home situation. It was the one thing she knew would be her undoing if things got worse. Liam got extra attention. She left the office early on many days. Jim noticed the changes in her, and he guessed why. His gentle side came out when they were together. Steady, a bit too watchful, but caring. Still, when she saw him in action with the other Guards, at a social especially, she wondered if he was the same man at all.

She had to put it down mostly to the anniversary, the ten-year mark for Declan. It was almost eight since she had remarried. She was glad that she had decided to drop the Eimear. The married name had been no big deal, but she had wondered if she should have stuck with her maiden name instead. Lots of people had done that.

Herlighy, the psychiatrist, wouldn't say right or wrong to it, of course. And when she got in touch with him again, he was the same as he had been a decade before. A bit stouter, a bit greyer, she could see, but it was as if the ten years had passed in a day. He told her after the first session this time that she'd been right to try a bit of therapy instead of asking for a prescription.

It was the summer then, and she had been going twice a week to see Herlighy. He talked to her about refocusing on her goals. Goals? At first she wanted to laugh, but it wasn't funny. This she tried, and it made a bit of sense. He brought in the lack of success with the fertility treatment, and how her husband was taking it. She'd spent much of that winter and spring attending courses on management and human resources.

Of course she knew her husband was proud of her. He was also relieved that she was coming out of something he didn't understand, but had begun to make him worry more and more. She loved him more for his puzzlement, not in a passionate way, but because he couldn't help showing her he needed her. The baby thing didn't really matter, he kept on telling her. She did not believe him, but she believed that he wanted to persuade her so that she'd get well again, and that seemed to have been a signal she allowed to get though. She began to surface again.

She found herself becoming more the foil for his bluster and high spirits when they had people over, or when they were out. As though to reward her for her trials, she made a friend whom she grew to like more and more. It was odd because she was the wife of another Guard, and she was from Dublin too. Yes, Kathleen was a Dubliner, and she was funny and tough, and well able to kick up her heels at a do. Her husband Maura didn't understand, and while she was leery of him, liked his company and the dry wit that came out every now and then. Jim said that he swore at Matt Minogue as much as swore by him.

They had been told earlier in the year that the fertility treatment should be stopped – wait: *discontinued*. Jim took it well, she thought, but one night she discovered he had been crying. Liam it would be then, it looked like.

She had new energy then, a restlessness that bordered on agitation. If she hadn't had Herlighy to tell her that she was okay, she might have gotten stuck there. But within a week she had quit Mitchell, and opened up her own agency and told Jim that it was time to move up. Up where, was his reply, caught between bafflement and suspicion. A different house, different area: didn't he feel the way things were going in Dublin now, all the money flooding in, the factories going up like mad, the dozens of calls she was getting each and every day, for staff?

And, of course, that was the year of the House Fiasco, what started the other thing. The house she wanted, she saw on a drive out by Foxrock. She knew it right away. She also predicted Jim digging in his heels when he found out the price. She bided her time, and she'd driven by on her own a half-dozen times during the week to see it. The place didn't sell. The owner was in no hurry. He had jumped the gun on what he thought the house would get, if things continued in Ireland the way there were. She found out that he was going to take it off the market. All this she told Jim, and then a plan to go to the man and offer him something a bit below the price.

Well. That was the worst row since their marriage. Liam

had heard some of it too. She told her husband he was a stick-in-the-mud, a pessimist, for expecting things in Ireland to collapse again. That he had no real ambition, because he didn't see outside his bloody job. That he had a typical civil servant mentality.

There was a truce after a few days. The best they could come up with was, give it a year and see then. The auctioneer's sign was gone that same week. She continued to show Jim how house prices were going in the newspaper. He stuck to his guns and got fierce stubborn, something he was all together too good at, and insisted to her that they had an agreement to wait one year. She tried to tell him that waiting a year in this market was way too long.

She did not tell him that she had driven back to the house in Foxrock and knocked on the door. The owner of the house seemed surprised but she saw in him his belief that he had the edge, and was going to keep it. The price he told her was a quarter as much again as what it had been listed for. She wasn't sure if she had hidden her shock, or her anger. She thanked him, said she'd consider it.

That was a lie, but it was important to keep her cool. The truth was that she'd already considered it: they simply didn't have that kind of money – yet. They would, she felt certain, as soon as her own agency was up and running, but that wouldn't wash right now. She also understood that and she had made a decision that had nothing to do with the house in Foxrock, or the seller, but with her husband and her own hopes. It would never happen again that she would be thwarted like this. This house was lost, and even if she could have bought it over her husband's grumbling, it had been poisoned really. In fact, the mention of the place even would remind her of this time, and she couldn't see herself ever living there now. Well, Foxrock wasn't the only tony area. Killiney was up there too, and that is where she'd begin her search.

Still, it bothered her all that week, and for a long time afterwards. She snapped at everyone. Catherine, the new girl, actually cried. Maura took her aside and apologized, and meant it. Everyone was getting as stressed out as they were buoyant with the new money, she realized. Everybody sneaked that Celtic Tiger expression into conversation. She made or tried to make a joke with Catherine about being mauled by this tiger they were talking about.

It turned out that Catherine felt overstretched. That wasn't right, Maura told her, and she'd fix that right away. She went with Catherine through her files and, over Catherine's protests, began plucking some out. It almost became a joke, but still she kept the files. The atmosphere in the office eased. Every day of that first week back that New Year she brought in cake and wine and even Chinese food one day.

The files stayed in her desk drawer all week, unopened. On a Friday afternoon – and Maura remembered the time to the minute, the sight of the bus on the street below pouring out people – Catherine came by with a worried look.

It was a client, and he was annoyed. In fact he was a bit scary. He wanted to know what was keeping the agency from returning his call. He wouldn't be called back, no: he wanted the boss right now. Who was he, she asked Catherine, and Catherine bit her lip and nodded toward the drawer where she'd dropped the files she'd taken from her that day.

Much later, she'd remember everything so clearly: the oh-oh, the grin for Catherine's sake, the Hold button flashing. A bit of bad language, so watch out, was Catherine's almost apologetic warning when she shushed her out.

She took up the receiver and turned the same hand to let her little finger prod the Hold button. She decided in those few instants that this would be her first client she would tell to go to hell. Big contract, little contract, hectic or not, no-one would speak to her staff like that.

She gave her name and straightaway asked his. He didn't give it. Instead he told her it was about bloody time. And furthermore, what exactly were they doing that he had to wait all this time? Was this normal?

She cut him short and asked him his name again. She moved in closer to the desk, her free hand ready to swoop on the button that'd cut this fella off.

The name is on the bloody file, he told her. Didn't the other girl tell her? As though he sensed she was about to drop the call, he told her: Victory Meat Packers. Didn't they send in the papers a fortnight before Christmas? It was more a raw Dublin accent than the tone, more sarcastic than hostile. They'd been crying out for meat cutters for months, and they were still waiting for word.

She'd give him a chance. She heard him say something about Yugoslavia. Didn't he know there was some kind of war going on there, she wanted to say, but his humour had improved. She asked for a minute to get the file and he didn't have any rude comment.

Victory Meat Packers was near the top. She flicked through the correspondence. They wanted general labourers. "General labourers," not packers or meat cutters? They had already taken several people on one-year permits from Eastern Europe – that must have been what he meant by the Yugoslavia remark.

She looked down for contact names and then she stopped. Next to her fingernail was the name Rynn.

She had difficulty lifting her arm. Whatever it was that passed through her then felt like it had run to the top of her head, like an electric shock. She had to remember to breathe, and breathe again, and from somewhere she knew she had to try to breathe slower and deeper if she was going to be able to do anything. Her eyes did not want to go to the phone and its dumbly flashing light, but it seemed to be even more the centre of her thoughts now.

She lifted the receiver off the desk and pushed the Hold button. He asked if everything in the agency took so long as this. Had she gone out for her dinner and forgotten him or something?

She asked whom she was speaking to. She had to repeat it. Was the name too hard to read, was his answer. Four letters, rhymes with "win"? And that's how the company was called Victory, did she get it? After a few seconds his voice bore in on here again: Hello? Was she after falling asleep or something? Anybody home? Like, was she still there?

♣ ♣ ♣

She deliberated for a week. It gave her time to try to find out more on Victory, and what she could get from Jim.

"Rynn?" he said to her when she'd brought it up first.

He'd given her that look, that trademark Guard look, delivered sideways. She wondered if he had picked up on her turmoil. She had waited for a dinner out to ask him.

"Rynn is an out-and-out gangster. A long-standing low-life Dublin gangster."

"Really?"

"He certainly damned well is. Why were you asking about him?"

"His name showed up somewhere."

"Somewhere?"

"On a request for people at work."

"You're joking me," he said. "At your place? Looking for staff?"

"Not for himself, exactly. A company of his – so far as I can make out."

"'Who's going to win? / Jimmy effin' Rynn!' Ever hear that one?"

She hadn't. He sat back and looked around the restaurant. It had only opened last year but he liked it. She didn't mind that she couldn't crowbar him away from the meat and two veg. Her appetite hadn't come back, and she wondered how much she could eat of the chicken she'd ordered.

Jim hadn't seemed to notice her picking at her food more.

"Well I'll tell you," he said. "This Rynn is the second smartest crook in Ireland. The smartest one is not in Ireland. He's in jail in Holland and will be for another eight years. Guess who got him put in there?"

"Rynn?"

"Well done, girl of my heart. That is correct. But that doesn't make Rynn the smartest. Are you wondering why?"

She poured him more wine. The waiter came by again, and Jim had some comment for him. It was preparatory to a joke, she soon learned. She mostly enjoyed the banter that he inflicted on everyone who came in range, even this running joke about mad cow that the waiter was obliging enough to listen to. Liam, though, Liam got very embarrassed about it. At his age, of course, it was all about embarrassment, wasn't it, and crabbiness. If he was like this when he hit eighteen, she'd have to think twice about the plan to tell him about his real father.

The waiter actually enjoyed the joke.

"So that's what you do if a fish won't oblige," Jim said, and the waiter laughed again.

She realized she hadn't been listening.

"Grand lad," Jim said and put down the glass. "I could eat that every day of the week. 'To hell with poverty, we'll kill a hen.' Matt does say that when he gets a bit of wind in his sails. In a session, you know the way it is. Ha ha."

She smiled and searched for a way to get him back on the topic of Rynn.

"There's smart and there's smarter, I suppose."

"What, the waiter?"

"No, this gangster."

"Rynn? Well he is definitely a breed apart, so he is. It's common knowledge he got people over there to set up the other lad. I'll say that for him. Rynn's a thinker."

He leaned in again, and he placed his finger along the side of his nose.

"Tell you the truth it's only lately we copped on to just how far he's gone. That journalist one, what's her name – Guerin – she's great at digging up stuff. God, she's annoying, but she gets her stuff."

"What stuff?"

He squinted at her. Then he spoke in a whisper.

"He has companies, tax scams, drugs – anything you can think of, he has it. He has people on the continent – not just the usual bunch in Amsterdam, oh no, that wouldn't be good enough for him – but personal connections with big lads there. I even heard Russian, can you imagine that? What year was it that that Berlin Wall – four, five years?"

"Four," she said.

"Well I do listen, as you well know. Oh yes. Now I shouldn't be passing this around because, well for one thing, we're only beginning to see how big this thing is. Rynn, he's way ahead of us. Oh yes, it's a fright to God in actual fact, how far ahead. I heard that the IRA – even the IRA – has gone to him for stuff they couldn't do themselves. How about that?"

"I never imagined."

"To be sure! Keep what I tell you under your hat. I mean it. If this were known . . ."

"Now it's not as bad as maybe I'm painting it but, by Jesus, it was a big freak entirely last year. It started with a fella found in somewhere . . . Germany, I think, yes . . . with shall we say, acute and terminal lead poisoning. They traced a phone number to an associate of Rynn's. So it's not like Rynn can be looking forward to a free run much longer. All the accountants and barristers he has up his jumper aren't going to help him dodge what's coming his way."

She tried eating, smaller morsels now, but swallowing wasn't getting any easier.

"Task force job one is going to be Rynn," he said and winked. "It'll go big, I hear. He won't know what hit him."

"Not many would be knowing about it though," she said.

"You're right there. Oh yes, but you know me. I hear everything. I am an actual Hoover for information. God, yes. The thing is, we found a Judas. Do you get it?"

"Judas?"

"Ah come on – an informant. Everyone has a Judas. We found Rynn's, and he's going to do the business. Any day now, you-know-who's going to show up on the front page in his nice new boiler suit and his State bracelets."

She had to think what the slang meant. It must be handcuffs.

"Victory something, did you call this outfit?" he asked.

"Yes."

"And was it himself who you dealt with?"

"One of the girls did, but I go over them all. She didn't know."

"Of course she wouldn't. God, how cocky can you get,

phoning up like that. No doubt he'd be keen to call himself a businessman. Classic, isn't it, this Dublin crowd? So bloody cheeky about it."

She watched her husband's scorn ebb.

"'Victory,'" he said after a while. "I get it. He's bloody obsessed about beating the law. Spends a fortune on the legal side. Well, it's worked for him so far. But we'll see about that shortly – oh, wait, I remember now: a young lad of his was shot to death a good number of years back. Maybe that did it. Maybe that made him get smart."

Then he sat back and began to chortle softly, waving his knife and fork around. It was a habit that annoyed the heart and soul out of her still. She took it to be a relic of growing up far from the delicacies of proper dining.

"I have me own one for the same Rynn," he said.

"What do you mean, your own one?"

"Hah. I doubt I'll ever get to say it to him. But somebody should."

"Somebody should what?"

Mischief glittered in his eye as he whispered over the food between them.

"It's only a matter of weeks. That's exactly the words! Oh I'd give my eye teeth to see his face. Never happen of course. That'd be giving things away."

He sat erect again and looked around the restaurant. She hoped he wouldn't make some comment about how much of the price of their meal was going on the flowers and the fancy fittings.

"My advice to you is put that bloody file through the shredder. Get one of yours to tell him you don't offer the services. Make up something. You wouldn't have him on the books for long anyway. A matter of weeks, oh yes – I like that, if I say so myself."

She waited. He set down his knife and fork.

"What you're on about, this 'matter of weeks' thing."

He dropped his head and nodded to get her in close to his, almost touching the flowers.

There was a hard set to his eyes now.

"This Rynn's not the only one that can play with his words. Not by a long shot. The fella we have, the Judas that's going to put Rynn in the big house for twenty years? His name happens to be Weekes. We nailed him just a while back, on armed robbery and he went over right away. Oh yes. Do you get it? His name . . .? Only a matter of Weekes . . . ?"

Chapter 20

MALONE RAN ON AHEAD. He said nothing to Minogue before he began his run, but merely caught Minogue's eye before he took off, and flicked his head in the general direction of the Temple Bar.

Minogue half trotted and half walked through the crowds on the footpaths, and tried to keep Malone in sight. He lost track of the weaving-and-darting detective, rounded the post office in Andrew Street, and slipped between the waiting cars at the lights below.

He squeezed the mobile, trying to think what he should do with it. He skipped down the hill to Dame Street, more on the roadway than on the footpath, and he ran across toward the Bank of Ireland, straining to gain the broad footpath there before traffic roared down on him. One car horn he got, but mercifully, none of the kamikaze motorbikes that Dublin bred to rocket out suddenly from traffic lights.

He slowed to walk, felt the tics in his legs, and tried not to think of an overworked heart. He glared back at a man staring openly and a little condescendingly, he decided, at this flustered, panting countryman. Malone was already gone under the Central Bank building. He checked his watch and marvelled: literally three minutes since the woman from the Orient Express had called him, and Malone wasn't more than a minute away.

He took the steps three at a time, impressing and alarming

himself. The smooth granite looked greasy, as if it could sweat up
the decades of drizzle and smog that had been its companions
since being blasted, torn and hammered from the Wicklow
Mountains.

Down the narrow street he managed a brief trot again. His
sliding belt and the shirt tail straining to be free didn't bother him
now. There were more people eyeing menus by the doors of the
restaurants, and clusters of people, men mostly, stood near the
doors of the pubs. Still, the streets had not taken on that real
evening feel.

In sight of the Orient Express now, he saw no sign of
Malone. He tucked in his shirt just before he got to the window
and tugged his belt up. The lights were on at the front of the
restaurant and an elderly couple with a continental look to them
were looking in. The woman was smiling at some newly seated
people but she saw Minogue immediately. He waited by the
window, tried to catch his breath, and marvelled a little at how
her expression could change so quickly between her customers
and him.

She was pointing. Around the corner? Malone was stepping
out of a pub and scanning the street. He jogged over, drawing
looks and several passersby to stop and move aside. Minogue was
glad to hear him panting and taking deep breaths. Malone reached
for the door but Minogue tapped his shoulder.

"Leave her, Tommy. She's scared enough."

"Get out of it!" Malone snapped. "Forget 'scared.' We're
after a bad guy."

Minogue grabbed his arm then.

"Leave her. There's other stuff going on. She'll never help if
we barge in now."

"Who's running this circus here? Us or the monkeys?"

"Try up the street, come on."

Malone waited long enough to send a slow burning glare
through the glass.

"One out, one in," Minogue said to him. "Same as before?"

He watched Malone's heaving chest while he looked up and
down the street.

"Okay. Let me start, I'll go in here again."

Minogue found a spot against the wall of a pub, and he began a slow survey of the passing faces. She'd said the man was alone, that he'd paused by the window, looked in, and walked on. He'd been carrying a motorbike helmet.

Some men came out of the pub and gathered in a final group of four on the street. It was the English crowds they had bumped into earlier. They were only getting started on their soiree, by the look of things. Minogue looked away. He left it to the last moment before turning back to cover this end of the street again. They weren't moving. There was a lot of laughing, cigarette lighting, throwing comments across to one another and shifting their feet around. He tried looking by them, over their heads, looking at the faces of the people passing between them.

The wag from earlier had seen him now, he knew, and he was nudging his friend next to him. Another glanced at Minogue for a moment, and then let a spitball drop with slow deliberation to the pavement. The men's faces turned toward Minogue. There were more words. One of them buckled with laughter.

Malone appeared from the side door of the pub.

"We'll go this one," he said to Minogue, nodding toward the next pub a half-dozen doors up.

"Wait, Tommy. I'm calling it in. It's just too hard here for the pair of us."

"You're not serious."

"Look, I want him as much as you do. I just think we're going to lose him here."

"Don't be worrying," Malone said and set his mouth in a grim line. "I'll find him. Him and me have to have a little chat. Come on."

Minogue held up his mobile, but Malone was off. He called out after him, held up the mobile again, but Malone waved it off.

This is what keeps you from Sergeant, Minogue felt like shouting after him. This is what'll have you in the dock yourself for doing a number on this George character, if you ever catch up to him. If he doesn't hammer the crap out of you again.

Malone paused by the group of men and said something to

them. The wag had some fast answer for him. It had an immediate effect on his friends. They fell away laughing. Minogue knew what was coming now by the way Malone changed his stance and faced the man.

Minogue saw Malone's arm come up and his finger settle inches from the man's face. He heard something about intoxicated. Some of the passersby moved away, others slowed to watch. He called out Malone's name again, saw the tilt of his colleague's head that meant trouble for sure. Four of them, he thought, and they've been drinking. Were there no uniform patrols here? What happened to all the promises and crackdowns after the stag-party knifings there a few years back?

He looked for the fluorescent green-and-white figures of any foot patrols, none. It was Malone's voice he heard say something about a night in the tank, and then an English accent in protest, something like *wotivoidanthen*. Another voice said *chasing oilyins then?* Aliens, he meant, Minogue realized. Then he heard Malone pull obstruction, disturbance, and arrest out of the bag. Things were getting out of hand.

Two of the men stepped in next to the wag, and began arguing. The wag seemed happy enough with how things were going now. Something in the vacant smile and the folded arms told Minogue that this fella was more than the designated clown of the group. He'd gotten his way. Maybe he was a soldier on leave?

He stepped around the wag and told the others to shut up. He made a quick sweep of his card.

"Calm down the lot of you!"

To which he was told, almost in harmony, by at least two of them: you tell him to calm down.

"Wait for your mate over there," Minogue tried. "We'll talk to him."

One of the men, he couldn't tell which, invited him to talk to his arse. Minogue glanced down at the keypad as he dialed, and he tried to ignore the voices that had risen around him again. The wag was getting straight about his rights and discrimination, bloody *roy-cizm*. Racism? Irish people against English? Wasn't it the other way around?

Minogue thumbed Send, and he eyed the gathering lines of watchers again while he waited for a connection. Still no uniforms. He looked over his shoulder toward the Merchant's Arch that framed the Ha'penny Bridge over the Liffey behind. Nothing: nothing except some girls, an old man and a man in a leather jacket. His eye lingered a moment on the man, and saw him shift something he was carrying as he descended the steps toward the quays. A white helmet?

"Tommy," he called out over the others, and pointed at the figure now bobbing down the first few steps.

Malone took a step to his side and then, with one more hesitant step while he craned his neck, he broke into a sprint. The men all shouted at once and turned to watch him. The figure in the arch turned at the noise and for a moment watched Malone running his way.

"What the hell's wrong with that copper?"

It was the wag, and he seemed almost disappointed.

Bloody lunatic, Minogue heard from another, and then effin' head case. He closed the phone and started out after Malone, but one of the foursome stepped into his path.

"Bad idea, Nigel," he said. "Get out of the way!"

"What the hell's this? Are you real cops? Candid bloody Camera, right?"

Minogue reached out, but the man danced aside and again blocked his way. Enough, Minogue decided: this one at least was going to get the treatment, in spades.

"You're under arrest for–"

He stopped as he saw Malone careen to a stop and slam his back against the wall.

"What," he heard the taunt, but ignored the sneering face on the man in a half-crouch waltzing around ahead of him. "You want to do something, do you? Come on."

Something happened on the wall above Malone – dust – and Minogue heard a crack high up behind him. He turned to look and saw a spot in the hand-painted sign for the pub.

The man with the helmet had come back up the steps. He'd stopped a couple of steps from the top, and was pointing in

Malone's direction. Malone crouched and half rose again, his head bobbing and weaving like a boxer.

Someone in the small crowd called out the word "shooting," and several broke away. Minogue shouted out Malone's name again.

The four yobs had scattered, but beside him the wag had scuttled over in one crablike move.

"Someone's bloody shooting!"

There was boozy breath in the air around him.

"I know shooting, so I do!"

Minogue saw a small flash now from the end of the man's arm. Shouting started behind, and Minogue heard shoes scratching for a grip, footsteps running.

"I didn't mean no 'arm," said the man beside him, blinking hard. "It was just a bit of a laugh, wasn't it?"

Malone was backing away now, his hands guiding him along the wall. The man with the helmet turned, but then came around again for what looked like another shot.

"My grandmother was Irish," the man said. "I didn't mean no 'arm, right?"

The man lifted his helmet and pushed it over his head in one movement, and then skipped down the steps. Malone ran backwards in a crouch, his hands touching the laneway. The bobbing helmet had disappeared over the edge of the top step now.

Minogue pushed Redial, and waved Malone over.

There was a look on Malone's face that Minogue hadn't seen before. Malone's eyes darted from the archway back to Minogue as he spoke into the phone. Minogue reached out and grabbed his shoulder. Malone's tongue seemed to go like a snake's, side to side, so fast over his lips.

"No 'arm, mate," the wag kept repeating to Malone now. "No 'arm?"

"I think he has a motorbike parked down on the quays," Minogue said. He repeated the location, spelled his name, said yes, it was Inspector.

"And he'll be long gone down the same quays in no time, on a motorbike."

He gave his mobile number again. He was told to leave the connection open.

Malone's face was white. Minogue saw that his hands were shaking.

Malone seemed to want to say something. The Englishman's beery breath was all around them now. He was reaching out to try to shake Malone's hands. Over the talk and the odd shout Minogue heard a siren.

He knows what he's about, he thought. He'd be through traffic like a flash and he could go anywhere with a motorbike. He left his hand on Malone's shoulder, watched the darting eyes and wondered if Malone might vomit or something.

"Look," he heard several people in the crowd say. Suddenly there was a siren close by.

In a few moments he saw the flashing blue from a second squad car on the walls, and he pressed his mobile to his ear harder. He wondered, but didn't care, if Malone might erupt on this half-drunken iijit now trying to shake his hand.

"I been under fire mate, I know what it's like, okay? Irish Guards, you know? The Queen Mum's boys? No 'arm, okay? Really. I'm Garry, mate. Okay? No 'arm?"

Malone let his hand be shaken, but kept his eye on the Arch. Minogue was finally driven to turn on the drunken yob turned maudlin conciliator, Mr. Nigel Englishman.

"Will you just give over there?"

Minogue wasn't much pleased to be taken seriously at last.

"Just go," he said to the outstretched hand, and watched as the man made off sideways, still trying to keep up eye contact while he kept mouthing something that could have been remorse.

The sets of running footsteps were winded detectives with their guns drawn. Over the siren Minogue still heard muffled yells, even yelps, from people nearby. In moments, a fainter siren joined the first. It remained out of sync, but grew stronger as it was funnelled up to them through the arch from the quays. Two older women were making their way up the steps there now. He heard Malone take a deep breath and exhale.

"That was close enough, Tommy."

Malone nodded but didn't take his eyes off the two women who had now stopped.

"Why is crap like this always happening to me," he whispered, hoarsely.

Slowly, Minogue stood upright. The crowd, began to reform, and seemed to be getting bigger fast. Mouths were dropping open, and Minogue guessed by some expressions on others' faces that they were skeptical. Blue light from the roof lights pulsed on the metal and glass of the shops opposite; an engine was racing in high gear, tires shrieking.

He waved one of the detectives over. Someone spoke to him from the Emergency switch, a different man's voice. He asked if there were personnel at the scene now. It took Minogue a moment to figure out what personnel meant again. He'd been thinking of how shock might take hold of Malone, of what 'no 'arm' that gobshite had been going on about.

Two more Guards appeared, running up the steps from the quays, and Minogue watched the women almost fall to the wall. The bastard is long gone, he decided.

The voice on the phone asked again if the Guards had arrived.

"They have," Minogue said.

Could he hang up now but continue to make the line free? He could, he told him. He stepped over to Malone. The first detective over had two orange-red spots high on his cheeks from his exertions running here. Minogue wanted to tell him to put the gun away.

"George?" the detective repeated. "That's the name?"

Some uniforms had arrived now. Minogue's chest felt achy and full of something swollen, and chill. This was the time your brain catches up a bit with what happened, he knew. Malone too seemed suddenly exhausted, and he stood now with his head down, answering the detective in small nods and shrugs. Once he turned his head, bruise toward the detective, and shook his head to a question.

"A motorbike," the detective next to Minogue muttered. "He'll cover plenty of ground on that."

Minogue let his eye contact last a few moments. The detective got the hint. He had to rip the Velcro back twice after settling the pistol, to place it snuggly in the shoulder pouch. The detective said something to another, who turned away and spoke into a walkie talkie.

"Let's go over to the car," he said to Minogue. "You and your mate. Malone, is it? Get some details?"

Minogue ignored, as did Malone, the four men now turning their way as they passed. Again he heard the "no 'arm mate." Malone snapped his head up and turned and took a quick step toward them. The uniformed Guard brought up his notebook to stop Malone. Minogue didn't hear what Malone said between his gritted teeth, but at least two of the words started with an F.

Chapter 21

September 11, 1993

R YNN'S BUSINESS, Victory Meat Packers, was nothing to do with meat processing, Maura Kilmartin found out. It wasn't a nothing, it was a shell, a tax hole probably. She'd asked Róisín to see if there was anyone she knew in the Revenue Commissioners who could do a little digging for her. Róisín said she'd look into it. By the way she said it, Maura believed she would prefer not to, and she was glad she hadn't mentioned who she'd wanted to find out about. It didn't come up again.

When she phoned the number for Rynn, a woman answered. Was this Victory Meats? Who wanted to know, was the answer. Maura asked if this was the right number for a Mister Rynn. In the few seconds' delay before the woman answered, Maura heard a hand rubbing over the mouthpiece at the far end, and the woman shouting out "Da."

"He says, who are you?"

"An employment agency, Mr. Rynn contacted us."

She heard a man's voice in the background, and then a cough.

"He'll be with you in a minute," the woman said, and held her hand over the mouthpiece again.

Her own need to take a breath made Maura gasp. How long had she been holding her breath, and not even noticed? She tried to breathe steadily, slowly.

She looked at the bank statement again, and remembered

272

the tone in the meeting with the branch manager, the one about the loan to re-do the offices she had rented. It was the nerve of him, just assuming he could talk to her like that, more than anything else. He accepted that it was a good location, but wondered if she was not a little over-optimistic in her business plan. The banks never changed. It had been bad luck that Jim had asked her casually whatever had happened to that house out in Foxrock anyway, and she had ended up shouting at him.

He had been shaken by her outburst. He'd muttered something about not being "nobs" or "Foxrock types," or "keeping up with the Joneses" before withdrawing. Later, conciliatory and tender as he was in bed, he tried to ease things. If she could win the lottery, ha ha, or if she could get money out of the agency. But everything in the agency still got ploughed back–

She jumped when the voice came on.

"Yes? Are you that agency crowd?"

"Mr. Rynn, you were looking for people to work for your company, and we kept you waiting a bit by mistake. General labourers, was it?"

"That's right."

"How many openings?"

"I'm only starting up, amn't I? And if I can't get me workers, how can I get started?"

"Did you say four or five, was it?"

"That'd be a start."

"A start?"

"What's this, question time? I don't know exactly. I can't predict exactly how many. You don't know the business, do you? Obviously. All I know right now is there's no-one wants to work at that that's born here. That's why I'm talking to you. Right?"

"But you could save yourself money, if it's only four or five people. You could find them yourself, maybe?"

"Says who? There's nobody wants to do it. And them foreign ones are good workers, aren't they?"

"Seasonal work, is it?"

"Yeah. That's a good way to look at it. Look: say a friend of mine, say he gets an order of beef for some place – Saudi Arabia or something. I'm not joking, that's what's going on now, did you know that? Did you?"

She said that she didn't.

"Well, that's not going to last forever, is it? So he doesn't know how many months, or how many people exactly. I'm just trying to help a mate out here. He's fierce busy, you know? Things is really taking off. He says he'll have to build a new place and all. Right?"

"Well, I'm not sure we're the right people here."

"What are you talking about, 'not sure'? There's people telling me they already have to go outside the country to get people. I mean, I'm hearing there's places like yours, they'll get people in from Yugoslavia and that, if that's what the factories want."

"We don't do much of that, and it's only skilled trades really."

"Well, don't you think you should? I'm telling you. It's going to be big here, like it is already on the continent. Nobody's full-time hiring anymore. You pick up the phone, a fella says 'how many?' And out they come, to your factory or your green-houses or whatever – in a van, they're for the day, or the week, whatever – and they're gone. No problem, right? Building sites even, the foreman is short so he only wants lads for a couple of days, mixing cement, brickie's helpers and that."

She placed her hand flat on her desk and pushed slowly to try and stop her heart racing.

"That's the future," he said. "There's work for these people, and if I'm thinking straight, there's going to be lots more. Get them in from Mongolia, anywhere. Look, we'd be giving these people a start, that's my way of thinking, right? Maybe learn a bit of English, see? You have to start somewhere. Do you see what I'm getting at?"

"I think so, but Mr. Rynn–"

"What? If the Irish won't work, I say, give someone else the chance. Here, I'll bet your outfit hasn't considered that now, have you? Ah, it's obvious I'm barking up the wrong tree with yous. I mean I can't be waiting and explaining here. You don't know what's going on out there at all, by the sound of this. Let's just forget it, there."

"Mr. Rynn," she began but stopped, had to clear her throat.

"No. I can tell I'm at the wrong place."

"I have to pass on a message to you."

"What message? Look, I'm not interested in 'a message.'"

Everything rushed up at her then. She almost put the phone down. She squeezed it harder instead, and she opened her eyes again.

"Are you listening?"

She could tell by his voice that he was suspicious now, irritated.

"What? What do you mean? Are you going to give me the brush-off here, what's your name again? You never told me your name."

"Maura. Someone wants to meet you, today."

"Who does? What are you on about?"

"It has to be today. In an hour. She says she has a very important message."

"She? She who?"

"Eimear Kelly wants to meet you."

"Eimear who?"

"Eimear Kelly. Declan Kelly's wife. Garda Declan Kelly."

She waited for the line to go dead. She looked down at her hand. She had twisted the telephone cord around her finger enough to leave a criss-crossed red weal.

"And what would this person have to tell me?"

"I believe," she said, pausing to swallow in her throat gone suddenly dry. "I believe she can tell you something that could stop you spending your life in jail."

"Is that what this person told you, now? And when did she tell you this?"

"She says to meet her, in a pub near Kimmage Cross Roads. She said you'd know it. Come on your own."

"Who are you? Who put you up to this?"

"A quarter to four."

"This is a joke? Who the hell is this?"

She held the receiver an inch over the base for several moments, watching it waver as she tried to still her hand. She heard his voice grow louder, he started to curse, she put down the receiver and then she let her forehead down on the desk.

Chapter 22

THEY BROUGHT MINOGUE, AND MALONE, down to Pearse Street Station. They: a hyperactive detective named Brendan Somebody and an older, untidy-looking sergeant with yellow teeth and a sagging look to him that his moustache did not bolster, one bit. Minogue had already forgotten the sergeant's first name, twice. He waited with some embarrassment for the chance to hear it from the other Guard, or even Malone. Malone still looked shook. He didn't offer even the slightest bit of humour that might ease the tension. Minogue saw his hands shake, even under the fidgetiness and finger work, the drumming, the incessant patting Malone kept up to hide the shakes.

The evening had set in. Minogue had felt stupid being driven through the pedestrian area. Stupider still when the driver put on the light to cross four lanes so he could swing around Pearse Street. A taxi man braked hard during this. Minogue didn't need to be a lip-reading expert.

"Come on up," said the sergeant when they got off Townsend Street, and the door of the car park closed behind the car. "We'll be done in no time."

To Minogue, something in the voice's inflection came over as a subtle tilt to whimsy. While he conceded that it had probably not been intended at all, he still speculated on the origins of the man's accent. He couldn't decide Carlow, Wicklow, or even Wexford behind how the words were spun and set in the air.

"Or do ye want to slip into Mulligan's there, maybe apply some lotion?"

Minogue offered a tight smile but declined the bogus offer to go to the well-known pub around the corner. He was thinking about the small cloud appearing from the wall above Malone's head back near Merchant's Arch, the pulverized mortar thrown out by the bullet, hanging in the air a few moments.

"The Naas Road, you said," said the sergeant and held open the door. "This fella? 'George'?"

"If it's him, yes."

"And if it wasn't? Who else would be taking potshots at you two?"

Malone paused to give the sergeant a look.

"You did time here in Pearse Street, I understand, er, Matt?"

"A good long while ago, yes."

The sergeant nodded, as though in sympathy. Then he rubbed his hands

"A cup of something then?" he asked. "Those statements will be typed up, I mean word-processed, in no time. No time at all."

Minogue knew that someone, likely the sergeant, would be comparing his with Malone's before he'd give them a look for corrections in the signing copy.

Inside what passed for a canteen there were four uniforms lazing about. Their patrol gear was strewn on other chairs. A few nods ensued, a non-committal "how's it going." Malone started looking for a kettle or something but tipped a cup on the floor. He stood staring at it for a minute.

"I hope you're not the team's goalie," Minogue heard one of the uniforms say.

"Sorry about that," said Malone.

"How well you might now," said another. "And it being the most important cup we have here."

The lush and twisting accent of Clare arrowed straight to Minogue's brain. He looked over at its issuer, a heavy, ginger-headed loafer sunk into a deep slouch against the wall. He was now observing Minogue with a testy eye.

"You'd better have your prayers said, lads," he said. "that was Big Joe's cup you destroyed."

"Big Joe?"

"Ah now, go aisy on yourself. We don't want to be frightening you."

Malone was fetching about for something to sweep up the floor. Minogue filled the kettle.

"Bicycle Joe," said another Guard. "You don't want to mess with Bicycle Joe."

The door opened and a Bean Garda came in. She was hatted and kitted, ready for the streets already. One of the Guards laughed.

"Speak of the divil. Joe, this man's after destroying your cup. Lookit."

Malone turned and nodded.

"Were you the two caught up in that fooferaw down in the Temple Bar," she said. "I heard it on the radio downstairs."

Malone nodded. One by one, the Guards began getting up from the table. There was a loud, long groan from one, and the lazy-eyed Clareman stretched himself and wheezed.

"Clareman, are you?"

"Straight up my spine," said Minogue, "to the top of my big, thick head."

"Well, you can break every damn cup in the place so."

Malone kept at his sweeping. One of the Guards asked if he'd gotten the bruise just now.

Togged up, their walkie talkies tested, the Guards began to file out. The Bean Garda took out rubber gloves to check them and then pocketed them again.

"The times we're living in," she said to Minogue.

"Tell me again when you're Commissioner," he said.

"The charm just rolling off you," she said.

"What's the Bicycle Joe thing, do you mind me asking? If it's salacious now . . ."

But she laughed.

"Not a bit of it, no. It was a stunt I had to pull one night. Not by design, I can tell you. Me and one of the lads – Mikey Mac here, the Clare Superman you were talking to – we were doing closing times down O Connell Street. Two gorillas came our way, fully intending to do the business. Fierce drunk, and looking for trouble. Mikey Mac and one of them got into a tussle. But the other one was no gentleman, let me tell you. Equal opportunity and all that. So, well . . . I had to throw a bike at him to settle his hash."

"A bike. How did that turn out?"

"He was a bit surprised. And then I took a leap at him. I pinned him under the bike until the clown car showed up."

"She pushed the handlebars into a delicate spot on him," a Guard called out. "Had him saying his prayers right quick – tell the truth, Joanne, you fecking hooligan."

"Mind yourself," Minogue said. "We'll talk again."

Malone scooped up the pieces of china. The kettle began ticking and soon purring. Minogue walked to the window. It looked out on a lot of barbed wire over the wall that ran along Townsend Street. There were a lot of lights on now, and the sky was beginning to glow.

The cupboard door closed behind him. He wondered again what Malone had thought when that lunatic had come back up the steps, shooting.

"He'll turn up," he said to Malone. "That I know. He's our man, and he's going to pay for this."

Malone was leaning against the cupboard. He seemed to be studying the floor.

"Right, Tommy?"

Malone nodded, and then he looked up.

"How many casings, would you say?"

Minogue had counted eight shots, he thought.

"Seven or eight, I think."

"Nothing yet from where they found Lawless?"

"They haven't said, that I know."

"You know what I'm saying," Malone murmured. "Right?"

Knowaramsane echoed in Minogue's mind. *Ryigh*? He should phone Kathleen. He wouldn't say a word unless she asked him straight out.

"I get where you're going there," he said. "I'll be very keen to find out too."

Malone had to go to the toilet. Minogue stayed by the sink and waited for the kettle to finish. He heard – felt, more – the low hum from the public office below. Then he went to the window again, and soon the afternoon's doings began to replay in his mind.

Malone came back smelling of the industrial soap they had in the dispensers now. His short bristly hair was wet and his bruise darkened the pale face almost as much as the dark-ringed eyes.

"Don't tell me," Malone said and eased himself into a chair. "No sign of the bastard. And never will be."

Minogue wondered why no other Guards were coming through the canteen. Had someone told them to give the place a wide berth, because these two were in it? Two detectives that seemed to drag all kinds of calamity in their wake?

"Be nice if he dropped it somewhere," Malone murmured. "Broke a leg maybe."

The motorbike, Minogue realized. Dropped: crashed.

"Just the one broken leg would do. For now, like."

Minogue brought over the teapot. He thought of begging one of the Guards or staff for a smoke. He determined to wait out Malone for a few words, or even for Malone to start drinking his tea. He studied the Formica faux-granite tabletop, the walls.

The detective who had driven them over arrived.

"How are we doing, lads?"

"We're managing," said Minogue. He eyed the way this Detective Brendan Mad-energy was rubbing his hands and then clicking his fingers. It was of a speed and a pattern too complex for him to divine yet.

"They found the bike, the motorbike. Yup! They think it's the one."

Malone sat up. Minogue took in the darting eyes, the way Brendan kept running his lower lip under his top teeth, in and out, chewing and releasing.

"Registration?"

The finger-clicking and the hand-rubbing stopped.

"Well guess what," he said, very still for the first time Minogue remembered.

"Fake? Robbed . . .?"

"The first. We've started a search with the importer. Kawasaki."

"Anybody spot him though?" Malone asked.

"No. Not yet – but that won't last."

"Well, he's a huge big tall bastard," said Malone, "wearing a helmet. Hard to miss. Know what I'm saying?"

"Oh, someone saw him – or someone – ditch a helmet. They think. It's up in the Liffey there, at the end of the quays. But we have feet on the ground there right now and plenty of squad cars."

Kingsbridge–Heuston train station, Minogue thought: right by the Phoenix Park too, and the start of the motorway. Gone for sure.

"Sergeant says will ye come down, he's just printing out the statements."

"That fast?"

"Voice recognition. It actually works now."

Minogue and Malone followed him down the stairs and threaded their way over to the sergeant's walled-in cubicle.

"Take your time," said the sergeant. He rubbed both ends of his moustache with the thumb and middle finger of one hard. The sergeant's head was doing the moving, Minogue noted, while the elbow remained planted on the desk all the while. Like a cow rubbing its neck on a fence.

"Mark it anyway you want. We have it all – delete, search, and replace. Oh yes."

Minogue sat on the edge of one of the chairs jammed into the partition wall, and he glanced over the first page. The sergeant answered the phone. Minogue stopped reading when he heard the sergeant speak, after a pause.

"He's right here with me now. I'll ask."

"Are you able to take a call?"

That'll depend, Minogue wanted to say.

"Work?" he said instead.

"That too, I imagine," said the sergeant. The whimsy in the tone grated hard on Minogue, more even than the wildly annoying stroking of the moustache that the sergeant had resumed with. It felt like teasing now, and slagging he didn't need at the minute.

"A Superintendent Kilmartin," said the sergeant, more prescient than Minogue had allowed. "Inquiring after your welfare, I believe."

Minogue couldn't help himself. He put down the papers, glanced at Malone, and scowled.

"God damn it," he said, but with little bile. "That Mayo tinker has his nose in everything."

He was a little pleased to see Malone's mouth twitch a little at his utterance.

Chapter 23

September 11, 1993

SHE WAITED IN THE CAR until the panic ebbed. Then she hurriedly opened the door and stepped out onto the footpath, lest she changed her mind. A few doors down, beyond that young woman pushing the pram, oblivious to what was happening here, was the door into the lounge section of the pub.

She almost forgot to lock the car door. She was glad of the excuse to backtrack the few yards. That wasn't as bad as the near miss she'd had going through traffic lights that must have been red. She had pulled over not long afterwards, not even halfway from her office to the pub, and tried to decide for once and for all. Call it off, follow through? It wasn't about that place in Foxrock – that was gone. But whatever was raging away in her head had rushed unexpectedly out of her mouth in a shrill yell on her way here. It had first terrified her, but after a few moments it had felt right.

It was the time of day when the kids were out of school, the lull before the rush hour started. She stopped at the door of the pub and checked the time. She wanted to be here first, to give her time to settle a bit. She looked back at her faded red Fiat before she pulled open the door.

The lounge was empty. A man was moving around, laying beer mats on the tables. He glanced over, gave her the once-over, and a too-friendly hello. He was hiding his curiosity about a woman on her own coming in at this hour reasonably well, she thought. He said he'd be with her in a minute.

She chose a spot along the wall where she could see the door in. She had brought a newspaper and some work in her carry-all.

"An orange juice?" he repeated after she ordered.

"That's it," she said, annoyed at how he repeated it. As if she had no business on her own in a pub in the afternoon, ordering an orange too.

She watched him pull a bottle up with a flourish and open it on the opener attached to the counter. He moved to the side, to reach a bin of ice. The swing door behind him flapped open and a younger barman came through with a crate of some drinks. With the door jammed open, she saw the face clearly. The hand came up with a cigarette and put it to his mouth, but the dull, faraway stare still stayed on her.

She was on her feet without realizing it, grabbing at the bag. The barman had noticed.

"I have to go," she said. "I can't stay."

She pulled on the door when she should have pushed. When she did get out on the footpath, a dark-haired man was there already. He was trying not to look like he had run out. The bar, that's where he was, went through her mind again. Hadn't she said lounge on the phone?

She didn't know why she stopped. Maybe it was curiosity, to see if Rynn would join the other one here. Fifty feet away, this man was. If she made a run for it, would he run after her?

The hand with the cigarette emerged first, and then Rynn. He said something out of the side of his mouth to the other and then began a slow stroll toward her. She looked from him back to the other man. A lorry passed slowly, straining and filling the air around her with the diesel rattle from a broken exhaust, but it didn't break this spell.

Then he was beside her, scrutinizing her.

"That was you made that phone call?"

She said nothing.

"You haven't changed," he said.

She watched the lines of smoke coming out the corner of his mouth. Declan had said Rynn could find out anything. He even knew their bank balance back then. Why wouldn't he have had a picture of her, then.

"Are you Eimear, then?"

It wasn't a question, she knew. Her knees were gone to jelly.

"I was," she said. It came out as a croak.

"Was? What are you talking 'was'?"

"I am her."

"And now you want something."

"Not here," she said.

His expression began to take on a sneering look. He turned on his heel and held his arms up, and came around again.

"What? Not for the cameras? Or do you have that in your bag?"

"Not here," she said again. "I mean, no there's none of that."

"Tape recorder? Wires . . . ?"

She shook her head. He looked her up and down, drew on his cigarette.

"What exactly do you want?"

She nodded toward the door of the lounge. He looked her up and down and then stared at her. She wondered if she'd be able to walk now. She looked away, waited.

"Okay," said Rynn, in a voice that sounded like he was conceding something to a child. "Surprise me then."

He held the door for her. She felt she would totter and fall with each step. His stare lacerated her as she got by him and into the dim, smelly and suddenly quieter confines of the lounge.

The barman's face changed when Rynn stepped in behind her. She made it to where she had sat before, and she put down her bag. She watched the barman approach, kept her eyes on him, and ignored his wheeze and squeaks as Rynn settled into a leatherette chair between her and the door.

"Nothing," she heard Rynn say, and looked up from the glass of orange whose bursting carbonated bubbles she had been watching. The barman had become much busier now. He barely looked over at the door when the dark-haired man came in.

Rynn was speaking to her, saying something about the agency. She waited until the dark-haired man sat.

"I went on my own," she said.

"That's not what I said. I said, who put you up to this?"

"Nobody. Nobody did."

"Then you won't mind if we make bloody sure you weren't wired, will you?"

She stared at her drink again. She heard him exhale smoke.

"You're scared, aren't you?"

She fought to keep her head still, watched more bubbles surface and pop.

"That's good. You should be. When I meet someone I don't know, that's what I look for. 'Cause if they're not scared, they're on drugs, see. Or they're out to do me harm. How about you, Mrs. Kelly? Are you here to do me harm?"

She couldn't be sure how her words would come out.

"Well?" he said, not unkindly, after a few moments.

"I know some things," she started out, but a catch in her throat interrupted her.

"Good. So did your husband, if I remember."

It was a taunt, she knew, to see if she'd crack. She had expected it.

"Some things that will affect you," she went on.

"Me?"

He sat back and rubbed at the tip of his nose with his thumb.

"Now why would you care about that?"

"You know they're always trying," she said. "And that you think you're one step ahead all the time."

"They?"

"The Guards."

"Oh. And how would you know this?"

"My husband is a Guard."

"Your husband is dead, missus."

She stared back at him. When she didn't look away, he almost smiled.

"But by Jesus he caused a lot of trouble before he went. Now tell me something. Are you out of your mind or what? Do you think you're dealing with an iijit here?"

"I remarried."

He flicked his cigarette over the ashtray.

"Another Guard."

"A habit, I see. Do I know him?"

"No."

"I will in an hour," he said quickly.

She returned his gaze.

"You'll be wishing you'd listened to me better."

He straightened.

"I'm not the kind of man listens to talk like that," he said in a slow, monotone. "Even from a woman."

"I didn't come here to threaten you."

"What's your thing, exactly? Are you on heroin or something? Drank everything away? What?"

"Nothing."

"But what do you want?"

She took out the manila envelope with the notes for Victory.

"What's to stop me from going out the door and picking up the phone and telling someone the wife of a Guard is trying to put the heavy hand on me? How'd your hubbie like that?"

She placed the applications on the table.

"They'll send the fellas in the white coats for you," he said. "Off to the funny farm."

"I'm just meeting with a client," she said, and sat back. Rynn lit another cigarette and looked over to the bar. Then he smiled.

"I get it," he said. "You're going to tell me you found out this whole meat-packer business is bollocks. Is that your gig? Pardon my use of the English language and all."

"No," she said.

"Oh. It's even trickier, is it? Do I detect . . .?"

He narrowed his eyes until they were almost closed.

"Are you making a proposition to me here, is it?"

She shook her head.

He crossed his arms and rested his thumbnail on his lower lip, the cigarette inches from his nose, and he watched her.

"I know what you want. You want revenge. Don't you?"

She felt the weakness return to her arms and legs now.

"Don't you?"

"You can do all the thinking you want in jail," she said.

She saw the anger flash across his eyes then. His voice was almost a whisper.

"Listen, you stupid bitch. Do you have a clue who you're dealing with here?"

She knew that the man at the bar was looking at her now. The barman was pretending not to.

"Now I'm going to do you the biggest favour of your life," Rynn muttered. "You hear? I'm going to let you walk out the door and go home. You won't get a better offer than that. I don't deal with head cases."

A thrill ran through her. Far from frightening her, something about his anger had made him weaken in her eyes.

"How much is a year of your life worth?" she asked.

"Go home," he said. "Don't push your luck."

"Say, fifteen years in jail."

The man at the bar was on his feet as Rynn's hand came up from the backhanded sweep of his arm that had sent the papers flying. Rynn hadn't taken his eyes off her. He held up his hand, and the man at the bar sat down. She watched the last of the papers unroll and flatten itself on the carpet.

"Got the message?"

She looked back to him.

"You're not the man I thought you'd be."

"Your husband tried to pull something like this on me. You are messing with the wrong man. Now get out of here before I change my mind."

"This time next month," she said. "Phone me. If they let you, of course. And I'll tell you what you could have had."

It was a hateful glance, she recognized, but the dread she had felt was gone.

"You won't even know who did it until later," she said. "By then they'll have all they want on you."

He said nothing. She wondered if he'd lash out again.

"Say you behave yourself inside," she added. "Maybe you'd be out in twelve years. If you didn't run into any trouble in there, I suppose."

"You," he said then, in a voice barely above a whisper. "You are suicidal. You need a shrink. As well as a few slaps. But it won't be me. No way. I see your plan, you know. You want me to give you the hiding you deserve, so they can charge me on it."

"You're getting it cheap," she said. "It's a once-in-a-lifetime chance for you."

His face suddenly creased into a smile then.

"Once in a lifetime," he said. "I like that."

"Sixty thousand," she said.

He sat back suddenly, mock horror on his face.

"To get me slappers in for the clubs? Me 'general labourers' I'm looking for?"

"I don't want your business."

His face set again.

"That was a joke," he said. "Do you even know what a slapper is?"

She said nothing.

"You're from the country, I can tell. Well a slapper is a whore. But, thank God, that's only me trying to get a rise out of you. I'm just a businessman trying to get a factory up and running. Do me bit for Ireland, see? And if we need to go abroad to find people who'll do the job, well I can't be flying around East Germany or Czechoslovakia or whatever interviewing people, can I? That would be your line of work."

"Twelve years," she said. "Five thousand a year. That's nothing to you."

He looked down at the ashtray. She braced herself.

"You've got some nerve," he murmured. "I'll say that for you. Some bloody nerve."

"Pay after you get proof," she said then.

She could see confusion in his look now. He stared at her for what seemed a long, long time.

"You think I'd give you sixty thousand quid?"

She nodded.

"You'll be glad you did."

"Okay then. Tell me what you want to tell me. Right now."

She looked at the papers sprawled across the carpet.

Islandbridge

"I think we're getting ready to finish up here then," she said and reached for the pages that had fallen by the chair. She felt his hand on her arm.

"Leave them. You have something to tell me."

"You have something to tell me first," she said.

"You're scared," he said. "And you're not scared. You are one peculiar bird, I'm telling you. Tell me, do you leave little stories lying around, like your husband did, maybe?"

"Give me your word," she said.

"Jesus, my word? Should I be flattered or what? You mean . . .?"

She met the barman's eye for a moment.

"If it's true, what you're going to tell me?"

She nodded.

"Before we leave here, today?"

"Yes. I'll tell you."

"And I don't have to pay until I find out, later on sometime?"

"Right."

"Even if one millionth of this bullshit is true, you think I'm ever going to?"

"If you give your word," she said.

He shook his head and smiled, and drew on his cigarette. She took her first sip of the orange and realized she hadn't paid for it.

"Okay," he said. "This is one weird day. But like they say, miracles happen."

"I'm going to tell you a name. This person is working with the Guards. They're getting ready for something for you."

"A name?"

"A man the name of Weekes."

She had already shifted slightly in her chair, ready to move aside. He was very still, thoughtful.

"Did I hear you right?"

"Yes. That's what I was told."

"You," he said and paused. "You have just done something very very very . . . stupid. You hear me? Do you?"

He looked up from the tip of his cigarette he had been studying.

291

"If you think, for one minute–"

She flinched and turned away as his arm swept across the table. The glass went a distance before it began to cartwheel across the carpet and break up. She heard someone else's voice, and a small shriek that could only have been herself. When she took her hands down, Rynn was standing. He looked down at her for several moments, nodding, as the sneer took over his whole face. The dark-haired man was by his side now.

Rynn fumbled in his pocket and looked at the notes in his hand. He pulled out a ten-pound note and let it drop on the table. She heard the faint hiss from the spilled drink in patches across the Formica.

"Go buy yourself an overdose of whatever it is you're on," Rynn said. "You lunatic."

There were spots of orange on the papers too, she saw. She only looked up when she heard the door being kicked open. The barman turned from the door. She knelt on one knee and began picking up the papers.

"Leave the premises there Miss, Missus," she heard him say, but she kept on.

She stuffed them into the carry-all. He was coming toward her now, saying something about cleaning it up himself, and that she shouldn't come back. She grabbed the handle of the bag. She didn't want to look him in the eye.

"You won't be served here again," he said.

She got to the door, fumbling and clutching her coat. She made it to the car. Once inside, she burst into tears.

Chapter 24

MINOGUE'S EYES STUNG NOW and he looked away from the screen. Malone kept at it, clicking the mouse in an almost regular tattoo, his head in toward the monitor.

Sinnott had been eyeing the proceedings this past while. Malone had asked him when he was going home. That was when they first arrived into Immigration and Sinnott met them there, three floors up, in the near-deserted offices that adjoined the old CDU in Dublin Castle.

It was after nine. Weariness came to Minogue in his joints now. He rubbed at his knees. There was still a sizeable strain in one where he had knelt in the Temple Bar after the shots. Knelt there, he thought: Iseult would laugh at that.

He looked over the already tired-looking evening paper that Sinnott had left there, and studied the photo of the black family. Chad. Chad? It had been taken in a church by the look of it. The man had a suit and tie, his beaming wife and children – five – were dressed up too.

It was a tabloid headline for sure.

"Our new Irish family? *Fáilte!*"

Talk about manipulative, he thought. He rubbed at his eyes and opened them when he heard Malone's mouse-clicking stop. Malone grunted, it sounded like a no. The face was olive, the man's on the screen, but the eyes didn't look right any more than the fat lips.

"How tall?" he called out. Sinnott looked around and then back to the screen.

"One eighty," he said.

"In real numbers, Joe. Come on."

"Five eleven, yes. Five eleven."

Malone went on to the next one, then another. Minogue took out his mobile. He had promised Kathleen he'd leave it on, after she'd tracked him down an hour ago. She was annoyed, she wanted him home. Jim Kilmartin had let slip what had happened. He'd phoned the house to see how Minogue was doing. It didn't take long for Kathleen to get it out of him.

Sinnott got up.

"You're a divil for work, Joe," Minogue said. "Go on home, can't you?"

"And leave your man here in front of the database?"

Minogue had to remember what a database was again: Sinnott meant the pictures and the vitals, right.

Sinnott sat on the desk.

"No," he said. "I'm interested. We'll give it a while yet."

Malone swore slowly and carefully. It wasn't George, Minogue saw when he glanced at the screen. Malone had tripped into some other area.

"Click. 'FY,'" said Sinnott. "Former Yugoslavia. Put in the male and age again."

"Like I say," Sinnott said turning to Minogue again. "This is something we're working on, bit by bit."

"Prostitution, you said?"

"The whole bit. Drugs, contraband."

"Trafficking."

"That's the man," said Sinnott. "You've got the lingo, I see."

"Where else could we look for this thug?"

"You mean if he's not carrying fakes?"

"I get it, Joe, I get it. Don't rub it in."

"You've been through the talent catalogue earlier, right?"

Minogue remembered turning the pages with their pouches over, pushing down the plastic sometimes to get the glare off the photos beneath.

"I have."

"Well, you're pretty well coming to the end of this search, so, with the PIA stuff."

Minogue didn't want to ask what the acronym meant again. He let it bounce gently around his mind until he got it.

"Persons of Interest and Associates."

"Nice," said Sinnott. "You should come over here on your next tour. On your way to Euro-land."

Minogue didn't mind Sinnott slagging a little. He hadn't met him before, only heard about him from Malone.

"Thing is," said Sinnott, and drew up his legs so he was seated completely on the desk now, "thing is, it's always moving. I mean these are very organized people in their own ways. It's not 'Russian' or 'Ukrainian' or 'Romanian' just. There's crossovers. One crowd will do a favour for another, if it suits them. Or have a feud – kill one another. How long is this George fella in Ireland?"

Minogue shrugged.

"Long enough to have his own fake numbers on a motorbike," Malone said. "Long enough to know his way around."

He swivelled around slowly.

"Long enough to be having dinner with the likes of Jimmy Rynn."

Sinnott nodded and began swinging his legs.

"That's disturbing," he said. "That's disturbing, all right."

"I'll bloody well disturb him when I get a hold of him, I can tell you," Malone said.

"Rynn," said Sinnott. "Now there's someone. How in the hell is he still around, walking the streets?"

"He's not an iijit like a lot of them," said Malone. "I'll give him that. He figured out the whole 'arm's-length' thing years ago. You know? He's a 'businessman' now."

"No-one's untouchable, Tommy," said Sinnott. "Don't be crying the blues there, man. His day will come."

"Me bollicks," said Malone. "He's like an old crocodile or something, just his eyes over the water. Sees everything, waits. Takes his time. Pays people to look out for him. Pays well, I hear.

Like it or not, we haven't made much of a dent in him yet."

The talk died out. Even Malone seemed ready to call it a day. Outside their island of light the storeys of darkened offices loomed. For a few moments, Minogue imagined the three of them were on an island of light, alone, and a world away from the middle of lopsided, swollen Dublin.

"There's fierce amount of headers floating around all over," Sinnott murmured.

"You can learn a lot from looking in a mirror," Malone said and yawned. Sinnott looked up in a lazy half-smile.

"No wonder you got that puck in the snot. I meant fellas like your lad, 'George.' After all the wars and that over in Yugoslavia. That sort of thing."

"Ah, he's gone to ground," said Minogue and stood. "For tonight anyway. I wouldn't doubt but he had a car parked handy enough too."

"You know," said Sinnott, "from what I hear in England, they have a system down pat. I don't want to disillusion yous now but . . ."

"Disillusion us, Joe," said Minogue.

"I dare you," yawned Malone.

"Car. Local associates, affiliates—"

"A few identities tucked away under the mattress?"

"I wouldn't doubt it."

"Jaysus, Joe," said Malone. "You're a cheerful bastard."

"I'm going," Minogue said. "Nothing's getting done on this tonight."

Sinnott went to the monitor, closed the program, and then shut down the computer.

"You two didn't see that," he said.

"Right," said Minogue.

Sinnott left two lights on. He locked and tested the door out to the hallway. Minogue waited by a window that looked across the park toward the Clock Tower. There was a faint vibration, a distant melody from music being played somewhere. To his right the dark bulk of the oldest part of Dublin Castle, the Tower that had housed the Garda Museum for a decade now. From that same tower chiefs had been imprisoned and tortured, and Fiach O'Byrne had escaped some time in the 1500s, fleeing on foot over the snowbound Wicklow Mountains.

Minogue's mind went out over the rooftops now, in the glare of Dublin's lights, into the suburbs and finally over the sprinkle of lights that petered out where the mountains took over.

"Prostitutes," Malone murmured. "I'm telling you."

Traffic, Minogue thought, and kept his inner eye on the empty nighttime folds of West Wicklow.

"How can we thank you, Joe," he said outside.

"Keep your gob shut about that database will do," said Sinnott.

Minogue affected a smile but sought out Sinnott's eyes to signal otherwise. The floodlight by the Upper Castle Yard showed through the sparse hairs in the beard he guessed Sinnott must have grown to cover the pits left by ferocious acne.

"Maybe Tommy here will stand us a pint," he said. "Being as it's him got us drug into this caper."

Malone didn't protest. The night air felt clammy and tired out itself on Minogue's face as they headed over to where they'd parked. It was some concert somewhere he was hearing far off he decided.

The sound got louder as they approached the gate out onto Dame Street. He heard lots of tambourines and bits of a choral sound that sounded different. Plenty of tapping. Shakers? Drums?

There was a Guard manning the gate, and he seemed to know Sinnott.

"Join in, outside," he said. "Some craic out there, I never seen the like, I tell you."

"What is?"

"There's some class of a concert thing, to do with that African man."

"What man?"

"The plane, the man who fell down out of the plane," said the Guard, and shifted his jacket. "They want to bring the man's family here, twenty something of them. I don't know how or when it got going, but it's getting bigger by the minute. Go on, have a look."

There were groups gathered by Dublin Castle gate, and they were thickening into a pretty sizeable crowd. It had no amplification for the instruments. People were swaying and clapping hands. The traffic had almost stopped.

In the Millennium Park, under the plaque commemorating the three IRA men that had been tortured to death here by the Black and Tans, a group of about a dozen had found some way to get up on a height. Most of them were black. There were drums and tambourines and the shakers he had suspected. He didn't know what they were singing. He asked Malone.

"I don't speak African," Malone shouted back.

A hand-done sign wobbled as someone tried to attach it to a pole. Miracle? Then the music faltered and a cheer went up. A camera flashed. Minogue saw the figure bound up beside the singers and raise an arm in a fist. Black clothes, wraparound glasses . . .

"Jaysus," said Malone. "Look who it is."

Chapter 25

October 24, 1999

S HE LEFT THE WINDOWS OPEN all day, even with the late autumn nip in the air. Hallowe'en was a week away. She had lit a fire under the builders, so she had. They hadn't been one bit pleased. But if they'd had their way, they'd still be foostering about here at Christmas – or even into the New Year, for God's sake. Some days she had even wondered if they had some plot to deprive her of a proper, finished, renovated house in time for Christmas.

Liam had moaned about the cold in the house. She tried to explain the need to get the smells of cement and paint and everything out as much as possible, especially before the guests arrived. He was still in a bit of sulk at having moved, to be honest. She'd had words with him, and he flounced out. She called after him to be here by four but he didn't answer. He'd probably get the bus over to his friend Shane's house, three down from the Kilmartins' old home. Ah, The Single Child Syndrome, she thought again: The Little Emperor. But what odds, she decided yet again: he could be managed, and he was on the right track towards his Finals.

Jim came home early. He had been on night work twice in the past week, with a case near the canal, and then when someone was found in a house on fire.

"Can you smell the cement or the plaster now?"

"No," he said. "But they'll need to keep their bloody coats

on when they come over if we don't get cracking."

Promotion was the excuse, and Jim had been nervous all week about it. The squad lads would be here, most of them. Hoey was going through a bad patch, Jim told her. Someone'd needed to keep an eye on him, and the drink.

"Kathleen and Matt?"

"'Course they are."

"He'll watch out for Seamus . . . ?"

"Hoey? Matt will. He misses nothing. He only lets on he's an iijit."

She watched him try to close the new window in the dining room. They did a lot of squeaking, but the man said that was normal.

"Will we put on a fire, Jim, what do you think?"

He swore and there was a harsh click from the window. She surveyed the plates and the napkins she'd found in Switzers, and the silverware from the Kilkenny Design. You had to be careful, she knew, not too overreach, not to have fancy things in cutlery. The flowers weren't overdone either.

"I love a fire," he said. "But you don't want people sitting around, that's the trouble."

"Oh God," she said, remembering. "What does the Assistant Commissioner drink, the new one, is it Italian?"

He gave her a glare.

"Arra Sweet and Holy Jesus, Maura, will you not be worrying about him. He's easy pleased. Sure isn't he a Monaghan man?"

"His wife, what's her name?"

"Noreen."

"What does she like again?"

"I don't know. But if she's anything like the man she married, she'll drink a pint out of a whore's boot."

"I hope you're not going to be talking like that tonight."

He gave her a mock salute.

"Come on, Jim. Don't be like that."

He tugged on the new curtains and gazed out at the rubble still left in the garden.

"I know we're high-mucky-mucky now, girl of my heart,

but you can't take the bog out of the man. It's a party we're having, right? In our house?"

She thought of reminding him how much engineering had gone on to get him to this 'our.'"

"It's a dinner party," she said. "Not a tinker's bonfire."

He made a face and walked over to the bottles of wine. He began to study the labels.

"It's mixing business with pleasure," she said.

He started humming, "Lannigan's Ball."

"I'll have my crowd from work too, you know. It's social of course, but we're going to be enjoying ourselves."

He hummed louder and slipped in words.

"Networking," she said. "As much as celebrating the promotion and that."

"And your goings-on," he said.

"Certainly," she said. "That's why I asked a few clients along, but easygoing."

He looked up from his study of the label.

"Well Christ, there's one you'd better not be bringing."

"Who? I don't get it."

"That Rynn fella."

The name seemed to hang in the air for a moment.

"That's not funny. Where did that come from?"

He beamed, and he came over and grabbed her.

"I know. I know," he said. "I'm only trying to get a rise out of you. His name came up, I was talking to a fella starting up that new section in Serious Crimes."

"Did you tell them that he once tried to get the agency to get people for him?"

"No I didn't. Of course not – are you mad? But he's bulletproof, that bastard. We thought we had him but our man disappeared, no sign of him."

She put her hands on his forearms.

"This is my outfit for tonight," she said.

He nuzzled her neck.

"God you're like a plank" he murmured. "Have a glass of something."

The doorbell still squeaked: the workmen hadn't looked at it she told one of them.

"Already?" he said, detaching himself a little.

"That'll be the caterer, the waitresses, I think."

"Waitresses? Jesus, in my house? You're joking!"

She grabbed his shoulder.

"Jim, listen! Will you wake up? You're in 1999! You're a Chief Inspector. My job's going great. Ireland's woken up – haven't you read the business pages? We're not going to be standing around handing out little ham sandwiches like a wake. All right?"

He looked back into her eyes.

"You're a fierce bossy woman," he said, but there was no sting in it.

"Just enjoy tonight, will you?"

She headed for the hall.

"Where's Liam?"

"Ah, he was a bit crooked after school. He's probably back at Brian's house."

She glanced back at him and for a moment was pierced by the frown that had come on his face.

"He'll be okay, love. It's an age thing."

It was very short waiters carrying tableclothes and a bag of something. Just as she closed the door, she saw figures at the gate.

"Perfect timing," she murmured. It'd get Jim off to a good start tonight.

"Are we allowed in?" Kathleen Minogue called out. Her husband was closing the gate behind them.

Maura called out to them.

"Welcome the pair of ye, come on."

She smiled back at Kathleen. That woman always seemed to be in good humour. It was infectious. Things would go great.

She watched Matt closing the gate and something cold spread though her. He had dark hair and he was tall, a bit like that fella that had come with Rynn to the pub that day. His bodyguard, or helper, or picker-upper – whatever you called someone who worked for a criminal. Weekes. He had a nasty look to him, and bad eyes. Sometimes she had wondered what he'd done at Rynn's bidding over the years.

The money had been put into her locked car sometime during the day, in broad daylight. It wasn't the slow mocking Dublin accent on the phone when Rynn phoned at the end of the day. He had spoken quietly. He hadn't sworn or raised his voice.

"Whatever else you can say about me," he had said, "I keep my word, don't I."

The face was Matt Minogue's of course it was, and that boyish look to him that made you think he was half-preoccupied with something else.

"There's a nip in the air already, isn't there?"

It was Kathleen's voice, and then she was beside her. A small look of concern, she noted, as Kathleen's face came in and she felt her cheek on hers.

"Gorgeous," said Kathleen. "Way better than moving to mouldy old Foxrock! Wasn't that the place years back . . .?"

"Yes, I'd almost forgotten that."

Maura knew Minogue didn't like the hug stuff. It was a shyness she liked. Since getting Matt on the Squad, her own husband had changed, and she was sure it was cues Jim picked up from him.

"Tell his highness to get the apron off, Maura," Minogue said in that reluctant way he often spoke. "His betters are here."

Kathleen elbowed him, but he had been expecting it.

He stepped back and held out something with a bow on it.

"A bit of art," he said. "Iseult."

Maura drew Kathleen into the hall, enjoying the oohing and awing from her about the decor.

She pointed out defects with the floor where the stairs stopped and rolled her eyes toward the bare patches of plaster still by the door they'd hung on the cloakroom.

The waitress had gone straight to the kitchen. That seemed to be enough to eject Jim from there.

"Look," said Kathleen and rubbed her hand along the banister. "Is that oak?"

"Bog oak, Kathleen," Jim said, and leaned in to give her a hug.

"Are we the first?"

"Kathleen Mavourneen, you'll be the first ones in that door to toast the goings on. Here, I'll get a few glasses from the servant girl."

She looked from Kathleen to her husband.

"They'll all be along," she said. "Róisín's coming up. Ma too. A crowd from work. The Commissioner even. Oh I hope I don't call him God Almighty by mistake."

Kathleen said something about the new one, a rumour about an Assistant Comm. Tynan.

"But Jim'd know the day or the hour, I'm sure," said Kathleen, as he returned with glasses and a bottle of Italian bubbly.

"Let them take the coats off Jim, will you?"

"Oh, are ye staying? Ha ha!"

"Don't you, Jim," said Kathleen.

"Don't I what– Jaysus, don't let me spill this."

"Don't you know every move that goes on in the Guards?"

"Bedad and I do," he said. "And, I'm not ashamed to admit it."

He almost overfilled Minogue's glass. Maura felt the twinge again and tried to fight it off. What was done was done – there was no going back. Ever. Weekes had been a criminal all his life.

"Somebody has to know what's going on, don't they, Matt?"

They touched glasses. The wine wasn't cold enough; she should do something about the ice. The doorbell went again and Jim wrenched it open. Róisín, Tom. It was starting. Her chest began to lose the tightness and she tried harder to focus on what was going on around her. The laughter from Jim – Kathleen's peculiar giggle – Róisín's husband Tom's new glasses.

The phone now. She was nearest. She picked it up, tried to guess who it was needed directions.

"How's the party going?"

She put down the glass and held her hand over her other ear.

"I said how's it going? Party started, is it?"

Her shoulders went rigid and the rush of heat seemed to race up her neck. "Who is this?"

"Oh, I know you'll have to do the who is this bit. Don't you have a second phone in that place of yours?"

"This isn't a good time."

"Oh, I think it is, Mrs. Kelly."

She followed the line to the box at the bottom of the wall, where it connected.

"I'm phoning back in five minutes. That should be enough time. We're still in business, aren't we?"

"I told you, I don't want to do it anymore. And don't call me here."

"You haven't told me anything for months."

"There's nothing to tell, that's why."

"Well, start listening to your husband again, then, will you? What am I paying you for?"

"I told you–"

"Now you shut up," he said, calmly. "Let's have no more of this 'I told you' stuff! This is a two-way street. Five minutes."

He hung up.

She had to keep things going, she knew.

"Okay," she said, and she put down the receiver.

She smiled back at Kathleen.

"Are we okay, Maura?" Kathleen asked.

Did it show?

"Can I . . . ?" Kathleen started to say.

"Don't you want your drink?" Jim called after her as she headed upstairs. She thought she heard someone, a man, say upset and then overwork. It would hardly be Minogue saying it.

She closed the bathroom door. She considered taking a knife, a pliers or something to the telephone line.

It was cold here. She opened the valve on the radiator and sat on the edge of the new bathtub. Jim, the slob, had left his razor out. She reached for it, turned it over. The edge of the blade had soap rime and whiskers. The steel was ice cold.

Chapter 26

INOGUE SAID NOTHING after he got home, nothing, that is, about the latter part of his day. He ached. He went straight to the Jameson's, all the while carrying on a strained but reasonable conversation through the door into the living room where Kathleen sat, watching the English news.

"Anything about the African thing?" he called out.

"What African thing?"

He waited until the whiskey had gotten by his gullet.

"I came across some kind of a concert going on there in Dame Street."

"No. But there was plenty of other excitement in town later on, I see."

"I heard something about trouble down in the Temple Bar," he tried.

"Trouble is right. Somebody fired off a gun. That place is, God, I don't know. Iseult's place is right there in the middle of all that, God almighty."

Not for long, he didn't call out.

"She phoned anyway," Kathleen said. "She got her contraption put together."

"She's a welder now, is she," he replied, and took another swallow of the Jameson's. "That's a good skill to pick up."

In the light cast out from the window, he could see some of the results of his tentative efforts to relocate the rockery.

Rockeries are not supposed to migrate, he had been telling him-self for quite a number of years now, but somehow his efforts here each year had become almost a habit. He almost enjoyed Kilmartin's slow surveys of the rockery in transit, as it generally was, when he'd look over the latest effort. Bizarre, was Kilmartin's latest term, delivered in a murmur that was more curious than dismissive.

"Aren't you coming in?"

Hint, hint, he knew.

"I'll plug in the kettle first," he replied.

He headed for the living room, and flopped down in the sofa beside her. She eyed him.

"I'm glad that day is over," he said. "It was brutal, all the running around."

"You're back to the eighteen-hour-day madness, are you?"

"Temporary."

"A temporary posting," she said.

He didn't let on he had registered the leaden tone.

"Me and Tommy were ready for a bit of, well, you know."

"A pint after work."

The ads were over. The announcer told them a Special Report was coming up later. To prove she was not fibbing, the screen was taken over by a view of some dusty plain with a few sparse trees, and African faces.

"Is that what's-his-name?"

"It is," said Kathleen. "Look, it's Africa – Chad, it says. Is that a coinicdence?"

The famous reporter looked like he was being boiled red by the heat there, and he was surrounded by children, their brown heads like large eggs.

The children laughed about something. Several of the kids had baseball and basketball logos on their T-shirts. This released a strange dismay in Minogue. What could you expect, he thought then? Were Africans supposed to stay in loincloths? He remem-bered the picture of the dead man's family, all in their Sunday finery. They could as easily have been at one of those gospel churches in the American South. There was a sweeping shot of a hut with lots of kids in it, clapping hands and swaying.

"I heard there's a church group wants to sponsor the man's family here," she said.

"Presuming they'd want to come here," Minogue said, unwisely.

"Why wouldn't they?" she asked. "We're well on here now, aren't we? There's tons of less deserving landing here anyway, isn't there?"

"They'd better like rain, then. Long nights in the winter."

She gave him a hard look.

"You're missing the point here," she said. "The poor man probably hadn't intended to come here."

"The point is what?"

"That there's somebody pulling strings, Matt. Someone is making it happen like this."

She glanced up to the ceiling.

"Things don't just happen for no reason," she said.

Kathleen muted it, and sighed.

"When do you think you'll be finished this, what is it again?"

"A case review."

"Shunted over to Kilmainham, or Islandbridge, is it?"

"That's it. Not the most salubrious of environments, but sure, that's that."

She finished her survey of his profile and turned to the television too.

He stifled a rising bubble from his gorge and held his breath so the smell of Jameson's would not escape. It was a bad plan. The first hiccup was massive.

"Cleaning up someone else's mess, it sounds like," she said. "Is that what you want to be doing now?"

"I suppose I should have told Commissioner Tynan to shag off."

"It's Tommy Malone you should have told that to."

"'Shag off, Tommy. No offence, like?'"

"I like Tommy," she protested. "I really do – and I feel sorry for him. But if you'd have stayed away from that place . . . God, I suppose there's a funny side to it: the only time you go inside a church – willingly – and look what happened."

"No-one would have known that in advance."

"Says you. But you know yourself that Tommy is, well, he's not himself."

"Tommy might have been on to something. There are leads."

"Leads? Can't the others do that? Why does it have to be you?"

"To make a long story short, it's that Tommy got a tip on someone who might be able to bring us to someone else. . . . Who could open up the investigation. The team on the case never got that far, so Tynan wants to go with the one who seems to be able to make the progress."

"'Someone else,'" she murmured.

"She would be a good source for this case. If, well, you know."

He had been caught, and he knew it. She looked at him.

"If what?"

"I think, well, we think," he said. "We think she's out there still. So, well, that's part of it. We can only see how far we get."

"You're delighted," she said. "Admit it. It's back to the old line of business."

He concentrated more on the screen. A shampoo that conditions as well as makes you look like a model.

"A one-off," he said. "Then I'll be back on the Euro beat. The glamour, all that."

She gave no sign of receipt of the peace offering.

He looked over at her, and took in the lines on her neck, the greying strands above her ears.

"*Frère Jacques, Frère Jacques, Dormez-vous, D–*"

She laughed and batted at his roving hands. It was warm under her arm. His finger traced the straps of her bra.

"Full marks for trying," she said. "But when the French comes spouting out of you, I know you're covering up."

"Why would I want to do that, *chérie*?"

He had her laughing now. It was a good time to press home the advantage.

The phone echoed in the hall. They stayed still, his chin on her neck, his hands flat. It rang again.

"Like I said. Cleaning up somebody else's mess again."

"What?"

"That'll be Jim again. He's after phoning twice. You promised you'd try harder with that stupid bloody mobile, Matt. Come on now. I'm not an answering machine."

"What's he want?"

"(A) 'Turn on his damned phone'; (B) I don't know. Answer it, will you?"

Minogue listened for another ring. Kathleen stirred under him.

"Leave it," he said. "He's been annoying the heart and soul out of me this past while. You think I'm bad, not being able to shake off the Squad. Leave him."

Her voice was soft now, serious.

"Answer it, Matt. He sounds, I don't know. A bit lonely or something. Maybe he was drinking. I don't like to think . . ."

Minogue took his time. He went through what he'd say: do you know it's nearly eleven o'clock at night; buy a bloody ticket to the States and drop in on your son and don't be waiting on him; grow up, move on, stop looking over your shoulder.

He took the receiver but didn't lift it until there was another ring.

"Matt?"

"Yourself."

"Where were you? I was trying to get in touch with you."

Minogue absorbed the hurried tone, the odd flatness and almost accentless voice coming from Kilmartin.

"Kathleen said you were looking for me."

He stopped immediately he heard the voice in the background, a woman's. She was upset. Kilmartin put his hand over the mouthpiece but Minogue still heard the raised male voice and a faint reply.

"Jim," he said when he heard the scruffing again.

"I need to talk to you. Are you listening?"

"Jim, I'm jacked. I had a day of it today, let me tell you."

"Did you watch the news earlier on?"

"I'm only after getting in the door."

"But did you?"

"No, how could I?"

"Okay, look. Come over to the house, will you?"

Minogue looked at the photo of Eamonn that Kathleen had mounted in the hall.

"It's ten o'clock at night, Jim."

"I know what the goddamned time is," said Kilmartin, but his voice hadn't changed from the deliberate, slow intonation.

"Whyn't you have your phone on?" he asked. "I could've reached you then."

"Can it be in the morning?"

"No. That won't do. No."

An explanation would go a long way, he wanted to say. But it would only draw him in deeper.

"Did you see the news at all?" Kilmartin asked.

"No. What did I miss?"

Kilmartin waited a moment.

"Nothing. When you think about it. So come over. It's important."

"Has something gone astray on you?"

Kilmartin didn't speak for a moment. Moniogue was sure he'd heard a glass, or a bottle.

"I'll tell you when you get here. I need your advice. Matt?"

"I'm half-jarred, Jim."

"It doesn't matter."

"But I've had the worst day–"

"I know. Believe you me, Matt. I know."

However Kilmartin had said that stopped his words. He knew he wouldn't be able to get anywhere with the poor mouth routine.

"Couldn't you come up here?" he tried.

"No."

"Are you drunk?"

"Not yet."

"Well get in your fancy car and drive over here."

"Matt! I can't! Okay?"

Minogue waited a minute in the hall and then returned to the sitting room.

"Well?"

"I'll be back in a while," he said. "I have to go over to Jim's place."

"At this hour of the night?"

"Something that can't wait, he says. I won't be long."

He took Daithi's old Adidas jacket, the one that had become his gardening jacket. Kathleen demanded to see his mobile. She turned it on and locked the keypad.

"I'll go in late tomorrow," he said to her. "Maybe come down and walk Dun Laoghaire Pier with me?"

"The nerve of you. Incorrigible. I can't be bought off, got that?"

"I want to ask you something," he said. "Something that was on the news earlier."

"The news?"

"Oh now I get it. You must know something about it then – yes, were you in on that?"

"What?"

"You were! That thing down in the Temple Bar. Why would you be asking me, if you weren't? You are a–"

She paused.

"Please, Kathleen?"

"You and Jim Kilmartin, honestly! You can't give it up, can you? Do you know that Maura told me he's forever phoning his old pals and asking around, any time there's a murder or that? Oh yes – it's that bad. The lads in the State Lab? The 'Scenes Men'? Well, why doesn't he phone one of them then, and not be bothering you at home here?"

"Kathleen–"

"You're . . . *obsessed* or something. Maura even told me that he gets emails with pictures from the lab. He does! He says they do be asking him for any tip or thing the others would miss. You know what Jim thinks of ordinary Guards handling his old job."

"Kathleen, do you mind? He's upset about something. I

haven't heard him like this. Something he asked me, about the news. Okay?"

"As if you didn't know. It was something about some man in a car, out in Kildare. The Guards found a man, yes."

"Kildare?"

"Somewhere off the Naas Road there. They said it might be some man they were looking for over something else this afternoon in town. Maybe even the thing down in the Temple Bar – yes."

Chapter 27

MINOGUE OPTED FOR the Bray Road. Doing seventy-five in the short stretches between the lights didn't stop him from being passed by others. One, he was almost sure, had been a Maserati.

He got off at Loughlinstown, and wound his way over through Ballybrack and up the back of Killiney village, where the Kilmartin family, all two of them, had resided for a few years now. How long, he tried to remember exactly: hadn't there been a do there for the millennium New Year?

He let the Citroën onto the avenue where the Kilmartins' house was, five down from the turn in. He spotted two Range Rovers in adjoining driveways. Audis and midsized Beemers seemed to be favoured on this road. The Kilmartins' house was an Olympian stone's throw from the back end of a pub that Minogue despised, the only pub in the old village of Killiney.

Timing is everything, he said to himself as he came in sight of the gates. Maura Kilmartin was the brains behind the move here, there could be no doubt, and James Kilmartin, many years removed from being the bogman-in-the-ditch, had wisely coasted in her wake. Maura had gotten them moved in here just when people wondered if the house-price boom was over. It was not. Kilmartin had confided one night last year that the place had more than doubled in price. Shrewd in every way, was Maura, and she had parleyed a small employment agency into a well-known "recruitment office" over the years. Then Minogue remembered the flat tone in his friend's voice on the phone. Illness? Maura? He hoped not.

He pulled in by the gate. Kilmartin's Granada was in the driveway. Maybe he was daring someone to steal it, with car theft so endemic here. Maura's Audi, the "little red number" as Kilmartin called it, was probably in the garage already.

Yes, Minogue reflected again: being in the right place at the right time. Iseult had said that enough times lately for him to take notice, almost always with a mordant cynicism that made him anxious for her for days afterwards. She had surely meant talent or originality, or the Arts themselves, he believed, and that these meant little enough in the New Ireland. Then a thought came to him as his hand settled on the gate: his own daughter had no place to go. She had no real home anymore at all.

He ran his hand along the railing. How could anyone ever afford to buy a house here? Iseult could rent a flat maybe, or a small house, if she were lucky, but she had no home of her own, and no prospect of one here in her native city. And where would people in Iseult's position go, if they didn't want to move in with their parents again? Migrate, emigrate?

So too did that African man, desperate enough and naïve enough, to stow away on a plane, not knowing where he'd land. Anywhere but where he'd come from, he might have thought. Was it some cosmic curse to be born African these days, to scramble for any home, or any opening in the fortress of a rich white, European world?

The gate had not been latched, he saw now. He looked at the dark windows. In an upstairs window, though, he thought he spotted some movement. But the lights in that bedroom did not go on. Maybe Kilmartin had been standing up there, waiting for him. Had he gone to bed or something, after phoning him to ask him over?

The hall door opened as he was reaching for the bell. Kilmartin, in shirt sleeves, pulled open the door. The hair was skew-ways on him, Minogue noticed. Maybe he'd been having a snooze. Smells came to him then; whiskey, he believed, and some kind of food maybe, but not from cooking.

"A bit early for Hallowe'en there, Jim. The hair. Did I wake you up?"

"No," said Kilmartin. "Come on. The front room there. Wait–"

Minogue turned and looked down toward the gate.

"That your jalopy there, down by the gate?"

"It is. Are you expecting someone else?"

Kilmartin looked at him, but Minogue wondered if he saw him at all.

"Are you all right?"

"Come in, there."

Minogue felt the hand on his shoulder, turning him toward the doorway to the left. The "office" he'd heard Kilmartin calling it once, half-seriously he had thought then.

"Do you use lights here at all in these parts, Jim?"

Kilmartin reached in and flicked on a light.

"Jemmy?" he said. "Bushmills? I have cold beer."

"Cup of tea?"

"No," said Kilmartin. "I have Jemmy in the dresser there. You don't take ice."

Minogue had already made a plan to pour it back in the bottle when he got a moment.

Kilmartin put a tumbler half-full of Jameson's by the monitor. Then he filled his own.

"Come here," he said and reached in over the keyboard to grasp a mouse.

Minogue took his time ambling over. The screen came to life slowly. He saw windows being opened. He noted Kilmartin's shirt tail out, how he took a measured, savage gulp of his own whiskey.

"I'm going to show you something. You ready?"

Minogue knew enough to recognize an email program. Kilmartin scrolled down from a line of poorly edited text, something about "fresh off the presses."

The pictures that came up began with night shots of a car. Someone in the driver's seat was leaning forward over the wheel.

"See that?"

"Jim."

316

The next one inched up and it showed a profile. There were streaks of blood down the cheeks and nose, a diffuse gloss to the front of the head that was almost purple.

"Okay? Wait."

The third one showed the swollen face, with the top of the forehead distended. The exit wound the size of a tennis ball. The man's eyes were half-open.

Minogue stepped back. Kilmartin turned from the screen, the light washing over his face.

"Jim. Listen to me–"

"–This is your man," said Kilmartin. "Isn't it?"

Minogue kept his eye on how Kilmartin's eyes seemed to be vibrating.

"Isn't it? The fella thumped Malone? Turned up there in the Temple Bar this afternoon?"

Minogue nodded. Kilmartin seemed satisfied. He grasped his glass, looked down into it and then threw the last of its contents into the back of his throat.

"How," Minogue began. "I mean when . . ."

Kilmartin gave him a hard look.

"Why?" said Minogue.

"Why? You think I just happened across this? Oh right. You probably heard I keep in touch with the Bureau mob. Right. No, this isn't because of that."

He leaned around Minogue to pick the bottle from the table.

"No," Kilmartin said. "Sometimes they ask me to have a gawk at some of the Scenes photos. You know, me being the old hand. Your name doesn't be on the list for that extracurricular, I'm sure."

"Are you involved in this thing?"

"Involved is it? Well now Matt, me oul stock . . ."

Kilmartin spun on his heel a little, and looked up to a corner of the ceiling for a few moments.

"God, how far do we go back? Ah donkey's years. Ah yes."

Kilmartin's eyes went to window out. Over the hedge there Minogue could see some lights all the way over beyond Shankill, the hills behind part of the dark.

"I'm going to make a cup of tea. Come on."

"Don't. Just sit down and we'll talk."

Minogue pulled open the door and headed for the kitchen. His foot caught on something and dragged it along the run. He stopped and looked down and then stooped down. A piece of pottery?

"Forget the damn tea, will you!"

Minogue pushed open the door of the kitchen. The light was off but he could still see pieces of things against the tiles. He forgot for a moment where the light switch was. Kilmartin was next to him now.

"Leave it," he said. "I told you. Don't mind here. Come back in and we'll talk."

Minogue shook the hand off his shoulder.

"Where's Maura?"

"Maura's grand. Don't worry about Maura. Okay, come on back now."

When Minogue resisted again, Kilmartin stood at the wall, his back to the light switch. Minogue didn't want to cross the floor to find another light on the cooker.

"Look Matt, we had words. All right? I'm ashamed to say. Now come on out. I don't want to be reminded. Really."

"Is she all right, Jim?"

"She's fine. You know she gets, well, emotional sometimes. Seldom enough now."

"Liam?"

"What about Liam?"

"Is he okay?"

"He is. Now stop, will you, and come back inside. I'll fix this later."

Minogue couldn't see Kilmartin's face.

"Maura's a great worker, Jim. We all know that. Is she maybe ready for a break?"

Kilmartin said nothing.

"Maybe yourself and herself would consider taking off and heading over to see Liam? Sure he'd be delighted, and Maura–"

"Will you for the love of Christ stop talking? And about Liam? Will you?"

Minogue looked at the column of dim light in the doorway as it opened again.

"Come out of here," Kilmartin said. "I don't want to be reminded. Okay?"

The catch in Kilmartin's voice changed everything for him. He went by Kilmartin and heard the kitchen door close behind him. Kilmartin's voice was almost a whisper now.

"Jim, if there's anything I can do . . ."

Kilmartin's eyes had a weariness in them now when he stared across at Minogue.

"Do . . .? I think you already have, Matt. Yes."

"I don't know what that means."

Kilmartin sat back and let his arm rest on the dresser. He looked up at the dresser then, seemed to take in the quality of the trim, the glass doors, and then down to the brass handles on the drawers below. He let out a big sigh.

"What do you know about that man, in those pictures? Jim?"

A weak smile came to Kilmartin's features but left quickly and the bleakness set in deeper.

"Oh Christ," he said. "Me and my foolish ways. Digital this, and digital that. Do you know I have a damn phone, a mobile I mean, that even takes videos? But, no. These ones I asked for. It took me an hour but there's the beauty of the gadgets – I was able to reach Jack still at the site. You remember Jack Mooney?"

"Scenes? Photo man?"

"Who else. Jack is as mad as I am for this stuff. So I get his mobile and he says he'll download a few. Do you know what that means?"

Minogue nodded.

"Well, there's progress. Maybe soon you'll graduate to finding the power switch on your phone."

Minogue waited for a smile, even the hint of one.

"I've a confession, Jim," he said finally. Kilmartin, stopped stroking his nose.

"I know what I'm doing, acting the gobshite. I leave it off on purpose."

Kilmartin's face eased but then his eyes lost their focus again.
"As if I didn't know."

A minute passed. All Minogue heard was Kilmartin's fingertips moving over bristles on his chin.

"What did you phone for, Jim?"

"I can't tell you."

Again Minogue waited.

"I can't."

And then Kilmartin's head went down. His shoulders
heaved and he drew in his arms to bring his hands over his face.
Minogue heard huge tearing sobs. His own mind went wild. He
felt his own limbs had seized up, a gaping tear open in his guts.

"I can't," Kilmartin sobbed. "I can't."

"I can help," was all Minogue could think to say.

"Where's Maura? I just want to see her, Jim."

Kilmartin wiped his nose with his hand and gradually sat
up. He took a box of paper hankies from the drawer and blew his
nose. The minutes passed.

"Sorry," he said then. "I'm sorry."

"Nothing to be sorry for, Jim. Nothing. It's good you
phoned. I am."

"Is it? Is it really?"

Kilmartin's hand ran up and down the handles of the drawer
behind him.

"Do they know who he is? This man in the car?"

Kilmartin's hand stopped stroking the drawer handles.

"Well, do you know who it is?" he said to Minogue.

"Tommy and I met him over in a big drinking barn on the
Naas Road. He's the fella knocked Tommy's head off."

"But who is he?"

"I don't know. Maybe you can tell me, now. A foreign
accent; calls himself George."

Kilmartin's fingers began to move again, tracing the out-
lines of the embossed brass, dropping the handles one by one as
he went to each.

"George," he said. "You caught up with him again there
down the Temple Bar?"

"Jim."

Kilmartin didn't react.

"Jim?"

The face that turned to Minogue had lost its hardness, that set of folds and lines that Minogue had bundled forever with James Kilmartin.

"How long again, Matt? Twenty what . . . ?"

"Over twenty years," said Minogue. "That's as high as I can count."

"You were in rag order when I took you on, do you remember. Very shaky."

"I was that."

"But I knew," Kilmartin went on. "I knew who and what I was getting on board, didn't I? And we done all right, the Squad, didn't we?"

"We did."

"But too good. There's something in human nature wants to tear things down. There is, you know. Everything always goes back to that."

Minogue couldn't make sense of this. He eyed the almost empty glass. He wondered how would he convince Kilmartin not to have any more, to call it a night.

"Matt, tell me something. And don't try to get around this one, okay?"

Minogue nodded. The Jameson's had his mind drifting a bit now.

"Serious now?"

"Serious."

"Is there a hell? Come on now – you said you'd be serious. Stop looking at me like that. Tell me – look, I know you're one of them deep thinker types. Really. So tell me, will you?"

Minogue shook his head.

"But you can't get it out of your head, can you? Remember, the priests, and the sermons before Good Friday – all the fires? And the worms and that? Forever . . .?"

Again, Minogue shook his head.

"I have it in my head since then too," he said. "I just can't get it out."

"And you the pagan too," Kilmartin murmured.

Minogue understood that something had been closed now. Maybe now that Kilmartin was calmer, something would come out.

"Things always look better in the morning," he said. Kilmartin didn't let on he'd heard him.

"All that philosophizing," said Kilmartin in the same slow monotone. "Christ. 'There's no going back.' Isn't that what they all say? Why am I always hearing that these days? Are you hearing that a lot these days, are you?"

"Well, I don't believe the 'they' mob half the time."

Kilmartin gave him a look that Minogue at first took to be annoyance, but ended in a something between a grimace and a bleaker smile.

"I'm always blathering, amn't I. And now look at me."

"Is Maura upstairs, Jim?"

A glint of anger came to Kilmartin's eyes, and his face changed.

"You have me worried," said Minogue. "What happened here? It was hardly those fellas redoing your kitchen are after throwing the crockery around."

Kilmartin didn't take up any of the effort at humour.

"Worried, are you," he said, his voice regaining some strength.

Minogue held back from saying any more for the moment. Kilmartin rubbed hard at his eyes.

"Everything going great," he muttered. "Deep down you always know there's something else, though. But you ignore it. You forget about it."

He stopped rubbing, and looked at Minogue.

"Do you know how much I hate what I do every day? My job?"

"I thought you liked it."

"God, I tried and I tried. The golden parachute out of the Squad, the new office and the perks. Everyone telling me how lucky I was – I began to believe them. I wanted to. All this guff about electronics and databases and – and everything. You know what? I couldn't give a tinker's curse. And I bet you're the same, with your Mister Eurocop gig there. I'm right, amn't I?"

Maybe Kilmartin and his wife had had a row about money. It had been a sore point years ago, he vaguely remembered. But why? Maura's business was going great. She could well afford to pay for any decorating and building whims herself. Maybe Kilmartin had had a few jars too many, and something was said, and then it popped. Maybe the pressure had built up too much.

"Here," said Kilmartin. "No way, no *way* are you not having a proper drink. No way – and not on the worst night of my life. Wait and I'll get you a glass. Wait there!"

Minogue heard Kilmartin's leather soles crunch more stuff on the floor going into the hall. Kilmartin was muttering to himself, but Minogue could not make out the words. He took out his phone, and wondered where, or whom, to start calling.

Chapter 28

KILMARTIN WAS BACK QUICKER than Minogue had expected. "What's with the phone? Who are you phoning?" Minogue waited until Kilmartin stood still and looked at him.

"The truth is, Jim, nobody. I don't know who I should phone. But you're in bad shape. What's Maura's mobile?"

"Forget Maura's mobile, will you!"

Minogue stared at him.

"Come on, damn it all now," said Kilmartin. "Let's not have a falling-out, for Christ's sake! What were we talking about anyway? Here, take this."

Minogue held the glass but didn't drink from it.

"Right," said Kilmartin, letting himself down with a sigh. "Right – you and Malone, the pair of you. You're like, I don't know, magnets or something, yes, magnets for trouble. I mean to say, one day the pair of you saunter into a church, to listen to some scut, what's his name . . ."

"Lawless?"

"Right! Jesus, how could I forget a name like that. Anyway, next day he's dead. Then, for God's sake, you find some big lug of a fella you think is connected to someone in the Condon case, and that one turns up dead in a car – this is four hours after he has a run-in with you two, with bullets flying in broad daylight right in the middle of Dublin today! Now how does that happen?

Answer me that one if you can."

Minogue watched him reach for the whiskey bottle. Halfway to it, Kilmartin stopped and looked across at him again.

"I know," he said. "It's Tynan. He knows; he's copped on. Oh but he's a cold, calculating bastard – and I don't care if his missus is at death's door with cancer, or whatever. I don't. I just wish he'd have come to me, and put it straight out. Christ, that would have been bad enough – but not this! He used you, Matt. Tell me the truth now, come on. How did he brief you? What did he tell you?"

The bottle swayed in Kilmartin's hand as he held it over the rim of his glass, and it splashed in more whiskey than he was ready for. The neck of the bottle bounced off the rim as Kilmartin tried to correct his hold, but nothing broke.

"Just to review the Condon case."

"My arse for a yarn! Why the hell were you chasing this fella today then? Or after Rynn?"

Minogue watched Kilmartin take a hurried gulp. He tried to remember when Rynn's name had come up with Kilmartin, but couldn't.

"Well?"

"You know a lot about this, Jim. Don't you?"

"Answer my question!"

"You've been keeping on eye on us, haven't you. What we're working on."

Kilmartin put his glass down.

"Are you ready? Do you really want to know who this man is, was? Do you?"

Minogue nodded. His mind wouldn't let go of wondering how Kilmartin had come up with Rynn.

"Okay then. He's a fella works with Rynn. He came over first two years ago. He's in and out of the country a lot. Want to know what he does?"

"Go ahead."

Kilmartin moved in over the table, and he held his fist over it.

"He's a pimp. That's what he is."

The fist came down, but not with the clumsy force Minogue had expected.

"He's a drug importer."

Down came the fist again.

"He moves money around – from Eastern Europe to that other great Irish country where my goddamn son is probably going to spend the rest of his goddamn days, America. This man sells women, rents them. And he beats them if they give him any bother. Now what kind of a man does that?"

"A criminal, I suppose."

"Damned right! He drives a fancy car. He has three or four places he lives in, here and in someplace the arse end of Masi–, Mace–, a place that's half Greece and half not."

"Macedonia?"

"That's the one. His parents were mixed in there somehow. Oh yes, this fella likes to move around. He did some kind of national service, and he knows his guns and how to beat the crap out of people. A paratrooper, he was. He's in and out of places I barely heard of: Sofia, Budapest, or Bucharest. That Moldova place. Christ, when I heard that place, I thought it was a type of a cake or something. Did you know any of this?"

Minogue watched the hand circle the glass.

"He talks to these people here in their own language. He *is* one of those people, do you get it? Rynn brought him in, or let him in, I should say. And he lets Rynn think that Rynn's the boss, when in actual fact, Rynn is the one who got hired by these people."

Minogue took advantage of the pause while Kilmartin lifted his glass.

"What people?"

"Don't be stupid, Matt. The place is overrun with them – the continent anyway, and we're getting like that. And I'll tell you something else. When Rynn's not useful for them here anymore, this fella will get the word and do for Rynn, so's they can run things the way they want. He's a Michael, or however they spell Michael over there, Arcacop – Christ, I can't remember how to say it. George's his middle name. Now *that's* a bit ironic, wouldn't you say?"

"You mean he's not actually Greek?"

"No! Middle names. Sure amn't I married to a middle name, for God's sake?"

"Jim, I don't get this– I'm lost here, you have to– "

"*Eimear* Maura," Kilmartin said, his voice near a shout now. "You iijit! Come on, you knew that for years, I mean we all knew the story there."

Minogue tried to remember the year Kilmartin had gotten married.

"I know what you think," said Kilmartin. "All these years. I'm not a gobshite, you know. I know what people think, yes I do. 'Ah, Jim loves to be in the know – a great man for the contacts.' 'Ah, Jim's a divil for the oul gossip, isn't he.' Isn't that it? Come on now."

"And you're good at it," Minogue said. 'That's why you come out on top.'

"Oh really," said Kilmartin with a whine in his voice. "Now isn't that sweet of you. You're doing a bit of what here, social work, is it? Charity? Counselling? Poor Jim. Jim needs a hug. Jim's crying his eyes out. Poor oul Jim's off the rails."

The screen saver stopped suddenly and the screen went black. Minogue's eye lingered on a small orange light that began to pulse slowly under the screeen.

"No," Kilmartin declared, and planted his glass hard on the table. "This time, you'd be very goddamned wrong, so you would."

His voice was soft then when he spoke again.

"But by Christ, how I wish you could be right. How I wish that now."

Minogue did what he always did, dithered. He thought about trying to get Kilmartin out of the house, down to Dun Laoghaire Pier even, or the Strand, to sober him up. He saw him reaching for the bottle again.

"Don't, Jim. It'll just make it worse."

Kilmartin's arm stopped. He looked down at it as though it had unexpectedly disobeyed him. Minogue thought his friend was going to cry, again.

"No it isn't," Kilmartin muttered. "We're not going back. We're just not."

James Kilmartin was beyond proud, Minogue knew. He was defiant, supreme, a man from a different age. Kilmartin would not be able to face Minogue again for a long, long time after tonight. Maybe never. The loss his mind predicted but his stomach wanted to hold back began to ache hard now.

Kilmartin threw back a noisy gulp of whiskey.

"You're forgetting," he said. "How do I know all this, right? Didn't you want to ask me that? Didn't you?"

"It's not important right now," Minogue said.

"Oh, is that so, now?"

"You need a night's sleep. Can I see Maura before I go . . .?"

Kilmartin held his glass up and studied its contents.

"The laughing stock of every Guard now," he said. "And I never knew. Never! But, sure, who'd ever believe that? Nobody."

"I just don't get it, Jim. I'm missing out on something."

"You still don't get it? Well that's funny now. Because I don't get it either."

Parts of Kilmartin's words were getting mashed more and more, Minogue realized. The whiskey would have him asleep now, if only he'd give it the chance.

"All those years, Matt. All those years. Right under my nose. Who'd believe that? Who, I ask you? Not a one of them, that's who. I'll get dragged down with her."

"Maura–"

Kilmartin was suddenly on his feet. His chair bounced off the computer table, and rolled sideways where it settled. The screen glowed alive again.

"Will you for the love of Christ shut up about that? Maura this, Maura that. You go on, and on, and on about her. Jesus!"

Kilmartin couldn't stand steady. Minogue prepared to stand himself.

"Don't you get it yet? Didn't you hear a word I said?"

Minogue stood slowly.

Kilmartin had both hands on his head now. He looked like a prisoner-of-war on one of those programs about the war, Minogue thought.

"It was Maura did all this," he whispered.

Kilmartin swung out an arm, and moved it in a slow arc.

"The house, the Waterford glass all over the kitchen floor. The holidays. The marble in the toilet. The fancy car. Didn't you ever wonder, didn't you?"

"Wonder what?"

"I mean how could a farmer's son from the bogs of Mayo ever do this?"

"Maura's done great, Jim."

Kilmartin looked over at Minogue, and nodded once.

"It's Maura," he said. "Yes. Maura, Maura, Maura."

He dropped his arm and stared for a moment at the window. "She met him."

Minogue took a step away from the table.

"Rynn?"

"Yeah, *Rynn!*"

The quiet in the room after Kilmartin's yell was intense.

"When did she tell you?"

"Tonight," he said, his voice barely a whisper now. "I told her about that fella you and Malone were after. The way I tell her any news, Christ, like I've done since the day we got married. The way any couple would. Come on: 'Any bit of news today, love?' Thousands of people, millions, ask the same question over the tea table every night. Tell me that's true or not, isn't it?"

Minogue nodded.

"It was a coincidence – as if there's such a damned thing. It had to do with work. Rynn's a 'businessman' now, if you please. He was looking to hire people, a type of part-time I-don't-know-what scam he had going. Meat products or something. Rynn, who should have been under lock and key years ago."

"What coincidence, Jim?"

"We had him back then, for the love of God! Oh, this is ten years ago, yes. Why do I remember it? It was just before the big turnover, the millennium thing – a fella in Serious Crimes, he says, Jim, bejases, we have him now. They were lining him up – we had a sidekick of his was going to do the business, to grass on Rynn – the whole works. But then he disappears. Christ, we used to make a sort of a joke about it. 'A matter of weeks' – the fella's name *was* Weekes. He never turned up, never."

"I wondered how he's still on the streets," Minogue said. "Rynn, I mean, if he's a big wheel."

"Oh by Christ, I'm telling you! He got even bigger! He never put one foot wrong after that. We came close a few times, but somehow he was always one step ahead of us. Some . . . how."

"Maura talked to you about stuff like this, Jim?"

Kilmartin gave him a short, disdainful look, and turned away.

"'Talked,'" he murmured. "She certainly did 'talk.'"

"Why this evening?"

"She went a bit odd after I told her about your shenanigans. I even think I mentioned Rynn, you know. So she got a funny look to her. I sort of noticed something, but what would I know to say, or to ask?"

"Jim, stop a minute. Why this talk of Rynn?"

"So," Kilmartin said, going on as though Minogue hadn't spoken. "Out she goes. Where, I do not know. She's gone down to the shopping centre or something, I thinks to myself. Maybe Cornelscourt, I don't know."

Minogue did not take advantage of the pause. He watched instead, as Kilmartin seemed to gather himself.

"She's back inside of an hour. She looks a bit shook, I says to myself, but I says nothing. Why would I? But then she sees me fiddling here at the computer. 'Any email from Liam?' No, says I. Then she sees the pictures, you know, bits of them. After I see that thing on the news, I had this feeling – so I calls Paddy, Paddy down at the Bureau, and he eventually ponies up three pictures. The ones you saw there."

"He's still doing that, is he," Minogue said, the urge to say anything strong now.

Maybe Maura's car was in the garage. He could just wander upstairs, with the excuse of using the toilet there.

"Are you listening to me?"

"I'm with you on this part."

"So I'm yapping away, you know the way I go on some-times. Telling Maura I had a notion this fella might be the self-same fella who had been giving you two such trouble. So she looks at me, right? What's wrong, says I. Are you poorly? I mean, she looks like she's going to pass out on me, or something."

At that Kilmartin paused again, and took a breath, and glanced over at Minogue.

"That's when everything went haywire, Matt," he said in a whisper.

"Haywire."

"Actually, not right then. I went to the jacks, and when I came back, she had looked on the desktop thing there and she'd seen the pictures. She . . . She . . ."

Kilmartin pinched his eyes and breathed out several times. Minogue checked again that he had his mobile in his jacket pocket. He tried to get eye contact with Kilmartin.

"Will you come out a while with me, Jim?"

"Will you drive me somewhere?"

"Well, I could, I suppose, but where?"

"Near to town."

"Where?"

"Not that far. I'll tell you when we get there."

"I was thinking maybe a little bit of fresh air. Walk the roads here a half an hour?"

"I'll bloody drive meself then, won't I? Then we'll see who's going to win, so we will. Oh yes we will."

"Jim, you're too far gone to be doing that."

Kilmartin frowned at him.

"I'm too far gone? Me? Don't you get it, Matt? Don't you get what I'm telling you?"

Minogue felt the hairs going up on the back of his neck: so this is what a nervous breakdown looked like?

"We can go out a while, Jim. Would you like that? Just tell Maura we're going out for a pint. Will you do that?"

Kilmartin shook his head.

"Can I tell her then?"

Again Kilmartin shook his head.

"She told me things, Matt. You know?"

Minogue waited.

"She says he could do it to us now."

"Do what, Jim? Who would?"

Kilmartin's eyes were wide now. He blinked.

"Rynn. She told me. She told me everything."

Minogue's mind had gone empty.

"Rynn," he said.

Kilmartin nodded. His eyes were still on Minogue but they had slipped out of focus.

"She," he began. "Maura, I mean. Maura met him. It was her husband. Everything got screwed up. She tried to get out, but she couldn't."

Minogue moved slightly, but it didn't work. Kilmartin's eyes stayed fixed.

"She thinks Rynn is gone mad, that he'll kill anyone. Like that fella. She says . . ."

With that, the intensity returned to Kilmartin's eyes.

"She says, Rynn's the type would do that, just to be sure."

"Do what?"

"He'd kill everyone, to cover himself. She did it, Matt. Did you know that? She did it. I believe her."

"What did she do, Jim?"

"I never in a million years would have known," said Kilmartin. "Me who knows everything. Do you believe me? Do you?"

"Maura, Jim: what did she do?"

"She– What's that out there? Out on the road there."

Minogue turned to the window. Through the reflected room around him, he saw car lights slide between the gate pillars, and drift slowly down the road until they were swallowed up by the hedges.

"He's stopping," said Kilmartin. "He had his brake lights on. Did you see?"

Minogue turned back toward Kilmartin.

"That's my car parked out there."

"It went by," Kilmartin hissed. "But it stopped up the road."

"You need a rest. We'll work it all out afterwards. Soon, all right?"

"There's another one."

Kilmartin was on the move. He said something Minogue didn't understand, but he heard "business."

Kilmartin pulled hard at one of the drawers, making the wood squeal a little. He drew something out, and with his back to Minogue seemed to push at it, or pull.

Minogue knew what it was, and still he refused to believe it. He glanced at the door half ajar.

"We'll see about that," he heard Kilmartin say.

He saw the gun held down near Kilmartin's knee as Kilmartin lunged at the light switch.

"What the hell are you doing, Jim?"

"You shut up now. Enough out of you, with your let's go for a walk. Hit that damned screen – quick!"

Kilmartin's whiskey breath seemed to have filled the room.

"Jim, don't."

Kilmartin said something under his breath, stepped over, almost missing his balance, and stabbed at a button under the screen.

"Get over the back wall, behind the forsythia there. Into the O'Neills, and then– have you a phone?"

"Yes, but–"

"Don't 'but' me, for Christ's sake! Get going! These fellas won't be polite about it. Get! Go!"

Kilmartin brushed by him and slapped at a switch in the hall. Minogue heard his shoes crush something and scrape against the kitchen floor. He looked down the driveway. Nobody.

"Jim, slow down, it's nothing. Nothing, okay?"

"Get out," Kilmartin called out. "Out the back. They might be there already."

There was a swathe of pale light from somewhere across the kitchen floor. A moon, Minogue wondered. He saw shadows of broken things, some with the soft glint of glass or china. Kilmartin had pulled open the back door. Minogue couldn't see his face.

"Out!"

"Jim! It's probably just kids coming home late or something."

"Shut up, you gom," Kilmartin said. "Don't you know anything? They know where you live, they know everything – what's that? Jesus, they're out there."

Minogue ducked down alongside Kilmartin. Through the open door he heard something, a footfall maybe. He peered around the edge of the cupboard.

The doorbell went then. Kilmartin started and brought up the gun. He turned on his hunkers, holding out his hand on the floor. Someone was definitely in the garden. There was roaring in Minogue's head now, but still Kilmartin's croaking whisper came to him.

"It's too late for the back, come on!"

Kilmartin began to creep across the floor, scattering fragments and shards, crunching others, as he went. He pulled up his hand sharply after a few steps, swore, and lost his balance. Minogue's heart leaped then: something was crossing the dimmer light bathing the garden. There was a hat to the figure though, a brim. It was standard if they were coming to a house where there'd been trouble, he remembered.

"Jim, it's Guards, stop! I saw one."

"No! – Jesus I've cut meself here, that stupid Waterford glass . . . ! We're going out the front, Matt. It's our best chance."

Kilmartin had slurred half his words. Minogue saw another movement, a figure detach itself from the shadows and begin to approach the side of the house.

"Jim, put it down, they're Guards!"

Kilmartin was on his feet now, in a crouch. Minogue rose, felt his knees get some strength, and the dizziness and his racing jackhammer heart crest higher. He kept his eye on Kilmartin's right arm, saw the pistol pointed to the floor. It took two steps to get to Kilmartin's side. For a moment he thought of Maura, of something terrible Kilmartin had done to her. Then, with Kilmartin's muttered curses coming through the roaring in his ears, he grabbed at the forearm with both his hands.

With his left on Kilmartin's wrist, he ran his other hand down over his knuckles to where he gripped the pistol. Kilmartin let out a shout that didn't come close to drowning out the gunshot. Minogue had him off balance, and he pulled more. A man shouted outside, and something passed by the open door in a hurry.

Kilmartin's finger was locked inside the trigger-guard still. Minogue got his shoulder into Kilmartin as he turned, and he felt Kilmartin lose his footing and come with him. He had the gun and Kilmartin's knuckles on the floor now. As Kilmartin came down, Minogue backed in harder. Kilmartin tried to turn, but Minogue pushed back while he pulled the arm against the joint.

He couldn't make out what Kilmartin was shouting now. He knew he couldn't be sure that Kilmartin was so drunk he couldn't get out of the lock.

"They're Guards!" he yelled again. "Guards!"

He hadn't been able to get anywhere trying to pry Kilmartin's fingers out from the trigger-guard. He considered trying to thumb the safety, or even to eject the clip. Kilmartin began to push back slowly now.

"I'll break your goddamned arm, Jim," he hissed. "I will!"

Then there was somebody in the doorway, and they were shouting. He felt Kilmartin's arm slacken a little, as the man shouted again. Somebody else had come in behind them too, a second voice, not yelling.

Minogue looked down the arm that held the pistol trained on him, saw no uniform, and his heart went cold. In one instant he believed that Kilmartin had been right all along. He saw the man framed in Merchant's Arch, Malone ducking, flinching. Maura, he thought too: what had happened to Maura?

"Flat!" the man with the pistol yelled again. "Arms out – straighter!"

Minogue's face pressed into tiles.

"I'm a Garda officer," he said.

"Face down!"

"We're Guards," Minogue said again, just as his arm was grabbed and pulled up.

"I know," the man above him said. "Just shut up a minute, will you."

Minogue's left arm was yanked then and he felt the cut of the plastic restraints bite into his wrists. He knew they'd not turn him over, but he didn't care. More footsteps came through the kitchen now. A piece of broken something went by on the tiles beside him. Still he heard the other sound, above the drag of feet scratching across the debris.

"Jimmy," he said. The sobs continued.

"It's him," he heard a voice say. "Okay, we have it."

"Jim?"

The sobbing paused.

"Where's my wife?" Kilmartin asked. "Where is she?"

One of the detectives came down on one knee.

"She's outside," he said. "She came with us."

"Is she hurt?" Kilmartin sobbed. "I would never . . . I didn't mean to do that. I never did a thing like that in my life, I'd never raise my hand to a woman, I wouldn't."

He began sobbing again, and Minogue heard his shoes scraping across the fragments on the tiles.

"Watch him!" a voice called out. "He's moving."

"It's okay," came the other voice, as the detective stood. "We have it. It's okay."

"Let her alone," Minogue heard his friend whisper between sobs. "She's had enough trouble in her life."

Chapter 29

MINOGUE WAS DOWN TO his last cigarette. He listened to the wind, and watched Jacky's eyes. His brother's dog was a tired and ancient collie, content enough to have trailed along at an easy pace with Minogue when he had started his climb up on the rocky Burren headlands above the farm, hours earlier.

"Go down to the village and buy me some fags," he whispered to Jacky.

The tail wagged gently, and the eyes passed over Minogue. Soon the dog was resting its muzzle on its paws again, and looking out the doorway of the stone shelter. The drizzle had not quite obscured the line of Atlantic cradled between the hills.

Those were Minogue's first words since the ones this morning in the kitchen, to Kathleen. She had taken a few days off and come down with him here, to the family farm. She and her sister-in-law had gone into Ennis the other day. Today it was Galway City. Back at the farmhouse earlier on, Minogue had lifted the phone back in the farmhouse to phone Kathleen on her mobile, ready to apologize for snapping at her. But he didn't. He had just glanced at the front page of the newspaper, and on it he had seen enough in those two photos. Rynn, in cuffs, was being put into a patrol car. Sister Imelda Foran had her arm around someone who was wearing a coat over her head.

"Natalia," Minogue murmured. The dog's ears went up a little.

It was her real name. She had been brought over from England, along with some others who had already been forced into the racket there. It had been Rynn's idea to let George – or Mike, or Mikhail, if the papers they'd found weren't bogus – run things here for a while yet. Apparently he spoke the language.

They'd found a Bulgarian passport as well, and a Russian passport too, in the man's place, a swish flat on Pembroke Road. One was in the name of Mikhail somebody, the other a name that translated as George. There had been a hundred and something thousand euro in envelopes about the place. They'd also found a small pistol – not the one he'd pulled on Malone that day, it turned out – along with plastic bags of amphetamines, one of cocaine, and a collection of pornography. There were keys for safety deposit boxes, airline tickets, phone numbers to places Minogue had to check out on a map: Skopje, Belgrade, places near the Black Sea, more.

There were first names that matched people known to Interpol. Entry stamps from Moscow airport, Heathrow, Athens, everywhere. And Kilmartin had been right about the paratrooper bit. The man also had the women's families' addresses, even phone numbers for them, and sets of some of the best fake papers that the Guards had come across yet – including passports from Canada and Spain and some other places.

There had been headlines for several days: 'A shocking glimpse of the reality of Eurocrime.' 'Syndicates come to Ireland: are we sitting ducks?' Sullivan had told him before he'd left that even Moser was helping out on it, from over in Austria, and wanted to send his regards. It had made front pages in papers over there one day. Serious Crimes were holding one of Rynn's fixers on a drugs charge from the day after the shooting. They were going at him night and day to give them any piece of Rynn. But Rynn was holding tight: he hardly knew this Mike character at all, friend of a friend, etc. He had hired two barristers. He was out on bail. He'd even given an interview where he said he was getting advice on suing the Guards for interfering with a legitimate entrepreneur and businessman.

None of this Minogue wanted to know.

But Malone was almost sure they were going after Rynn for both Lawless and this shooting of George/Mike too. Rynn was saying nothing about Emmett Condon. Malone was confident that as more of Rynn's people were brought in, something would give – especially now the girl had turned up alive.

In the same phone call that Minogue himself had cut short, Malone also told him there was no word yet on the raid the Guards in Portlaoise had done on the poultry plant there, or the house where the other girls had been kept. The man they'd arrested there was local – "the foreman," he described himself, and claimed he was running a legit business with people who wanted to work there. Chickens, Malone had repeated the man's protestations: chickens is my only concern!

Mister Chicken-tycoon denied ever meeting Rynn, or even this Mike. That he was shielding the girl from Rynn did not occur to him, apparently: if it had, he would have jettisoned her, no doubt. Fear would put things in perspective, no doubt, and any fees or earnings from it would become suddenly very, very unimportant if he'd known Rynn was involved. Defying Rynn, and running the girl out on the Naas Road along with the others, had been his erstwhile foreign partner's fatal calculation.

Minogue reached into his back pocket, and felt around for the page he had torn out of yesterday's paper. It was a bit the worse for wear already. He spread it out on the rocks underfoot, pausing again to study the photos of the African man's family getting ready to board a plane for the first time, before turning it over to the coverage of Kilmartin. Hand in hand with an equally haggard-looking Maura, Jim Kilmartin had been caught by a photographer coming out of some barrister's office up near The Four Courts. The charge of assault (domestic) had been tacked onto the firearms one. There was no word on the rest, whatever they would be. Could you be charged for talking to your wife? For having a big mouth, for resorting to that most Irish of habits, the heroic tales of struggling, merry and wily, against an enemy?

Minogue couldn't stop thinking about Kilmartin. Somehow he looked much smaller here in the picture, this man in whose company Minogue had been so often over the years. Maura had lost a lot of weight. There was shading on her right side still, but the eye didn't look as bad. Their son had flown home from the States to help out. Some homecoming. Nobody answered the Kilmartins' home number. His mobile went straight to a message.

But Minogue would not give up. He looked around the shed that had always been here, even before he was born. It hadn't changed in decades. It was the first place he thought of when Kathleen had suggested going away for a few days. Its drystone walls were imperfectly capped by rusting corrugated iron, and that roof itself was held down and almost covered with smaller stones.

His mind was made up: he pulled out his mobile. A weak signal. He dialed anyway. The same message. He'd do the same as he had done every day since, anyway.

"Jim, it's Matt. Phone me. I swear I'll have it switched on."

Just as he readied to End it, he stopped, and lifted it again.

"Jim, you have to believe me. I never for a minute thought . . ."

He lost track of what he should say then. He closed the phone slowly, in the hope that he'd remember what he should be saying before the connection went. Jacky was staring at him. When he looked back, the tail wagged.

"You'd talk if only you could, wouldn't you? Same as myself."

Minogue leaned over, his eyes still on the view over the stone fields that led off to Black Head, and took out the bottle.

"Don't let on you saw this. We have enough misery."

It scalded a bit. His stomach was empty; it didn't matter. He felt for the letter, and confirmed with his thumb under the flap that he had sealed it. A stamp too, he felt. Dear Sir/Madam, This letter is to inform you of my decision to . . .

His eyes glazed over. They were then drawn to a distant movement, barely visible through the drizzle. It was a bus, a tourist bus, no doubt, and it was making slow progress, winding its way toward far-off Corkscrew Hill. Minogue had seen no walkers here since he'd come up across Corcabawn earlier, the long way that wound around the unmarked graveyard and the ruins of Cathirmore. The grey from the limestone had long closed in on the leaking sky, and only the fissures in the rocks kept them apart in places. It'd be dark in a couple of hours.

"And so what," he murmured. The dog's ears quivered.

Soon Minogue's eyes slid out of focus again. The dog had closed his eyes, he noticed.

He closed his eyes, but his thoughts wouldn't stop churning. The whiskey wasn't helping. Still things swirled and paused, and they came back worse, before moving on around again. As though burned on his eyelids, he saw Maura Kilmartin's desolate face out on the driveway again that night, and the bruises on her face worse than the closing eye. He had heard Kilmartin wail once in the house, and then something being hammered a few times. Two squad cars showed up very damn fast after the gun went off. The sergeant who came tearing in from Dalkey Station started out very belligerent. He soon backed off. Still, Minogue had felt like hitting him, hard.

Blake had shown up within the hour. He got nowhere with Kilmartin, who was still drunk. He had taken to long silences which he'd interrupt with a curse at whoever was asking him something. They had charged Kilmartin the same night all the same, with the firearms charge. There was no bail set. They'd put him on paid leave, pending.

Kathleen heard that Maura had gone down the country to her sister's, and that Jim might be with her. They were worried about Maura. Nobody had said they were worried about Superintendent James Kilmartin. And what were they going to charge her with, she'd asked Minogue several times, until he'd snapped at her. He didn't know, and he didn't want to know. He had even told Tadhg Sullivan he'd wipe that grin off his face if he thought he could say anything about Jim Kilmartin and his doings. Power, his head of section, had met him the first day in, and said why didn't he take a few days' leave, and he wasn't asking. Great idea, Minogue had told him, as though to let him know he wouldn't be back anyway.

His mind slowed, or rather went sideways, and the breeze

against the stones and whistling low in the roof took over. In his dreams, if they were dreams at all and not some delirium, he saw the African man. He was picking up all the wreaths and cards from the footpath, and giving them to Iseult, who dropped them into something and then hammered a piece of metal to another, and said something that sounded like Moravia. Then there was a gavel, and Sister Imelda, smoking, in front of a collie who guarded some red stains on a roadway, and Maura Kilmartin saying something. She said it again, and she turned and ran into a river, or was it a lake. Then the dog was back, baring its teeth and growling low in its throat.

Minogue opened his eyes. He was blind! No: it was dark. It was Jacky growling. The growl began to rise, and just before it tore into barking, Minogue heard a voice, something scuffing against stones outside.

"Turn off the dog, will you?"

Jacky wouldn't go beyond the doorway. Minogue called to him, and tried to get up. The stiffness had almost locked his joints. The bottle was by his hand. He got the neck of it, and tried to hear the words between the barking.

"Boss, the dog? Can you switch it off?"

Minogue rolled slowly to his knees, and ran his hand down the dog's back to the collar.

"I brought a big stick, I don't want to use it on him. Boss? Are you there at all?"

"Give me a minute, Tommy."

He stayed on his hunkers and got through the doorway. Malone's silhouette against the last of the sky to the west showed a sizeable blackthorn stick. The dog lunged, almost pulling Minogue over.

He held it for a while, whispering to it.

"Put away that stick, so he knows you're not worth a bite," he said to Malone. "Let him smell you awhile."

"I have a torch. I'm turning it on, okay?"

Jacky started growling again. The light went from Malone's shoe across the stones and back. "To find our way back."

"I don't need it. Turn it off."

"I brought this, here."

Minogue felt the bottle, and grasped it.

"You certainly took the wrong turn somewhere. How'd you get here?"

"From Dublin? Easy. I just asked someone where a head case would hide."

"But up here."

A voice came over to Minogue then, and Jacky's tail went off.

"I showed him, Uncle Matt."

"Is that Sean?"

"It is. Da sent the little something. No fags though. He has orders not to."

Minogue let the dog go. Malone stepped over.

"I'm here for a reason, Tommy. So I'd be obliged if you'd leave me to it."

Malone didn't say anything. Minogue tried to see Jacky's antics with his nephew. Sean was the baby of the family, too shy by far. He loved animals. It looked like he'd get the farm now.

"Well, I'll leave you to it," Sean said. "Ye're all right for the way down, are ye?"

Minogue let his eye go from light to light below the headland, and settled on the yard light for his brother's farm. He listened to Sean's footsteps over the stones, the dog's paws as he bounded from stone to stone ahead of him.

"Nice here," said Malone. "Except for the fact it's frigging wet and cold and dark, and we're in the middle of frigging nowhere."

Malone shifted a little where he sat when Minogue made no response.

"Nothing personal, okay? I don't mean that in a bad way."

He heard Malone's breath, as though about to say something but deciding not to.

"I was going to phone you, but I decided not to."

"How'd you know I have a phone? Or that it's even on?"

"Kathleen told me."

Something insinuated itself into Minogue's mind then, and he grew suddenly alert. He thought of how Sean had spoken, how there was something quieter than usual in it. And how quickly Sean had left. It wasn't like the boy at all.

"You were in the house below?"

"Yeah."

There were no slags from Malone either, none of the comments about country people and cows he had prepared for without even knowing it.

"You came all the way down here today, from Dublin?"

"Yeah. Sonia's idea."

"Sonia? She's here?"

"She is. She's in the kitchen below."

Alarm welled up in Minogue now.

"Something's happened," he said.

"I didn't want to be the one, boss. I really didn't. Tynan phoned, the bastard."

"Tell me."

Malone's breath came out in small gasps, like he'd been winded.

"Don't," Minogue said then, and he pointed at Malone. "Don't!"

He brushed by Malone, almost tripping on a ledge. He could make out the darker shadows where the stones gave way to patches of grass. He heard Malone saying something, and he shouted back at him to shut up. He stumbled once and his knee hit off the side of a stone, sending a flash of pain that made him close his eyes.

Up again, he walked through the pain, and even picked up speed. He was cursing now, he knew, and he had already made up his mind that he'd make it over the side of the hill and down into Gortaboher, a small scatter of houses in a valley where even the tourists didn't linger much. There was still a green road from there that would lead him back into the village three miles or so away. What he would do there, he hadn't thought about. He knew he had some money somewhere.

He heard Malone's shout again, farther away.

"Find your own way down!" he yelled back.

He stopped to massage the knee. It didn't help. There was

still a dim, manila sliver of sky over the darker line that marked the sea's horizon. But if he fell up here, he thought. He swore again, and he pressed on.

His phone was tearing apart the quiet now. He slowed and took it out, and opened it. Kathleen was crying. She got his name out just before he threw it in a long, slow arc into the rocks.